UNMASKED

A Psychic Visions Novel
Book #14

Dale Mayer

Books in This Series:

Tuesday's Child
Hide 'n Go Seek
Maddy's Floor
Garden of Sorrow
Knock Knock…
Rare Find
Eyes to the Soul
Now You See Her
Shattered
Into the Abyss
Seeds of Malice
Eye of the Falcon
Itsy-Bitsy Spider
Unmasked
Deep Beneath
Psychic Visions Books 1–3
Psychic Visions Books 4–6
Psychic Visions Books 7–9

UNMASKED
Dale Mayer
Valley Publishing

ISBN-13: 978-1-773361-00-0
Print Edition

About This Book

Childhood dreams can come true—so can nightmares ...

Lacey always dreamed of a trip to Pompeii but never thought it would happen, until her cousin calls out of the blue, asking if Lacey would like to replace their photographer on their archeological dig.

Sebastian wasn't expecting Lacey to be, well ... Lacey. But he's intrigued from the start, and then he sees what she can do—even before she does.

As the images of the past rise in front of Lacey, taxing her artistic ability to document them, strange events start happening. Without reason, the atmosphere on the dig shifts to something supernatural that scares her, intrigues her, then consumes her.

For Sebastian these events all bring back memories of the worst dig in his life, and he can see history repeating itself. He needs to stop it this time. He must protect his team and his friends, but especially Lacey ... before everyone dies— just like they did last time.

Your Free Book Awaits!

KILL OR BE KILLED

Part of an elite SEAL team, Mason takes on the dangerous jobs no one else wants to do – or can do. When he's on a mission, he's focused and dedicated. When he's not, he plays as hard as he fights.

Until he meets a woman he can't have but can't forget. Software developer, Tesla lost her brother in combat and has no intention of getting close to someone else in the military. Determined to save other US soldiers from a similar fate, she's created a program that could save lives. But other countries know about the program, and they won't stop until they get it – and get her.

Time is running out ... For her ... For him ... For them ...

DOWNLOAD a ***complimentary*** copy of MASON? Just tell me where to send it!

http://dalemayer.com/sealsmason/

CHAPTER 1

LACEY PAULSON STEPPED outside of the Naples International Airport building, stepping away from the crowds where she could take a moment to realize she truly was in Italy. Not just Italy but Naples, almost at her last stop, Pompeii. She was a long way from Kansas. Lacey tilted her face to the sun and took a deep breath—loving the hot dusty air. Inside, she wanted to shout and cheer and scream for joy. This was her dream trip, the one she never thought she'd take.

Lacey wouldn't be here if it weren't for her cousin Chana phoning to say their photographer had just quit on her archaeological dig. And that Lacey could come join Chana for a couple of weeks this summer and take the other photographer's place. Lacey had screamed *yes*. What perfect timing. She was a teacher, and her summer holidays had just started. But she'd have done anything to make her dream trip finally happen.

Ever since she was a little girl, she'd dreamed of Pompeii—as in *seriously* dreamed of that place.

She didn't understand why, but her fascination was soul deep. The older she got, the more Pompeii had taken over her life.

This was an opportunity of a lifetime. And her first trip overseas. Her first true vacation in years. And this one was paid for. What luck!

She'd never had a chance to go into archaeology, even though she was a history buff. Still, her hobby was photography, hence Chana's suggestion. Lacey slung her duffel bag over her shoulder and walked toward where all the cabs were lined up. Chana had said someone from the dig would pick her up. Lacey stood still, her gaze glancing across the multitude of faces, wondering how she was supposed to find anybody in this crowd. There—a big white placard with her name on it caught her eye. She walked toward what looked to be a twenty-seven, twenty-eight-year-old male, still dusty from being on the dig, but his smile was bright when he saw her.

"You must be Lacey," he said, holding out his hand. "I'm Tom Masters, one of the interns working the dig. Chana sent me to collect you."

Lacey gave his hand a good shake and smiled back. "I'm glad to see you. I haven't traveled much, so I was worried how I would find you."

He chuckled and motioned at the vehicle behind him. "Not a problem. Come on. Let's get out of the crowds and head to the apartment."

"We can't go to the dig first?"

He shook his head as he turned on the engine and carefully pulled the vehicle out into the traffic. Of course many others were leaving the airport too. "No, it's after five o'clock. There's no point. Chana should be at the apartment when we get there. Hopefully there will be time before we go out for dinner. Gives you a chance to freshen up or to take a nap to help with jet lag."

Lacey nodded, holding back her disappointment. What did she expect? Of course it was too late today. "How's the weather these days?"

"For the work we do, it's not too bad. It'll get hotter and dustier as the summer deepens. But, at the moment, it's quite nice out there."

"And where exactly are you working?"

"We enter at the Stabian Gate then continue into one of the back, less traveled corners. We're not interested in a dig with all the big mansions and temples. We're doing the work on the common people. It's a much less popular area of Pompeii for both archaeologists and tourists. But, for us, it's very satisfactory to uncover the day-to-day routines of the people who supported the city of Pompeii."

Lacey sagged back in her seat with a happy sigh. "Sounds fascinating."

"It is," he said, "even for those of us who work here day in and day out. It's like opening small windows into people's lives, seeing what they're doing, and how they did it, even though it was thousands of years ago."

"I've been dreaming about coming to Pompeii for decades," she said. "I'm sure that's the only reason Chana invited me."

"She speaks of you very highly and very affectionately," Tom said with a laugh. He turned the vehicle onto a big roundabout, caught another right-hand exit and kept going. "I think she's really looking forward to your visit."

"Not as much as I am," Lacey said, staring out the side window, watching so much new and old whip by, enjoying the surrounding areas. "It's really beautiful here."

"Have you ever been to Italy?"

"No," she admitted. "I had always planned to visit, but I never seemed to quite have the time or the money."

"Right. Both of those things need to happen at the same

time for vacations. Unless, of course, you find a way to make the holiday your job."

"Which would be absolutely wonderful," she said, "but hasn't happened so far."

"Are you looking for paid work over here?" he asked in surprise. "I mean, there's lots of work, but it's usually internships. And often you have to be an archaeology student to qualify for most of the ancient sites."

"Understood," she said, her gaze never leaving the world outside the window. "I haven't been seriously looking. It was just in the back of my mind." She pointed out several buildings. "The architecture here is something else."

"Very different from North America, that's for sure."

"Where are you from?" she asked, suddenly turning to look at her companion.

"I'm from Indiana, but I've been over here now for most of the past eight months. Long enough for it to be home but not so long that I've lost that joyous awareness of how lucky I am to be doing what I love."

She appreciated that about him. "That's a good thing," she said. "Most people forget very quickly."

Tom drove in silence while she gasped, oohed and aahed at the world around her. She twisted as they went past something too fast to take a close look and then bounced in her seat to lean forward and see what was happening on his side.

Finally he laughed. "I'll be happy to take you around the city a little bit when you're ready to do some touristy day trips."

"And I'll take you up on it," she said, beaming. "I'm sad I'm only here for fourteen days."

"Well, if you love it that much," he said, "I'm sure you'll

find other opportunities."

"I hope so," she said fervently. "I've thought of nothing else for years and years."

"About coming here?"

"Coming to Pompeii," she confessed. "Sometimes I think it's in my DNA. It started as a little girl, and that dream never disappeared."

He slowed in the traffic, took several more corners in quick succession and said, "We're almost there. We have several apartments we all share. There can be up to fifteen people here at any given time. But there are always a couple coming or going. You'll be sharing a bedroom with your cousin. I hope that's okay."

"It's absolutely perfect," she assured him. "We've shared living spaces before."

He nodded. "She said you've done some weekend trips with her when you both lived in the same town."

"Exactly," she said. "I was in Washington when Mount St. Helen's blew. But I was young. That was just another reminder I needed to come to Pompeii."

"Did you like Mount St. Helens?" he asked curiously.

She nodded. "I did, but it's not the same as seeing an entire city reawaken after such a catastrophe."

"And such a volcanic catastrophe is one of the reasons why I'm here," he said slowly. "I try to never forget that what I'm doing on a dig and everything we're learning about a place and a time was brought about by a major catastrophe with a massive loss of human life."

That sobered her up. "I know. It's a terrible reminder. The only way to make it any easier is to realize it happened so long ago."

"But it could easily happen again in another location,"

he said. "For all intents and purposes, the original people of Pompeii had no clue they were living on top of a massive volcano. And, when it erupted, I don't think any of them knew how to protect themselves."

"Do we even know now?" she asked him thoughtfully. "I guess we evacuate, but I don't imagine it would have been very easy to have escaped a city as large as Pompeii back then. It's not like they had vehicles to clear people out or to move the lava flowing through to the ocean in any contained manner."

"True. There were other dangerous elements besides the lava too. The gases, the ash, the lack of oxygen, the panic … it's amazing anyone survived. Many sites in Pompeii have been excavated, but massive amounts of the city remain undiscovered to this date."

"But you're not working the main tourist spots?"

"We call it the *forgotten corner,*" he said with a laugh. "It's close to the Stabian Gate, but it's a hell of a long way out of the public paths, overgrown with plants and greenery because nobody started any work thereabouts. We're not expecting much in the way of wealthy individuals at our dig site. Like I said, we're more interested in the way of life of the common people."

"I like that," Lacey said. "So often people are only concerned with the royalty of a civilization. But, in order to keep that royalty functioning, thousands of people work for them."

"Exactly," Tom said. Finally he pulled up in front of a small apartment building and shut off the engine. He turned and grinned. "We're here."

Lacey bounced out of the vehicle, reached into the back seat and grabbed her duffel bag. There she stopped and stared. "You can see the ruins from here?"

He nodded. "It's only a couple blocks away."

She gasped. "Oh …"

"Tomorrow," he said firmly. He grabbed her elbow gently and nudged her toward the corner of the block. "The front entrance is around here."

Twisting her head so she could still keep an eye on the ruins and the surrounding area, she allowed herself to be led around the corner until the ruins were out of sight. With a sad smile she said, "I guess I'll be there tomorrow."

He just shook his head with a smile on his face, pushed open the door to the main entrance and let her inside. "We'll take the stairs." He glanced down at her bag. "Do you want me to carry that?"

She shook her head. "No. I only travel with what I can carry. If I can't lug this around the world, then I need to learn to take less."

He shrugged as if he didn't care and led the way upstairs.

She followed along. By the time she got to the top of the second landing, her arm had registered the extra weight. She sighed, shuffled the bag so it was slung over her other shoulder and carried it on up.

The air was even different here. She wasn't used to the heat and humidity. And it sounded silly, but there was no dirt in the air back home, while a fine dust floated around her here.

She was thankful when Tom opened the door at the top of the landing of the third floor. She followed him into the hallway as he stepped to the door right across from the stairwell.

There he pulled out keys, unlocked the door and pushed it open. She stepped in behind him, sadly disappointed to see it wasn't a whole lot different from a basic apartment in the States, except no carpeting was anywhere. Probably due to all the dust in this region. She wanted to experience Pompeii as authentically as possible. And yet, of course, she wanted to live in today's contemporary world too.

Running water, electricity and cell phones weren't something she wanted to do without. At least not for long.

He motioned toward the bedrooms and said, "Yours is on the left with your cousin."

She walked into the bedroom on the left, saw two single beds, one messed up—evidently her cousin had been sleeping there—so Lacey put her duffel bag on the other.

As she turned around, she walked over to the window and smiled. This window showed her the entranceway to the Pompeii sites. She gave a happy sigh and returned to the living room.

She could hear voices as she stepped into the living room. She caught a look on Tom's face. There was worry. He held out his hands, his voice whispering something she couldn't quite hear. The woman he was talking to, her face also creased with fear, caught sight of Lacey. A serene mask immediately dropped down on the woman's face, and then, as if realizing who the stranger was in her apartment, her face exploded with joy.

She raced over to grab a hold of Lacey. "Oh, my goodness, you're finally here."

The two women hugged joyously. They'd always been the best of friends. Very similar in age, with Chana about six months older.

Finally she stepped back, held Lacey by the shoulders and took a good look at her. "I'm so happy we could finally get you here."

Lacey chuckled. "Not half as happy as I am."

The two women hugged yet again, and then Chana turned to speak to Tom, but he had left them alone. She glanced at the front door, but it was closed.

"I'm sorry. Did I interrupt something?" Lacey asked. "I should have just stayed in our room."

Chana chuckled. "No. It's just there's been a bit of an upset. We've had a couple accidents on the site. Tom left early today, and, of course, something else happened at the end of the day." She shrugged. "Not a whole lot we can do about it now." She glanced down at herself. "I need a shower before we go out for a meal in an hour or so, unless you're really hungry now."

"I'm fine for a little while." She waved at her cousin. "Go. I'm sure you're hot and dusty after a day on the excavation site."

"That I am," she said. "No matter how much I tell myself that I'll take it easy, I just can't. I end up working long physical days, and that's just part of the job."

Chana had said it so simply and without any anger or regret that Lacey realized just how much her cousin enjoyed her work. "I have some emails to send," Lacey said. "You go have a shower. We'll talk when you come out."

Chana smiled and nodded as she walked into the bedroom. She called back, "Thanks. You're a doll."

Lacey waited until her cousin had whatever she needed from the room and headed into the bathroom; then Lacey went to her carry-on bag and grabbed her laptop. She took it over to the little table in the kitchen and sat down. She'd forgotten to ask her cousin for the internet password. She walked over to the bathroom door and, not hearing the water running yet, called out, "Chana, what's the password for the internet?"

"Pompeii," Chana called out with a laugh. "What else would it be?"

Smiling, Lacey returned to the table, sat down, typed in the password and crowed with delight when the internet connected. With that up, she opened her email and sent off several messages to friends and family, letting them know she was happily here at Chana's apartment.

After that, she went onto Facebook and downloaded a couple photos she'd taken with her cell phone, posting them on her Facebook page with the caption, I'm finally here.

As soon as she posted it, she got comments from lots of her friends. She answered a few until she looked up to see her cousin walking in, a towel wrapped around her head and the rest of her covered in a light cotton shirt and shorts.

"Did you get on the internet?" her cousin asked.

Lacey nodded. "I did indeed." She finished the last of her comments, shut down her social media sites, closed the lid to the laptop and smiled up at her cousin. "I don't know how many times I'm going to say it, but thank you for inviting me."

Her cousin smiled, waved a hand at her and said, "Are you kidding? I had to get you over here. All I've heard about all these years is how much you wanted to visit Pompeii."

"When I found out you were here, I did hope I might get an opportunity to come. I could have made the trip sometime in the last five years, if I'd really tried harder. But you know what it's like. Sometimes the money and time just don't sync up together."

"More like both went into caring for your mother."

Lacey's smile fell away. No reason to argue with Chana's statement because it was true.

"You've also been working your ass off to keep your mother's medical bills paid," Chana said. "You deserve a vacation more than anybody I know."

At the second mention of her mother, Lacey's shoulders sagged. "I was happy to do it. I wish all the money had gone to something beneficial. At the end, all we could do was manage the process so she could die peacefully."

"Finding out you've got breast cancer at that late stage, there really isn't a whole lot anybody can do."

"True, but she fought the good fight. It just dragged on to a painful end. It was sad because she was still so young."

"She was always quite …" Chana fell silent, and then she shrugged. "There's no real easy way to say it, but your mom never seemed to quite recover from your father's death. Maybe, in the end, she was happy to go."

Lacey nodded. "As much as I hate to admit it, I think you're right. Dad died a good ten years ago, but she never got over the loss."

"And I think, at that point, maybe slowly, but a definite shift in the roles happened between the two of you. You know we've talked about this many times. But your mother became more and more dependent on you, as if she was already taking that one step across the line. As if she were waiting for you to be old enough so she could join him."

In spite of Lacey's attempts to hold back her tears, they still burned in the corner of her eyes. She gave a misty smile to Chana. "And, in that case, I'm very happy to think she found him."

"Me too." Chana walked to the fridge, opened it and pulled out a bottle of wine. "Will you have a drink with me?"

"Absolutely."

She poured two glasses of chilled white wine and

brought them to the table. The women clinked their glasses gently together with a cheer to the days in front of them.

"Now that you've relaxed a little bit, what kind of problems are you having on the dig?"

"It's really hard to say," Chana said, "but definitely a couple of unexplained accidents that shouldn't have happened. Like, a wall more than strong enough to be standing on its own suddenly falls, tools go missing, one long-handled shovel snapped in half."

Lacey frowned.

"See what I mean? Nothing major in each event, but it adds up. Some of the locals working with us say we have a site with bad juju to it."

Lacey laughed. "Wouldn't that be something? Almost like a scary movie where you excavate something horrific," she joked.

But her cousin was serious when she replied, "We have to accept that not everybody holds our views, and some people here are very superstitious. Compounding that are the thousands of buried people who lost their lives here, and it's their graves we're disturbing. That can bring on a lot of different beliefs and fear factors."

"I hadn't considered that," Lacey said. She nodded slowly, thinking about what it would be like to live in a world where religious beliefs were being tampered with by strangers, foreigners who came into your country, your world, and were, maybe in their minds, desecrating graves of their ancestors. "I guess it's a balancing act between the locals and the tourists and the researchers, isn't it?"

"It is, and that's stressful. You get down, emotionally, mentally. If some unknown person is causing trouble, you look at everyone else suspiciously," her cousin said wearily.

"This started over a week ago, after we opened up one new section of the dig. But there's nothing new or unusual about that area. It's another house we opened up. So far, we've reached a room in the back, but it's empty as far as we can tell. Quite possibly it's only a storage room."

"So it's likely not connected to what you're doing but maybe more about the fact that you're even in that corner perhaps?"

Chana opened her mouth to say something, but two men walked into the apartment, and the women's conversation was over.

CHAPTER 2

A
FTER INTRODUCTIONS, THE group set off for the restaurant. Dinner was a little later than planned. By the time they walked into the small café and ordered, it was almost nine o'clock. But then it was Italy, and that seemed to be pretty normal for them.

Lacey was in love with everything she saw—the atmosphere, the smells, the cheerful happy voices. Very little vehicle traffic occurred in this area, but there were loads of foot traffic.

They sat outside in a small enclosed patio, people from the dig site on both sides of the long narrow table, and watched the world go by as they waited for their meals to arrive. Before the food came, the rest of the dig crew arrived. Lacey was quickly introduced to the gang and was told several more would arrive in a few days.

"It's a popular time for vacations among the interns," Tom said. "One's traveled to a wedding, and one's gone back for a family vacation."

Lacey loved hearing the insights into these people's lives. And this archeological-dig life seemed so normal to them. And yet, to have a job like this was anything but normal to her.

When her pasta arrived, she was enthralled at how pretty it looked. After the first bite, she fell in love all over again.

"This is fantastic," she mumbled around a mouthful.

Chana laughed. "It is, isn't it? It's also one of the cheapest places here. In the midst of a heavy tourist spot, we have to watch where we eat. Otherwise our budget money doesn't go very far."

"What about buying groceries and cooking?" Lacey asked.

"We do that too. We always have breakfast at home and make our own lunches, but dinners out are just the perfect thing at the end of a very long hot day."

Agreed. How many times did Lacey come home from dealing with a classroom of difficult kids, their homework laden in her arms, knowing she had hours and hours of marking to do, and the last thing she wanted was to cook a full meal? "I tend to go for salads at a time like that."

"But it's hard to keep functioning in a physical job on just salads."

She winced. "Never thought of that." Her pasta was made with olive oil, fresh tomatoes and some local cheese she'd never heard of.

It was simple fare but extremely tasty. When she finished her meal, she pushed away the empty bowl, picked up her glass of wine and settled in to listen to the conversations. There had been a lot of muted discussions about the troubles at the site. She could hear some but not all of it. She was at one end of the table, so it was hard to hear the conversation at the other end. She leaned closer to her cousin and said, "They seem to be worried."

Her cousin nodded. "They are." But she didn't elaborate.

Not wanting to intrude or to bring up issues while they were still in public, Lacey sat quietly. By the time they made it back to the apartment, she thought they were all returning to the same place but then the group split into two.

Back in the apartment she was still keyed up and didn't think she could sleep, but she knew her cousin was desperately in need of rest. Not only had the worry of the day taken its toll, but Chana had put in long physical hours.

After Chana finally changed into her pajamas, she lay down in bed. "I know you probably still aren't ready to go to sleep yet, but I'm just beat. I'm sorry."

"Don't worry about it," Lacey said. "I can sit here in bed on my laptop for a little bit. I should be tired, but jet lag is a funny thing."

"See you in the morning."

Lacey wandered through the internet, stopping at her favorite news sites and then checking out her daily horoscope. She read them with a wry expression, always wondering how much these people got paid to make up this stuff. But, every once in a while, they noted something so on target that Lacey found it very difficult to completely dispel astrology. As it was, all her horoscopes had mentioned her upcoming trip. Sure, she was reading into it what she wanted to, but it was interesting to see what they would say. The weekly one though caused her a little concern. *Danger stalks your footsteps. Be careful. Be extra-vigilant. Don't trust anyone.*

Lacey slowly closed the lid on her laptop, tucked it on the floor beside her bed and pulled the blankets over her. That last horoscope was hardly guaranteed to help her sleep. Still, she was someplace she'd been trying to get to for a long time, and it was hard for that euphoria to calm down.

Eventually though, she did fall asleep. She woke several times in the night to audible footsteps in the strange space. At one point, she got up and walked out to the living room to see who was up. But the area appeared to be empty. The bedroom door to the other room, where the two men slept in similar beds, was closed. Lacey could have sworn she'd heard somebody leave. And, of course, they could have. They could have walked right through the living room and out the door. It wasn't like she had come out of her room immediately.

She looked out the window to see a city covered in darkness. Enough lights were all around to shine in an odd, eerie glow. But nothing was ominous about it. To her fascinated gaze, it was just one more fantasy element to her trip.

She turned and walked back to her room, feeling an odd chill to the air. She dashed into her bed and pulled the covers up. The bedroom was warm, intensely so. Eventually she fell asleep again. When she woke, it was six a.m. Her cousin was already up, making coffee from the wonderful aroma reaching her nose. Lacey quickly dressed and joined Chana in the kitchen. "What time are we starting?"

"We'll try to be there at seven," Chana said calmly. She poured Lacey a cup of coffee, placing it on the table. "The earlier we can work the dig, the cooler it is."

"That works for me." Breakfast was granola with yogurt and fresh fruit. She enjoyed it. At home she tended to either skip breakfast or to grab a piece of fruit or toast as she raced out the door. She knew it wasn't healthy, but sometimes she didn't care. She was so busy that breakfast seemed too much effort.

By the time they had packed up and were ready to go, she was beside herself with impatience. Her cousin just laughed at her.

"Look at you. You'd think we were going on some big trek or something. We'll cross to the gates and head up to the site. It's a fifteen-minute walk."

Lacey bounced from side to side. "But that's okay. You know how I feel about this."

"I do indeed," Chana said, shaking her head. "What I don't know is why?"

"I can't explain it rationally," Lacey said.

On that note, they left the apartment, walked down the stairs and outside.

Lacey continued, "But I've had a ton of dreams, and I've always felt drawn to this place."

Her cousin nodded, watched the traffic, led Lacey across the road and moments later they walked through the ruins.

Lacey gasped in joy. "Just look at it," she cried out. "How can anybody not stop and stare?"

"I've done this trek a thousand times," Chana said, "and it never fails to astound me how advanced the society was for their time and how absolutely devastating the volcano eruption was."

"That's the thing to remember, isn't it?" Lacey nodded, rushing to catch up with her cousin. "All of this joy inside me came about because of a great human catastrophe."

"Well, technically it was Mother Nature's catastrophe with an extremely high count of human devastation."

They kept walking until Chana pointed out Stabian Gate. "This is the entrance we use. This gate, in itself, is very famous." She launched into a historical recital about when it was unearthed and opened up in the early 1800s, but it wasn't until the early 1900s that people came back to do more. "Pompeii is a never-ending archaeological site," she explained. "And still probably ninety percent of it is buried."

At that, Lacey studied how much was open and un-earthed. "It's absolutely amazing that so much has been excavated already."

"It is," Chana said. "And it's ongoing. A vast number of houses and walkways and tunnels and markets are left to be explored. But it won't all happen in my lifetime."

That hint of sadness in her cousin's voice had Lacey turning to glance at her. "Is that just the passage of time you feel, marking your life, or is something else going on?"

Chana looked at her in surprise. "Nothing is going on. Why? Did I sound sad?"

"Yes, you did," Lacey said with a laugh. "I was afraid for a moment there that you had some sort of illness you hadn't told me about." Her cousin didn't answer, so Lacey pushed the issue. "If something was wrong, you'd tell me, wouldn't you?" Her cousin had been *off* all morning, pensive, as if thinking about all the problems at the site—or something else. It was the *something else* that bothered Lacey. "Right?"

"Of course I would," her cousin rushed to reassure her. "You know I would."

Lacey frowned, not sure she believed her cousin. "How is your family, by the way?"

"You'd probably know better than me. I understand Mom attended your mother's funeral, but I haven't talked to her much since then."

"I saw your mom a few weeks ago, before I left."

"Did she know you were coming over?"

"Not until I told her," Lacey said, remembering she found that odd too. "I wondered if you were going to tell her."

"I don't think at that point you had booked your flight, so I held off, in case something came up and you didn't come."

It was on the tip of Lacey's tongue to ask why Chana

hadn't wanted to let her own mother know about Lacey's arrival here in Pompeii. But it wasn't any of Lacey's business. *Chana and her mother.* There was a distance between them from way back when. They were more cordial strangers than relatives.

Chana's mother, Lacey's aunt Charlie, had married four times already. Chana had walked away from any remaining relationship with her mom somewhere around the time of the second husband's divorce, not approving of her mother's system of catching her next husband or those individual partners. But Chana had gone her own way early in life, so she had a tough edge to her, whereas Lacey was the nurturer. She'd stayed home to look after her mother, and losing her had devastated her. She'd buried herself in her work and in the kids she loved so much.

"Mom is Mom," Chana said. "I learned early on not to get too involved or to tell her too much. She reads things into the conversations that I never intended."

"I can understand that."

"Can you? Aunt Millicent was absolutely divine. I'd have done anything to have had her as my mom," Chana said. "I'd have given everything for that kind of a relationship."

"I'm sorry. I know Aunt Charlie wasn't the easiest to live with."

"Not in the slightest," Chana said. She motioned up ahead. "We're just around the corner."

Lacey had been busy looking around and keeping track of the conversation, but there was just so much to see. She knew she'd be dazed this whole two weeks, just sitting and absorbing the completely different geographical looks to the place. So much history was here, and so much of the finds they uncovered here on a day-to-day basis were steeped in personal stories. She said out loud, "Two weeks won't be enough, will it?"

"Nope, not even close." Her cousin glanced at her and grinned. "What happens if you don't go back in September?"

"I won't have a job," she said simply. "I could stay for the summer though."

Her cousin nodded but didn't say too much. "We'll see how it goes," she said.

"Besides, it's not your decision anyway, is it?"

Her cousin shook her head. "Nope. None of us ever has job security here. These are all charity foundation projects. I know I have a job for the rest of this calendar year, but, past that, it's anybody's guess."

"Hey, at least you know that much," Lacey said with a big grin.

"Absolutely," Chana said. "Some things in life are just what they are. One day at a time. That's what we work on here. But it's a slow process. There's only so much we can excavate."

"And you must get value from your finds, whether intrinsic or economic or historic."

"Which is why you're here," Chana said. "Take pictures, find the story of what we're unveiling and make it real. Something people can relate to."

"That's a tall order," Lacey said lightly. "Pictures, yes. Maybe a story, yes. But making it magical so everybody can relate? I don't know."

"I do. Our photographer isn't coming back. We're not paying you because we can't afford to," she said.

Lacey interrupted her. "You know I don't want a paycheck."

"Good thing," Chana said cheerfully. "Because there's

no budget money. But, at the same time, you could make a huge difference here, and I think it could lead to an incredibly valuable change in your career, if you wanted, if you did it successfully. You're very talented in many ways. I know you think you suck but you used to be a great sketch artist too."

"Ha, I haven't done any artwork in a long time. Besides two weeks isn't terribly long though to accomplish all that."

"Well, two weeks will give you plenty of time to take many photographs," Chana said. "Afterward, when you're back home for the rest of your summer vacation, how you pull it all together and present it, now that's a different story."

Lacey thought about that as they approached the wide-open dig. It went down approximately twenty feet at one side and was only about ten feet deep at the other. Some of it was surface level. It was fascinating because it looked into several houses, a stone walkway between them—those stones laid by hand by people and used to build roads and homes and businesses from centuries ago.

Lacey walked up to the first building and placed her hand on one of the cornerstones, amazed at the sense of homecoming she felt. And yet, there was no reason for it. Maybe it was just the years of wanting desperately to come here.

She sat down—more a leaning against the cornerstone—and studied the world around her. "It's amazing how much you've done," she said.

"Oh, no, it's not," Chana said. "It's slow. We can't use any heavy equipment in this area, so it's all done by hand. Lots of trowel work." She tossed a laughing look at Lacey. "Don't worry. You might get roped into doing some of that too."

"I can't say I've done much hard physical gardening-type work in my life," she said, "but you know I'm up for anything at least once."

"Well, no complaining if you do, you're forewarned," her cousin said. She walked to a far corner. The site was approximately fifty feet by maybe sixty-five. "I'm working on the house over here. We've unearthed the kitchen area. Little bits of pottery are showing up. We're identifying each piece, tagging it for the foundation to take back to the center to do some research. I highly suggest you get out your camera gear, take a bunch of test photos, figure out where and what lighting you need, how it'll work with all this rock, so you can get the best photographs possible."

With the reminder how she was here to work, Lacey put down her bag and pulled out her camera. She'd splurged on new lenses before coming over, money she could ill afford with her mother's estate still hung up.

But the probate process was already many months in, and she did have enough money to handle her day-to-day needs because of her own teaching position. Only she'd thought her mother's mortgage was paid off, and it wasn't. Her mother had never once mentioned it. That left Lacey covering the costs of her mother's house atop Lacey's own monthly bills, along with everything else pertaining to her mother, including her funeral and medical expenses, out of Lacey's own pocket. She'd taken a big hit. The legal paperwork had just gone through a couple months ago that had given her access to her mother's bank account. That had gone a long way to ease things while paying her mother's ongoing bills.

As Lacey put the strap around her neck and took off the

cap, checking the light around her, her cousin called out, "Is that a new camera?"

"No. It's the same SLR I've had for about two years, but I did buy a couple new lenses."

"The lenses cost more than the camera, don't they?" her cousin asked in a dry tone. "Remember how we told you not to spend too much money on that stuff for this dig?"

"It gave me an excuse to buy the lenses I've always wanted," Lacey said, mollifying her cousin, who appeared to be irritated at the concept. "Besides, it'll take some practice shots for me to figure out the lighting and the subject matter."

"The other photographer only had a simple point-and-shoot camera," Chana said, waving at Lacey's camera with all the fancy lenses. "You've got a lot of money tied up in those." She chewed on her bottom lip, as if considering how much Lacey had spent.

"Are you worried something'll happen to my gear?" Lacey studied the bag at her feet, frowning. Indeed, she had a lot of her money tied up here. And it wasn't insured.

Her cousin shrugged. "Like I said, we've had some incidents around here. Could you at least make doubly sure you look after your stuff? I'd hate to see you, or your camera gear, have any kind of mishap."

Her cousin's wording was kind of odd, but obediently Lacey closed up her camera gear in its camera bag, but it had double shoulder straps, more like a backpack. So she wore it on her back and then walked around the area. She focused first on the rocks, trying to get the different striations to show up with only the natural light. With so much gray in those rocks, she wanted to highlight the light bouncing off each one in this pathway between the two buildings. It was stunning to think how many people had walked on each of these stones. How many years these blocks been here, helping people to go where they needed to go? Then in hiding, until brought into the light again.

Thinking of the hands that had touched each of these stones, she lost herself in her work, snapping photographs of her surroundings. She started wide, laying a grid of what she would be looking for as reference points later. Then she went in closer, making a grid out of each quarter section.

By the time she put down her camera and reached for her bottle of water, it seemed everybody else had shown up for work too. She walked over to join them. There were smiles and a couple of teasing comments about the size of her lenses. She'd heard it all before. "What are you all working on this morning?" Lacey asked. There was a sudden silence. She raised an eyebrow. "Did I say something wrong?"

They shook their heads. "We're chipping into a new section this morning," Tom said, "if you want to take some photographs before we start."

She walked over to the indicated area, about eight feet long, three feet wide at the one side and about five feet high. "If this is a room, why the strange shape?" she asked as she picked up her camera and clicked. The roof was slopped off to the side.

"We suspect something's underneath it or in it, but we don't have any way to know until we get there."

Tom, Mark and two other men gathered around and chipped carefully away at one corner. Lacey took several photographs and realized this would entail long hours of tedious work. She stepped back a little to take more photos and then lost interest as they worked intently. Chana was right about how slow the handwork was.

She heard a cry and turned around to see Tom standing, holding his finger against his mouth. Chana walked over. "Are you okay?"

He nodded. "Just a foolish accident." He headed to where they had their bags gathered and pulled out a large Band-Aid. He wrapped it around his injured finger, then picked up his bottle of water and took a drink.

Lacey kept clicking, thinking about the human efforts that went into all this work. The blood sweat and tears to open up these places of interest. As she watched, one of the other men, Brian, cried out when a rock crumbled from above, striking his shoulder. They all turned to look at him. "Lots of accidents," Lacey murmured.

Silence.

She glanced over at the interns. "I'm not accusing anyone," she said hurriedly. "I was thinking of all the effort that goes into this work.

"There are always accidents on sites," Tom said brusquely. "As long as no one is seriously hurt, our work keeps its integrity."

"Lots of times it's Mother Nature, … and sometimes it isn't." Chana nodded. "We came in one day, and one of the mummies had been damaged." She glanced at the others, then added, "At least that's what we reported, but the damage looked more human oriented than due to Mother Nature."

Lacey winced. "I'm sorry. That's not easy to deal with."

"It's catastrophic," Tom said harshly. "Our reputation is only as good as our work is. And, if people see damage like that, then there's a good chance we'll get run out of here."

"Sabotage?" Lacey asked slowly. "Maybe the locals wanting to stop the dig?"

Tom and Chana both looked at her and nodded slowly.

Lacey's stomach sank.

Chana pointed at one of the new spaces they'd opened. "Somebody cracked open the coffin cover and attempted to steal the mummy inside and damaged it in the process."

Lacey stared at them. "That's terrible. Why would someone do that?"

They looked at her, looked at each other, then back at her. "We have no clue."

"And you should have reported that to us," a voice on ground level announced in exasperation and anger.

CHAPTER 3

S HE SPUN TO see a man in jeans and a T-shirt but also wearing a mantle of authority that had everybody backing up slightly.

"I know that," Chana said quickly. She stepped forward as if realizing what her instinctive step backward had meant. "I was going to tell you …"

He waved a hand and cut her off. "When?"

She glanced helplessly over at Tom.

Tom stepped forward and said, "I asked her not to, until I could figure out what the hell was going on."

The stranger stood with his legs in a wide stance and his hands on his hips as he glared at them. His gaze drifted from one person to the next before coming back to land on Lacey's face. He frowned. "Who are you?"

She stepped forward. "Lacey. I'm the new photographer."

His frown deepened as if sifting through faces and people's names and relevant memos in his head. Then he gave a clipped nod. "Right. I do remember that." His gaze returned to Chana. "I want to know exactly what's happening here. And I also want to know why nobody contacted the office. The only way this foundation functions is if we have complete transparency."

"We do understand that, sir," Tom said. "It was a misjudgment on my part."

"No," Chana said sadly. "I was okay to go along with it. We were hoping we could solve it before we had to tell you we were having trouble."

Lacey's gaze went from Chana to the stranger. This must be the Sebastian Bentley she'd heard about. She took another step forward. "It's nice to meet you. I'm sorry it's not under better circumstances."

Some of the tension eased from his shoulders. He dropped down into the dig site so he stood on the same level as she was, reached over and shook her hand. "Ditto." He turned to the other two. "Now I want the full explanation. Then you'll show me all the damage."

A frisson of fear whispered across Chana's face. Lacey wondered what was behind it. There were undercurrents of something strange going on here. She followed along helplessly as they explained about the mummy they had worked so hard to excavate and how they had returned the next morning to find the back of the mummy's head caved in.

Sebastian stooped and took a closer look. Frowning, muttering to himself, he pulled out his cell phone, turned on the flashlight and tried to see inside the coffin. He nodded but didn't say anything. He straightened to look around. "Other accidents? Even small ones?"

Chana listed off the same events she had given Lacey last night.

"And then this morning, I cut my finger, but that was my fault," Tom said, holding up his bandaged hand. "Plus one of the guys got hit in the shoulder by a falling rock."

Sebastian nodded. "Show me where both happened." They took him toward the area Tom had been working on when he'd hurt himself.

Lacey went to follow, but Chana held her back. "Something is weird about those newest sites over there," she muttered in a low tone. "Better for Sebastian to see it right now, and, if there'll be a verbal thrashing about this, it's best it happens while we're a little farther away. It's hard on Tom to get a dressing down in front of us."

Lacey glanced at her in surprise. "It's hard on anybody. I don't know why it would be any worse in front of us."

Chana rolled her eyes at her. "That's because we're female. Tom's male ego might take a bit of a beating."

Lacey didn't think so. There didn't seem to be anything retiring or shy about Tom's ego. Thankfully though, she wasn't witness to any altercation as Sebastian crouched in front of the area where the rock had come down.

"How long ago was this?" Sebastian asked.

Tom looked over at Chana.

She checked her watch. "An hour maybe?" She glanced at Lacey for confirmation.

Lacey nodded. "It probably wasn't much more than that."

Sebastian studied the large oddly shaped room they'd been unearthing. "It's empty."

"That's not unusual, is it?" Lacey asked, curiosity piquing her voice.

"Yes," he said, "it is. Everything had a purpose in the Old World. Time, energy, money was all at a minimum. When you only live to be forty-seven, and that's considered a ripe old age, time takes on a very different meaning. To have an empty room like this, it's odd."

"Grain storage?" Lacey hazarded a guess.

He turned to look at her.

The expression on his face had her cracking-up laughing. "I guess that was a foolish answer, huh? I'm not a student of archaeology. I'm a history teacher. Although not of Pompeii. They would never allow me to teach much on that curriculum. I really wanted to though," she confessed.

He nodded absentmindedly and wandered off to one of the other corners, Tom anxiously at his heels.

She glanced over at Chana. "Are you guys in big trouble?"

Chana shook her head. "No, but we should have told the head office. They can only minimize the bad press if we let them know what's happening, and too often this stuff gets ahead of us, and we don't see or hear anything until it's too late. That's not fair to the bosses. Control is a necessity if we want funds to keep flowing."

"Ah, grant funding. Yes. Got it."

Leaving the others to sort out the problems, Lacey returned to her photographing. Now that she was where the mummy's coffin had been opened up, she took a moment to take photographs of the entire thing.

No matter what she did, she couldn't stop looking at Sebastian. He was obviously in great physical shape. Not exactly required for an office worker or an overseer for a group of workers. Something about that heavily muscled chest under his T-shirt and his bulging biceps as he shifted and moved. She felt like an idiot for even thinking about it. She put it down to hormones and too long since she'd had a serious boyfriend.

Yet it was more than that—he had *presence*, radiating power just standing here. It was very attractive. When she'd decided to move in to look after her mother, her boyfriend at the time had decided Lacey was more of a burden than he was willing to bear. She'd watched him go and hadn't felt a pang of regret. Because, if that was his attitude, she wanted nothing to do with him.

But it had meant the next year and a half had been sometimes very lonely as the grief threatened to overwhelm her for her upcoming loss. There was no cure for her mother's condition. It was a case of taking every moment they had together and enjoying it. And, for that, she was grateful her former boyfriend wasn't in the picture, so he didn't steal any of those moments from her and her mother.

Almost an hour later, intent on capturing the photos she'd been asked to take, Lacey heard that deep rumbling growl of Sebastian in the background.

He didn't fit her concept of an archaeologist in any way. Yet he seemed just as comfortable here among the rocks as he would commanding a big company. It had something to do with that presence of his.

Heavy footsteps sounded the team's approach. Trying not to make it obvious, she took photos as they studied their array of broken tools, making notes of the tools now gone, *stolen.*

Sebastian's striking voice was hard as he demanded, "Are you sure you locked everything up, put everything away?"

Her cousin Chana said, "Yes. We have a routine. We do it every night. And the locks weren't broken."

He straightened and pivoted slightly to look at her.

Lacey pointed her camera and caught that jaw, that nose, those aquiline cheeks. *Click. Click. Click.* Then catching Chana's gaze, Lacey quickly turned away.

Chana frowned as she understood what Lacey had been doing.

Feeling the heat roll up her neck and cheeks, Lacey hid

behind the camera. She changed the angle ever-so-slightly to get a panoramic view. She slowly, methodically took pictures of the entire circle around her. If nothing else, it would provide a hell of a memory afterward.

Finally the group walked away with Sebastian. Lacey stayed behind, taking pictures of the broken tools and visible footprints. It was so fascinating to see where people walked now versus where they had walked thousands of years ago. She couldn't help it. She bent close and took photographs of one shoe imprint and then another and then another.

"What are you, a detective?"

She gave a shriek and spun around to see Sebastian glaring at her. She took a deep breath, stabilizing her shaky hands. "I was thinking of the contrast," she said steadily but had enunciated very carefully, so there was no misunderstanding. "Of footprints today versus the footprints of nearly two thousand years ago."

He stared at her suspiciously for a moment before he relaxed and gave her an approving nod. "That could make quite a story." He turned and strode away.

She let out her pent-up breath, only to suck it in again as Chana whispered angrily in her ear, "What are you doing?"

"Taking photos," Lacey said, hating her defensive tone. "What was I supposed to be doing?"

"You don't need to be taking pictures of the boss." Chana spun on her heels and followed Sebastian.

Lacey stayed where she was, needing a few minutes away from the group and Chana's prying eyes.

Calmer, Lacey wandered this section, seeing stairs appearing out of the dirt. No way to know how far down they went because the undisturbed ground met the seventh step downward, still not fully uncovered. They hadn't excavated any farther. She walked to the top of the stairs and snapped a photo as she took every step down, thinking about the people who had walked these stairs, carrying burdens, holding children by the hand—the old, the young, the weak, the pregnant. She moved carefully, and, where the stairs stopped, she bent to capture that partially buried step from many angles. The wonder of the past meeting the present flowed through her.

She gave a happy sigh and slowly straightened to find she wasn't alone. She looked up to find Sebastian staring at her, an odd look on his face. She frowned and asked in a low voice, "Have I done something wrong?"

He shook his head and pointed to where she'd been crouched. "What is it you see?"

"I see where the past meets the future," she said quietly. "And I guess that probably sounds frivolous, but I look at it from behind the camera. I see the collision, not of the past with the volcano, but as the future reaches deep into the past."

That odd look crossed his face yet again. His gaze intensified as if probing into her psyche, holding her captive by his will alone. She stood uncertainly, her fingers fidgeting on the camera. And then, as if she had been finally released from his hold, he gave a quick nod and spun away again. Shaky, she sat down on one of the steps and took several deep breaths. What the hell just happened?

SEBASTIAN WOULD HAVE to find out more about his new photographer. Something about her was … familiar, … odd, … insightful. She was a puzzle. He loved solving puzzles of the past. Puzzles of the present never interested him. They were too young, held no mystery, no depth. But something about Lacey went beyond deep.

He really liked the answers she'd given him. He could see an old soul reaching through the centuries. Did she realize she'd been drawn here and why?

He glanced back to see Lacey sitting, taking several deep breaths as if he'd unnerved her. Fine if he had. She'd unnerved him too. He walked toward Chana, seeing her stiffen, waiting for his condemnation. "If anything else happens, no matter how minor it may seem to you," he said in a stern voice, "I want to hear about it, and I want to hear immediately. Do you understand me? You don't call anybody else, including the rest of the team. You pick up your phone, and you dial me." He leaned forward just a bit, satisfied when she leaned back reflexively. "*No* exceptions."

She took a deep breath and nodded. "I am sorry."

"I know you are," he said absently. His mind had already moved forward. "I'll be in Pompeii for the next week. We have several board meetings. I'll be on-site a lot. So, when you least expect me, I'll be here."

And with that warning and a hard look at the rest of the group, he turned and walked away, satisfied the team would follow his orders. Still, there was nothing like seeing things from his own eyes too. What he really wanted was to see what Lacey saw. He stopped at the edge of the dig, turned and called back, "Chana, come here please."

She raced over.

"What's the deal with Lacey again?" He watched the color blanch from her face. He shook his head. "It's fine that she's here. I just don't remember what the arrangement was."

"She's a middle-school history teacher, out for the summer holidays. I told her how we had lost our photographer, and she volunteered to come. She's really, really good. But she's not a pro, and we're not paying her," she said very clearly. "But we are covering her costs."

He shot a glance toward the woman who, even now, was absorbed in a pattern of rock on the ground just off to the side. The mystery of what it was, what it had been, remained buried beneath the ground. Her aura was cream-colored and glowing brightly, even from a distance ... "Okay, that's fine."

"I'll keep an eye on her," Chana said quickly. "She's my cousin. She's really doing this as a favor for us."

He nodded absentmindedly. "I said it's all right. I do want to see the photos she takes."

"I didn't get her to sign a nondisclosure agreement," she said quickly. "If that's something you want."

His mind contemplated the issue. "I'll think about it. Depends on how willing she is to share her photos."

"She does this for the joy of it," Chana said. "For the love of the world around her. She has a very unique insight into everything."

"And why is that?"

Chana lowered her voice. "I honestly think it's because she spent years caring for her dying mother—tried to make each moment count before she lost her. No treatment was working, so they knew the end was inevitable, and yet, every day they tried to do something to make that day special. After her mother passed away six months ago, Lacey continued the practice. And coming here has been a dream of hers since forever. All I ever heard from her was how she wanted to see Pompeii."

He'd taken a step away when he heard that last bit. He spun around and looked at Chana hard. "What do you mean?"

He watched as his team leader shrugged her shoulders. "Honestly? She saw a documentary when she was young, like six or seven. Since then it's all she's talked about."

"And this is her first time here?"

Chana nodded. "I really want to make it a good visit for her. She deserves that. She's a good person, and she spent a lot of years of her life making her mother's life easier."

He kept his thoughts to himself, but he couldn't keep his gaze off Lacey. *What did she see behind that lens of hers? Did she see the people of the past? The death and disaster? The good? The evil?*

Voluntarily taking that walk of grief with her mother was difficult. He'd only seen one person do it well—his own mother had nursed his sister to her early end. It took a lot of spirit, a lot of heart, but it could also break someone. And the breaks could be hidden inside where no one knew. That could make them weak, make them easily accessible, make them susceptible to all kinds of dangers. All kinds of evil.

He could admire what she'd done, but she needed watching.

A lot was going on here that nobody knew about, that nobody understood because they couldn't relate to the dark forces underneath. But anybody who had been *called* from halfway across the world, with a need instilled at such a young age—well, that meant that person needed to be here. He didn't know why. But he'd find out. His visit just became open-ended. He didn't dare leave the site or Lacey alone …

Things were happening. Or maybe evil Mayan god-driven things were happening considering people were doing things they weren't aware of. He'd seen the anomaly before—starting, as a young man, at a Mayan ruin dig where there'd been similar incidents to what he saw here. Only back then, things got much worse, starting with accelerating verbal squabbles among the crew, for no good reason, but they saw the negative energy coming from one very strong and powerful male energy who was very, very, *very* angry ... ending with several deaths.

The locals blamed Kisin, the Mayan god of death. Sebastian didn't know what to call it. It was a violent nightmare he was desperate to get out of and by the time it came to a stop, there were only a couple of them left alive.

Deaths that had haunted him ever since. When he'd heard about the incidents on this site, his heart had damn-near exploded in his chest. That was partly why he'd been so angry that his team hadn't contacted him. They didn't understand the danger. And they definitely didn't understand how the darkness underneath was attracted to the light above.

The darkness especially liked the innocence, the energy, the purity of someone like Lacey. More than *liked*—it fed on it ...

CHAPTER 4

B Y THE END of the day, Lacey was tired, dusty, exuberantly overjoyed, and oddly at peace. She walked back with the crew as silent as they were jovial. They had survived the boss's visit and had spent the afternoon joking about always looking around to see if he was close by.

Lacey hadn't felt the same amusement, the same hilarity or release from the tension of having him here. Because she didn't feel like she was released from it. Something dark and intense had been in his gaze. Something knowing, something powerful that scared the crap out of her. But, at the same time, it attracted her like nothing else. It was otherworldly. It had nothing to do with a male-female sense of attraction; more like a moth to a flame, knowing it would get burned but unable to stop the flight into the direct path of destruction.

"Why are you so quiet, Lacey?" Tom asked. "Your first day too much for you?"

She gave him a bright smile. "It was perfect." Her tone was a happy one. "It was absolutely perfect."

He shook his head. "Then you obviously didn't have a trowel or a small brush in your hand." That brought out everybody's hilarity.

She just smiled and nodded.

When they got home, they split off and had showers in

turn. When they were all clean and redressed, Lacey walked out to the kitchen to see the group waiting for her. She raised an eyebrow. "Sorry. Am I late for something?"

"Tonight is a beer-and-pizza fest at one of the pubs," Mark explained. "We always try to hit it every week."

She smiled, hooked arms with her cousin and said, "Well, don't leave me behind."

They walked out, all of them laughing and joking.

She stared at the sun sinking slowly and commented, "The days seem so long here, and yet, it's already eight o'clock. I'm really tired but too pent-up to sleep yet."

"I know," Chana said. "It took me a long time to get accustomed to it. But it'll be dark soon enough. The town comes alive at night."

"With the ghosts of the dead," Tom said jokingly.

Lacey wondered about that. "All joking aside, have you guys ever felt any ghosts around?"

They all looked at her and broke out laughing.

Chana shook her arm. "Of course not, silly. These people died quickly and a long time ago. No haunting spirits here."

"I was reading some books about that," Lacey said, trying not to feel mocked by their comments. "Sometimes spirits who die very quickly don't know they have passed away, so tend to haunt, not understanding why nobody's talking to them."

"Can you imagine?" Katie said. She was the only other woman in the group. She stayed in the other apartment with Matt.

"I think it would be pretty horrifying myself," Chana said. "Can you imagine everybody walking past you and never seeing you?"

Lacey nodded, turned and stepped off the curb into the street.

"Look out." Chana grabbed her arm, but it was too late.

Lacey took a blow as the vehicle slammed to a stop, tires screeching as it hit her, sending her flying. Instantly she was surrounded by the others. She lay there on the street for a long moment in shock, pain radiating up and down her left side. Yet feeling very stupid.

She tried to sit up, trying to make light of it, she said, "Wow, that was a really stupid thing to have done."

"Don't move," Tom warned.

"I'm fine," she exclaimed. "Help me up, please."

Tom bent and slowly helped her to her feet. "Are you sure you should be standing?" he asked worriedly.

She nodded. "If you give me a minute to assess the damage, I'm pretty sure I'm fine." She gently stood on her left foot and was delighted it could accept the weight. She checked everything else. "I'll be fine. Nothing's broken. I'll end up with a little bruising that's all."

Trying to minimize the attention she was getting, hating that it was due to her clumsiness, she motioned ahead. "Could we please go to the restaurant? I can sit down then. And I'm sure food will help."

"Absolutely," Tom said, but he hooked his arm through hers and half supported her.

"I'm fine," she said. "Honestly."

Only he wouldn't listen.

She glanced over at Chana, who just shrugged.

At the restaurant, Tom let her go. They walked in as a group but waited until they were seated.

Lacey gratefully sank onto a bench seat at the back of the table. "This is nice." She glanced over at Chana, who was busy texting. Everyone did these days. Considering so much of her hurt right now, Lacey looked forward to that beer and pizza they'd promised. By the time the pizza arrived, so had the beer, except the guys wouldn't let her drink.

"No. No alcohol for you."

That just frustrated her. Why didn't they believe her? She was fine. "Come on. That's exactly what I need right now," she pleaded.

"No. Because, if you need any medication," Chana said quietly at her side, "you can't have any alcohol first."

Lacey groaned and accepted the rationality of what Chana said. Just then the double front doors blew open, and everybody turned to look at the new arrival. Sebastian strode across the restaurant. Everybody cleared a path as he came to their table. He caught sight of Lacey, his gaze pinning her in place as he headed toward her. When he reached them, everyone fell silent.

He glared at Lacey. "What the hell happened?"

He plunked himself down in an unoccupied chair directly across from her. "Talk to me. What happened?"

Lacey wasn't even sure what to say. So she said nothing.

After a moment Chana spoke up. "She was hit by a car."

Lacey winced. She didn't know anybody would use that term. "I stepped onto the road without looking. I got hit."

He frowned as if thinking about it. "How bad?"

She shrugged. "It's not bad." But the truth was, she felt pretty shaky and tired, and everything on her left side burned.

He wasn't fooled. "We'll take you to a doctor after this."

"I'm sure it'll be fine," she protested. The thought of all the damn insurance forms she'd have to fill out was a nightmare in itself. "Nothing a hot bath and a good night's sleep won't help."

The second round of pizzas arrived then. She tried to eat, but it was a little disconcerting having Sebastian sitting here. He was moody and frustrated, possibly angry, and she didn't know what she might have done to have deserved it. She wanted to keep a low profile so her trip was not cut short, but, ever since she'd been here, it seemed like there had been nothing but problems. And he might be the biggest of them all.

She wasn't sure how to get back on the right track with him. Everything she said seemed to be the wrong thing. And because she felt just rough enough, she decided to say nothing since talking might make it worse.

She waited until the group finished eating, and then, with a nudge at her cousin, she asked, "Do you mind if we leave early? I'd like to go to bed soon."

Chana studied her face in worry. "You aren't looking all that good."

With effort Lacey bolstered a bright smile and said, "Thanks."

Her cousin flushed. "You know I didn't mean it that way," she said quietly. "I think you should listen to Sebastian."

Lacey glared at her. "That's not what I wanted to hear."

"Too bad." Sebastian stood, tossed some money on the table, motioned at Chana and said, "You can either come with us or go home, and I'll bring her back afterward."

Chana looked at Lacey, as if wondering what she should do.

Lacey shrugged. "You might as well go home and get some rest." Her tone held a little resentment that she couldn't quite hold back. "I'll be fine. The doctor will check me over and send me off anyway."

With everybody getting up at the same time, Lacey waited and squeezed out from the table, desperate to hold back her cries from pain that just moving her body created. Everything was stiff for having sat so long. She knew it'd be better when she walked around a bit again, but right now trying to get outside would be brutal.

Her right arm was grabbed gently but firmly, and she was led to the front door. There she stopped and took several deep breaths.

Chana turned to look back at her. "Are you sure?"

Lacey gave her a bright smile. "Go. I'll be home in less than an hour." She turned to look at Sebastian, adding, "Right?"

He stared at her steadily. "I guess it depends on how bad it really is. You think I didn't see the sweat coming off your forehead? You think I don't see how much pain you're in?"

She winced. "And here I thought I did a great job of hiding it," she muttered.

He led the way around the corner. She followed him without having any choice in the matter as he had retained his grip on her arm.

"How far are we going?"

"Luckily not far," he said. "A friend of mine is a doctor here. We'll take you there. I've already contacted him. He's expecting us. He'll give you a quick glance over and see if it's any worse than you think."

"Oh, good. Okay," she said, feeling better. "I was thinking of sitting at a hospital for hours, waiting for somebody to take a few minutes to look at me."

"No, this is much faster."

He kept walking, and she followed. However, with every

step the pain seemed to kick in heavier.

Finally he paused in front of a large door, hit several buzzers, and a resounding *click* replied on the other side. He pulled the door toward him. "The good news is, he also has an elevator."

She stared at him, her brain fuzzy. "That's a good thing," she said faintly. "I hadn't even contemplated how hard stairs would be."

It was only a few steps to the elevator, and thankfully it was open and waiting for them. He led her inside, propped her against the back wall and said, "Don't move."

She snorted. "There aren't a hell of a lot of places I can go right now."

The pain was getting worse. She knew it was just fatigue, but that ache was deep and intense. The elevator opened directly onto somebody's apartment. She frowned. "How does that work?"

"You have to have a pass code to get in."

He led her forward a few steps, calling out, "Juan, where are you?"

"I'm coming. I'm coming," a man called out from somewhere in the depths of the apartment.

It was dark, but then it became super bright as an overhead light came on. She closed her eyes and bent her head against the light.

"Oh, interesting," the stranger said. He stepped forward and grasped her hand gently. "I'm Juan. Let me take a look at you."

She smiled as much of a bright cheerful smile as she could, hiding the pain she was in. "Thank you so much for seeing me."

He shook his head rapidly. "Oh, no, no, no, no. When

Sebastian says he needs help, we help."

She chuckled. "That's good to know."

Juan led her to an upholstered chair and said, "Now sit down. Let me take a look."

She looked at the chair, then at him. "It's much easier if I stand," she admitted.

His gaze sharpened. "Tell me exactly what happened."

With a hesitant look in Sebastian's direction, she nodded and proceeded to tell Juan about walking out into the traffic without looking and getting nudged by the car.

At the word *nudged*, Sebastian snorted. "You can see how she can barely move that side of her body. The whole way here, she moved slower. She'll seize up in agony in no time."

"That we can deal with," Juan said. He glanced at her. "I have to lift your shirt."

She nodded and leaned sideways so he could lift her clothing out of the way. It was just a loose tank top, thankfully, a light, filmy material he could lift easily. But she studied his face as he watched her skin appear.

A grim look came over him.

She asked, "Does it look bad?"

Sebastian strode forward so he could take a closer look.

She twisted and then gasped at the pain it caused. "Okay. So I don't get to look myself," she muttered.

"No," Sebastian said, his fingers gentle as he took over holding up her shirt while the doctor poked and prodded.

Pain lanced through her when he got to her ribs. But she was determined to not get sent to a hospital because of a busted rib and her own stupidity. She gritted her teeth and, with neither of the men focused on her face, she scrunched it up to stop herself from crying out.

Juan asked, "What about your legs?"

Sebastian lowered her shirt, and she straightened slightly, lifting her left leg as instructed.

He said, "I need to see your hip."

She nodded grimly. "I landed on my hip, but I think I took the initial blow on the ribs."

"What kind of vehicle was it?"

"A van," she said with a frown. "Some kind of a delivery van, I think."

He nodded and gently lowered her shorts to her knees so she stood before both men in her underwear. Embarrassed, yes, but in too much pain to care.

He poked and prodded some more. "Nothing's broken," he announced as he slowly pulled her shorts back up. "But you'll turn many shades of green and purple over the next week. You'll need heavy muscle relaxants. Otherwise you can't get out of bed in the morning nor will you sleep." He helped her to turn around slowly. "Now sit."

She sat slowly, trying hard not to cry.

"You must feel terrible." His voice was sympathetic and caring. "You take a blow like that from the vehicle, and then you get hit by the road as well—that's a second blow. Your body is in shock. Your muscles have tightened up because of the injuries. You'll have swelling with a lot of soreness." Then he glanced down at her feet and frowned. He crouched down. "Your feet too?"

She leaned forward. "I don't remember my foot being injured."

"They're both scraped and bleeding." He unbuckled her sandal and removed it from her foot. "Wait a minute. I'll get some antiseptic water for a foot soak." He hurried away.

She sighed as she looked at her feet. "Are you going to

send me home to the States?" she asked Sebastian in a low voice. She felt more than saw his startled surprise. That was a good thing. Maybe he wouldn't feel so inclined to cut short her visit.

Now she wished she hadn't mentioned that. Suddenly he crouched in front of her, that magnetic gaze of his locked on hers. "I should, you know."

She stared at him. "Why?" Her voice was low, plaintive. "I've been looking forward to this trip forever."

He nodded. "Chana told me. I understand how you feel about it, but some really serious issues are happening at the site, and you've been hurt once now. I don't want you to get hurt again."

"That's not likely, surely? And," she added after a moment's hesitation, "it was my fault. It's not like somebody did this to me. I'm the fool who stepped out into the traffic."

He didn't say anything for a long moment. "I guess there's no hope of you having seen the driver?"

She shook her head. "Honestly I think he drove away, not realizing. I'm probably such a lightweight he didn't even know he hit me."

At that Sebastian snorted. "Oh, he knew. He definitely knew. I wonder if anybody else caught sight of him."

"I doubt it," she said. "But I can't be sure. You'd have to ask them."

Just then the doctor returned with a basin filled with warm water. He placed the basin down in front of her and said, "Put your foot in it carefully." He unbuckled her other sandal, removed it from her foot, noticed she had scrapes and scratches along that calf. "You soak. I'll get antibiotics to clean this off. Then we'll take a look and put some ointment on it for you." He disappeared once again.

She sat there, her eyes closed, loving the warmth on her feet. She knew she should be home in bed, but right now this was worth the trip over. The thought of walking to the apartment was almost heartbreaking.

"We'll see how you feel in the morning," Sebastian said abruptly.

"I'm fine," she snapped. "I really don't want to be here." She didn't understand what was going on behind that deep gaze of his, but she could see a turmoil she didn't understand. "Surely it's not that big a deal."

The doctor returned again, cleaned the scrapes on both legs, checked her over again, making sure nothing else needed to be attended to. As he lowered her shirt once again, he said, "How are your feet doing now?"

She wiggled her toes and admitted, "They're much better." She lifted her feet and saw they were also a little puffy.

"I'd say you should stay off your feet for the next few days, but I doubt you'd listen to me."

"Nope, I won't," she said, laughing. "I spent too long trying to get here."

He nodded as if nothing she said would surprise him.

She glanced at Sebastian and quirked, "You must have brought in some interesting characters if he assumes I'm like the rest of them and won't listen to his instructions."

He shook his head but remained silent.

She shrugged and watched as the doctor dried her feet and put an ointment on her toes, which he then bandaged. In a surprising move he took her sandals, placed them in the water, giving them a quick disinfectant washing, and then banged them together to knock off the water and put her feet back inside them.

The doctor said. "Better to have them cleaned off and

not bring any possible infection with them."

It made logical sense, but it felt weird to stand up in wet shoes. "I'll track water all over your floor."

"Could be worse," he said cheerfully. "You could be tracking blood."

She winced, "Good point."

"I want to see you in a couple days if other injuries arise. Do you hear me?"

She nodded. "I can manage that. I don't know how to pay you."

"It's already taken care of," the doctor said with a wave of his hand at Sebastian. "That's his problem, not yours."

She wasn't so sure about that. She felt bad as it was. She'd hardly been working for him when she got hit. But it wasn't the time or the place for that conversation.

Moving slowly she made it to the doctor's elevator. Sebastian pressed the button so they could go back down. It opened, and they stepped inside. She waved at the doctor, and they sank slowly out of sight.

"He's very nice," she murmured.

"He is. Very caring. He's the epitome of a man doing what he should be doing. He has the right personality and passion for it."

She thought about that and nodded. "I agree. It's not always easy to know what one should be doing in life."

"Chana said you're a teacher?"

"Yes. My parents adamantly discouraged me from going into archaeology, so the closest I could get was being a history teacher," she said with a laugh.

"That's too bad. There's still quite a field left for those with the right passion for it."

"When Chana went into it, it was like watching her do

what she was supposed to do and feeling like I'd missed my opportunity."

The elevator doors opened, and they stepped out.

She caught his intense gaze and smiled. "I am okay, you know."

He seemed to relax. "Maybe," he said, "but I feel responsible nonetheless."

"Why?" she asked. "It's not like you were there. You didn't push me into the vehicle."

"Do you think anybody pushed you?" he asked.

She frowned. "Honestly I felt a nudge, but it was so light it couldn't have been a push. I think it was just us jostling for space to cross the road." Her smile brightened. "Besides, I was with the team. It's not like anybody there would hurt me."

He nodded but kept his thoughts to himself.

He was so hard to read. Normally she was good at understanding what people were thinking, but, in his case, it was like a blank slate. "So you'll let me stay?"

He slid a glance at her.

She shrugged. "I know I'm pestering you. But I won't sleep tonight if I'm afraid you'll send me back tomorrow."

"You can stay," he said abruptly. "But if anything else happens ..."

"It won't happen to me," she said "There's no way. I only have a couple weeks here as it is."

"Chana said you're on vacation?"

She nodded. "I am. I have the whole summer off. Chana explained how this job was only for two weeks." She looked at him hopefully. "Unless you can use my services longer?"

"No cats to look after at home?"

"No. The family cat, my mother's baby, passed away just

a month before my mother did."

She was so lost in the memory that she didn't realize he'd clasped her hand with his own. He squeezed her fingers and said, "I'm sorry. That's a double loss."

"It is, and one certainly is more minor to the other, but together they were a double blow." She was about to step forward again into the street, but he caught her and held her close. She looked up and sighed. "That's what I did last time too."

He didn't say anything, and they waited until the traffic had cleared; then he escorted her across the street.

As they walked to the apartment, she asked with a frown, "Are you coming up?"

"Not to your apartment. I have my own on the same floor." He took her to her apartment door. "He gave me medications." He handed her two bottles. One was a muscle relaxant, the other painkillers. He pointed out the labels on each. "Two painkillers to be taken every four hours, two right now and go to bed. If you wake up in the middle of night, take two more. Same for the muscle relaxants."

She smiled, thanked him and went to open the door. It was unlocked. Of course it was. She wasn't with Chana, and Chana would have been inside waiting for her.

But Sebastian didn't like it. "Do you have a key?"

She shook her head. "No. I just arrived last night. I don't even know how many keys there are for the apartment."

"Lots," he said. "Keeping track of them is a pain in the ass."

That startled a laugh out of her. "I can imagine. If you have lots of interns back and forth, that must be hard." She walked inside, turned and smiled up at him. "Thanks again. And good night." She went to close the door, but he put his foot inside.

"I need to check to make sure everything's okay."

Disturbed and wondering why he was so protective, she watched as he circled the living room. Chana's bedroom door was open. She was asleep on the bed, easily visible from the hall. The men's bedroom was also open, and both beds occupied. The place was silent and calm.

"Satisfied?"

His lips quirked, and he nodded his head. "At least I've checked. Now get to sleep." He then turned and walked out.

SOMETHING WAS WRONG with the apartment. Sebastian took the stairs back outside to track whatever energy he'd seen in there earlier. That was disturbing. How long had it been since somebody had been in that place? And who had left the energy? And when? And why was it leaving a trail? All questions that normally he'd have answers to, but he wasn't getting any. Just that it was old energy. He hadn't seen it on any of his team, and he didn't know if it was masking itself or if he had yet to see whoever had that energy.

He'd started seeing auras as a child but didn't understand what they were. It's only later he got an inkling of how different his view of his world was to others and delved deeper into the field. Who knew there could be so many differences between people?

When he had first opened the door, he had seen a little faint energy, footprints on the tile floor, so he'd gone in to check. But whatever it was, the energy, the footprints, had led right back out again. He hadn't seen them as he and Lacey had come up the elevator, just that they had been up here on the third floor. And he hadn't asked her about it either. But now it would be hard for him to sleep. He hadn't seen footprints like that since the Mayan ruins. Footprints glowed from the vestiges of energy of the spirit walking. He'd been new to auras and footprints at the Mayan dig, he often wondered if that dig hadn't brought it all into his awareness.

Almost every dig since had some paranormal events too, but minor. He'd often wondered if he'd attracted them. It was a disconcerting thought.

But there was something familiar about these footprints. It couldn't be. It shouldn't be. But … his mind was already saying it was.

And that was too disturbing to contemplate.

All energy had a unique signature. But sometimes events or spirits could hide or transform that signature to something or someone else. He knew there had to be something missing here. Because there's no way that could be the same signature he'd seen before …

Yet it was close enough to make his stomach heave.

He had a quick shower and got ready for bed. But, as predicted, couldn't sleep. He rose, entered his bedroom and pulled out his laptop and turned it on, checked his emails and responded to a couple that needed to be done now. Then he looked at his saved documents on his notes from the Mayan files. There were two versions: the official notes, and then there were his paranormal notes. As he delved into them, it took a frustrating ten minutes to find the references he was looking for.

But finally he read his own words from ten years ago. *The footprints glowed as they led across the temple floors.* So he hadn't been wrong.

Of course there was no note on the identity of the signature—he hadn't understood that unique identifying appearance to each back then. Even if he had, it's not as if he could say in what way it was unique.

There was no visible sign in the physical world, but, in the paranormal world, the footprints could be easily seen. He hadn't seen them at the restaurant or on the way to his buddy's place. But now that he'd come back to the apartment building, they were here—or rather he was not seeing them. He wondered if he should move everybody to a new place.

Who had been in the crew's apartment recently? The landlord, cleaning ladies and any number of guests or friends of the team probably. He opened a document and wrote down every person who could have been in Lacey's apartment the past day.

And then he stopped and considered ... Were the footprints fresh, as in the last day? Or, since he had not been in that apartment building in weeks, could the footprints be older? It shouldn't be so strong as to stay around that long. Most times energy dissipated within hours—a day at the most. And with that thought uppermost, he widened the list of potential people in the apartment building to weeks ago. Intuitively he figured they had been there recently, as in since all the problems at the site had started. But he couldn't be too careful. Nothing made any sense, yet he knew it would. Eventually.

He shut down his computer and walked into the kitchen for a glass of water before bed. Usually his instincts were decent. He contacted Jeremiah, asking about his plan, adding:

Mayan dig incidents are happening here at Pompeii dig.

So Golden Boy needs my help?

Sebastian ignored his taciturn tone, noting Jeremiah's attitude was getting worse. But Jeremiah always came through for Sebastian. So he let Jeremiah know about all the incidents so far and what Sebastian had just come up with.

Almost instantly his response was *WTF?*

Sebastian chuckled. *Right? Not sure what the hell is going on, but it's serious.*

No, that's not serious. That's sinister. That's deadly. That's evil.

I know. It's early days. I don't have any answers. I don't even know what questions to ask to get those answers.

Of course you know how I've visited Pompeii many, many times over the decades. I was just there ten days ago, and nothing had gone wrong. So what's changed? Do you want me to come over?

Not yet. Sebastian tapped his fingers on the counter. *But I might need you here if things get any worse.*

I can come to Naples now.

Sebastian made a sudden decision. *If you don't mind …*

Hell no. I'm not going through that shit again. Better to stop it now.

Right. That's what I was thinking myself.

I'm only a few hours away.

Check in with me once you arrive or after you get a feel for things here.

Not a problem, Jeremiah answered. *I'll see you soon.*

Sebastian put his empty water glass in the dishwasher and turned off lights in the apartment as he reached his bedroom, stretching out on his bed to attempt to sleep again. But his mind burned with the painful Mayan expedition memories. It had been his first experience into supernatural events, and, as an initiation, it had been terrifying. He'd spoken to many experts afterward, but, without anything to show for what he'd gone through, some of them had been dubious of his claims, while others had been excited and wanted to go back in, yet only one person had understood the trauma Sebastian had gone through. Stefan.

It was late and, even with Jeremiah coming to help, Sebastian still couldn't sleep. He tossed and turned, his mind filled with bad memories of so long ago. He couldn't remember much about the powerful psychic he had spoken to way back when, right after he had escaped the Mayan site with his life and right before he began his own research into these psychic happenings. Stefan had been young to be touted as the best in his field, about the same age as Sebastian is now. He'd warned Sebastian ten years ago how according to the locals, the energy released at the Mayan site, Kisin—or his servant the jailor—would always be attracted to him in the future. That once a connection was made … it was always there. And connections could be made in many ways.

Sebastian dozed, woke up, suddenly alert, sitting up in bed and looking around his apartment. He pushed his hair off his forehead wishing he could talk to Stefan about his current mess. But it seemed so minor compared to their last conversation.

But just the reminder of the steadfastness, the deepness of that man's voice, reciting his message almost ten long years ago as if in a trance, had been beyond freaky. Stefan had had a profound impact on Sebastian, which led to his further studies of all things paranormal and supernatural, looking for answers. Hell, he was still looking.

Sebastian tossed off the bedcovers and headed to grab his

laptop from his study. "Well, Stefan, maybe you were right. And maybe that energy always lives and breathes around us. Whether or not it knew me back then, it's certainly back in my world now. The question is, what has it been doing in the meantime? And what are its plans for me? Is this personal? If so, why?"

Settled in bed again but with his laptop, he looked through his emails for the name. But he had nothing with Stefan at all. He searched the internet for contact information, a website. But again found nothing. He frowned.

He remembered coming across something about Stefan years later, seeing some of the paintings the man created. They were incredibly difficult to look at and yet transfixing. It was even worse trying to tear his gaze away. Sebastian still couldn't remember what Stefan's last name was. He typed odd things into Google—*Stefan psychic, Stefan artist*. And very quickly Sebastian came up with a name—Stefan Kronos.

The darkness had settled heavily into his bedroom as Sebastian stared at that name. Feelings of fear and panic rolled through him as he remembered the Mayan ruins. He worked on his breathing to stop from hyperventilating at the onslaught of the younger version of himself crowding through his mind and warning him to stay away from Pompeii, to get the hell out of Italy and to leave this thing alone.

He glanced around his bedroom and said, "Well, Stefan, I'm not sure how I'm supposed to contact you, but you're the only one who made any sense back then."

There was, of course, no answer. Sebastian tossed out another attempt to contact Stefan. "If we're meant to connect, find a way please." Still nothing happened.

He slammed shut his laptop, tossed it on the other side of his bed and slipped back down so he was prone again.

Until a ball of light shone in the center of his bedroom.

He roared in surprise, jumped out of his bed, grabbing the weapon he always kept hidden under his pillow and backed against the wall, the small snub-nosed handgun pointed at the light. "Who are you? What do you want?"

A man's face appeared. No body, just a glowing orb and a face.

Sebastian frowned at it. "Do I know you?" The face in the orb had shoulder-length blond hair, pulled back in a low ponytail.

"You just called me," The glowing ball said, the voice tired but tinged with humor.

"And you always answer everybody who calls you?" Sebastian asked in astonishment.

The man shook his head. "No, I don't. But, just like you have a prior bond with that evil from the Mayan ruins, I have a prior bond with you."

Slowly Sebastian lowered the revolver and admitted the impossible was happening. And yet, after what he'd been through, he knew nothing was impossible. He didn't want to let go of the gun, just in case, but it was foolish to shoot something that wasn't even here.

Stefan nodded. "I appreciate you not shooting me," he said humorously. "It takes a lot of energy to be here as it is. It would be instinctive for me to protect myself, and that would be a foolish waste of energy—I'd like to think—because I don't imagine you can shoot around dimensions."

Sebastian stared at him. "But you're human. You're alive. Yet you're acting like a spirit being. How are you doing what you're doing?"

"Lots of practice and lots of energy," he said quietly. "You called me because of that energy you found in the Mayan ruins. Have you come into contact with it again?"

Sebastian nodded slowly. "Back then you said that energy could always recognize me again. Did you mean that?"

Stefan said, "All energy has a signature. It's unique to who you are. Just as you should be able to recognize that energy again, it too will recognize you." He hesitated then added slowly, "However there have been several instances where that energy has managed to change its appearance. So although I say you should recognize that energy, it's also possible that you won't be able to."

Sebastian ran a hand through his hair. He dropped the handgun back under the pillow and sat down on the side of the bed. He was still wrapping his mind around the fact he was speaking to a ball of energy, projected from God-only-knows-where to his rented apartment in Pompeii. "You're really here talking to me?"

"I'm really here talking to you," Stefan said, but the humor had gone. "Look. I can't maintain this. Maybe we can talk via phone or email." And he started to fade.

Sebastian jumped to his feet and walked around the corner. "Wait," he said. "Things are happening on the dig that I'm working on. It feels like the same energy. But I didn't see it at the dig, just down the hallway from here. I thought I saw the same footprints, the same pattern of footprints."

"What kind of footprints?"

Sebastian took a deep breath. "Psychic footprints."

Stefan stared at him for a long moment. "The glowing outline of a footprint?"

"Yes, and a trail, where it's going forward and back."

"And do you recognize its energy signature?"

"As much as I can recognize anything from ten years ago, so yes and no, but it feels the same." He hesitated then filled him in on the Kisin lore.

"I remember hearing something about that back then," Stefan muttered.

Silence fell.

"Don't doubt yourself," Stefan finally added. "You know by now, this many years later, and I'm sure you've researched the topic thoroughly, just how much danger this type of evil can cause."

"I don't know why it's here and if it is *exactly* the same."

"It might not be exactly the same," Stefan murmured. "Once a negative energy awakens, it causes ripples underneath, giving other energies much-needed power. So it is possible an energy, an old entity, has now been released from the site you're at currently. Could it be connected to this Kisin energy—maybe? But as we know there are no gods of death, just men with hearts willed with evil. Chances are your Kisin made a reputation for himself slaughtering many people. Once he was finally dead, the locals would have blamed any catastrophic event on him for centuries." He sighed. "Sure it's possible this Kisin is back. His servant's energy could have been sealed in that tomb you opened, but it could be any number of other assholes trying to reclaim all they lost and live again—in whatever form they can."

Dread filled his heart as he stared at Stefan. "That sounds like the absolutely worst thing possible."

Stefan gave him a sad smile. "It isn't. It's unpleasant, and it's definitely not anything we want to deal with. But think about hundreds of these gathering in one spot. That would be worse. And you can't lump all entities into being evil. There are many spirits caught between—neither alive nor dead—through no ill will of their own."

"A battle between good and evil again."

"There is no *again*," Stefan said quietly. "Because it never stopped."

"What do I do now?"

"It's important that you track each energy you feel, see how strong it is. Every time you see those footprints, try to figure out if its energy changes. Try to communicate with it and see if it will give you any answers as to what it wants." Stefan stopped for a moment. "How serious are these incidents?"

"Minor yet," Sebastian said cautiously. "Which is why I had worried I was overreacting. But then tonight I saw the footprints, and that terrified me." He had no problem admitting it. He'd be a foolish man to see something well beyond the scope of his personal experiences and beliefs and to not be concerned about it. "And what about other specialists nearby? Is anybody local around who you might know? I will contact Hunter too."

Stefan frowned. "No one I know. I can contact Hunter too. Send him your way if he's free from the current job he's been working on for me."

"Anything you can do would be appreciated," Sebastian said. "I have a good team of young people to protect."

Stefan nodded. "You need a support system to stop your doubts. Preferably energy workers like myself. If you have other psychics, other people who can see these footprints, it will give you validation that you're not crazy." He started to fade. "Get my email from Hunter as that's the best way to contact me after this, but I'm always available if it's an emergency."

And just like that he faded from sight.

CHAPTER 5

G ETTING OUT OF bed the next morning redefined
Lacey's understanding of what pain was. She sat on the
edge of the bed, catching her breath. She hoped a hot shower
would allow her muscles to move. Right now she felt ninety
years old. All her joints had seized. Using the headboard, she
got into a standing position, then hobbled toward the
hallway bathroom—the only one in this apartment and to be
shared by all four who lived here. It was early, but she
needed to loosen up her body. And definitely time for more
painkillers. She had to at least look like she wasn't badly
hurt, so Sebastian couldn't bar her from going onsite today.

Standing under the hot water in the shower helped a lot.
It was all she could do to keep her moans of joy to herself as
she leaned against the shower wall and let the heat pound on
her side, back and hips. Not wanting to steal too much of
the hot water supply, she reluctantly turned off the taps and
dried off. With her hair braided to one side, her teeth
brushed, she headed back to her room, still wrapped up in a
towel. She had never thought to pack a bathrobe. Luckily
nobody else seemed to be up to care. When she walked into
the bedroom, she saw Chana was already dressed. She was
bent, making her bed.

She turned to look at Lacey and, with a critical eye, said,
"You look better. I wasn't sure when I watched you get out

of bed."

"Yeah, getting up was a bit rough," Lacey admitted. "But a hot shower helped." After her cousin left, Lacey quickly took her muscle relaxants and one of the painkillers. She stored the medicine bottles in her camera bag, making sure she took a bottle of water with her, and headed to the kitchen where the others stumbled around, looking for coffee and breakfast.

"Do we wait for Sebastian?" Lacey asked.

"You tell us," Brian said cheerfully from the kitchen doorway. "You're the one who went out with him last night."

That brought on a lot of teasing and joking from the others.

Lacey shook her head. "Yeah, he took me to a doctor who checked me over, cleaned my scrapes and bandaged me up," she said blithely. "Very romantic."

As a conversation stopper, it was pretty good.

"How are you feeling now?" Mark asked in a solicitous tone.

"I'm feeling much better," she said. "Looking forward to getting out there today."

"Make sure you don't overdo it," Chana said. "No more mishaps for anybody, got it?" Her gaze went around the group.

The rest of the team from Katie's apartment—Brian, Matt and Denny—had come in the kitchen right behind Tom. Most had coffee and waited while the others ate breakfast. Apparently this was their informal meeting as they discussed the day before and headed to the site every day. Lacey listened in as they made plans for the day. But soon enough it was time to pack up and go. She made sure she had extra water and packed a pair of socks, in case blisters formed on her heels after the scrapes. She had checked her ribs in the shower but figured she'd be good enough to go. As long as she had on a loose shirt and didn't sweat too badly, nothing should be touching her bruised ribs, and she'd be fine.

The group crossed the street, heading toward the entrance to the excavation site. This time several people were around her, maybe subconsciously making sure she didn't step off the curb into the street traffic accidentally.

She didn't say anything. She just wanted her camera out to take pictures. The crew was somber as they approached the site. And their boss had beaten them to work. She realized just how much Sebastian's presence was a bit of a downer.

"Does he come very often?" she asked when a lull in the conversation came.

The others nodded.

"But normally he's the most amiable person you could ask for," Chana said. "So he's worried about something. Otherwise he wouldn't be so short-tempered and so tense."

"Is he the only one who comes?"

"No, Colin, his business partner, comes every once in a while," Chana said, as they all neared the Stabian Gate. "He was here a few days ago, and the foundation warehouse has a manager who pops by irregularly, but I haven't seen him in a while. He might be on vacation. Sometimes it seems like too many bosses."

"Like any job then," Lacey confirmed with a smile. "My students like to think they're my bosses, but the school board in the school district I work in are my bosses."

"I couldn't do your job," Katie said.

"It's fun most of the time," Lacey said comfortably. "But there are lots of things I don't like about it."

"I think that comes with every job," Chana said.

They were at the site now. The place was deserted at this hour.

"Do you guys start the earliest here?" Lacey looked around but couldn't see anyone else at their dig site.

"We want to get in a lot of work before the heat gets high," Tom said. "So the earlier we get here, the better. I don't know what other archeological groups are doing, as we're not working anywhere close to them anyway. We don't see them very often."

"I thought I saw a group here yesterday," Lacey said, sure she'd seen several people close by.

They looked at her and frowned. "Nobody's around here at all except for us. Never has been."

She stayed silent, wondering, wanting to get her camera out so she could take a look at the pictures she'd taken yesterday without doing so right in front of everybody. Regardless she was pretty damn sure she'd seen people working on another site close by.

Soon as the crew got busy, she pulled out her camera and studied the shots she'd taken. She hadn't had a chance to download anything yet, so they were still on her SD card. She flicked through again and again until she got to the spot where she'd been near the stairs. She stopped at one of the images, showing the stairs disappearing into the ground, and smiled. It had an incredibly powerful impact. A few photos earlier, she came across the ones she had taken of the other team. It was really hard to see them through the trees. She thought she'd captured more details there. But found only black smudges.

"I'll have to get in closer next time," she said, then realized that might not be the smartest thing to do. Because she probably had to have permission from the other team in order to photograph them. "I'll discuss it with Sebastian later," she muttered as she flicked through her pictures.

"Do you always talk to yourself?" Sebastian asked as he stopped in front of her. "And what do you want to discuss with me?"

She looked up and, since she was one level down, he stood just above her at ground level.

He crouched in front of her. "Ask me now."

She motioned to where she'd seen the team. "Yesterday I saw a group working over there. I tried to take photos, but I see only black smudges on my camera."

He stiffened, and the smile on his face fell away.

She quickly added, "I just wanted to know if we were allowed to take pictures of other people or if we needed permission first." As the look on his face darkened, she held up her hand and straightened. "Look. I'm sorry. I'm still figuring out what I can and cannot do."

Slowly he stood up tall above her. He had to be at least six-two, maybe six-three, as he towered high over her. "The rule is, you can only take pictures of our team and the site," he said almost too quietly. "And, if we have a reason to take photos of another group, we get permission and signed waivers."

"Oh, good," she said with relief. "In that case, it's a good thing those pictures didn't turn out."

He motioned at the camera in her hand. "Do you have them up?"

Thinking he was more concerned about the legal aspects of her taking those pictures, she nodded and flicked back to where she had been so he could see the sequence of photos. "See? Right here. I came upon them and took a few photos, and then I was talking with you and taking the photos of the stairs."

He stared at the photos with the dark smudges, pointing. "These dark … *smudges* here and here and here?"

She nodded.

"Can you email these to me please?" he held out a card with his information.

His tone was so neutral and seemingly not angry that she was happy to comply. "Sure. As you can see, absolutely no new faces are captured there."

"Still, I need a copy of them."

"Right. Legal departments and all that." She wrote down the numbers of the images. "When I download them later this afternoon, I'll send them to you."

He nodded. "And make sure you watch what you take pictures of, right?"

She beamed happily. "No problem." As she bent to put her notepad in her bag, she caught her breath as she moved the wrong way. There was a sudden silence around her. She realized that, up until then, he'd completely forgotten about her injuries. She grabbed her camera bag, straightened and put it on her shoulder, deliberately not letting him see any kind of reaction as she moved. "Maybe I'll start today on this segment."

He shook his head. "No, a lot of pottery pieces need to be photographed. Start over there and catalogue every piece we've unearthed."

"I can do that," she said with a bright smile. She stepped up to his level and walked past him as he grabbed her arm.

"How are you?" he asked softly.

She threw him another cheerful smile that she knew didn't fool him in any way. "I'm feeling much better. The painkillers and the muscle relaxants overnight helped a lot."

He nodded. "Don't do too much today. And keep taking your pills. Especially the relaxants."

"I will." She pulled her arm free and walked away. She really wanted to turn back and see if he was watching her, but she instinctively knew he was. And that was unnerving in itself.

Back at the dig site where they had tables laid out, Katie worked on the samples.

"Sebastian wants me to take photographs of all the pieces found so far," Lacey said.

Katie nodded. "Everything that we pull out, we name, tag and bag, and then you can take photographs of them."

"I can do that." Lacey changed out her lenses, adjusted her focus and set up for the first piece. After several discussions back and forth with Katie, Lacey changed and tweaked her process a little bit, and then, when they agreed the photos were good, Lacey went ahead and took serious photographs. Not just one but four or five of each piece.

When they broke for lunch, she looked up in surprise, completely stunned that so many hours had gone by. "It can't be lunchtime already." Her gaze went from one of the crew to the other.

They all looked at her in surprise. "Don't be too eager and too efficient here," Tom said. "The boss won't let you go if you do that."

Pleased, Lacey just smiled at him. "Not likely to happen but I'll do my best regardless."

They sat in the shade and ate sandwiches. She looked at the sandwich Chana had handed her and said, "I didn't even see you make these."

"I didn't," she said. "Sebastian brought them. It's time for a break anyway, so we might as well eat. It's supposed to get very hot this afternoon, so we'll work as late as we can. But, once that heat hits, we may have to break for a while."

"For a while?"

Chana shrugged. "What I really mean is, we'll be done for the day. Could work on paperwork back at the apartment."

"I can get behind that," Lacey said. "I have to sift through a few thousand photos."

"Are you really taking that many?" Tom asked. Honest curiosity was in his voice.

"Not quite," she said, "but I wouldn't be at all surprised if I wasn't up over six hundred already."

"That's still a ton," he said. "It'd be nice to think we could get caught up. We need your photos to document boxes and boxes of materials we've found." He turned to Katie. "Where is all that stuff?"

"It's all still in our apartment because we didn't know where else to send it. We can't ship it to the foundation until it's been cataloged, and we didn't want to leave it here with the trouble we're having on the site."

"In that case maybe I should go back with you this afternoon," Lacey said to Katie. "I could get on that cataloging."

Katie shrugged. "You could. I know Sebastian has plans to set it all out on the table and get you to work on it."

"Do you have a big table in your apartment?"

She shook her head. "Sebastian does. His apartment is just down from us."

"In that case I'll talk to him when he comes over."

"Except I'm already here," Sebastian said in exasperation. "That's twice you've said something along that line today."

She chewed the bite in her mouth as she thought about how to respond, but he just waved at her.

"Make sure to take your muscle relaxants with that food. Minimize any chance of a stomachache. You'll also find the heat hits you a whole lot worse this afternoon, so I want you to knock off by three o'clock at the very latest."

"Katie said boxes of samples and retrieved items to be catalogued are at our apartments. I thought I could work on that when we leave here."

"No," he said, his tone curt. "When the day is done, the day is done. I don't want you overdoing it, particularly when you're not feeling good."

"I'm fine," she snapped.

At her tone everybody else went silent.

She sighed. "Okay, so I'm not a hundred percent fine, but I'm feeling much better."

"Good," he said. "In that case we aren't going to push it, are we?"

She just rolled her eyes at him. "Do you worry like this about everybody?" she muttered.

He nodded. "I do." He looked at his watch. "I'll be back in an hour and a half or so." He stopped and looked at Lacey. "I'll come and collect you at that time."

"Do you want me to come with you then too?" Katie asked.

"Yes. Pack up what she has already photographed here. We'll take that back to my place, sort it out and ship it on to the foundation."

It seemed like almost as soon as he'd left, he was back.

Lacey straightened, groaned at her sore muscles and walked over to a cooler spot in some shade. Sitting down, she pulled out her water and painkillers. She didn't want anybody to see what she was doing because she didn't want anybody to question her about it, but she was hurting. She'd love to go back to the apartment, have a shower and collapse in bed, just letting the painkillers work.

As she sat here, she picked up her camera and studied the area where she had seen the people before. She took several more photos and put down her camera, resting her head against the rock. She took several deep, slow relaxing breaths but heard bushes crackling behind her. She didn't think much of it, but, when heavy footsteps came closer, she froze and wondered what animals were around here. She glanced at her team, but they were busy working away. The sounds came from the right. She slipped down to a ledge below, holding up her camera.

She waited, clicking several images just for reference, until it sounded like the crunching brushes were closer and closer. She frowned and then heard a branch snapping in two. Her fingers clicked her camera madly, but she hadn't seen anything.

Suddenly Tom called out to her, coming up on her left side. "Hey, you okay?"

He'd come around the bush from where she'd been watching. "Hey. Sorry. I heard you crashing around in there," she said with a self-deprecating laugh. "I thought maybe I was about to get attacked by some wild animal." She held up her camera, waited a minute and said, "But obviously it was just you."

He chuckled, jumped down and said, "It's a sign you've been here too long when you see the boogeyman around every corner."

She gave a one-arm shrug. "Well, I am tired. However, I'm heading back with Sebastian and Katie soon."

A whistle ripped across the open pit. She turned and winced at the movement, jarring her leg. She caught the side of the stone wall for a moment, catching her breath. There was Sebastian, waving at her.

Slowly she clambered back up to where she had been sitting originally, grabbed her bag, smiled at Tom and said, "The boss calls."

Tom walked back with her, slow enough so she wasn't pushing herself. When they reached Sebastian, he grabbed a big box.

Katie grabbed another one. "Let's go. Otherwise we won't have any time to work today."

She exchanged a glance with Katie. "Was I late?"

Katie just chuckled with a nod to Sebastian. "No, he is."

"Oh, okay." As Lacey left, something caused her to turn and to stare at the spot where she'd heard the noise. She hated to think her nerves were getting the better of her, but she swore something was coming toward her, and she thought she'd heard a branch break—not just bushes rustling—but that was stupid as she never saw a person or any animal.

Because nothing could make a branch break and not be seen. Right?

Back at the apartment they carefully lowered the boxes on a large dining room table in Sebastian's apartment. He told Lacey, "You'll have to adjust your lights and filters. The light in here is pretty bad. I'd rather do it outside, but, with all the problems on the site, we decided it was better to bring everything inside."

She nodded and sat in a chair at the table, fiddling with her camera. She took several photographs, adjusted the light again and then decided on a different lens. By the time she was ready to go, Sebastian and Katie had a good forty different items laid out. Standing carefully in front and leaning down over the top of the items, Lacey clicked several photographs from a few different angles to make sure she had a good visual identification of what the item was. Then it was flipped, exposing a card identifying what it was and where it had been found, along with its ID number.

By the time she had taken six photographs of every one of the items, Katie came behind her, packaging up the finds and checking off each on her datasheet with matching ID numbers found there. And, just for safe measure, Lacey came behind her and took photographs of each of the items now numerically marked and resting in the box. With the table completely empty, everything collected and boxed, they laid out another whole set.

Lacey lost track of time as they did table load after table load after table load. Finally she straightened and gasped as her back seized up.

Katie rushed to her side. "Are you all right?"

Lacey took a deep breath, let it out slowly and gasped. "Straightened too fast. I forgot how sore my side is. But I'm fine."

Sebastian walked over and handed her a large glass of water. She took the first sip and then couldn't seem to get enough. She completely emptied the glass, then handed it back and asked, "May I get a refill please?"

He raised an eyebrow but went to refill the glass for her. When her second glassful came back, she drank half and just held it close for a moment.

"I hadn't realized how dehydrated I was getting," she said.

The two of them stared at her with odd looks on their faces.

"What did I say?" she demanded.

"You've been drinking all afternoon," Katie said. "I'm surprised you haven't been running to the bathroom every thirty minutes."

Lacey chuckled. "Now that you mentioned it ..." She looked around the apartment, then back at Sebastian. "May I use your washroom, please?"

"Of course you can," he said, pointing down the hallway. "It's over there."

She made her way to the bathroom, used the facilities and, when washing her hands, she looked into the mirror and grinned. Her face was still dusty from working onsite earlier. She didn't even remember getting so dirty. She took a moment to quickly wash her face. But, when she looked up again, it looked like she'd only smeared the dirt.

Doing a more thorough job with her second washing, she thought she should get down the hall to her place and have a shower. She looked a little closer at her face in the mirror and noted big baggy bruises underneath her eyes and an odd look to her at the moment. She stood, figuring out what was off. There was something, but she didn't know what.

Shrugging, she walked back out again to see Katie packing up the last box and saying, "We're done. Sebastian will send the rest of this to the foundation tomorrow morning, and we'll be back on the dig site."

"Wow, that went faster than I thought," Lacey said in surprise. "Nice."

"We're all heading out to dinner in half an hour," Katie said to Lacey. "The others are already in the showers in our apartments, so that doesn't give you time for a shower."

Lacey shrugged. "I guess I'll have mine when I get back. It depends on how bad I look though." She glanced down to see a fine layer of dust all over her. "I don't understand how I got so dirty," she said in amazement.

"You can stand out on the porch, and I'll brush you off. Then, if you put on a clean T-shirt, you'll be good to go."

And that was what they did. Fifteen minutes later Lacey came out of her bedroom, now dressed in a clean shirt, her hair brushed out and rebraided, ready for dinner. Her stomach growled as she walked out. The others looked at her.

"Did you eat lunch?"

She nodded. "I think it must be all the fresh air," she said. "I'm not usually this hungry, but I am right now." She glanced up and caught Sebastian's lightning-quick frown. "What? Now I can't eat either?"

The others looked confused.

He shrugged and said, "She was drinking enough water earlier that I wondered if she was okay."

"Not used to the heat," she said lightly. She glanced at the door and everybody sitting around. "Are we leaving?" She tried to interject a note of humor in her voice. "Otherwise I need a shower. But I'd really like food first."

At that, they all jumped up and headed outside. She stepped in front of Sebastian and felt a *zap* as he reached forward. She jumped back and said, "Wow, that was quite the electrical charge."

Chana glanced at her in surprise. "That normally only happens when there is carpet underfoot."

"Lately my body and my senses seem to be reacting off the wall," Lacey said. "Who knows what the hell is going on."

"Maybe it's just your change in location," Chana said. "I wouldn't worry about it."

"I'm not worried," Lacey said, but, as soon as the words were out of her mouth, her gaze flew up to land on Sebastian. And the look in his eye had her really worried now because he looked terrified. She opened her mouth to ask him, but he gave a sharp shake of his head, cutting her off.

She frowned and followed Chana out. But she couldn't help but turn and look back at the apartment. For the first time since she'd arrived, she sensed something was going on here that she didn't know anything about. And she didn't think anybody else would let her in on the big secret.

THE CHANGES IN Lacey were definitely worth watching her closely, to see if things got worse. Her extreme thirst and growing appetite reminded him of the guys on Mayan site— before they died. Yet Sebastian didn't want to scare Lacey or his other interns. Obviously she had been outside, working physically in a job she wasn't used to. But a hell of a lot more was going on in her aura now than before.

Her energy had a blur, almost a cloudiness to it, but that could be from all the excitement going on in her system.

As he well knew, sometimes entities affected people by just being around them and could make them hungrier, thirstier or angrier, changing their moods, changing their energy. He'd seen it happen before. One of the team members he had worked with in the Mayan excavation had gotten extremely thirsty to the point they couldn't stop him from drinking too much water so fast, and they were seriously worried he would kill himself via water intoxication. Then the same guy started gorging on the food. It was like he couldn't squelch the appetites inside him.

He was the first one to die.

After her traffic accident, Sebastian had observed Lacey today, with several items of note, but it was her latest comment about being "hungry" that had made his heart freeze. Yet her symptoms weren't as severe as those seen on the Mayan site. Thankfully.

Once everyone was seated in the open-air café where they took up two tables, Sebastian sent a message to Jeremiah. *Are you still coming?*

Be there before you go to bed tonight.

Next he texted Hunter again. He'd tried three times but this time his response was instant.

I'm already in town. You'll see me tomorrow.

With relief, Sebastian sat back as large plates of pasta were delivered. He ate slowly, keeping an eye on the rest of the crew, looking for any signs of something being off. He felt protective about this group.

He'd worked with them several times, knew most of their personal issues. Chana and her mother never seemed to see eye to eye and fought on the phone once or twice. She'd had a boyfriend who she had dumped before coming back out here this summer.

Katie was engaged to be married and wanted her future husband to move to Italy so she could continue working on the dig. But he was a student back in New York, and it looked like they would continue their long-distance relationship for a while. He came back and forth when he could, sometimes spending weeks at a time with her.

Mark ... well, Mark was an interesting one. He was a new intern to the area, but he held a fascinating interest into the history of Pompeii, almost a macabre interest. That alone was enough to set off the warning lights. But he appeared to be normal—a laughing, enjoying-life young adult. He was maybe twenty-four, twenty-five. Sebastian would have to check his file to get a better idea.

When he glanced around the table, his gaze landed on Lacey. A woman who was still interested in more than she should be, for her own safety here. She glowed with an unearthly glow from the inside. She lit up with every conversation that touched on her passions; otherwise she had this muted soft warm light. He didn't know how to describe it, but, if you were looking for the good people in the world, she was it. He hadn't met too many like her, and, as such, she was someone he wanted to stay close to, if only to experience what it was like to be around her. She teased and joked, but her jokes were always funny and gentle. Everybody else could get crude and rude, and she would smile and laugh, not be offended, so she wasn't prissy to be around by any means.

And then his gaze landed on the empty pasta bowl in front of her. He frowned as she reached for the garlic bread still on the table and slathered it with extra butter. Finally she sat back with a happy smile and said, "Good food."

The others glanced at her and chuckled.

"You were hungry, weren't you?" Chana said.

Lacey smiled and said, "If you can't finish yours, just let me know."

At that, Chana slid her bowl toward her. "Go for it. I ate sandwiches at lunch, and I'm still full."

Lacey didn't hesitate. She leaned forward, popped the

last of the garlic bread into her mouth and dove into Chana's pasta. Sebastian's own appetite fled as he watched her genteel way of inhaling Chana's food. When she was done, she reached for her water, drank the whole glass, refilled it from the water pitcher on the table and drank that glassful too. He realized he could no longer toss this off as a light suspicion. Something really ugly was going on here.

The conversation around them was lighthearted. Katie told them all about having finished the cataloging with all of Lacey's photography expertise, so everything was done and boxed and ready to be shipped back to the foundation now. They all cheered, patting Lacey on the shoulder.

"I knew she could do it," Chana said proudly. "Being here is her big dream."

Lacey lifted her wineglass. "To dreams."

At that, a big cheer went up around the table, and they all chinked glasses.

Sebastian watched to see how she would handle the wine. Lacey took a big sip and then choked. He leaned forward as he realized what was happening. She didn't understand though. She put down the wineglass and reached for the water and drank another glass of water until she stopped coughing, but she never picked up the wineglass again.

"Dammit," he muttered. He drank down his wine and said, "Lacey, how about a quick second trip back to the doctor to make sure you're okay?"

She shook her head. "Don't need to. Not only am I fine," she said, "but there's no bruising." She twisted slightly so he could see the back of her arm where it had been scraped.

The wound was almost gone now. In less than twenty-four hours. His breath caught in the back of his throat, and his hand trembled. "That's amazing."

But he wasn't amazed; he was pissed. He was terrified. This was well past stage one of something he'd seen before. Lacey had headed into this without passing go, without stopping at any of the signs that he had seen before. She'd headed straight into stage two. And now he knew they were all in deep shit. Well past the help of a *normal* doctor.

CHAPTER 6

THE WINE TASTED funny. As she held out her glass to Chana, Lacey whispered, "If I eat your dinner that you didn't like, will you finish my wine that I don't like?"

Chana's face lit up with a smile. "Anytime," she said, accepting the wineglass. She tossed the wine back and said, "I'm surprised you don't like this one. It's a favorite here."

"Doesn't taste right tonight. Maybe it was the pairing with the pasta, or maybe I'm cheerfully happy from dinner," she said.

The group rose soon afterward, ready to head back to the apartments.

With an arm linked with her cousin, Lacey loved the short walk. She pointed out the stars. "I can't believe you can see Orion's Belt from here."

Chana chuckled. "I forgot you were as crazy about astrology as you are about Pompeii."

"Well, that would be astronomy," she said, "but I do love astrology too."

"Do you check the daily stars to see if the love of your life will show up today?" Mark teased.

Everybody had a good laugh.

"Not today I didn't." Lacey took their good-natured teasing with a big smile. It was great having a group of friends to enjoy the evening with. She squeezed Chana's arm and whispered, "You have nice friends."

Chana chuckled. "I do."

Back in the apartment, Lacey said, "I'm the only one who didn't get a shower earlier, so if you all don't mind …"

"Please do," Mark said, pinching his nose, "as a favor to the rest of us."

She rolled her eyes at him, grabbed her nightclothes and headed into the shower. She stripped down and looked at herself in the mirror. She hadn't lied when she had told Sebastian that she had almost no bruising. She looked incredibly fit and healthy. She didn't know when she'd started to feel that much better but figured sometime around early afternoon. Maybe she'd just needed to sit down and recharge.

Feeling stronger and more limber, she stood in the hot water until her hair ran free of dirt, then shampooed and conditioned it gently and washed the rest of her thoroughly. By the time she was done, she figured she'd pretty well emptied the hot water tank. She wrung her hair of most of the water, then put it into a braid for the night. Redressed, she walked back out, wondering about the pain pills and muscle relaxants. Should she take more? It seemed foolish when she felt good.

With her dirty clothes and the pills in hand, she went back into the bedroom. "Not sure when we do laundry, but I didn't bring a ton of clothing and will need to wash some soon. I didn't consider how dusty everything is here."

"If you can make it until the weekend," Chana said, "we can do a wash then."

"Perfect. Maybe we should go shopping so I can get a couple more outfits."

Chana was already deep into her book, but she nodded.

"No boyfriend for you these days?" Lacey asked. "I thought maybe you and Tom had something going on." She glanced at her and caught color rolling up her cousin's face. She chuckled. "Or was I not supposed to notice?"

"It's a little hard to have a relationship in a gang like this," she said with a sigh. "Still I'd try it if it weren't for other issues."

"Who made these sleeping arrangements?" Lacey asked. She sat down on the bed, tucked her legs under the covers and stretched out. She might be feeling a hell of a lot better, but she loved being here in bed, relaxing for the evening.

"I think Sebastian set up the roommates," Chana said. "Besides, it's probably not a good idea to have a relationship with somebody you're working with."

"It's great when it's all good," Lacey said. "But it sucks the minute things go bad."

Chana agreed. She reached over and turned off her bedside light. "I don't know about you, but I'm tired. Good night." She rolled over and almost immediately fell asleep.

Lacey, even with all the pills she'd taken that day, wasn't tired—she was hungry. What the hell? She'd eaten a huge amount of food at dinnertime. Besides, there was nothing for her to snack on here, so too bad.

She lay in bed, the lights out, when she heard people walking through the apartment. Somebody went into the kitchen, got water, opened the fridge, and she wondered if they were snacking too. Such a strange feeling to be sharing an apartment with other people after living alone for so long. It had been different when she had lived with her mother too, because her mother hadn't been very mobile. All the audible footsteps in the house, all the noises had been mostly Lacey making them. Here, however, any number of people walked around.

The two crew apartments also had connecting doors. Both belonged to the foundation. Another door opened and closed again. It could have been either of the apartment doors. *Whatever.*

She closed her eyes and tried to sleep.

But raised voices quickly had her fully awake. She glanced at Chana, only her cousin slept heavily. Lacey bounded to her feet, quietly opened her bedroom door and stepped out so she could at least hear who was talking. It was Mark and Tom.

She walked into the living room, frowning at the two of them.

Mark saw her enter and apologized. "Sorry. We didn't mean to wake you."

She shrugged. "That's all right. I hadn't fallen asleep yet." She glanced at Tom, then back at Mark, wondering if she should just go back to bed.

"Isn't it a bit late for this?" Tom asked Mark.

Mark struggled to bite back words, spun on his heel and walked out of the apartment, slamming the door hard behind him.

Lacey glanced at Tom and said, "Not everything is happy in heaven, huh?"

He gave her a wry look. "Definitely not." He walked down the hallway and shut the connecting door—quietly.

With nothing else to do, she headed back to bed to get some sleep. But her mind wouldn't let it be. She swore she'd heard Tom say something about theft. What she didn't know was what the hell had been stolen and by whom?

JEREMIAH ARRIVED AT midnight. Sebastian studied his face, then his friend's appearance, normally a calm person with an eternally young attitude, he looked frustrated, frazzled. "What happened to you?"

Jeremiah rolled his eyes. "Nothing, just having an off day ..."

"Any particular reason?"

Jeremiah shrugged. "You know me, moody as hell. Today is just one of those days." "So what the hell's going on here?" Jeremiah sagged into the big living room chair. "Never thought we'd see this again."

Sebastian watched him, seeing the fatigue on his friend's face. "You didn't have to come, if it was too much, you know."

Jeremiah just waved it away. "Anything new developing?"

"Not necessarily. The woman hit by the vehicle is doing better in that respect."

"I don't think you told me about her."

Sebastian filled him in. "The thing that bothers me is she is doing *very* well."

"So, you'd be happier if she was doing badly?"

"No. But she's doing better than she should be."

"In what way?" Jeremiah asked slowly, leaning back into the recliner. He glanced around. "You don't have a beer, do you?"

Sebastian walked into the kitchen, grabbed two cans of beer, popped the top of his and came out, placing Jeremiah's on the coffee table beside him, even though Sebastian knew it would remain untouched. He always asked and never drank but it was part of his social routine.

"She's healed remarkably well is what I mean. Just yesterday she was in the accident—last night on their way to eat—but the scrapes have already closed over, the bruises and scabs have almost disappeared. She's moving a lot better than she was even this morning."

"Good drugs? Good ointment? Lord, you think it's related?"

Sebastian had to ponder that. He'd been disturbed at the fast healing of Lacey's system. He was grateful she wasn't seriously hurt, and obviously it could have been so much worse. But the fact was, she was moving as if she wasn't injured at all, and she didn't show any lingering signs of pain. Yet he'd seen her hip and calf immediately after the accident. They had been scraped up pretty bad. A bit of redness remained, but he suspected, by tomorrow, that would be all gone. "It's possible she's got an incredible immune system, but it doesn't feel like it." Then he remembered the other issues he'd noticed. "She has a crazy appetite and is thirsty all the time. Then tonight alcohol didn't agree with her."

"We've certainly learned to listen to our feelings, to our intuition," Jeremiah said.

"I know, and in this case it feels off. But we've never seen anybody heal this fast. Down in the Mayan ruins, they were getting stupid injuries that had no explanations. Sure there was the crazy hunger and thirst, but there were also headaches, blurry vision, aches and pains, even open wounds, but we never saw any open wounds heal completely overnight, so I don't see how they could be related." Sebastian didn't know what else to say. He knew no two incidents would be exactly the same. It was never that neat and tidy when dealing with energy. There were always slight differences that add to the confusion. "It was the weird zap between us that really got to me. It happened once between one of the doctors and myself. It was like a foretelling of something to come. Immediately I wanted to take her back to the doctor and have him take a second look, but she refused."

"You could have insisted."

"I could have, but it seemed strange to insist when she's doing so well. I'm trying not to set off any alarms as it is."

"Is anything else going on at the site?"

"Yes. I just don't know how serious it all is," he said. "I'm not sure the team is being honest with me, and they seem to be fighting among themselves, tempers flaring. I feel like I need to be here every day to see for myself and stop things from getting worse."

"I didn't notice anything when I was here last." Jeremiah leaned forward, resting his elbows on his hands. "But if you can't trust your team …"

Sebastian hopped up and paced the living room. "I've never had to question their honesty or integrity before, so I'm not sure what to think. It could be something as simple as one having an affair with another, or two who were having an affair have broken up, and things are difficult now."

"That's always the worst, isn't it? And it happens all the time." Jeremiah was quiet then asked, "Maybe it's the new arrival. Is she pretty, young, single?"

Instantly the picture of Lacey's fresh innocence slammed into Sebastian's brain. "Yes, to all of them." His voice was softer than he had intended.

And, of course, Jeremiah wasn't fooled. "Ahh. You like her."

"Nothing not to like," he answered in a mild tone.

"And yet?"

"And yet, there's something about her. There's a glow within—a special light. If there's any evil energy around, it'll be attracted to her like bees to honey."

"Now I'm really fascinated."

Sebastian shrugged. "You'll meet her tomorrow."

While they sat here talking, he heard an apartment door slam shut in the outer hallway. Frowning, he walked to the front door and peered out. But nobody was there. It could have been one of his team, or it could have been somebody else who lives on this floor.

He closed the door slowly and walked back to his friend. "It'll be good to have you around," he said.

"I have been around. Remember? Just not always where you can see me."

The two friends exchanged long looks. They'd been friends since way before the Mayan expedition. The love of the past and an opportunity to work in a corner of Pompeii was too irresistible for either of them.

"Anyway, it's bedtime," Sebastian said. "See you early tomorrow morning—trying to beat the heat."

"Can't wait," Jeremiah said. "I'll see you in the morning." He got up and headed to his room.

Sebastian sat in the living room for another long moment, finishing his beer. He felt like he was on the cusp of something momentous. But it didn't feel good. It wasn't a place he wanted to be. He didn't like the undertones and the undercurrents and especially didn't like all he didn't understand.

He carried the beer cans back into the kitchen, putting his on the counter and Jeremiah's back into the fridge. He stared outside at the sky, then turned his gaze in the direction of the ruins. There was almost a malevolence out there—waiting, watching. What he didn't know was what or who it waited for. He turned and headed to his bed. He needed to have all his strength for whatever tomorrow would bring.

CHAPTER 7

A NEW PERSON arrived the next morning. He walked onto the site to cries of welcome.

"Hey, Hunter."

"Good to see you again, Hunter."

Hunter. A man who stared at Lacey a little too intently. She smiled and excused herself, finding his presence too strong to ignore and needing to step back while everyone else appeared to welcome him. By noon, Lacey had completely forgotten about her injuries. She felt fine, back to her happy, contented self. Even Hunter appeared less interested in her. She smiled easily at everybody as she worked through the photographs she needed to take and then shifted to more location-based shots.

She found what appeared to be a partial footprint set in a path. It looked old, as in baked into the mud and the dirt of the surroundings. Potentially when the rock blocks were formed, as if a child had stepped where he wasn't supposed to. Fascinated, she took several photographs.

As she wandered, she took more and more photographs. She didn't think she'd ever get tired of it. She glanced past the area where they were working, wondering if she could take a few hours and just wander.

"Lacey?" her cousin called out.

She twisted to see Chana waving. Lacey walked over,

carefully making her way down to the level where Chana worked.

"Would you mind taking some photographs as we work on this?"

"Sure." It looked like they were unearthing a kitchen hearth.

As they worked at the slow and careful pace all archaeologists seemed to move at, Lacey took pictures of their progress. Several areas were being worked on at one time, and Lacey found it fascinating to see what was uncovered from one moment to the next. The longer she was here, the more addicted she became. It was a fascinating place. There was just something about the sun, the weather and the breeze, the old meeting the new, the digging into the mysteries that she found enthralling.

She wandered over to the odd-shaped doorless room they had broken into the other day. She took several more photos. Reaching down to remove a rock, she took pictures under and around it.

Changing her filters, she lowered her camera inside the dark room so she could take photos inside with a flash. It wasn't a very big area, and it was apparently empty. She moved slowly away from the group, taking photos of everything that interested her—a rock at a certain angle, a low-lying branch atop a stack of rocks, a partial wall not even yet begun to be excavated, a mound that hid who-knew-what. Tall grass. More odd indiscernible shapes to the landscape.

Moving back farther and farther, she kept clicking, fascinated by the world and what was hidden below. In her heart she was so sorry for all the people who had died here. The panic and the pain of the volcanic eruption would have been absolutely horrific. For most of them, death should have been fast. That didn't make it any easier to Lacey.

Lost in the moment, when someone touched her, she shrieked. She bounded back, her hand going to her chest as she stared in outrage at Sebastian and the stranger at his side. "You terrified me," she cried out. She took several deep breaths, glaring at him. "Why didn't you call out?"

His lips twitched. "I did. Several times."

She straightened and stared at him in shock. "Really?"

He nodded, watching her carefully, studying her.

She blew strands of hair off her face. "Sorry. I get so caught up in my work, I lose track of time and space. And my sense of hearing too, I presume."

He motioned at the area around her. "What are you taking pictures of?"

"Houses and pathways," she said with a big smile. "Children playing in playgrounds. Back doors and kitchens where families were created and grew."

The man beside Sebastian sucked in his breath and stared at her.

She glanced at him and smiled, stepping forward, reaching out a hand. "Hello. I'm Lacey."

He stepped forward, but they barely touched hands before he pulled his back. "Jeremiah. I'm a friend of Sebastian's."

Sebastian had the oddest look on his face when he turned toward Jeremiah. Lacey wanted to ask him about that, but now was not the right moment.

Jeremiah raised his eyebrows as he nodded to Sebastian, then asked Lacey, "What did you say you were taking pictures of?"

She waved behind her. "This whole neighborhood. It's

fascinating." An odd silence overtook the men, and she looked at them. "What?"

They didn't say anything, just continued to stare at her.

She brought up her camera and flicked through the pictures. "See? Look at this house. You can see the kitchen and the hearth that's the home of every family." She turned her camera so they could see.

The men looked in the small window in the back of her camera and then frowned at each other.

Sebastian reached out and tilted the camera back at her. "What do you see?"

She stared down at it. "A partial building that's been excavated," she exclaimed. She looked at several of the other pictures she'd been taking. "Why? What do you see?"

"A hillside," Jeremiah said bluntly. "One without any excavation."

She stared at him and then at the space around her. As she watched, it was as if a layer of dirt and grass filled in over the top. She touched her forehead. "I don't feel so good."

Sebastian grabbed her as she took a shaky step forward. He gently helped her sit on the ground. "I'm not sure what you were seeing," he said gently, "but it's fascinating."

She stared up at him blindly, confused by everything around her. "I could have sworn I saw everything here."

"If I gave you a piece of paper could you outline what you saw?"

She nodded.

He pushed his notepad forward and gave her a pencil. "Just from where you're sitting, what did you think you were taking pictures of?"

She sketched rapidly. She'd been an okay artist, never had the skill she'd seen in so many others. Still, she could certainly do this. She carefully filled in the paper with as much detail as she could. "This is pretty rough, but you get the general idea."

The men stood behind her, watching as she brought the image to life. Finally she sat back and surveyed her work. She pointed out where each of the pillars were and the markers she'd use. "It's all right here."

Sebastian gently patted her shoulder. "That's beautiful."

"Well, certainly not my artistry," she said with a chuckle. "But what's here certainly is beautiful."

"So, if you were to turn and look in that direction, what do you see?"

She looked up to see he pointed slightly off to the side behind her. She lifted the page, turning to the other site, poised the pencil and then sketched. "This is when I really wish I had some artistic skills."

"I don't know what you're talking about." Jeremiah said. "This is fantastic,"

The men watched as she sketched out yet another home with pathways between it and other houses.

As she drew on the page, she explained, "This goes to the park where the kids played. Here's a walkway where the community would sit sometimes and have meetings." She pointed out gardens, marking them with the pencil. "It's really beautiful." She sighed happily as she stared out. "How come I can see this, and you can't?"

Silence.

Slowly, she turned to look at both men, "What's wrong with me?"

"Nothing is wrong with you," Sebastian said, his voice low but reassuring. "But, for some reason, you're able to see beneath the layers that we see."

"I saw them first with my camera," she said, "and then, when I lowered the camera, I could see them in front of me."

"Explain."

She slowly turned to look at an area she hadn't been taking photographs of. "Walk with me over here." She hopped up and led them to a darker corner where there were more trees. "I haven't done any photography work here, so I see probably the same thing you're seeing right now—rocks, hillside, dark shadows, but there's a warm heavy breeze, almost a heavy atmosphere." She glanced at the others, and they agreed.

"Now I'll lift my camera and photograph the area. It takes a bit of time to see *more*. I hadn't really realized what I was doing because, for like the first ten, twenty, thirty photographs, I see this. But then it's almost as if I'm looking deeper and deeper, and I see it through my viewfinder. I take picture after picture, and then what happened last time was, I lowered my camera, and I'm still seeing what I saw before."

"Demonstrate please," Sebastian said.

She shrugged and snapped some photographs. "I know this shouldn't be happening," she exclaimed.

"Try to repeat what you did before."

She crouched, fascinated once again with the rocks, the way they were joined, the moss creeping over and under them, the mounds of weeds and dirt, forgotten areas of the world, the poor people who didn't get a warning ahead of time. Not that anybody did. Pompeii's destruction was indiscriminate. When the volcano erupted, it took out rich and old, young and poor, male and female.

She sighed. "This house was particularly unhappy." She stood up with the camera before her. "That corner in the back, something's wrong with that room."

"In what way?"

"There's no door," she said as she took more pictures. The more she took, the more clearly she could see. She lowered the camera but still couldn't see what she had seen in the camera. She lifted it again, and there it was. She kept working, going deeper, deeper into the woods. "Over here, this room, people are inside it, but it has no door. There's a small window but that's all."

"And the rest of the space?"

She described what she could see. She lowered the camera, and she now could see it all, almost like a holographic image in front of her she sighed happily. "I wish I could get a screenshot of what my eyes see right now."

Sebastian handed her the pad of paper and a pencil. "Can you try?"

She shot him a veiled look. "I don't think I can draw what I'm seeing, but I'll try." She crouched down and proceeded to transfer the image in front of her to the paper. The trouble was, once she got into it, she couldn't stop. The images took page after page after page. Her hand moved at lightning speed, drawing the lines, the elevation, the size, the shades, the shadows.

When she finally stopped, she could hardly move—her back was so stiff from being in the same position. She stared at the landscape in front of her. "And I can still see it all."

"Can you look back to the section you viewed before and see if you can see it there?"

She turned and nodded. "Yes, it's as if, once I see it, I can see it all the time."

"May I look at the pictures you drew?" Sebastian asked, his voice quiet, cautious.

With a heavy sigh she handed the notepad to him. "Like

I said, I'm not much of an artist. If I had Photoshop, I might recreate it a little better."

"How good is your memory?"

She looked at the camera and smiled. "I took photos of it."

They stood around her and peered into her camera.

She pointed out where her sketches were in her photos. "See this is where this is, and this is here, and this is there."

They turned and stared at her.

Her face thinned as shock reverberated through her. "You guys really can't see any of this, can you?"

Slowly they both shook their heads.

"How is that possible?" she asked.

Sebastian said, "Because you're seeing all kinds of stuff we have yet to see. It would take us days, weeks, years to excavate to reach the level of your ... images."

"Except what if ... what if I'm wrong? What if what I'm seeing isn't what's here?" She stared at them blankly. "What if it's my imagination?"

"Are you prone to bouts of pure imagination like this?" Jeremiah asked.

She stared at him. "No, not at all. This is the first time I've ever had this happen." She turned and glanced around in bewilderment. "It's so beautiful."

"I wish I could see it with you," Sebastian said. He crouched beside her. "Don't mention this to anybody else, okay?"

She gave a bitter laugh. "In case they think I'm completely nuts?" She lifted her hand. It was now trembling. "I don't understand." She shook her head. "I have to understand this. It's the only way I can function."

He reached out and held her shoulders firmly. "We'll

help you to understand. But right now I need you to calm down and to realize this is a special gift. Whatever it is you're seeing right now, we want to see it too."

She stared at him. "Do you really think I'm seeing what was here? That I'm seeing life before this disaster?"

"I would like to think so," he said. "We'll have to do some excavation, maybe underground radar imaging, to get a better idea." He pursed his lips. "The only thing is the expense to prove your visions. It would be fascinating to do so, though."

She shook her head. "Probably not necessary. I could go back to where we were, where they're currently working, and help identify everything that's right there." She took a deep breath. "But I couldn't do it without them knowing. That's not something I'm ready to let anybody else know at the moment." She glanced over at Sebastian's friend. "I hope you won't tell anybody either."

Jeremiah smiled at her gently. "No, of course not. This is something very special, and obviously we want to see everything that you've seen, so the more you can put down on paper, the better it is."

She nodded. "If you could get me some pencils and sketch pads, I could sit here and draw. I've doodled a lot but, well I'm not formally trained," she apologized again.

Both men chuckled.

"You don't need formal training," Sebastian said. "You're incredibly talented."

He lifted the page and flipped it to one of the last drawings she'd done. He held it out. "How could you not think this was brilliant?"

She stared down at it and whispered, "I don't even remember drawing this." Her fingers moved over the page.

"Did you see me do this?" She lifted her puzzled gaze to each of the men. "I know I was drawing, but I don't remember placing these lines on this page." Her mind was confused. She reached for her bag, pulled out and opened the water bottle and took several drinks. "What was in those painkillers your doctor friend gave me?" she asked suspiciously.

"When did you take the last one?" he countered.

"Last night, ... no." She frowned. "I decided I didn't need it. I'm not big on taking drugs in the best of times, so I chose to just go to sleep. I'm not sure when I took a pain pill. Maybe yesterday morning?"

"So do you really think there's any drug still in your system twenty-four hours after you took it?"

Feeling a sudden chill at the onset of the questioning, she wrapped her arms tight around herself and rubbed her arms. "Is it cold?"

They walked her back out toward where the bright sun was.

Instantly she could feel the rays of warmth pouring down over her. "That's better," she said. She turned and looked at the corner. "Something ugly happened in that place."

"Ugly, like what?" Sebastian asked her.

She shot him a shuttered look. "I don't want to say. I don't have any proof."

"It's not like you can accuse anybody here," Jeremiah said. "None of us were alive back then."

"I know," she said softly. "But still it feels odd."

"What does?"

"To see where people were kept like in a jail. Where they were walled in as prisoners."

The men turned to look in the direction she talked

about.

She studied the walls in her camera. "I don't know how they would have gotten out."

"So you're saying, they were never intended to get free?"

"Exactly. And I think the window might have been for the jailer to feed them and to give them water. At least in the beginning. But I think, at the end, he used it to watch."

"Watch what?" Sebastian asked urgently.

She took a heavy breath, reached out and squeezed his fingers, relieved when he squeezed back, one of his arms coming around her shoulders, hugging her close. She whispered, "He wanted to watch them. He wanted to watch them die."

IT WAS HARD to imagine the kind of shock Sebastian felt right now. It never occurred to him such a thing would be possible. He knew from the look on Jeremiah's face that he had been equally stunned. Sebastian couldn't help but wonder if Hunter had experienced this. Sebastian and Jeremiah kept looking at the drawings and again around at the surrounding areas Lacey had sketched. They could see from the corner stones, how the buildings lay. Lacey's diagrams were completely plausible, and that was the part that got to Sebastian.

How could she possibly know this? Even imagine this? She couldn't, unless she'd seen it before. And that brought up a whole lot of questions he wasn't ready to answer. Hell, he had no answers.

Jeremiah's expression said he had none either.

Lacey sat down, pulled her knees up against her chest, her arms wrapped around them tightly, and rocked back and forth, dealing with the shock, and yet, absolutely certain in what she could see.

That amazed Sebastian. He loved the concept of seeing into the past. It was what his life's work was all about. In all of his energy and supernatural research he'd never come across such a skill. And certainly not to see the past in 3-D through a camera lens and then to draw such detailed architectural drawings. How did that work? Because, in his mind, it didn't work at all, and yet, the proof was in Lacey's diagrams beside him.

He had some historical drawings that he could potentially use to confirm her diagrams. But, because everything happened so long ago, it wasn't like he had anything definitive.

She'd done a best guess, and it seemed eerily accurate. Her renditions were spooky with realism. She said she wasn't much of an artist, and, of course, that left a lot of room for interpretation, but these diagrams said something different. He patted her on the shoulder. "Come on. Let's join the others."

She shook her head. "No. I don't want them to know anything about this."

"I have no intention of telling them," he said calmly. "But you're obviously upset, and I think being around the others will help you."

"I'm not so sure about that." She got to her feet unsteadily.

As he helped her regain her balance, he asked, "How are you feeling today?"

Startled, glancing up at him, she shrugged. "Honestly? I felt great this morning. I felt like a big to-do was made over nothing."

"Well, it wasn't nothing," he said. "Have you always been a fast healer?"

She considered that for a long moment and then nodded. "Essentially, yes. Plus I don't get sick very often."

"Lucky you," he said. "Not everybody has a strong constitution."

"I think that's because I always had to be healthy and strong for my mother's sake." She gave him a sad smile. She turned to look behind her, her gaze drifting through all the buildings she could see so clearly. "It's like I'm right there," she murmured. "Like I'm in Pompeii before 79 AD. Before Mount Vesuvius erupted and destroyed the whole town." She held up her forefinger. "No. Let me amend that. I think I'm seeing Pompeii as it would appear if completely unburied, showing all the destruction done by Mount Vesuvius."

"And I want to know all about that," he said.

"I'm not sure what I can tell you, other than what I've already said. If you think about it, this shouldn't be happening."

"Sometimes," Jeremiah said, "we don't need to think about things. We just have to accept."

She mulled that over. "And not question?"

"Who would you question?" he asked in a sensible voice. "Lots of things are completely unanswerable in life. This looks to be one of them."

She came to a stop, turned around and took a long gaze at the buildings that seemingly lived here. Following her gaze, he saw a slightly whitish-blue energy instead of stone gray, but it was so clear, so crisp, that she could see the openings for doors and windows. "What if I can't see this tomorrow?"

"I hope you can," Sebastian said. "Because this is incredibly valuable information."

"Oh, you can't count on anything."

"Why's that?"

She turned and stared at him. "What if I made it up?"

"Did you?"

She shook her head. "Of course not."

He nodded. "I didn't think so." He grabbed her arm gently and nudged her forward. "Act normal except maybe appear like you've had a very long day and need to go home early."

"Are you escorting me home?"

"I'd like to confirm if you can see more of the buildings around where everybody is currently working, taking some pictures you might remember later, and then I want you to go home."

She picked up her camera and clicked away as they approached. It seemed like she didn't have to work quite so hard this time as the buildings quickly took shape in her viewfinder. Finally she lowered her camera and looked around. She said quietly to Sebastian, "It's all here. It's unbelievably amazing."

"That you can see anything is what's amazing," he said in a soft voice. "But remember to act naturally."

She smiled at Chana as they approached. "Do you need me right now? I was wondering about going home. The heat is hitting me, and the painkillers aren't taking the edge off."

Chana was concerned and solicitous. She gave Lacey a quick hug and said, "Go. Go lie down. Get your shower first. Just relax. We'll be over in a couple hours."

CHAPTER 8

WITH A SMILE Lacey headed toward the gate. She cast one glance back at the team, catching sight of Sebastian and Hunter, with Jeremiah standing in front of them, their heads together in a deep conversation. Hunter looked up, as if knowing she watched them.

Turning to face forward, she kept walking. She thought the men might come with her, but it now seemed like they wouldn't, which was probably best so the crew wouldn't get more suspicious as to what could be going on with her. She felt eerily disconnected from everything around her. At the gate she stopped and turned back to the portion of the dig site where she had been looking at the last time. She could easily see some buildings rising aboveground, other buildings still buried. The roof of this one, the smokestack of that one. Like the ground receded and she could see the buildings in all their glory. Except that most had fallen into disrepair from the damage of the volcano.

But her mind potentially pieced this all together, imagining what she thought should be there. She had no way of knowing and certainly wouldn't talk to a shrink about it.

She scrubbed her face and turned resolutely toward the apartment.

When she crossed the street, she was careful to look both ways. She made it across, turned once more to look behind her, but found no sign of Sebastian—or Jeremiah or Hunter for that matter. And somehow Hunter appeared to be connected to Sebastian more than the other team members. Just the sight of that conversation between the three men had looked so intense, ... and maybe it was her insecurity, but it seemed she'd been the topic of conversation. She walked up to the empty apartment and was delighted to have some time in this space to herself. She took a quick shower, and, when she was dressed, she sat down on the couch. She wasn't sure if she should make coffee or just sit and relax.

She heard a knock on the door. She got up and answered it, finding Sebastian standing there ... alone. He stepped inside and asked, "Anybody else here?"

She shook her head. She glanced at the big book he had under his arm. "What's that?"

"Something I want to talk to you about." He motioned toward the kitchen table, set the book down and opened it up to a chapter about one-third of the way in. "There is talk of energy at some ancient ruin sites around the world."

"Energy?" she asked cautiously. She sat down and studied the old texts and the images. "Are you saying, *ghosts?*"

"Essentially, yes."

She stared at him. "I'm not sure I believe in ghosts at the best of times. But in a ruin as ancient as Pompeii?"

"Why not Pompeii?" he asked curiously. "Think of all the souls who died here."

She winced. "I've been trying hard not to think of all the people who died in the volcanic eruption. They've been gone thousands of years. Why would their souls still be hanging around?"

"A couple theories involve the dead being disturbed with all the various excavations."

She settled back and studied his face. He looked so calm and sensible and normal. And then he had brought up the energy, the ghosts. "Do you believe this stuff?"

His lips quirked. "I gather you don't."

She shrugged. "I believe what I can see, feel, taste and touch."

"Maybe you have no experience with them, but how do you explain what you saw and did today?"

She turned her gaze to his book. "I've been struggling hard to not think about that either."

He chuckled, brought out the sketchbook, which he had also brought with him. He quickly flipped to the last pages and showed them to her. "How's that working out for you?"

She leaned forward and studied the diagrams. "They're quite good," she admitted. "But I'm not sure I've ever done anything like this before." She glanced at him suspiciously. "Are you sure I did them?"

He brought out his cell phone, clicked on something and held up a video. Sure enough, it captured her doing the sketch she now stared at. The world around that area held nothing in her drawings supposedly, but she could see something which she had rendered on paper.

"Wow," she whispered. "You know this is all incredibly far-fetched."

"Sure it is," he said. "So either you tapped into an architectural side of your mentality and your creative imagination, or you were tapping into something already here."

"Yes, but ghosts don't draw architectural diagrams," she scoffed. "They rattle chains and moan down hallways."

At that, he laughed out loud. "Haunting ghosts certainly can. But there are supposedly other kinds as well."

In spite of herself she was interested. She leaned forward.

"So are those the ones who want to be here to protect their loved ones? In this case, we've got generations upon generations. They won't know who belongs to their bloodline anymore."

"And lots of times people, especially those who die sudden deaths, end up with their souls caught in a specific place," he said. "Sometimes spirits are so tied to events or things that they can't let go."

"Even though they can't take it with them?"

"Greed knows no boundaries."

His tone was too serious to think he was joking.

"That includes the divide between life and death."

She flipped through the chapters of his book, reading sections about why ghosts were surmised to be in existence. Everything was as he had said. "None of this explains what I'm seeing," she said softly.

"I know," he said. "But the fact is, you are seeing something. At least I trust you are."

She stared up at him, her eyes huge. "And the other option is, you don't believe me and, therefore, think I'm making this all up."

"What do you think?"

She sagged back and sipped the glass of water she had gotten. "I don't know how I could possibly have made it up. I've never seen visions like this before."

He pounced. "*Visions?*"

"I don't know what else to call it," she said. "But it's like these images just appeared. And although real looking, they kind of glowed."

"But you said they appeared only after you saw them through the camera."

"If I were you, I'd probably send me back home, me and

my weird drawings," she said bitterly. "Ever since I've come over here, my life has been odd. I was ecstatic to be here. Even today, when I was taking the photographs, I was so in tune with everything around me, so in awe. And it seemed like, the more pictures I took, the deeper and deeper I went. Down the rabbit hole apparently."

"That doesn't mean it's bad though," he said quietly. "I personally am fascinated by this. A couple of specialists are in town, and I wonder if you would mind if I took these sketches to them, see if they have any idea how to verify what might be versus what was."

She waved at the diagrams. "Go for it. At the moment I can still see everything, so I'm not sure how or why I would want to keep the sketches." But, as he grabbed them, she said, "Except maybe digitally." She frowned, grabbed her camera, stood and took photos of her drawings. "So I have something for myself."

"I understand," he said. "I'll stop tonight and talk to one. I also would like to take you back to the doctor."

She glanced up at him, surprised. "Do you think I hit my head harder than I thought?" She reached up to her temple.

He waved at the diagrams "Did you ever think you might have done something to your brain?" He waved at the diagrams.

She laughed a little wildly, a little out of control, as she stared at the diagrams. "So, … what? I take a fall, crack my head and all of a sudden start drawing pictures?"

He reached over and laced his fingers with hers.

When he did, she realized she'd been clenching them so tightly together that she had left crescent-moon-shaped indentations on her palms.

Then, still holding her hands, he nudged her chin up. "It's possible. Just because it's never happened to you before doesn't mean it couldn't have this time."

She didn't want to look him in the eye. At the same time, she couldn't take her eyes away from their hands clasped together. A glow seemed to surround them. "Do you see that?" she asked in a daze.

"See what?"

She snapped her lips shut and refused to say anything else. The last thing she wanted was for him to think she was completely off her rocker.

"See what?" he asked in a more determined voice. He gave her hands a shake.

She watched as the white luminance rippled outward and dispersed into the air. She groaned. "Just another sign I'm going crazy," she muttered. "But, around our hands, there's a glow. Like a white light."

"Oh, that," he said calmly. "Yes, I can see that."

She froze and stared up at him. "What?"

He raised one eyebrow. "Sure, I see auras. So?"

She slowly sagged in place. "As in real auras?"

At that, he burst out laughing. "Real auras versus fake auras?" He motioned at the diagrams. "Real cities versus fake cities?"

"You know what I mean," she snapped.

"Yes, I do. And the answer is, yes, I can see auras. I've always been able to see auras. I didn't know what they were when I was a kid. I thought everybody could see the glowing lights around people. Apparently not."

She stared at him in bemusement.

He just smiled, gave her fingers a squeeze and gently dropped her hands. "We're meeting the others for an early dinner. Are you ready?"

She nodded and stood. "Aren't they coming to the apartment?"

He shook his head. "We're supposed to meet them at the restaurant."

"What excuse will you give for us arriving together?"

"I don't have to give any excuse," he said in surprise. "Why would I?"

She didn't know what to say. It sounded more ridiculous the more she thought about it. She shrugged and stood. "I don't know. Apparently I have a concussion," she announced. "And I can't trust anything I say … or do."

"That's what I was trying to look at, but you wouldn't let me see." He rose and gently checked her head under the light. "It's hardly noticeable."

"Can you see that in my aura?"

"Yes," he said quietly. "And it did look to be slightly off before but not too bad." He smiled. "And before you ask, no I can't see anything off in your aura that would explain what you're seeing and drawing."

"Good. If you do, please let me know." She collected her purse and the new keys to the apartment that Chana had given her. "Shall we?"

He nodded. They let themselves out of the apartment and headed to the restaurant.

As they walked down the street, Lacey wasn't surprised when Sebastian continued to question her.

"So auras are less of a surprise than drawings of ancient ruins?"

"The drawings are a surprise," she said. "I can see what's there. So it seems completely normal to put that on paper. What's not normal is that you can't see the buildings too."

"That's exactly how I feel about auras. I can see them, and no one else can. So it's hard to know if people believe me or not."

"Do you think that's what this is?" she asked, wondering. She stared down at their hands. "And why is it I can see it right now?"

"I hate to say the blow on the head started this," he said humorously, "and I don't know if that has any connection to what's been going on today at all, but it is the one anomaly over the last few days."

"You don't know that," she said. "Because you don't know what my days were like before that. You don't know anything about me."

"Only what's in your file," he agreed.

"File?" Her voice rose higher. "What's in that file?"

He stared at her steadily. "Do you really think I'd let anybody come onto a site such as this who I don't have some background information on?"

Her shoulders sagged, and she nodded. "Yes, of course. I'm sorry. Apparently it's my day to be completely out of touch with reality."

"Doesn't matter," he said. "Your photographs and drawings are one issue. Are you having any other trouble with your eyesight? Do you have a headache? Have you had any kind of pain in the back of your neck? Are your glands swollen?" His hands reached up to check under her chin and her throat.

"No, no," she said, twisting away and taking several steps back. "I told you that I'm fine."

"Okay, but it's what you haven't told me that's now a problem," he said. Without asking, he crouched to look at the scrapes she had sustained earlier on her calf. He stopped and stared. "You know that's not normal."

"Now what?" she asked in exasperation, bending to see. "Oh, that's looking much better."

"Nobody heals that fast."

"Of course we do," she scoffed. "This is not abnormal. Now my sketches *are* abnormal."

He grinned, looped her arm though his and steered her down the street.

"Where are we going?"

"Ancient Stone Restaurant," he said. "It's just around the corner."

At the restaurant he led her upstairs, down the hallway and out to a rooftop deck. There the rest of the team was gathered at one end of the deck across several tables. As they joined them, everyone shouted out their welcomes.

She slipped into her position beside Chana and smiled at her cousin. "This," she said, "is spectacular." She tilted her face to the evening light above them. "It must be truly glorious when the stars are out or when the sun sets," she murmured.

"It is." Chana gave her a hug. "How are you feeling?"

Feeling like it was easier to be a little honest and only use a little white lie, Lacey said, "Much better, thanks. A little lie-down helped a lot."

"You did have a pretty rough accident your second night here, still worked the next day and worked hard all day today too." Chana's tone held worry. "You don't have to push yourself here. You know that, right?"

Lacey squeezed Chana's hand. "You know I don't want to get sent home."

Chana shook her head. "Honestly, you're better than the last photographer we had anyway. We're all fighting to keep you here right now."

Mark piped up. "Absolutely. So far you've done a terrific job."

She gave him a grateful smile. "Thanks so much. It's always nice to be appreciated."

After that, the conversation turned to dinner and the history of the restaurant. Content to sit back and listen, Lacey studied the surroundings, amazed at the architecture and the openness of the whole region. It was spectacularly beautiful. Her gaze swept the other diners on the restaurant's rooftop.

The dress code was everything from jeans to dresses. It was lovely to see one table filled with couples in evening clothes. Lacey instantly felt underdressed and dirty. She'd had a shower but didn't feel quite as refreshed and as classy looking as she would have liked. As she studied the diners, one of the men turned toward her. She'd been caught staring and quickly shifted her gaze to another part of the rooftop. In the back somebody sat alone. He had a tall glass of something dark in his hand. He sipped it gently as he studied everybody around them. Somewhat like she was doing.

"Lacey?"

She shook her head, pulling herself back to her table and smiled at Sebastian. "Sorry. A little lost in thought."

His gaze was direct, and yet, considering, as if analyzing her response.

She gave him a brighter smile and said, "Honestly, I'm fine."

He nodded. "We've decided to order multiple plates. Everyone can share, if that's all right with you."

"Sounds like fun," she said, glancing around at the others. "Providing you guys leave me something to eat," she said with a chuckle.

Mark patted his stomach. "I don't know about that. I'm quite hungry today."

The others all chimed in to agree.

But Chana said, "Honestly, I'm not. The heat's hitting me this time around."

"But you didn't eat much of your dinner last night either," Lacey protested.

"No, but I ate several sandwiches at lunch," Chana said. "Don't you worry about me."

They'd been friends and family for so long it was hard not to. From where Lacey sat, she couldn't hear all the conversations the crew had. She was missing out on a lot. And that kept her gaze wandering to the table with the well-dressed people and on to the single man sitting in the corner.

When she shifted her gaze yet again, she noticed Sebastian had moved and now sat directly in front of her. She frowned at him, and he frowned back. She sighed. "Now what?" she muttered.

"I'm trying to figure out what you're doing."

Her gaze widened. "I didn't think I was doing anything. I'm just studying everybody else up here, wondering about a restaurant with such a beautiful open rooftop deck, a space like this."

"It's special, isn't it?"

"It is indeed. It's also got to be a pain in the ass when the weather is ugly."

"Which isn't very often," he said. "Remember where you are."

She smiled. "I'm never going to forget," she said sincerely. "Thanks again for not sending me back."

He sighed. "I told you that I wasn't planning on doing

that."

"It doesn't mean you won't change your mind. I'm just trying to be good and not get in your crosshairs."

"Honestly, I think you're already there permanently," he said with a note of humor.

She glared at him, but he held up a warning finger. She sighed and shifted her gaze back to the table full of well-dressed people. "I feel underdressed," she said. "I didn't bring anything really nice with me."

He twisted to view the table she was looking at. "What difference does it make?"

"None. Just that table over there," she said wistfully. "It's nice to dress up every once in a while. The men look so good in a suit," she said. "It's always nice to see them dressed up."

"Suits or men?" he asked in mocking confusion.

She just smiled at him.

Just then six platters of some incredibly aromatic foods arrived, all holding various items from rice to what looked like fowl of some kind, plus some oranges and figs. She stared in awe. The platters were passed around. She took bits of every item so she could try them. The Moroccan rice was absolutely delicious.

She couldn't stop eating. She quickly finished her plate and looked to see if there would be any leftovers. Sebastian reached across the table, grabbed the closest platter and put half of what was left on her plate.

"There's tons," he stressed. "You're the one still healing. Make sure you eat lots."

"If I eat lots, I'll get fat."

Chana chuckled. "You'd need twenty pounds to even begin to cover all your bones."

"That's not fair," Lacey protested. "I regained twenty pounds after Mom died."

"I can imagine. You were staying up night and day for her and wearing yourself down."

"I used to sit and read to her all the time," she said with whimsical remembrance. "And she never cared what I was reading, so it was history books about Pompeii."

The others stopped and stared at her. Mark raised an eyebrow. "Really?"

She grinned. "What can I say? I have always been addicted to this part of Italy."

"Wow, you should have come here a long time ago then."

"I would have if I could have." She dug into her plateful again. "This rice is absolutely divine." She tried to slow herself down, but she was famished. Now she was past the point of thinking it was the fresh air and exercise. Sebastian's explanation that she was healing was the most likely theory, but it didn't really matter because all she could think about was putting more of this lovely dinner in her mouth.

She finished her second plate just as everyone else polished off the leftovers. She glanced along the table and asked, "Do you ever take leftovers home when you're out in a restaurant?"

Several of the men nodded. "We often do. For midnight snacks, sometimes lunch the next day."

She smiled. "Then next time we have pizza, we should order extra so we take it back to the apartments, even for breakfast the next day."

Mark chuckled. "A girl after my own heart. Pizza works for all meals in a day."

Privately she agreed with him. She loved her vegetables,

but there was just something about pizza.

With the boss handling the bill tonight because it was a treat for the crew, they all got up and trooped down the stairs. As she made her way behind the crowd, she caught sight of the man sitting in the corner again. He never smiled at her. She gave him a half wave, smiled and disappeared downstairs.

Sebastian came up behind her. "Who are you waving at?"

"The single guy in the corner," she said. "I'm not sure what he's drinking, but he's dressed all in black, and he looks really somber. I thought maybe a friendly face would cheer him up, but he didn't even smile." She stepped outside to the street, still feeling the heat of the day hanging heavily around her. She tilted her head up and studied the sky. "It's so very different here."

"Is that good or bad?" Sebastian asked.

"It's great," she said warmly. "Everything about it is absolutely perfect."

He grabbed her arm, tucking it into his as they walked behind everybody. "Good," he said. "We want to make sure your visit is as nice as possible."

"Now you sound like Chana," she complained.

"Hey," Chana said from just ahead of them, "there's nothing wrong with him sounding like me, if he's making sure you get a good vacation."

"But it's a working vacation," Lacey corrected. "I'm not here for everybody to take care of me."

"Then stop stepping in front of cars," Mark said in mock exaggeration, turning to smirk at her.

She just rolled her eyes at him.

He chuckled loudly and stepped up to walk with Katie,

who was farther ahead.

Back at the apartment Lacey smiled at Sebastian. "Thank you." As she was about to step inside behind the others he pulled her off to the side and said, "I contacted the historian friend of mine. He would like to meet you."

She frowned and chewed her lip. "He'll ask questions, and I don't have answers."

Sebastian smiled. "You let me worry about that."

She shrugged. "Okay. When?"

He checked his watch. "He's at a coffee shop this evening. He sings there sometimes. How about we go and have a coffee right now?"

She frowned but nodded.

"I'll grab the sketchbooks from my apartment," he said. "If you want to, I'll meet you back here in five minutes."

At his suggestion, she nodded and stepped inside.

Chana asked, "What happened to you?"

"Sebastian wants me to meet someone."

Instantly the apartment fell silent.

SEBASTIAN WALKED INTO his apartment. There was no sign of Jeremiah. He picked up the sketchbooks and walked back out, locking the door behind him. As he reached the other apartment, he could hear someone talking inside but not clearly enough to understand what they said. The door opened as he approached, and Lacey stepped out.

"What's that all about?" he asked with a tilt of his head toward the apartment as he led her down the hall.

"They asked me what was going on, and I said you wanted me to meet somebody."

His brows drew together. "And?"

"Then they teased me," she muttered. "As if to say, we were going on a date. But I couldn't tell them what we were really doing."

He chuckled. "In that case"—he snagged her arm, hooked it through his bent arm—"we might as well look the part."

She tried to protest, but he wouldn't listen.

He liked being around her. There was something so damn nice about her. He also wanted to ask what the hell was going on at the rooftop restaurant too because she'd been so distracted. But he figured there would be enough questions once they got to the café.

He led the way to the coffee shop, pointing out little idiosyncrasies, facts about the stores as they walked past. "Bruno runs this little corner smoke shop," he said as they passed it. "He's on his fifth wife."

She gasped. "Five wives? Are you kidding?"

He nodded. "The first three he had at the same time, but he didn't tell anybody. Now he's down to just one, and it's a new one at that."

He had her laughing by the time they made it to the coffee shop. He noted with satisfaction her relaxed shoulders and the genuine smile on her face as they walked into the café. At least she wasn't stressed out at the moment.

As they walked in, Sebastian found Bruno sitting with a large group of people. He motioned to his friend and nudged Lacey to the back of the restaurant into a booth. He ordered coffees to be delivered to them there.

Bruno joined them after a moment. He bowed over her hand in an exaggerated flare and introduced himself. Sebastian could see that Lacey was enchanted with him.

"I'm sorry I missed your singing earlier," she said. "I imagine it was wonderful."

He beamed at her. "Aren't you the sweetest thing."

She chuckled. "I don't know about that. I'm nothing but a headache for Sebastian these days."

Bruno waved his hand at Sebastian. "That's not an issue. Sebastian is used to problems. And if he must have one it should be a pretty one like you."

Sebastian rolled his eyes at his buddy. Coffee was soon delivered, and then he pulled out a sketchbook and laid it down on the table.

Bruno drew it closer to him and flipped back the cover. He made several gasps of surprise as he flipped through the pages, and yet, stopped to study each one in more detail. "These are fantastic, and so accurate they are almost as if you were there." he said. He raised a sharp gaze to Lacey. "You do realize how talented you are, right?"

She shot Sebastian a look. He nodded. "I'm not sure about that," she muttered. "I've never really drawn much." She corrected, "I used to, then stopped, because I didn't have the same natural talent as everybody else in our class."

"What kind of art class was it?"

"Oils and still life. We did some nude models too, but I couldn't get the hang of it."

"Did you ever work on black-and-whites?"

She shook her head. "No. My instructors were really big on color."

"That's likely what happened. Too often you get forced into a medium that isn't your style, so you walk away. Whereas all you needed was to keep trying different art methods, different techniques that appealed, that made the art yours."

"Maybe so. I spent a few years thinking that, if I practiced, if I worked at it hard enough, I'd get there. Instead it seemed like I never got anywhere," she said in a plaintive voice. "And I haven't done any formal drawing until today."

He flipped through the images, until he stilled his hand as he lifted his gaze. "All of these today?"

She nodded. "All of them today."

At that point, Sebastian pulled out his cell phone and flicked to the video he'd taken while she sketched and held it up for Bruno.

Bruno watched, seeing the images appear in lightning speed in front of Lacey as she worked. "Wow, that is fantastic."

"What it is, is odd, weird and kind of distressing," she clarified. "I'm not sure about fantastic."

Both men turned their gazes to her.

She shrugged as if put on the spot. "I don't know how they came to be. So, of course, I'm a little worried about what's going on and what might be coming next."

In a low voice Sebastian picked up the story and explained about what she'd seen and what had happened. He prefaced the story by saying, "She was also hit by a car two nights ago. I didn't realize it earlier, but she hit her head. I don't know if that's a contributing factor to what's going on or not."

Bruno looked at her with gentle horror in his gaze. "Are you all right?"

Sheepishly she said, "I'm fine. I accidentally stepped out into the street when I should have waited for the traffic signal to change."

"And you didn't break anything obviously," he said with a hand wave at her body. "I don't see any casts, and I don't see any stitches or big gauze bandages."

"Exactly," Lacey said with a nudge toward Sebastian. "But he keeps hovering as if I'm seriously injured."

"He'll have a reason, my dear. Sebastian always has a reason for everything he does." Bruno stared down at the video, then hit Pause, handed it back to Sebastian and returned to studying the diagrams. "Any training on 3-D printed work or architectural or blueprint drawings?"

"No, I haven't done any of that."

"Interesting how very straight everything is," he said. "I bet we could set a ruler by these."

"Which also would be very strange for me." She explained further. "I usually paint free form. Dab paints on the canvas and try to make sense of it all." She laughed. "Often I was the only one who could make sense of my paintings. The teacher never did."

"Still, it's an interesting technique," he said. "So you're sitting there in that video, and you look up. You see where a line goes, where a window belongs, and you look down at your paper, and you draw it. Is that what happened?"

"More or less," she said. "I was just drawing what I saw."

"And yet, you couldn't see it?" Bruno turned to ask Sebastian.

"No."

Bruno tapped the pages. "Fascinating."

"Not really," she said. "As much as it's interesting that I might visualize what went where in this underground dig, the clarity, the detail, none of that is explainable."

"Oh, my dear. Not everything in life is explainable." Bruno settled back and reached for his coffee, took several sips, holding the cup with both hands. Finally he replaced the cup on the table and said slowly, "And the things that are explainable are not always things we want to hear the explanation for."

"I don't understand," she said.

"Just that the explanation we have here might not be something you're comfortable with."

"Do you have an explanation?" She leaned forward eagerly. "That would be awesome if you did."

"Let me start with, what do you think happened?"

She sat back, glanced at the images and shrugged. "I honestly have no clue. I'm obviously drawing something either from memory or making it up on the spot."

"Or you're tapping into the energy of the place and somehow seeing what buildings were there at the time."

"If that's possible, except that, of course, it's not."

"Everything in life is possible," Bruno said. "In this case, you have to look at the evidence. You could see what nobody else could see, and you saw it clear enough that you could draw it. Not only draw it but draw it with precision. So either you touched on a past life, touched on the energy of the space or connected with somebody else who was showing you all of this."

"Not one of those sounds like a good idea to me," she said suspiciously. "I'm very open-minded to a lot of this, but it still has to make some sense."

He flipped through several more drawings, then came back to one in particular. "And yet, in this one, you interjected a person. We know for sure that person wasn't there because no one was around but your own crew, right?" he asked Sebastian.

Sebastian nodded. "Right, no one else was there."

CHAPTER 9

"**I** DIDN'T SEE anyone around at the time," she said, "but there could have been."

"She also has an incredible appetite these days," Sebastian told Bruno.

Bruno nodded to Sebastian, noting the comments. In response to Lacey, however, he repeated, "An explanation is not always available. It's possible you're downloading somebody else's data. There's a term for it when people paint or write. *Spirit-writing* is one term, where you're given messages by a spirit, and you write them down. You think that either they are your own thoughts or inspiration from someone above, but, in actual fact, the spirit sends you the information."

"If the person doesn't know, that sounds like a mean prank," she said in surprise.

"It's not always possible to stop the process. Sometimes, like a medium, people connect with a spirit while they're painting. Next thing they know, they're painting what the spirit wants them to paint." Sebastian's lips quirked. "Sometimes literally. The spirit wants to sit there with a paintbrush in their hand and paint. Other times they have a message they need delivered. So the person painting somehow ends up painting what the spirit thinks will be an important message. And sometimes nobody can understand what the message is at all."

"That must be very frustrating for the spirits."

He gave her a look of approval. "Exactly. Glad to hear that you're more compassionate to spirits than many people."

"If they leave me alone," she said, "then I'm perfectly fine. But, if they don't leave me alone, that's a whole different story."

"How do you think you'd feel if you ever saw a spirit?" Bruno asked.

She stared at him, wide-mouthed.

Sebastian laughed. "First, she'd have to be aware of what she's seeing, and, second, I don't know if it would make any difference or not."

Bruno and Lacey both looked at him.

Sebastian smiled. "Because she just recently communicated with a spirit, and she didn't even know."

She stared at him, her jaw dropping open. "I did not," she argued.

"Yes, you did," Sebastian said. "At the restaurant on the rooftop deck. Not only was there no table in the corner but there was no man in a suit, drinking a glass of dark liquid."

He watched as the shock hit her face, and then her understanding dawned. Her jaw dropped a little more, and her shoulders sagged.

He wrapped an arm around her shoulders and tucked her up close. "Honestly, it's pretty special that you got to see him."

She shook her head. "I was feeling sorry for him. He was all alone. He didn't look like he wanted to be alone."

"I don't know if it's because of the bump on the head," Bruno said, "or if something happened on the dig site that, all of a sudden, has you seeing all this."

"But can we be sure it's *all of a sudden*?" Sebastian asked. "It's quite possible she's been seeing this kind of stuff for years. She's been beyond fascinated by Pompeii since she was a child."

She gave him a broken laugh. "No way I've seen spirits and ghosts for years. I live in a small town. Nothing ever happens there."

"What clothes were the people wearing at that other table you were so interested in?" He listened while she described what the ladies wore.

"The men had on black suits," she said. "I noticed because they all looked good."

He glanced over at Bruno and gave him a head shake. Bruno's eyebrows shot up. She glanced from one man to the other. Sebastian watched, waiting for her to get the message.

"What are you saying?" she asked suspiciously.

"That table was empty," he said. He held up his cell phone and showed her the picture of the table in question. "Here, right?"

She stabbed the image on his phone with her finger. "Yes, exactly there."

He pointed out the date and time stamp of this photo taken earlier tonight, then nodded as he put away his phone. "That table was empty."

"So who the hell were those people?" she asked in confusion. "What the hell is going on?"

Bruno patted her hand gently. "What's going on is that you're now seeing spirits. For whatever reason they've realized you can communicate with them. So now they'll be all around you all the time."

"No way do I want ghosts in my world." She frowned at

Sebastian, then spoke to Bruno again. "How will I ever know who's real, of this world, or not? Those in the restaurant looked just like you and me. And how do I explain talking to air to everyone else?"

Bruno smiled. "The thing is, I doubt this is a sudden event or a new phenomenon. I think the spirits have been around you for a long time, my dear. Only now your conscious is letting you see what your subconscious has always known."

SEBASTIAN COULD SEE how stunned she was by this turn of events. But did she realize how very special this was? He wanted desperately to have proof that what she saw had really existed. Her buildings as drawn were certainly done in the style of that era; the architecture, the living conditions were all spot-on. He was fascinated by this insight into the world she had created. But not half as much as Bruno, who pored over the sketches in front of him as if they were gold, and he lived in Pompeii. If he saw these were eerily accurate—then they were.

Bruno sat back with a sigh and looked at Sebastian and said, "Thank you very much for contacting me. Have you shown these to Hunter?" He motioned to the entrance to the coffeehouse where Hunter approached from the street.

Sebastian gave Bruno a small nod. "Not yet. I'm trying to convince her to let me show people, but she wants to avoid having anyone know. I needed your expert opinion. Hence the need to show you. I'm hoping she'll be fine with Hunter knowing too."

"They are fascinating," he said. "The question is, what to do from here?"

With raised eyebrows, Sebastian turned to Lacey and waited.

She shook her head, but then she said, "Okay. You can show Hunter."

"Good, as he's the other specialist I mentioned."

Hunter walked in the front entrance. Sebastian waved to him. Within moments he'd joined them, shaking hands with Bruno and tossing Lacey a bright smile.

She responded with a reserved one of her own.

Interesting, Sebastian thought. Hunter usually charmed everyone.

"Hey, Bruno." Hunter slid into the chair beside Bruno, his gaze falling on the sketches. "Wow, fascinating."

He glanced over at Sebastian. "Is this her?"

Sebastian nodded. "Yes."

"But you already knew that," she said softly, studying the new arrival.

"I wondered," Hunter corrected as he studied her face before shifting his gaze to the sketches.

"That's a mild adjective," Bruno muttered, his gaze once again locked on the pages before them. "Especially as Lacey here drew them."

Hunter made a startled sound reaching for the drawings.

"I don't even know what to do with this stuff." Lacey's voice showed the fatigue and the stress on her emotional senses. "I can't believe you guys think this is for real."

"Do you believe what you see?" Bruno asked pensively, his gaze drifting over her face as if searching for something.

"I know what I see," she said with a wave of her hand in the direction of the excavation sites. "But how do I know what I see is valid?"

"Well, it's valid in that you see it," Hunter said. "What

you're really looking for is confirmation that what you're seeing is what existed back in Pompeii's grand times."

Sebastian watched her nod slowly.

"Yes, that's exactly what I want. Confirmation."

"Your drawings appear to be as close a depiction as anybody could guess without having been there," Bruno said. "Accurate as far as building, style, materials, etcetera. They all match the times."

"The thing is, it's like I was there," she said. She leaned forward over the drawings. "Here is where she slept." She pointed to a house, saying, "She shared that room with three sisters."

"Who is *she?*"

"Linnea," Lacey murmured.

Sebastian looked closely to see her eyes slightly glazed over. He glanced at Bruno, who stared in fascination.

Hunter went still, his gaze narrowed on her face. "What does Linnea do?"

"Helps her mother. She makes pots and delivers water to houses."

"And foodstuffs?"

"Anything required." Lacey's voice came low, slow, in a tempered vein.

"Are you connected to Linnea?"

"Yes," Lacey said. "The city is beautiful. It is her home."

"What happened to you?" Sebastian asked, stilling Bruno's hand from moving in front of Lacey's eyes to see if she registered a change or looked any different.

"The volcano. There was just ash from one day to the next. Then fire blew into the sky, and dirt crumbled. Then hot liquid fire poured, and the skies rained upon us. We panicked and ran."

"But it happened quickly?"

"Yes," she murmured. "Very quickly."

"You were trapped inside the house?"

"No, not there." At this point Lacey's expression changed, became more alert. More ... herself. "She went to save her sister. Linnea struggled to free her." Lacey gasped and choked with tears. "The liquid fire ran along the pathway just outside the house. Everything is so confused, ... but she loved her sister so much ..."

Sebastian nodded. "What about your life there? Were you happy?"

Lacey seemed to focus on a faraway spot before speaking. "I used to be."

"And why weren't you at the end?"

Lacey shook her head, turned toward Sebastian, a deep sadness on her face. "Her sister, ... she'd been taken prisoner." She spoke bitterly. "Linnea couldn't stop it."

Bruno nudged the diagrams toward Lacey. Hunter spread them apart. She studied them and pointed to the room that had no door.

"What was her fate?"

Lacey raised her head, her expression a painful anger. "She doesn't know. She couldn't find her sister."

The men backed off on questioning about Linnea's past.

"Why are you here now?"

Lacey stared at them, her gaze haunted, but she knew the answer to the last question. "She is trying to find her sister."

Beside them, a waiter banged a platter of food down a little too heavily. Lacey gasped and collapsed against her chair. She looked around at the others, reached up to her temples and said, "All of a sudden, I'm not feeling so good."

"Headache?" Sebastian asked helpfully.

She nodded. "I guess." Her tone wasn't clear, as if not understanding what had just happened.

Bruno nudged Sebastian's arm, a question in his eyes.

Sebastian shook his head. He knew Bruno would understand this was hardly the time to bring up what had just happened. He told Bruno, "I'll see if I can get scans of these for you."

"I'd really like full-size copies if I could," he said.

Lacey picked up her camera and said, "I can send you images of them. I'll probably be drawing a lot over the next two weeks. I don't know. It seems to feel that way somehow."

"*Feel?*" Hunter asked in a neutral tone. "I'd like a copy too, if you wouldn't mind."

"Sure." She shrugged. "I can't really explain it. I have felt *odd* the last two days, since arriving here." She glanced around the room. "It's the wrong lighting in here. If you don't mind, I'll take the sketches home, separate the pages from the book, lay them down and try to take good photographs of them."

Bruno looked at her in delight. "I would absolutely love it. And, if you decide you don't want these ..." He tapped them.

"Not happening," Sebastian said firmly. "They belong to the foundation."

She shot him a look. "They do?"

He nodded. "They do. You created them for the bosses on working time."

She frowned as if not sure she liked his answer.

But no way would he have her giving away these diagrams, creating a ton of interest on the site they were still working. It was way too dangerous. Better to keep this a secret until he knew more. He quickly closed the sketchbook and stood. "Bruno, I'll contact you tomorrow. We'll try to get the photographs for you by then."

Hunter prepared to leave.

Bruno nodded, but his gaze was on the sketch pad in Sebastian's arms. "Find a way to copy them," he urged. "That information can't get lost."

"I'll see what I can do." Sebastian would love to have photocopies, but it would require a large copier, map-size, and he didn't know if the library here had one. He'd send out some inquiries to see who could possibly copy something so large. He held out a hand for Lacey. "Come on. Let's get you home." He nodded at Hunter, who rose as well.

"That's a good idea," she said. "I'm really tired now." With his help she stood, swayed ever-so-slightly and both men watched in concern. She gave them a bright smile. "I'm fine. Not to worry."

Sebastian held her hand, and the three of them walked through the coffee shop until they stood on the street.

"I'll leave you two here." Hunter raised his hand in farewell.

Calling out good night, Sebastian watched his friend slip away in the darkness. He'd catch up with him later. He really wanted to get Hunter's take on Lacey and the craziness she was caught up in. But that would have to wait a little. She spoke again. He pulled his mind back to the present.

"Why didn't you want to leave Bruno the originals?" she asked.

"Because they are special," he said. "We'll send him photographs."

"That should be good enough," she said. "I have to admit that I wouldn't mind working on a couple of them a little more. I can see details that need to be added that I didn't get a chance to the first time."

"Later," he said. "First, you need rest. Then we'll work on fine-tuning some of your artwork. But we also have to work on the dig."

She sighed. "So much to do and not enough time."

He chuckled. "If you're angling for a few more weeks here, I'll see what I can do."

She stopped in the street and stared at him in joy. "Really?"

"Really. As long as you can leave whatever it is you've left behind, I'll see about keeping your contract here open or extend it for a few more weeks."

She nodded. "I could do all kinds of diagrams then," she said enthusiastically.

"And yet, it's the photos we need first and foremost."

"Of course. The story. And what a story it is," she said almost dreamily.

"If you ever feel like you need to write it down, … maybe you should keep a voice recorder with you, to make note of the ideas that come to your mind."

"That's a great idea," she said, "but I don't have one."

"I'll get you one in the morning," he promised.

She chuckled. "Are you always this nice to your employees?"

"The ones who will potentially create something fantastic for the foundation? Absolutely." He linked his arm with hers again, helping her cross the street. "If you need to sleep in longer tomorrow morning, you can, you know? You don't have to start so early."

"No. Spending as much time with you as I am is already making the others talk. If I get special privileges, like sleeping in late, that'll just make the situation worse."

"Do you think people resent you?" He hadn't considered that, but people were still people all over the world. And, if he showed favoritism to one over the others, he could see how there might be some disgruntlement among them.

"No, I don't think so," she said. "But you never really know, and I don't want to start anything. If I'm only here for a couple weeks—or a month maybe—whatever disturbance I might cause will be just a ruffle in the wind at summer's end. However, if I'm staying longer, then it might potentially cause bigger trouble."

"I think your sunshiny disposition will make some of even the hardest and grumpiest of the team happy to hear you're extending your stay."

At that she set off in peals of laughter. "Oh, I wish. It would be nice if everybody was optimistic instead of pessimistic, that they'd smile instead of frown, say good things instead of nasty things about each other," she said impulsively. "The world would be a much happier place."

"Happier, yes," he said. "But I'm not sure so much sunshine makes everybody happy. Some people thrive on drama. Some people need strife and stress in order to surmount difficulties and to come up with incredible inventions."

"I guess," she said. "I'm the glue in between everybody that keeps the relationships all working."

"We need people like that too," he said. They approached the apartment building. He opened the main door. She stepped inside and froze. As he walked to the elevators, he turned, and she wasn't following him. A look of fear, almost terror, was on her face.

He moved to her side. "What's the matter?" he whispered.

She stared at him, her eyes huge, massive.

He gave her a little shake. "Lacey. Talk to me. What's the matter?"

She shook her head, her mouth opened, then closed. And then, as if released from some unseen grip, she took a shuddering breath and relaxed. "I don't know what that was. But, for just a moment, it was like an icy terror ripped through me." She grabbed his hand. "What's happening to me? Maybe I should go home. Maybe I should just forget about whatever's going on here and go home."

"No," he said firmly. "No panicking at the first sign of a problem."

She gave a bitter laugh. "This is hardly the first sign, is it?"

He took a deep breath and grabbed hold of his control. "You're fine. I suspect it was just a bit of a headache or something." Inside he was trying to figure out what the hell was going on here. He brushed her hair off her forehead and asked, "How is the head?"

She closed her eyes and whispered, "It's better, I think. But I don't like all this scary stuff."

He wrapped his arms gently around her and hugged her close. "Easy. It'll be calmer in a few days."

She pushed back and glared at him.

He wanted to chuckle. She was such a fascinating mix of temper and sunshine. Thunderclouds and storm warnings, and then the clouds would part and that beautiful smile would break free again.

"How can you say that? What does a few days from now have to do with what's going on?"

"Come on. Let's get you upstairs to bed."

"You're not answering me," she said resentfully. But she

let him tug her into the elevator. "I hope I don't feel that again. Something literally stopped me in my tracks, and it terrified me."

"I saw that," he said. He wrapped an arm around her shoulders and cradled her gently. "Stay calm. Stay focused. Whatever this is, we'll get to the bottom of it."

And just like that, once again her resistance crumbled. "Are you sure?"

"I'm sure," he said. "I will help you get to the bottom of this. I promise."

She sighed. "I hope so. I'm wondering if you are the cause of it."

Startled, he reared back to look down at her. "Really?"

She shrugged. "Well, it seems like it started when you came along."

"Hardly," he said. "You were hit by that vehicle before I ever got here."

"No," she countered. "I'd met you already at the site. I got hit later that evening."

CHAPTER 10

TOO MUCH WAS going on in Lacey's world right now. She knew she'd never sleep. But, when she woke up the next morning, she *had* slept, like a log. All of the events of the previous day seemed like a dream. She had none of the pictures with her to confirm whether it had happened or not, but she did have her camera.

She jumped out of bed bright and early and walked over to her camera, sat down, flipping through the photos. They were the ones she'd taken yesterday. And, sure enough, she could still see all the buildings as she'd drawn them. She sat, amazed, cross-legged on her bed as she went through them.

"That's a pretty happy smile on your face." Chana yawned and rolled over. "It's way too early to be up."

"I don't know why I'm awake," Lacey said. "But I feel quite energized."

"Good for you," Chana grumbled. "Wake me in another half hour."

Lacey made a mental note of the time, realizing it was just minutes past six o'clock. She kept looking through her photographs. When she looked up the next time, it was almost six-thirty. "Chana, are you awake?"

Chana mumbled, but that was all.

Lacey put down her camera, got up and gave her cousin a good shake on the shoulder. "It's six-thirty. Time to get up."

Lacey unpacked her camera cord, connecting the cable to her laptop, and proceeded to download as many of the photos as she could before they had to leave. She should have set this up last night before she went out, but she had forgotten. She dressed and headed to the kitchen to put on coffee. She heard only light murmurs from the other people in the apartment.

When the coffee was done, she took a cup and walked to the window. There was no patio, so the window would have to do. She studied the area of the dig. She could see buildings springing up all over the place. It truly amazed her. And yet, she was afraid to mention it, in case nobody else saw it.

Chana eventually joined her at the window. "What are you looking at?"

"The dig," she murmured. "It's so easy to imagine the glory of all the buildings as they must have been back then." She slid a sideways look at her cousin. "What do you see when you look at it?"

Chana snorted. "I see nothing but a dirt ground with some busted buildings and a gate. Don't ask me questions like that before breakfast." And grumpily she headed off to the kitchen to find food.

But her answer had let Lacey know exactly what Chana could see and couldn't see. She didn't see the huge buildings rising up in the midst. She couldn't see the stones visible, and yet, not visible. She didn't see the walkways, the streets, the cobblestones, like Lacey did. What she could see was both magical and terrifying.

She switched her gaze away from the dig site, now studying the rest of the inhabited town around her. But she witnessed no change in this scenery. No other buildings reared up from the streets. No other 3-D holographic buildings loomed atop anything. She looked back to the dig. And there they were still. She gave a happy sigh and just studied it, filling her with the bounty of the world that had been hidden. "Now if only I could capture all that," she murmured.

Mark wandered into the kitchen, groggy and unshaven. "Haven't you done enough picture-taking and drawing for a while? You've drawn more images than I've seen in a long time."

"Drawn?" She turned to look at him. Surprised he knew about them. "Well, I've taking a ton of photographs," she said cautiously.

"Oh, I thought the drawings in the sketchbook were yours," he said.

"Ah, so you know about those." She groaned. "Yes they are mine." She returned to looking out over the dig site. She didn't know how to explain this wonder, and she didn't want to lose it. It was so fantastic to see that Old World city come alive. She wasn't really seeing people or movement. More like she'd been an architect in another lifetime and saw the buildings as they had been.

"Are you coming?"

Startled, she turned to see Chana with her bag packed, ready to go. Lacey saw the team had all finished eating already. "Wow. I've been standing here in a daze?"

They all nodded.

She groaned. "Don't suppose there's any food to go with us there?"

Chana frowned. "You didn't eat?"

She shook her head. "No. Just daydreaming." She walked into the kitchen to see an open box of granola bars.

She picked up three and opened one, eating it as she walked with the others. "You're so lucky that you've been working here all this time," she said impulsively to her cousin. "It must have been quite the experience."

Chana was in a less-than-jovial mood though. "Yes. But, like any job, it becomes a tedious chore after a while."

That, of course, wasn't the way Lacey viewed it. But she was wise enough to keep her comments to herself.

As they walked across the street, she stared up at the dig and gasped, seeing the open gate, the walls rising high above on either side, showcasing the buildings behind it. Just the vast size of the former city was amazing.

Chana looked at her curiously. "You know it's the same as it always is? You've been here several days now. I thought some of that awestruckness would have worn off."

Lacey deliberately tried to pull in her enthusiasm again. "Sorry. I guess I sound pretty pathetic to you."

"No, ... I'm sorry. I'm just in a bitchy mood this morning," Chana said. "Didn't sleep well."

"Trouble with Tom?"

Chana shot her a look and sped up. Tom was a nonsubject as far as Chana was concerned.

At the site, Chana peeled off from the group and went to her corner, leaving Lacey feeling like she'd upset her cousin in some way. She wanted to apologize but figured, for the moment, it was better to stay quiet.

She unpacked her camera and started with more panoramic pictures. She didn't know why she felt compelled every day to take these broad landscape pictures, but it was like seeing minuscule progress, the weather change, the time of day change. It gave a snapshot look at life on this dig. As she checked the others, they were all much less than cheerful. As if something ugly had happened at the apartment that she'd missed.

She caught Katie walking alone to where the packing boxes were and asked, "Did I miss something? Everybody seems to be a little grumpy this morning."

Katie chuckled. "Nah, they're just jealous."

"Jealous of what?" Lacey asked.

"You," Katie said. "You appear to have bonded very well with the boss. Even though you just got here, you have a closer relationship with him than everybody else, and it's making others feel a little uneasy." She turned and walked away, picking up some tools on her way to where she'd been working.

Hearing her own worries spoken out loud, and much faster than she had expected, Lacey didn't know what to do. Would it help or hurt to let them know Hunter had been with them last night? She decided it would make it worse so stayed quiet.

It was one thing to bury herself in work, but now she felt like she couldn't even connect with the other people on the team. She really didn't have any connection with the boss, at least not one she had tried to create. It all had to do with her drawings of her visions.

But nobody knew that. And, even if they did, would that make them feel better or worse about her? Would they think she was making it up to be grandiose and to get more attention? That thought was enough to make her sick.

She worked on the items on the table Katie had left out for Lacey to photograph. When she was done, she put away her camera gear, but Katie came back.

"Just hang on a sec, Lacey. Let me ID them. We'll take photos again. Then it can be packed up and sent out."

Lacey waited silently while Katie put everything in bags and wrote down the identification number on them. And Lacey photographed them all again while Katie packed up the box. When they were done, Katie smiled breezily and said, "Well, that's one job out of the way." Then she turned and walked away.

Everything seemed normal with Katie, as if she wasn't holding anything against Lacey. But it was hard for her to forget Katie's words. Was everybody thinking Lacey had done something, like slept with the boss, in order to curry favor? She wasn't even getting paid, for heaven's sake.

Disturbed by the intrusion of the human element into her fantasy world, she walked to where she'd been and started photographing again. This time she focused on the outskirts where the pathways were. She wasn't looking for anything in particular, just everything. She photographed about twenty feet of path, loving how the road's stone blocks interlocked, how smooth they were, noting the little striations and marks that had been left behind over the years.

When she was done, she turned her attention to what appeared to be a series of old gardens or some kind of an enclave that could have held animals. She liked the idea of gardens. As she took photographs, what she had thought of as in her mind's eye became an actual garden. As she kept taking photographs, that same 3-D imaging system in her mind brought up outside her camera's viewfinder whatever it was that her mind saw. She frowned, dropped the camera so she could stare at her surroundings and wondered just how much of this was her own visualization. She was here; her mind said it should be a garden, so she had created a garden. That certainly wouldn't be very helpful if the garden didn't exist in Pompeii before the volcano eruption.

She continued to photograph anyway. The more she did, the more details she came up with. It was unnerving. She could see where animals might have lived, where people would have walked. She could almost hear the sounds of the wind blowing through the area. She sighed happily as she stepped closer to a bush. She reached out a hand to touch a vibrant green leaf, only her hand went through it.

She frowned and stepped back. "Good Lord. It looks so real," she muttered.

"What's the matter with reality?"

"What's the matter?" She stiffened at Sebastian's voice. "The reality is that everybody else is pissed off because you're spending so much time with me. I really don't need that. I came here to spend a couple weeks to live out my Pompeii dream. I didn't want to stir up any trouble."

"Maybe you should have thought of that before you became some kind of a 3-D architect."

His tone was wry and humorous. He obviously wasn't upset at her words. But his words bubbled laughter out of her. She turned to smile at him. "It's also foolish. Isn't that the way it is? Thousands of people died here. We are digging apart their lives, and I'm upset because the crew thinks I've done something to curry favor."

"You mean, like sleep with me?" he asked with interest. "Now that's an idea."

She snorted, sure he was joking. "Hardly," she said. "That's definitely not happening."

"Well, not as part of the job, that's for sure," he agreed. "Doesn't mean it can't happen for other reasons."

She shook her head and picked up her camera, taking a picture of his face.

He waved her away. "No taking pictures of the boss."

"Well, maybe if they see you upset with me," she said, "they'll calm down."

He seemed to realize she was serious. "Somebody said something?"

"In passing," she said, to protect Katie's identity. "It's my fault."

"It's nobody's fault," he exclaimed. "You have a rare talent that I'm trying to understand. You've also been hurt, and I don't want you to overdo it. Besides, I like you, and, if we spend time together, it's nobody's business but ours."

"But they don't know why or what we're doing."

"They don't want to know the real reason why," he said. "They're hung up on their own lives. Don't get involved."

She nodded. "I wasn't planning on it. I just want to keep out of trouble."

He nodded. "That's the best way to do it." He motioned at what she had been taking photos of. "What do you see here?"

She held up her camera so he could see the photos she'd taken. "See how beautiful and green the bushes are? I don't understand the species of this plant, but it's so vibrant and healthy, attracting the birds, now calling out to each other."

He stared at the photo, slid over to several more and then looked back at her. "So you can still see everything?"

She beamed at him. "It's stupendous really."

He nodded. "I wish I could see it."

She looked at her photos. "You don't see it in my photos?"

He shook his head.

"You don't see it here in your surroundings?"

Again he shook his head.

"Then what do you see?" she muttered, not knowing

150

what to say.

He glanced at her. "Just a partial ring here. Nothing in it, just dirt all the way around. No green bush. No sounds of birds singing."

She frowned, her fingers switching through the photographs. "Seriously?" She shook her head. "I was so sure. It's so vivid for me. I even tried to touch it."

"That must be nice," he said softly. "But I can assure you, nobody else sees what you're seeing."

She spun around to see where the rest of the team was.

He reached out for her arm. "Whoa, don't go there."

She glared at him. "If somebody else can see it, it would make me feel a hell of a lot better. Although, if not, they will all think I'm crazy."

"That would be too bad," he said. "But you can't tell them. They won't understand. They're not of the same mind-set as you are. You need to keep this to yourself."

She waved him off. "Go find somebody else to talk to. They all need some *boss love*. I have work to do."

"I want you to sketch what you see. Please?"

She noticed he had several sketchbooks in his hand and a box of pencils. He handed them to her.

"Which is more important, the photographs or the drawings?" she asked curiously. "I already photographed a box of items Katie had laid out, which is why I'm now shooting pictures here."

"Try to find a balance between the two." He nodded and turned away. He took several steps, then stopped, slowly turning back. "Did you hear that?"

She frowned at him. "I didn't hear anything. What did you hear?"

He studied her face for a long moment as if he didn't

believe her. Then he looked around, slowly pivoted, searching the area around her. "I'm not sure what I heard. But I didn't like the sound of it."

"Don't say that and leave me alone. I've never seen anything here that was scary."

"That's good, at least in my book. The thing is, stuff out here is scarier than anything you've ever imagined. I don't want any of it brought to life." He took off again, heading toward the others.

She plunked to the ground cross-legged, unnerved by his words. She didn't get it. She didn't want to. She couldn't hear anything scary. Everything she saw was light and bright and breezy. It went along with who she was. Everything she saw made her smile, had her gasping in awe. And yet, he seemed to live in a world of darkness and fear.

She opened one of the sketchbooks to the first page and snatched up a newly sharpened pencil. She didn't quite know what she was supposed to draw. A lone bush was hardly exciting. She sketched the garden plants around it too, but it wasn't a whole lot in her opinion.

Only after she was done did she catch herself drawing some weird design in the left corner. She didn't know what it meant. She walked away from it and then came back, and it still didn't give her any enlightenment. She sat back down again, turned the page and began the second drawing. This time her pencil moved on its own. She watched in amazement as Sebastian's face showed up. And then Hunter's beside him.

But her hand kept moving. It drew a temple behind them. She almost laughed because it could be a dig anywhere in so many different parts of the world. But obviously her mind seemed to think she needed a picture of the two men.

Just as suddenly her hand stopped. She smiled, turned to a clean page and said, "Now what?"

But nothing came. A little unnerved after having so many instinctive artistic ventures, she realized how much she had done and maybe she needed a break.

She pulled out her camera, putting the sketchbooks on the ground, and proceeded to take more pictures. She was looking for any bits of nature, even bugs. She bent close to the ground, studying, looking to find the soldiers of today versus those of the yesteryears.

Lost in her own thoughts again, taking photographs as the others came and went, doing nothing in particular and just letting her instincts turn her work alive, she finally realized that somebody was calling for her. She turned to find Chana standing there, holding one of the sketchbooks in her hand. "Are you doing more sketches again? Not photos?"

She shrugged. "Yeah, I am. Does that bother you?"

"Is that why you're spending so much time with Sebastian?"

"He wanted them for something," she said casually. "You know how I feel about my art. It's not really good enough. So I told him that he could just have them. I wasn't going to sell them to him."

Chana flipped over to the next page, and her breath caught. "Did you do this?" she asked in amazement. "It's really good, but, Jesus, it's scary as hell."

Lacey stood to take a look at the drawings, and she stopped, her throat choking down hard. "No," she said, "I didn't draw that."

"You just said you did."

She stared at the faces of the two men but with dark evil-looking masks on both faces. "No," she said. "I only sketched their faces. Not like that but nice pictures. You know me. I don't do ugly and nasty."

Chana nodded slowly, but her gaze never left Lacey's face. "What the hell is going on here?"

Lacey dropped the pencils and stepped back from the sketchbooks. "I have no clue," she cried out. She held up her hands as if to ward off Chana's approach. "I didn't do that. I promise I didn't do that." Her cries were creating a commotion.

Suddenly Sebastian was there. He held out his hand for the sketchbook. "May I?"

Chana reluctantly passed it over. Sebastian looked, his eyebrows raised. "Well, it's incredibly powerful," he muttered. "Not very nice but incredibly powerful."

But Lacey was having none of it. "I swear I didn't draw it."

"Are you sure?"

She nodded frantically. "I wouldn't have. That's not me. That's not the style I draw in. I can't stand scary stuff."

His gaze never left the sketches. "I'll close this and put it away for now. It's obviously upsetting you."

"Of course it's upsetting me," she said bitterly. She bent down and packed up her camera. "I'm going to work in a different area today." She turned and walked away.

CHANA ASKED, HER voice low and contained, "What's going on here?"

Sebastian shook his head. "I'm not exactly sure. I think she did draw these. I don't think she's aware she did though." He opened the sketchbook again and shot Chana a look. "I'm not taking advantage of her, if that's what you're thinking."

She shook her head. "No, that's not what I'm thinking. But I don't want her to come to any harm." She tapped the sketchbook in his hand. "This is not Lacey. She's literally sunshine and butterflies. This is nasty." She was at a loss for words. "So you tell me. How did she go from drawing pretty lilies and flowers, sunshine, roses and rainbows to something horrific like this?"

He studied the drawings. The longer he looked, the more he realized the power behind them. "She's incredibly talented."

"I'd rather she was not talented at all," Chana snapped, "if it means she isn't drawing this shit." She twisted to stare after her cousin. "I don't get it. She's been so excited to be here. Now she's evolving into somebody I don't recognize."

"What do you mean?"

Chana shook her head. "It's probably nothing. I'm just tired."

"Explain," Sebastian enunciated slowly. "Please."

She groaned. "I don't want to say anything. But, I mean, sure she probably could have walked into the street herself and got hit by a car at home. But, since that happened here, she's changed. She's eating a ton. I don't think she realizes it, but she finishes her plate, and then she looks at mine. If they bring us fresh bread, and some is left, she inhales it. She's drinking massive amounts of water all day, then complains she hasn't had any all day and needs some at home. Plus she's turned off of alcohol. It's bad, but I don't think she even recognizes what she's doing."

He studied her face. "I noticed she's eating more but not that it was obvious to anyone else."

"That's because you were so busy trying not to always look at her," Chana said. "The attraction is obvious. And it's making the working relationship here that much more difficult."

"Interesting," he said, "because there's no reason for anyone to be upset if there is any attraction. We're both single adults. She did some drawings that fascinated me. I asked her to do more. But I hadn't realized," he tapped the sketch, "this was coming out too."

"Too?" she said slowly. "In the same sentence, regarding my cousin, it doesn't sound like a good thing."

He gave her a crooked grin. "Let's just say that she has a great imagination when it comes to studying these ruins and filling in the details as they would have been back then."

"Yes, I can see her maybe doing something like that, but that isn't this." She tapped the sketchbook. "Where is that coming from?"

"It really bothers you, doesn't it?" He studied Chana. She'd worked for him for almost a year now. She'd always been a steady, stable worker. But superstition was one of those funny things that crept into a person's life and took hold in the oddest ways.

"It is scary. I don't want anything to happen to her. I'd like to have my old cousin back."

"You really think she's different?"

"Just different enough that it makes me uncertain," Chana said. "She hardly even sleeps while I'm dead tired. Of course, I'm doing some digging and I'm in the hot sun, but so is she. She sits in front of the laptop for hours sometimes. I'll wake up at like two or three o'clock in the morning, and she's still awake. And she still gets up at six-thirty with us. Sometimes before we rise. I just don't get it."

He filed away that information in the back of his mind, but it was worrisome. Excessive hunger and lack of sleep had more repercussions than he was prepared to admit, certainly to Chana. "I'll keep an eye on her."

"That's what I'm afraid of," she muttered and walked away.

He opened the sketchbook and placed it on the ground and, with his cell phone in hand, took several photos, getting closer with each one until they filled his viewfinder. As soon as he had a decent photo, he sent it to Bruno and emailed Colin, his partner. He'd kept him in the loop so far but they hadn't spoken. Then Colin was busy too and likely hadn't even read the texts. As an afterthought, he sent them to Stefan too. Sebastian had barely put his phone away when it beeped. He checked, seeing Colin's number. "Hey."

"What the fuck is that?" Colin cried out. "Is that from the same girl?"

"Yes. And she's horrified. She doesn't believe she drew that picture."

"Did anybody see her?"

"I don't think so. She's been sitting here alone. I brought her the sketchbooks and pencils about an hour ago, maybe an hour and a half ago."

"She drew those detailed sketches in that short a time?" Colin questioned, but now his tone was incredulous of her skill, not so much repulsed by the content.

"And a couple others," Sebastian said. "Obviously she's got some kind of entity attachment here."

"*You think?* Ugh you know how I feel about that stuff ..." Colin said. "That girl is damn scary."

"I'm not arguing that point," he said, "but, in truth, she doesn't realize most of what she's doing."

"And that's even scarier. I mean, I get that it's a good thing, at least for her sake, that she doesn't know anything, but we have to sort this out."

"I hear you," Sebastian said. "But this all happened very fast, and she's not inclined to believe the psychic angles. She's more into the scientific method—facts, figures, reality. It's not like I can make a big deal out of this quickly. I'm going slow so I don't spook her. If she ends up running back home, we're in trouble."

"Are you sure?" he asked. "Because, right about now, I'm not sure I want her anywhere on the site."

"The masks bothered you that much?"

"Hell yeah. They definitely did."

Sebastian hung up after the call ended and stared at the sketch. He wasn't particularly enthralled with the depiction of his face—especially when covered with that mask—but he wouldn't react like Colin did. Sebastian studied the two masks, realizing though that they were slightly different, they looked like a matched set. His covered only the lower portion of his face with high sides up the cheeks. It was a unique mask because it left the face mostly visible, just covered Sebastian's nose and mouth. Hunter's mask was the same but came slightly higher up on his face.

As a drawing, it was incredibly detailed, and the artwork itself was amazing. The concept, the actual subject matter, now that was a little out there. But Sebastian could still admire the artistic skill that had gone into this, even if no one else could.

He closed the sketchbook, tucked it under his arm and headed to the main part of the dig. He felt oddly protective of her sketches. She'd put so much of herself into them that it was hard for him to not see them as a part of who she truly was. She might not appreciate that insight, but it was hard to let go of. There was something very special about her work. He didn't know why or how, but it was as if it were already alive.

Or maybe …

His head filled in the answer.

Or maybe she was bringing something back to life.

CHAPTER 11

T HE NEXT FEW days went by in a relatively normal
pattern. There were no accidents, no injuries. Lacey
enjoyed the change of relative calm. She was no longer
hurting or aching. That had been a surprisingly fast recovery,
as Sebastian had said. She had no more visions, if that was
what they were. She refused to put pencil to paper, so that
cut out most of the problems with her drawings, should they
be of the scarier kind. And Sebastian not showing her any
untoward attention seemed to help with the discontent
among the rest of the team. She was so sorry it had happened
in the first place. She hadn't meant it to.

She settled into a rhythm, taking photos, wandering
around and keeping to the superficial areas on a geographical
level. She switched out lenses, tried different shots, different
looks. She brought her laptop one day, downloading and
sifting through the photos, discarding what she could,
deliberately avoiding the ones that had the controversial 3-D
architecture in them, putting them all into a folder with a
question mark as the label.

When she was done, she stared at that folder on her laptop and wondered. Unable to help herself, she double-
clicked on it and looked at the images. For her, even today,
the 3-D buildings were as clear as they were when she first
took these photos. She knew nobody else could see them in

her pictures, and that made it even more astounding. She wondered, if she printed these out, would she see the buildings still? And yet, nobody else would again?

It was a fascinating subject, and she had to admit she'd spent more than a few days sorting through research online to find something, anything that would help piece this together, help to explain it somehow. But instead she had found nothing. As far as she could confirm, nobody had ever had visions like this. And she wasn't even sure that was what she should call it. It was just too bizarre.

She closed the folder when she heard footsteps approach. She put down her laptop and looked up. And there was Sebastian. He studied her for a long moment. She frowned. "What's the matter?"

"Nothing," he said. "Just checking to make sure you're okay. You've been sitting here very still for quite a while."

She beamed a smile at him. "Oh, I was sorting through the thousands of photographs I've taken already. Finding ones that might work for the story of what you and others are doing here. Some are really nice shots. Plus some of the ones I took in the beginning weren't as good for identification purposes, so I was tossing those."

He nodded. "And the others?"

She winced. "I was trying to forget they exist. But I have to admit that I just opened them up to look for myself again."

"And?"

"And what?" she asked. "I still have no explanation as to how they came to be. I still see the 3-D images in my photos that you still don't see. I still have no clue as to what my sketches are about or why I drew them."

"And the ones with the masks?"

"I don't have a photo of that sketch," she said quietly. "And I'm not sure I want to."

"I'm pretty sure those are even more important than the others."

She studied him carefully. "I'm not sure what you mean."

He squatted in front of her, picked up a twig that lay on the path and casually scraped the ground in front of him as if thinking about what to say and how to say it. "Everybody has some sort of a symbol," he said, "for want of another word. When I saw you drawing the buildings, I thought maybe it was the architecture you were attracted to."

"Well, I am," she said, "but I don't know what that has to do with anything."

"Then you drew the masks. And that's a whole different thing altogether."

"I know," she whispered. She stared at his hand, mesmerized as it drifted back and forth across the dirt-covered stones aimlessly. When he didn't speak again, she lifted her head and caught his gaze. "What do you think the masks mean?"

"I'm not sure. I think they're the answer to this mystery. I did send a photograph of it to Bruno, and he was fascinated. He said there is some evidence of similar masks being used way back in the Mayan days. He's seen something similar to the one that you put on my face. He's going to look into it further."

"You can look into it all you want," she said. "It won't help us much with everything that has gone on here earlier."

"Maybe not. We found explanations very thin down in Peru as well."

"You never did explain anything about that." And she'd

love to know more. He was a fascinating man with lots of secrets of his own. Like seeing auras. Something else he didn't talk about.

"We had an unexplainable series of incidents when we were at a big ruin ten years ago. It was my first big dig. I was excited to be there and to follow along with all the big cheeses. My partners, Jeremiah and Callum were both there. All of us were ecstatic. It was a turning point in our careers. It was what we'd worked so hard to get, and we couldn't wait to deal with everything happening. We were excited by it all. But then things went wrong—odd incidents, odd accidents with no explanation. People getting hurt, weird noises in the night, tools broken, tools stolen."

At that, she gasped. "Just like here?"

He nodded. "Just like here. The thing is, it got much worse. We had one man lose an arm in a completely freak accident. A stone came down, crushing his arm, and we had to cut him free. And eventually, of course, after things got so bad, you know what happened."

"Someone died," she whispered in horror.

He nodded. "Exactly, somebody died. But someone else had died before him, and then a couple more died."

She reached out a shaky hand. "I'm so sorry."

He smiled. "You would say that. Everybody else would be freaked out, wanting to know the details, but you're more concerned about how traumatizing the experience would have been for me."

"Well, you were young," she said, "and living through that couldn't have been easy."

"It wasn't easy," he agreed. "But, more than that, we were left with this horrible feeling of something well beyond us, something we couldn't explain, something we didn't understand and something we couldn't stop. I think that was the worst part. I felt so helpless. No matter what I did—no matter what *we* did—we couldn't seem to make all the bad things go away. You know how it feels when you have no control over the stuff going on around you?"

She thought about her mother dying and all the treatments, the pain and the agony her mom went through, trying everything to save her life, and Lacey nodded. "Exactly. I have experienced that. I don't think there is anything worse."

His gaze deepened with understanding. "Then add in the fear and the shock and the horror of what you're going through right now only to find it just builds for days and days."

"How did you get out of it?"

"After our last man died, it was as if the tension snapped, and whatever was around had died with him. We buried him where he was, which was unfortunate for his family, but we didn't feel we had any choice. We couldn't take a risk of bringing him back. We took the opportunity to pack up and leave."

"I probably would have buried him with all his gear too."

"And that's exactly what we did. We didn't know if it was an infection. We didn't know if it was a curse," he admitted. "Something I would never have given credence to before this. But now it's like it couldn't have been anything but."

"Lots of people don't believe in the existence of true evil," she said.

"No," he said, "they don't. And that's more foolish of them because, once you've seen it, the existence of evil is never to be doubted again."

SEBASTIAN HADN'T WANTED to get into this topic with her. She seemed more pensive now, not as upset, as if she'd had time to assimilate some of the issues, which was pretty amazing, considering how shocking so much of it was. For himself, once he'd realized what was happening here, it was the masks that worried him most.

"What do you think is happening? At this dig site?" she asked softly. "Do you think I'm tapping into a dead person's thoughts? Am I possessed by a spirit? Am I reliving a past life?"

She *had* been doing a lot of thinking about this. "It could be any and all of the above," he said. "Personally I much prefer the third one."

She gave a trill of laughter. "Right. Isn't it a whole lot easier to think you're tapping into a previous lifetime's worth of memories versus somebody else getting their claws into you? But I also read that, once you do energy work or you tap into that kind of stuff, it leaves you open to other spirits."

He fell silent at that, wondering if she had made the connection he'd made.

She said, "So, if that is what's happening, do we think the masks are connected to a person? And, if they are, what could that spirit hope to do with them?"

He had to admit she had guts. She went for the gold on a very difficult question. He grabbed her hand and said, "I don't know. Bruno doesn't know. There is somebody who might be able to help us. But I don't really know myself."

"And who would that be?"

"The locals from the neighboring area of the Mayan ruins believe it was the god of death, Kisin, who was responsible for all the ills in the world. If it's connected to an old energy like that there's no way to know what he's after ... and yes that takes us into the twilight zone." He sighed. "The only way we got out of the Mayan ruins was with a special guide. All the others had left us. The scientist had called in somebody he knew who called somebody he knew. That got us out safe and sound," he admitted. "He got us out, and we never looked back."

"And you already contacted him about what's going on here too, didn't you?"

Sebastian nodded. "As soon as I heard about the accidents."

"And his response?"

"To let him know if it got any weirder."

"What do you think now? Is it any weirder?"

"He's already here at the site."

She studied Sebastian carefully. "He is?"

He smiled and nodded. "He got in a few days ago."

"Hunter?"

Sebastian nodded. "He's coming to talk to us now." She straightened and looked at the team member she'd seen earlier but had thought was known to the others. "The others acted like they already knew him."

"Hunter has an ability to do that."

She frowned at him. "Now *that* is unnerving."

Sebastian nodded. "It is. But he's very good at what he does, and he's really honest. He could be incredibly dishonest and get away with a lot of stuff, but the fact remains. He is honest."

She shrugged. "Okay, and now what?"

"He wants to ask us some questions."

She gave an eye roll as Hunter walked over and plunked down beside them. He took one look at her and said, "Hi. I hear you're having fun these days."

She glared at him. Something about his tone of voice set her nerves on edge. "Maybe for you it's fun."

"Why would you think it's fun for me?" he asked.

"Because you look like you enjoy the hunt, but I'd say you are more like a ghost hunter, vampire hunter, a hunter of some kind of supernatural otherworldly prey."

His gaze narrowed. "That's very interesting. Maybe I am." His voice was soft and humorous. "And why would you say that?"

"You're different."

Sebastian watched her shift, become warier, uncertain. Defensive. He wondered at the change, why she should react like that toward Hunter at this point. He could tell from Hunter's expression he was wondering the same thing. Then he saw things others didn't as Hunter's next actions proved.

"Okay let's go back to the beginning and start again. I don't think we were ever introduced," Hunter said easily. He reached out a hand. "Hi, I'm Hunter. Nice to meet you."

She stared at his hand, then hesitantly shook it. "Hi. I'm …" And she stopped. A confused look came into her eyes. She turned to stare at Sebastian. "I'm …"

Hunter leaned forward, refusing to let her hand go. "Yes?"

She gave a quick head shake. "I'm Lacey," she said firmly.

Hunter smiled. "Hi, Lacey. For whatever reason, you've always connected to Pompeii and another person who's lived here, haven't you?"

"Yes and no. I only heard about Linnea a few days ago."

Sebastian leaned forward, watching her face. "Is this a past life?"

She started to pull her hand away, but Hunter held it firm. Sebastian didn't know what Hunter was doing but could see the energy zip down his arm and across to hers, with little firings at her hand, as if she were struggling against the energy.

Finally Hunter released her hand. "It's not a past life though, is it?"

Lacey made a tiny shake of her head; then she cried out in sudden pain. As if somebody cut a cord inside her. She collapsed forward, pitching into their arms.

CHAPTER 12

LACEY WOKE UP flat on the ground, surrounded by the crew. Her gaze wandered from one to the other. "What happened?" Her voice was leaden and hard to use.

"You collapsed." Chana crouched beside her. "You let out a weird shriek and just fell forward."

Lacey stared at her, trying to remember what had happened. Her gaze drifted up to each crew member's face before landing on Sebastian's.

"I can't say I feel too good," she said, rubbing her head. "Did I fall on my head?"

"No," Sebastian said gently. He bent down and helped her into a sitting position. "How is the head when you're sitting?"

"Is there any water?" she whispered.

He reached for the water bottle he kept strapped on his belt, opening it up.

She drank greedily. When her thirst was finally quenched, she whispered, "Is it possible to go back to the apartment and lie down?"

"That's exactly what I'd order you to do." Sebastian helped her to her feet. "I'll take you back there now." He looked at everybody else. "She's fine. Maybe it was the heat."

The others looked at each other doubtfully and shrugged.

"Just another one of those weird things that's been happening since we got back this time," Tom said.

As she and Sebastian walked through the gates, back out to the main part of town, Sebastian said to her, "What happened?"

"I don't know what." Fatigue threaded through her voice. "But something on that site changed. Was anybody else there?"

"No, I don't believe so," he said. "It's been open to the public, of course, so there could have been any number of strangers. But nobody from my team was there."

She nodded slowly. "Somebody was definitely there," she whispered. "I could feel it."

"When?" he asked gently.

"Just before I pitched into your and Hunter's arms," she said. "Linnea was also back too."

"And how long have you known about this?"

She stumbled just then. He steadied her and held her close until she got her footing again. "Since I started the drawings. So I stopped sketching, thinking that kept them away from me. And I didn't want to tell anybody because, of course, it sounds like I'm off my rocker."

"Except to me."

"Yes," she said, "but, since we were already causing enough talk, I didn't want to add to it."

"Understood. Now you want to explain to me what you were talking about?"

"As near as I can figure it, there's a spirit whose name is Linnea. She was alive during the Pompeii time of the volcanic eruption. I can see a picture of her in my mind. I don't know how real she is. She overlaps with the documentary I saw so long ago. I was just a child then, but I think something from that documentary is what fascinated me about this place, that era. Or maybe I connected to Linnea through the drawings and seeing all those buildings nobody else could see. I don't know." With a wave of her hand she tried to dismiss that part of the conversation. "But I was trying to be calm and quiet, and I asked why she was contacting me. And she said she needs help."

"Help in what way?"

"She couldn't say. But she said evil has returned."

Sebastian stiffened.

She nodded. "I asked her, 'What evil? How was the evil coming? Where was the evil from?' But I couldn't get any more answers from her. She kept disappearing at that point."

"Did she appear afterward?"

"No," she said, "and this is why I can't guarantee it isn't my imagination. It's like she spoke in my head. I only saw her when my eyes were closed, which is in direct contrast to all the buildings I can see. I'm wondering if that car accident shook something loose in my brain," she said in disgust. "Because I'm definitely different."

"Chana said so too."

Lacey stopped momentarily. "She did?" At his nod, she groaned. "This trip was supposed to be a dream-come-true. Only it's completely changed my life and not in a good way."

"Some trips are like that," he said, a poor attempt at humor. "I think Hunter and Chana were speaking together when you pitched forward."

She shot him a look of disbelief.

"You weren't out for very long. Hunter disappeared then because, well, that's what Hunter does."

Sure enough, as they walked around to the corner of the

building where the apartment entrance was, they found Hunter leaning against the doorway. His gaze was on her face, checking to see how she was doing.

She gave him a wan smile. "Maybe don't talk to her again, huh?"

A smile flickered across his face. "Well, maybe not without more warning," he said. "It's a little hard to get answers if people don't talk."

"Sure, but both of us were talking in our head," she said. Then she froze. "God, that sounds so weird."

"Particularly when you use the pronoun *our*," Sebastian said. "That's curious."

"I don't know about *curious*," she said as they headed for the apartment, "but it's definitely a weird experience. I can't get very much information from her. I don't know who she is outside of her name or anything about what this evil is she's talking about."

At her apartment, Sebastian unlocked the door and let her inside. She gratefully collapsed on the couch. "I wouldn't be averse to a cup of coffee, if one of you wants to put on a pot."

Sebastian obediently walked over and made a pot of coffee, whereas Hunter sat on the couch beside her, his gaze intense. "What can you tell me about her?"

"She was young. But then they were all young back in that era, if old age was considered to be forty-seven," she said with a half-smile. "I'd guess she's fifteen, sixteen, maybe seventeen. I did understand she was part of a family with multiple siblings. And something about one sister being a prisoner." She tried to fill Hunter in on all she knew as she didn't know if he had a full picture of what was going on. "At the time I didn't realize I was really talking to her," she explained. "Only the last few days have I opened up the communication channel by simply asking her who she is and what she wants."

"And what kind of evil is she talking about?"

"She couldn't say, or she didn't answer when I tried to get her to define what the evil was. Back then it could have been anything from an illness to a crazy man to bad weather, I suppose."

Hunter nodded in understanding. "But it would be helpful if we got a little more information on her."

Lacey closed her eyes, leaned her head back and mentally called out, *Linnea, are you there?* There was a tiny rumble in her head. "She's here," Lacey said aloud. "But she's not explaining or saying much."

"Ask her how you can help," Sebastian said as he stood in the doorway of the kitchen.

Without looking at him, she relayed the request. No answer.

"Is there anybody else you've been able to communicate with?" Hunter asked.

"No, I don't think so," she said. "I don't know why I'm in contact with her."

"Sometimes these connections come and go. Maybe she was calling out, looking for somebody."

"But she doesn't seem to be calling out right now. She's not even responding."

"I might have scared her," Hunter said.

"Yeah, that's Hunter," Sebastian said as he sat down. "One scary dude."

She glanced from Sebastian to Hunter. "How come nobody else saw you there, when I passed out?"

"How do you know they didn't see me?"

She gave him a half smile. "Because I'm not a fool. For whatever reason, you seem to go almost into stealth mode, and nobody sees you."

He nodded. "That's a good description. Stealth mode. I like it."

"Maybe," she said. "But it's very freaky."

"A woman who draws 3-D diagrams from thousands of years ago? Well, that's also freaky," he said.

She thought about it and then grinned. "Yeah, it's pretty special, isn't it?" She glanced over at Sebastian. "Did you show Hunter the other sketches I did?"

"No idea at this point, but I'd like to see them again." He stood. "I'll get them from my apartment." He returned a few minutes later. She sat, zoned out, Hunter comfortably at her side, when Sebastian walked back in again with several sketchbooks. He handed the first one to Hunter.

He went through them and whistled. "Oh, wow. Even the ones I've seen before have incredible impact the second time around. You're quite the artist."

"No, I'm not," she said cheerfully. "I used to do some stuff when I was a kid, but I never carried on with any of it."

Hunter just nodded and flipped through the images. And then Sebastian handed him the other sketchbook. Hunter opened it to the page with the masks.

Her gaze was drawn to it like a moth to the fire. And her heart seized in her chest. She leaned closer so she could take a really good look at what she'd done. "I don't remember doing this at all," she whispered.

Hunter nodded, his fingers tracing Sebastian's features. "That's too bad," he said. "I'd really like to know what was in your mind when you did this. There's something almost familiar about these masks."

She stared at the sketch of Sebastian and then at Hunter, both of them strong, capable, proud men. Neither fighting their masks, both wearing them with pride. "I don't understand what the masks are all about," she whispered.

"That's okay. We never do right at the beginning," Hunter said. "It's amazing how much we can go through in life and not understand, and then, all of a sudden, something happens, and it's like doors open."

"So the door that opened was me arriving here?" she asked curiously. "Or was it the accident? I hit my head on the cement as I went down but I don't think I hit it that badly."

"Chances are it was both of those and likely much more," Hunter said. "We're like onions. We peel away layers. If you were meant to come to Pompeii, you listened and finally got here. That would have released a layer because the intuition tries so hard to get us to do what we're supposed to do. And, when we ignore it, it's frustrating. It has to start over again. When we don't ignore it, when we do listen, it's like a layer peels back."

"So landing here was already one layer of my resistance taken away?"

"That's a good way to look at it," he said. "And, when you went to the actual site and connected with that same joy, that same sense of pride and exuberance of being here, chances are another layer fell away. When you got hit that night and landed on the ground, knocking yourself senseless, I would say that a third layer drifted away."

"And so, with those three layers, whatever *this* is has thinned enough to be able to see things?"

"It's like that layer of density between now and then," Hunter said softly. "It thins and warps and changes. It softens. It gets hard again. Everybody thinks time is static, but it's not. It's dynamic. Physicists know this, but the common people can't interpret that properly in any way that they can deal with on a day-to-day basis, so they ignore it."

"And, in this case, for whatever reason, it thinned enough that I could connect with Linnea?"

"She probably connected with you first. Could she be the one who helped you with these drawings?"

"I don't think so," Lacey said. "I see those myself. I see those buildings, even see them in my camera." She turned to look back at him. "Nobody else can see those buildings like I do."

Sebastian nodded. "Nobody I've showed them to has been able to." He motioned to the camera she hugged in her lap. "Maybe show Hunter."

Eagerly she sat up and flicked through her photos. She had left the ones of the buildings on the camera, even though she had cleaned off all the others. When she got to the first one, she held it out for him. "What do you see?"

He looked at the picture and shrugged. "Hills, mountains, rocks, a few partial walls."

She nodded. "And the next one?"

He had the same answer to them all. He glanced up at Sebastian. "Is that what you see?"

"Yes," Sebastian said. "But not her."

Hunter looked at her. "Tell me what you see."

She motioned with her index finger where the buildings were and what she could see of them and how they were connected.

He grabbed her hand. "Now show me again."

She watched his face change. All of a sudden, it appeared he could see what she saw.

He stared into the viewfinder of the camera, mesmerized. "Oh, wow."

Sebastian joined them. "What? I can't see anything," he complained.

"By touching her," Hunter said, "I'm accessing her energy. All that she knows and sees is flowing through me. And right now, I can see these buildings like she sees them." With his other hand, he flicked back to the photos of her first sketches, bringing up the ones with the virtual buildings she'd drawn. "It looks just like that," he said in amazement. He flicked back through the next pictures, still holding her hand. "This is amazing."

"Right. And that's why I don't know what to do with this. Because, before now, this has never happened to me."

"How do you know?"

She stared at him. "Well, I guess I don't know obviously. But I haven't seen anything like this before."

He released her hand, letting Sebastian have a try.

But it didn't work for Sebastian. Disappointed, he dropped her hand and said, "You know what an archaeologist would do to see everything you see right now when it comes to the dig?"

She smiled sadly. "I'm sorry."

He shrugged, but it was obvious he was disappointed, more than disappointed, and quite devastated that Hunter could see, and he couldn't. As if somebody had said, *Hey, there's another way for you to do this*, only to find out you're the only one that, once again, can't do it.

And then Hunter asked the question that just blew her away.

He studied her face, leaned forward so he could look her directly in the eye and asked, "What's your relationship with death?"

WHAT A GREAT question, Sebastian thought. Obviously it was right on target too because Lacey looked completely pole-axed. He watched as the tears came to the corner of her eyes. She brushed them away impatiently. And he knew this would be about her mother.

She struggled to answer Hunter. "What do you mean?"

That was typical. Deflect a question with another question, so it gave her time to answer. But, at this point, she had Hunter's sympathy, Sebastian thought. Any discussion about her mother had to be painful.

"Has somebody close to you died? Did you watch them die over a long time? Did you have any involvement in their passing?"

At that last part she stared at him. "Are you asking if I murdered anybody?"

Hunter shook his head and patted her hand. "No, no, no. I know you're not the kind to kill anybody." And then he froze and said, "Well, you are, but it would be a mercy killing in your case."

Her bottom lip trembled.

"I meant," Hunter said, "if you had any experience with someone dying."

She took a deep breath and let it out slowly. "Yes. My mother. She was very sick. She had breast cancer, stage four. They couldn't do anything, though they tried. It was awful, right to the end. She passed away six months ago."

He settled back into the couch and studied her. "How did you handle it?"

Bewildered, she said, "I handled it the way I handle everything. I tried to make the best of it, to make every day special. I tried to let her know she was loved. I tried to do anything I could to make her days easier."

Hunter nodded thoughtfully. "Did you sit up with her through her last night?"

She stared at him, her eyes round as saucers. "How did you know?"

He gave her a small smile. "Did you not say on her deathbed that you wished you could join her? That you wished you could be with her? And that you would find a way to see her on the other side, wherever she ends up?"

Sebastian could see her saying exactly that and so much more. But then so many people would.

"Yes, to a certain extent," she whispered, tears in her eyes yet again. "But she never got over the loss of my father. I know she was really leaving me to go to him."

"So maybe you felt a bit of anger as well as a sense of betrayal, like she chose to be with him over you?"

Lacey shook her head. "No, that was in the beginning. And I felt terrible about it. Yet I knew she would be happy to leave. But the process ... The process was so unforgiving, so damaging to her soul and mind. Her physical body just broke down. Everyday something else didn't work," she whispered.

"Dying from a major illness isn't fun for anybody, I don't imagine," Hunter said. "I've lost friends but never from a slow wasting away of who they were."

She nodded. "That's a good way to describe it. Thankfully she stayed herself all the way through to the last few days. At the very end, she was there, yet she was almost not there, and I don't mean mentally." She struggled to formulate the words. "I know it'll sound silly, but it's almost like there was a glow to her, a translucent glow. Somehow she was not there physically anymore. Her skin turned thin and translucent. I don't know," she broke up. "It's so hard to explain."

"And how long did you sit with her at that time?"

"I stayed with her steadily," she said. "I kept telling her it was okay. If she was ready to let go, I'd be fine, that she was welcome to join Dad and to release herself from the pain she was in. How I was fine and didn't want her hanging on, holding on, fighting for my sake. I wanted her to go and to do what she needed to for her sake. It was obvious her organic body was done for, but, if there's a soul, if there's something on the other side, I really wanted her to be able to release earlier than later and to save herself all that pain. Not that there was much in the way of pain because she was on heavy drugs. We could only manage her passing."

Both men nodded, then Sebastian left the room. He reappeared with several cups of coffee and placed them on the small coffee table in front of the couch.

She glanced at Hunter. "How does that have anything to do with this?"

"I think it's an acceptance of the gate in between the two worlds," Hunter said. "An understanding that there is a spirit life on the other side."

Sebastian watched as Hunter talked. But Lacey stared at her cup. Almost ... hiding. "What aren't you telling us?"

She winced. And then glared at him. "You could just let me keep a secret or two, you know?" she snapped.

"This isn't the time." Hunter leaned forward, tilted her chin his way and said, "No secrets now. People's lives are on the line."

She groaned. "It has nothing to do with what's happening now."

"What happened?"

She shrugged. "It's just sometimes, when I would hold her hand, it would be like I was one with her. As if our spirits had melded into this incredible moment. And I was holding her hand when she died, and I could see this light around her body. I reached out to touch it, and it ran around me too. Holding me. It was like a hug, only she was already gone. I know that doesn't sound very normal, which is why I didn't bring it up. And then, the moment she died, I knew because ..." She fell silent.

"Because?"

"Because ... Because I saw her spirit separate from her body and leave."

CHAPTER 13

SOMETHING ABOUT SPEAKING with these two men had loosened her tongue. She'd never told anybody about that weird sensation or what she'd seen.

Sebastian leaned forward. "When you saw her spirit rise," he asked urgently, "what else did you see?"

She stared at him. "How did you know?"

Hunter squeezed her hand. "Tell us."

"It was like ..." She didn't know what to say. "It was like a doorway. Only it was open. Like staring out a window into a different world."

"And what did you see in that window?"

Tears came to her eyes. "I saw my father. He'd been dead ten years," she said in wonder. "But I saw my father. And he smiled at me. He held out his hand, not to me, but to my mother. As she grasped his hand, I let go of her. When I let go, that window closed. I sat there on my mother's sickbed, convincing myself I hadn't just imagined that for at least an hour. Just holding my mother's hand as her body cooled. She was gone in every way possible. But I couldn't leave that moment. It was so shocking, disheartening. I'd never been one of faith before," she said quietly. "But it made me realize there is so much more we don't understand." She let out a deep sigh, feeling some of the tension roll off her shoulders as she released that heavy weight. "I didn't realize how much I'd been holding that in." She looked from one man to the other. "What does it mean?"

"It means ..." Hunter said, "it means you opened the doorway to the other side."

"The other side of what?" she asked with a wide-open look. "Death, the divide between the two? Was that heaven? Is there such a thing?"

"If you believe in heaven," he said, "then you have to believe in hell."

She stared at him for a long moment. "That seemed very much like heaven," she whispered. "And that man was my father. I know it was."

"And then, of course, one has to question the existence of the other side of heaven too," Sebastian said quietly. "And I can tell you. I've seen that side. I've seen evil in many forms. Not for very long, not very deep. But what Hunter and I saw at the Mayan ruins belonged to the other side."

She stared at them softly. "So why is it we're together? Because I saw and believed in one side, and you saw and believed in the other? Are we the two halves of one experience? What exactly is the meaning behind all this?"

"I don't know," Sebastian said. "But I do know that darkness feeds on light. It consumes it, and then it goes looking for more."

She smiled. "I would have said that the light was something that is spread by touch, spread by caring, by kindness." She reached out and touched Sebastian's hand. "I felt so connected, so loved, so cared for when that door opened, revealing my father, while I still held my mother's hand. It's a feeling I don't think I'll ever forget. I can close my eyes and feel everything as it was at that one moment. Like it's glowing inside me. Their love for me is so strong, so deep into my soul, into my very being." She closed her eyes and mentally hugged that feeling ever-present inside. Her eyes flew open as she added, "Everybody says I'm a very warm, happy person. And I think it's because I found that peace, that center inside." She smiled up at both men. But they didn't say anything. Instead something odd was in Hunter's gaze. "What is it?"

He glanced over at Sebastian. "Did you see it?"

He nodded. "I did."

"See what?" she whispered. "Something in me, something around me?" She twisted to look behind her. "You guys are scaring me."

Sebastian squeezed her fingers. "Nothing to be afraid of. If anything, we are in awe."

"Of what?" she cried out, bewildered.

"Because inside you," Hunter said, "when you closed your eyes, you could feel that feeling of what it was to be so connected that your whole being glowed. As if this source of light came from the center of your solar plexus, moved up to your heart and then moved rapidly outward until you were a glowing bubble."

She laughed in delight. "You know what? I am so happy to hear that. Because that would be the ultimate ideal of what I would like to project to the world."

Both men settled back ever-so-slightly.

She gripped her hands together and smiled at them. "I don't know if you can understand how absolutely amazing it was to help my mother cross over, to have my father reach for her on the other side so she was never alone on her journey. How amazing would it be for everybody to know that's how it is or that's how it could be?" She squeezed her fingers together and then sank back into the couch with a happy sigh. "And yet, I have no clue why all the rest of this is happening."

"You opened the doorway to the other side," Hunter said quietly. "You opened it out of love. You opened it out of caring. But I don't know how quickly you closed it, and I don't know, while it was still open, who might have seen it and who might have been attracted to your bright warm light in this world."

"I hope everybody saw it. I hope everybody could feel it, could feel the love."

"Yes, if they needed it," Sebastian said. "If they were hurt and sore and lonely, dying, feeling depressed. Yes, yes, yes. But not if they were looking to consume it."

Slowly his words sank in. "You think the goodness within me, that joy I felt at that moment my mother was dying—and I know it sounds absolutely terrible to say that in one way. But you think that absolute bittersweet moment in my life attracted somebody who potentially wanted to destroy it?"

"Or who wanted to consume it literally," Hunter said. "Because they're so full of darkness, they're attracted to the light, like all things are. But they can't reach it because they're so deep into that evil persona that all they want to do is consume the light, whether to heal themselves or to eradicate the light so they can be bigger, badder, darker than they've ever been before."

She shook her head. "I can't believe something like that could happen."

"No, maybe you can't." Hunter pointed to the sketch-books. "But then you have to wonder where this came from."

She fell silent. Her mind was overwhelmed with the possibilities of what had been such a glorious moment in her life. "Was I was supposed to do something to protect myself?" she asked, chewing on her bottom lip. "I don't know how any of this works."

"Nobody *knows* how this works," Hunter said. "It could have been unlucky that you were seen by somebody evil. It could have been that you were there at that one moment where somebody was searching for a light, searching for more energy, searching for something to consume because they were angry or hurt or in denial about something in their world. Somebody evil, because they are filled with so much hate, could have been attracted to anything so bright and beautiful only to destroy it because that's what they do," he said. "That doesn't mean you were in the wrong. It doesn't mean you did anything wrong. But now we have to deal with the consequences."

"But we don't know for sure that's what happened, do we?" she asked. "I find it very difficult to believe that anything so beautiful could turn into something so very ugly."

Again Hunter tapped the masks and said, "You need to look at these and acknowledge they came from your hand. And, if there is all this beauty and light, where's all this darkness and ugliness coming from?"

For that, she had no answer.

HOURS LATER, BACK at his apartment, Sebastian's mind wouldn't let go of those mask sketches. There was something familiar about them but as he dove through his research and historical sites nothing was coming up.

When his phone rang, he answered almost absentmindedly, his attention still on the Mayan article on his monitor.

"I might have found something," Bruno said cautiously. "There are old manuscripts spouting on about the god of death we know as Kisin. Apparently there was a jailor back then who terrified the population, as he loved his job too much. Wanted his prisoners to suffer. His grave was kept secret so that the locals couldn't desecrate the site and stop his journey to join Kisin."

Sebastian's breath caught in the back of his throat. "But no word of masks?"

"No, but they do talk about his great evil. How he seemed to grow stronger, more evil with every death he facilitated?"

"We did find a sarcophagus at the site. That's about the same time all hell broke loose."

"Given what we know and gods being these theoretical entities the people worshipped," Bruno said humorously, "my money is on you disturbing the jailor."

"Do you have any history on the jailor? Maybe he was eventually killed—punished himself for a transgression. Spirits rarely come back if they are happy souls."

"Then again, given his job, the angry desperate souls …" Bruno chuckled. "Give me a few minutes. I've just found something else here."

The phone hummed as Sebastian kept the line open rather than having him try to call back and missing him at a later date.

"He was called Tialox, known as Kisin's servant."

"That's appropriate considering he served the prisoners to him."

"I'm not seeing much about him though. This is mostly anecdotal." Bruno's voice faded as he read more.

"Considering the work he did, something he likely loved, he'd have been a perfect serial killer in today's world. And of course, he'd have gloated at the pain and fear he brought about in those around him."

"I agree," Bruno said with a sigh. "A nasty man in life, quite possibly even uglier in death. Why he'd be hanging around I don't know …"

"He might have been murdered before his time, or maybe his soul couldn't rest with so much negative energy flowing through him."

"What does he have to do with these masks? Or the deaths that happened ten years ago?"

"No clue," he said groaning. "And I wish I did."

As he hung up, Hunter, working beside him on the couch, looked up. "I heard part of that."

"And here's the rest." Sebastian quickly filled him in on the conversation.

"Interesting and actually makes sense," Hunter said. "We do know how some entities die and don't cross over. Instead they stay and haunt where they died."

"True," Sebastian was quick to argue. "But it doesn't clarify anything—it only confuses the issue." He got up and paced his living room. "What does Lacey have to do with this? The two digs are thousands of miles apart. There's nothing to connect them. She was addicted to Pompeii since a child so now as an adult she comes and sketches death masks from an ancient Mayan culture?"

Hunter chuckled. "Maybe?"

Just then his phone rang. He glanced down and said, "He's always got perfect timing."

"Who?'

"Stefan? How are you?" he clicked the speaker button

and laid his phone on the coffee table.

"Wondering about ancient energy finding other ancient energy," he said in a crisp tone. "Sounds like you guys need to update me. And then send it to me in writing via email so I can ponder the evils of the world at my leisure."

At that Sebastian laughed. "Will do." And proceeded to bring him up-to-date.

CHAPTER 14

THE NEXT MORNING Lacey was still confused and disturbed. She'd hardly gotten any sleep, instead thinking about what had happened the previous night. Hunter and Sebastian hadn't exactly clarified what they'd said, but she'd understood enough to get the gist, and it was terrifying.

She'd been so joyful when her mother had passed over to meet her father, not at her mother's passing, but that it was so peaceful, so full of love and light. To think something like that could have caused a nightmare of the proportions that these men were suggesting, well, she wasn't sure she'd ever get a good night's sleep again.

She sat here in the kitchen in the early hours of the morning, waiting for the rest of the team to get up, staring at her sketchbook. The masks looked even more terrifying now. She didn't understand the details of them, but she knew they were correct. To think she was tapping into something here ... A past life of another soul was confusing in itself, and yet, made a cryptic kind of sense. She didn't know if she should reach out to this person or if she should deliberately try to tap into a past life, if that's what this was. She wondered about hypnosis, if that would help, but just the thought of even asking somebody for a recommendation was scary.

"What are you doing up so early?" Chana asked as she stumbled into the kitchen. She stood at the counter and stared at Lacey, a frown on her face as she tried to clear the sleep out of her eyes. "You should be sleeping."

"I would if I could," Lacey said softly. "But I can't seem to."

Chana nodded. She glanced around the room. "Did you at least make coffee?"

Lacey held up her cup. "I didn't want to disturb everybody so I just made a single cup."

Chana snorted. "Like that'll do any good." She made her way to the coffeepot to make more. "What's keeping you up at night?"

"Lots of things." Lacey smiled at her cousin. "But nothing worrisome."

She knew she'd said the right thing when she watched the relief cross Chana's face.

"Thank you so much for letting me be here," Lacey said.

Although her joy was somewhat mitigated by the strange events, she knew she needed to be here. She wasn't sure why or how, but her presence was important. And maybe this was the culmination of a lifetime of her dreams. Maybe it was a culmination of a lifetime of other people's dreams. If nothing else, she had to get to the bottom of this nightmare, to find a solution so she could go home again, free and clear of any curses or spirits, and to know Pompeii was not her be-all and end-all destination. Even as she thought that, a weird rumbling ran in her stomach, as if her intuition was saying something, but it wasn't getting through to her.

"I told you before, you're more than welcome," Chana said sincerely, but her gaze was on the sketchbook. "I'm sorry it's been such a weird time since you've arrived. Not to mention the accident."

The accident? The *car* accident. She waved it off with a hand. "That was my fault entirely."

"Still, I wish it hadn't happened," Chana said, shooting her a sideways glance. "I wonder if your head injury was a little more serious than we first thought."

Lacey lifted her mug of coffee and took a sip. It was well past cold because she'd ignored it for so long. "I'm fine," she reassured her cousin. "Honest."

She understood Chana was referring to the drawings. No way the team wouldn't realize something was happening with her. The fact strange stuff was going on in the dig site just added to the mystery.

She sifted through the sketches, studying the blueprint-looking ones, wondering how she could pick up two separate and distinct styles of artwork.

"Those are really incredible diagrams," Chana said, walking closer, her gaze locked on the blueprint Lacey had done of one house. "I knew you were an artist, but I had no idea you were this good."

"I hadn't realized I had such a love for architecture," Lacey said with the laugh. "But this seemed so clear and so detailed to me that I had to get it down."

An odd silence came from her cousin. Lacey looked up to see Chana staring at the image, a frown forming between her brows. "Something about it bothers you?" Lacey asked curiously.

Chana hesitated, then shook her head. "No …"

"That didn't sound very convincing," Lacey said. "What's wrong with it?"

"This corner's off. Something's not quite right here."

Lacey stood beside Chana, studying the upper right-hand corner of the image. "What's off about it?"

"I don't know," Chana said with a shrug. "You're the artist, not me. It feels like there's supposed to be something more here."

"I'll take a look at it." Lacey sat back down again, shifting the diagram so she could look at it from different angles and then held it back, propped up against the kitchen chair beside her so she could see it from a distance.

Chana went to the refrigerator and pulled out yogurt and granola. "It'll be another hot day in paradise," she said. "Amazing how blasé we get living over here."

"It certainly doesn't appear to be the same weather we had in North America," Lacey said, her voice distracted as she studied the corner Chana had been talking about.

Lacey could see what Chana meant. The lines, instead of being crisp and clear, kind of disappeared into a vagueness at that point. Where the rest of the edges appeared to be very distinct and coming to a final point, that corner didn't. She reached for her pencil and held it above the sketch pad, wondering what to do about it. But nothing inside her said to fill it in; nothing said to add something or to take away something.

After a moment of staring at it, she shrugged and put the pencil down again.

"Don't want to finish it?"

"I'll do it later," Lacey said. "I'm too tired right now."

"You kept me awake with all your tossing and turning," Chana said. "I couldn't figure out why you weren't sleeping."

Lacey looked at her and smiled. "Maybe it was something I ate." She could hardly tell her about the conversation with Hunter and Sebastian.

"Too much drinking with the boss," Chana said lightly.

She walked over with her bowl of breakfast and sat down beside Lacey.

"Do you think it bothers people?" Lacey asked, her voice sharper than she intended.

"Doesn't matter if it does or not," Chana said. "If something's going on between you, then something's going on between you."

"There isn't," Lacey said emphatically. "At least not yet."

That started a surprised look from Chana; then she broke out laughing. When she finally caught her breath again, she said, "Dear Lacey, I did miss you."

Happy to see the two had settled back into a more normal relationship, Lacey studied the food Chana ate, then said, "That looks really good."

Chana motioned to the cabinet and fridge. "Go get some. Whatever you need. You know that."

Lacey stood and walked over to make herself a bowl similar to Chana's. "What time does the rest of the team get up? Isn't it later than normal today?"

"Several of them were off drinking last night," Chana said comfortably. "They might be planning a late start."

"They're hungover then?"

"And there might have been some interesting pairings going on last night."

Lacey stopped in the act of putting the food back in the fridge, wondering what her cousin meant, then realized she was talking about some of them hooking up. She put the food away and joined her cousin at the table. "Does that work well on a dig site like this?"

"No," Chana said. "Look at me and Tom."

"You still want to go out with Tom?"

Chana shrugged, but the look on her face turned sad.

"Does he have somebody else?" Lacey asked.

"No, I don't think so."

"So … try again?"

"No, not doing that," Chana said. "We have to have a long talk first."

"So have the long talk, clear the air and decide what you both want," Lacey said. "I know it's not easy, but if it's what you want …"

"I'm not sure what I want," Chana said, her tone bitter. "You always seem to know *exactly* what you want. Whereas I feel like I'm out there sampling everything in life, not finding anything that's particularly right for me."

"I hardly think that's true," Lacey said gently. She swallowed a spoonful of yogurt and granola and smiled. "This is really tasty."

Chana chuckled, stood, grabbed her bowl and walked to the kitchen sink. "I think it *is* true."

She was obviously referring to their previous subject of conversation.

"I get that you didn't make this choice to visit Pompeii fast or easy, but you stepped up for it when an opportunity arose. In my case I don't have any real purpose. Yes, I'm here doing what I really love to do, but, beyond that—and there has to be a *beyond that*—I'm not sure what else to do with my life."

"Are you talking about relationships?"

"I'm talking *everything*," Chana said in a bout of frustration. She spun around to stare at Lacey, leaning against the sink, a fresh cup of coffee in her hand. "I want a family sometime in the next three to five years." She was restless and paced the kitchen. "I'm already twenty-nine."

Lacey felt a jolt as she thought about that. Because she

was only six months younger.

"Consider that," Chana said. "Do you really want to be older than thirty-five and having kids? And I know lots of people are out there doing it, but I'm not sure I'll have the energy or the inclination at that point."

"Six years is still a long time to get your act together," Lacey said. She took several more bites of yogurt, watching her cousin pace.

She wasn't sure what this was all about, but it was interesting to watch. They'd talked about having families, getting married, producing kids when they were younger, but they hadn't had this conversation in a while. For Lacey, there hadn't been any conversation to have. She hadn't had a male friend at all while nursing her mother and then dealing with her death. This was kind of like a new stage of life for her. But it did remind her that Chana had been ready for a while, and obviously she wasn't happy with the current stage of her life.

"What brought this on?" Lacey asked curiously. "I haven't heard you speak like this before."

Chana gave an irritable shrug as she stared out the window.

Lacey studied her cousin's face, seeing the frustration, maybe even anger. "Is this the reason you and Tom broke it off?"

"Partly," Chana admitted. "He doesn't want to have a family."

"*Aah*," Lacey murmured. She finished her yogurt but continued sitting there, watching her cousin. "And you always have," she said. It had been Chana's dream growing up. It would be hard for her to let that go.

Chana nodded. "I always have," she said softly. "And it

feels like I'm giving up something that's very, very important if I stay with him."

"Of course. Because he's making you choose between having that lifelong dream and him. Does he have any reasons for not wanting a family?"

"He has *his* reasons," Chana said. She walked toward Lacey and plopped down on an empty chair. "But they are reasons that don't matter to me. He thinks it's a terrible time in the world to raise children. He feels that we'd need more money for traveling and whatnot and that a child would cramp our lifestyle."

"Both of which are valid reasons," Lacey said, "but a cold comfort when you really want a family. And what he's talking about is all *now* stuff. Not *down the road* stuff. Short-term, not long-term focuses."

"And I said that to him," Chana said, "but I didn't seem to convince him."

There wasn't a whole lot Lacey could say to that. She finished her breakfast and went to rinse the bowl and refill her cup with coffee. "What time are we going to the site today?"

"I figured, if we went in a little earlier, we could leave a little earlier too," Chana said. "I've been really restless since I woke up. I want to get going now, if you want to go with me?"

"Absolutely I do," Lacey said with a big grin. "Let me grab my water and camera gear."

When she was ready, Chana was already at the door, waiting impatiently, most happy to leave now.

Lacey frowned. "I've never seen you this eager to get to work before."

But Chana was already out the door, heading toward the

stairs.

Still moving a little slower, Lacey followed behind and headed downstairs. By the time she reached the bottom, her cousin was already outside. She was surprised Chana wasn't waiting for her. Her cousin was normally a very courteous and caring friend.

She looked outside to find her already at the crosswalk. "You are in a rush today," Lacey called out, catching up with her.

At that, Chana slowed and waited. The two of them walked across the road.

"I'm not sure what the problem is," she said to Chana as they headed toward the entrance. Yes, Chana had mentioned Tom not wanting children. But there was something else bothering Chana. Plus the air felt odd this morning with a stillness to it that Lacey didn't recognize.

Or Lacey was letting the recent weird events color even her cousin's behavior.

Lacey loved the Roman road that led to the Stabian Gate. The archway, just the whole look, was so unique.

When they finally reached it and made their way through the gate, she turned to look behind her, sure she would catch sight of somebody following them. But nobody was there.

"If you think we're being followed," Chana said, "I've been thinking that for days."

Startled, Lacey stopped, then raced to catch up again. "What? You're just now saying something about it?"

"What can I say? I've never seen anybody. I'd sound like a neurotic female if I make any comments about it. It's not easy being one of only a couple women in a place like this. Women are very welcomed on dig sites all over the world, but it's still a male-dominated career. And, if you sound nervous or superstitious or say anything other than something the guys would say, you get labeled as neurotic or paranoid or just touchy, and I don't want that."

"Understood," Lacey murmured. She understood. It was also quite possible that it wasn't that they were being followed only that they were much more sensitive to the weird energy going on now.

They finally made it to the dig site, and, as she watched, Chana made her way down to where she had been working, picking up tools out of her backpack, and quickly got to work. It was early and maybe that was a good thing.

Lacey put down her backpack and pulled out her camera gear, realizing the light was unique because of the hour of the morning. Unable to help herself, she took pictures of places she'd already shot many, many times, but the light was so different this time.

She wandered the site, taking pictures of Chana, taking pictures of the site, the trees, the way the light hit the rocks. The shadows were amplified in the morning. This morning light offered a very unique look she hadn't seen before. She fast became lost in capturing the differences of today from the other days.

Only when she heard something behind her did she spin around to see what appeared to be a man walking toward her. She rubbed her fingers against her eyes to refocus. Only to realize nobody was there.

Straightening, she looked around, realizing just the two of them were at the site, and she'd wandered several hundred yards away from her cousin. "Hello? Is anyone here?"

There was no answer. But she was sure she'd seen something. She closed her eyes, trying to recapture that image in her mind, but it was gone. Disturbed, and yet, not having any discernible reason, she returned to work, always listening and aware somebody else might be around. Sebastian's words were never far from her thoughts. Ghosts? Surely not. She shoved that thought deep down and returned to work.

She was relieved to hear several other team members finally arriving. She smiled when she saw them, giving them a big wave. They waved back, joining Chana down below.

More comfortable now that she wasn't so alone, she continued to work on the deeper recesses of each section. She was drawn to the corner of her sketch that was still vague, wondering what was supposed to go there. Using her camera, she brought up the 3-D images she'd seen before. She sat in awe as she studied the lifelike images in front of her.

Both a fantasy-futuristic element and a historical element went into what she saw, as if the future and the past had blended into one, because she still saw the blue of a holographic structural image laid atop the broken stones. She carefully made her way to the vague corner.

As she approached the spot in question, she was stopped by an invisible wall. She reached out a hand but it was as if a force was stopping her. She froze, lowered the camera and looked around her. She was completely alone. It wasn't even nine o'clock in the morning. The place was deserted, and she saw no sign of animal or bird life. It was eerie, and yet, inspiring. Even though she felt like she wasn't supposed to go farther, she also felt compelled to.

There was an inner tug, as if somebody was pushing her forward, and another inner push, as if somebody was pushing her back.

Finally she called out, "Stop."

Instantly the sense of a tug of war paused. She frowned

and looked around. "I don't know what you guys are doing. I don't know who you are or what you want, but I'm not a pawn to be used in whatever game you're playing."

She took several deep breaths, centering herself, reminding herself where she was and why she was here. At the same time Hunter's words and Sebastian's comments flowed through her. She hadn't seen either of the men yet this morning. Instinctively though, she could feel them here somewhere.

She took a step toward the corner, and a force pushed her backward. She stumbled back several steps, only to feel a hand on her shoulder. She spun around in terror.

Sebastian reached out to steady her. "Easy. Just take it easy. I'm a friend, not a foe."

She slammed her hand against her chest. "I'm glad to hear that," she gasped. "Because I've just had a crazy few minutes."

"Explain," he snapped.

She told him about the tugging and the pushing and her yelling out.

"And when you just now took another step, you felt it again?"

She nodded.

"Show me."

She frowned up at him. "What if I don't want to?" she asked peevishly. "It's not very nice to be a pin cushion where people are moving you around at their whim."

"I think the proper term would be *pawn*," he said absentmindedly.

She waved a hand. "Semantics."

He chuckled. "I want to see if there's anything visible when you do get pushed back."

She froze and looked at him. "Right, you see auras. Do you think you could see the aura of whoever is doing this?"

His lips kicked up at the corners of his mouth. "Maybe. But, in order for me to see anything, you have to do it again."

She stared at him for a moment. "Might be better if you moved off to the left then, so you can see it from the side and not from behind."

Obediently he took several steps to the left and then took a couple forward. She closed her eyes, took a deep breath, opened them, turned and walked again toward the corner. Instantly she came up against that wall of energy, and, like a jab to her stomach, she stumbled back several feet from the force of the blow.

She stood, gasping. "Whatever it is does not want me over there." As soon as her words fell silent, she felt a tremendous surge of energy on her back, shoving her forward. "Are you seeing this?" she cried out, resisting the force shoving her forward. She took several steps, unable to hold herself steady. Then the other force came and pushed against her from the front. She held out her arms and roared, "Stop."

Both forces fell away. She stood trembling on the spot.

Sebastian wrapped his arms around her and held her close. "I did see something," he said. He rubbed his hands up and down her back. "I'm not exactly sure what's going on, but it's amazing."

She pushed back so she could stare up at him. "*Amazing*? That's all you've got to say? It was terrifying. It's like being caught in the middle of some strange wind turbine, where one is pushing me forward and one is pushing me back, and I'm getting flattened in the middle."

"I see two energy forces. The energy forces are very strong," he admitted. "I can see the outlines of the energy, but I can't see a specific human shape. Just a swirling force on either side."

"Outlines of the energy?" she questioned softly. "As in, you're seeing, like, wind?"

He shook his head. "No, I see two vertical forms with arms almost, but they are more ghostly. So more than an aura but less than seeing two full persons."

She took several breaths again and then sagged against him. "I don't like the sound of that."

He held her close. "You're doing just fine." He glanced around. "Why are you in this corner anyway?"

She gave a half snort. "Because, on the diagram I drew, this back corner was vague, undefined, and Chana asked me about it."

"Did she?" he murmured.

"She didn't have anything to do with it," Lacey's snapped, glaring up at him. "You leave her out of this craziness."

His smile was warm and caring. "So defensive when it comes to family. You're such a tiger, looking after those you love."

She gave a clipped nod. "And don't you forget it."

He grinned, but he turned so they were both staring at the corner. "Tell me what you see."

She raised her hands and described the pillars rising up from the corners. "A wall is there and a small window. Oh, this is the doorless room with just that small opening."

"Describe that room to me."

She did the best she could. But how does one describe a room with four walls and a floor and a ceiling but no door, just this little opening on the side?

"You think somebody was in there?"

The sense of knowing settled in her. "Yes." And then, off the cuff, she said, "It's her sister."

"Whose sister?" Sebastian asked softly.

"Linnea's," she said. "It's her sister Sabine."

"And why is she in there?"

Lacey closed her eyes, as if reaching for knowledge, and what she found were answers she hadn't expected. "I can see her," she said excitedly.

"Sabine?"

"No Linnea."

"Describe her to me."

She described the beautiful young woman, who was possibly sixteen or seventeen, standing in an off-white simple dress with her contrasting long black hair. "But she seems agitated," she ended with. "She keeps pointing at the corner where her sister is, then pushing me away."

"Why *away*? Doesn't she want you to save her sister?"

"She does, but it's dangerous."

"Why is her sister in there?"

"She was taken away."

"By whom?"

"A bad man." Lacey shrugged, as she watched and looked at him. "Linnea's gone now."

"So her sister was given to a bad man, and the bad man is keeping her in there? He's her jailor?"

"I think so," Lacey said.

"You realize we're talking in present tense, and this happened a long time ago, right?"

"I know," she said, "but, to Linnea, it's still present tense. Does she want us to dig her up?"

"No, and that would be the energy who's pushing you away from this corner. But whose energy is pushing you toward the corner?"

Lacey took a deep breath and looked up at Sebastian. "The jailor."

"WHAT CAN YOU tell me about him?" Sebastian asked Lacey. He was struck by the term jailor. Especially considering what Bruno had found. Bad man? Jailor? Still the two sites were far apart and a decade later.

Sebastian studied her face, to see if she would go into a trance to receive her visions, while using neurolinguistic programming cues to see if she was lying or searching in her past memories for answers. Those cues were subtle. But, at the moment, Lacey exhibited no deception, so he had no cause for that concern.

She shrugged. "I have no clue. I just sense he's a bad man. I can't tell you if he is the same bad man," she emphasized.

"Which, of course, is an important distinction."

"And why now?" Lacey cried out. "Your guys have been working this dig for how long? Other people have been on the Pompeii site for how long? Why is Linnea talking to me now?"

"Because you're here," he said simply. "Because she can communicate with you."

Lacey groaned. "So does that mean then she can't communicate with anybody else?"

"Maybe she's tried," he said. "Maybe she tried and failed. Maybe you're the first one who's been receptive."

"I guess the real issue is, what does she want?" Lacey

said. "This is so way beyond bizarre. It's hard for me to imagine what it is she wants from me."

"That's always the issue. It's one thing to communicate with these spirits. It's another thing entirely to understand what they want you to understand and to do. It's not like you can literally save her sister. She's been dead for thousands of years. Although maybe you could save her soul …"

"So why Linnea? Why Linnea and this other energy? Are they enemies? On the same side? Or do they even know about each other." She glanced at Sebastian. "Do I try to contact the bad man?"

His heart seized in a tight grip. He shook his head. "Don't ever do that."

She frowned up at him, not liking his tone.

"I mean it," he warned. "You don't know what you're dealing with and to try something like that is beyond dangerous. You need some defenses in your arsenal before you even *think* of dealing with evil spirits. Hunter's got to teach you the basics."

"Only he's not here."

Sebastian nodded. "First thing is to not do anything with negative energy alone. Not unless you're a pro. Next is to always—always—be surrounded by loving white energy."

She settled back some and nodded. "Makes sense. I'm not trying to be a hero," she whispered softly. "It just would be nice to have them talk to somebody else," she said with humor.

"I get that, but, for spirits who finally find somebody they can talk to, there's a desperation. They don't worry about social cues and niceties. It's all about getting the message across. So, although Linnea may not be trying to hurt you, her very desperate need will have a powerful impact on you. And she's the 'good guy' in this scenario."

"Oh, I get that," she agreed. "But the other guy ..."

"If someone is attempting to push you toward something, yet you're being sent away from it by Linnea. Then listen to her."

"Meaning, she is the voice of reason?"

"Maybe. We're more concerned about safety—*your* safety," he said.

"Okay, because I really don't want to get into some kind of an otherworldly argument here." She nodded emphatically. "I'm a schoolteacher. I'm only here because I felt compelled to be here." She heard her own words and winced. "Exactly the problem, isn't it?"

"I don't know that *that* is a problem," he said cautiously. "The thing is, these impulses are there for a reason. Whether you're here to help or for you to learn something about yourself or to do something the world needs you to do, I can't say." He watched as her gaze widened at his words. He chuckled. "No, I'm not asking you to be a superhero. I'm just hoping we can get to the bottom of this easily."

"And yet, nothing about this has been easy so far, has it?"

He glanced over her head to see Hunter moving through the bushes. He wondered if his friend had seen anything from her earlier display with the forces. "I think," he said, "Hunter wants to join us."

She spun around, saw Hunter and waved. "He sees stuff too, doesn't he?" she asked softly.

"It's not so much that he sees something, although he saw what you saw once he touched you," Sebastian said in a low tone, "but others don't always see him. He can turn it on and off." He watched her as she studied the trees, looking for

Hunter. "You always see him though, don't you?"

She pointed him out. "Yes, but he moves in a very smooth manner."

"He's always been very good at camouflaging his presence."

Hunter approached quietly. He smiled at Lacey. "That was an interesting demonstration."

Her face lit up. "Did you see them?"

"I'm not sure what I saw," he said cautiously. "But I definitely saw energy."

Her face fell. "What does that mean?" she cried out. "When you say *energy*, are you saying, like, a glowing golden ball? Are you talking about the wind? Just what is it? When you say you see *energy*, what do you mean exactly?"

Hunter looked at Sebastian.

Sebastian said, "What I saw was a tall form that looked like it could be human but covered in a glowing, moving stream of wind."

She frowned as if visualizing it.

Hunter added, "And I saw a large gray energy and a softer, smaller energy. Not white, but maybe with a lighter tinge, like a green to it."

Lacey's frown deepened. "I'd really like to see it for myself," she announced.

"Next time when you're buffeted by these forces," Hunter said, amusement in his tone, "maybe open your eyes and *look* at them."

She stared at him. "Were my eyes closed?"

He nodded.

She raised both hands in frustration. "Why would I do that?"

He chuckled. "I don't know. Why would you?"

"I think it was instinctive," she said. "The forces were so strong that I was leaning into them, trying to maintain my balance."

"You were leaning forward pretty substantially," Hunter said calmly. "I wondered what you were doing."

She shook her head. "I thought I was perfectly straight." She turned to look at Sebastian. "Did you see me leaning?"

He nodded slowly.

She glared at him. "But you didn't say anything."

His eyebrows shot up. "About you leaning? No. Because the way you were leaning also means the force behind you was stronger than the force in front of you." He watched as she digested that information, wondering how long it would take for her to click in.

She gasped, and her eyes grew wide and round. "So you were saying that the bad guy was winning." She worried her teeth on her bottom lip.

Sebastian pulled her close, stroking his thumb across her lip. "Don't chew on your lip like that. You'll end up making it all puffy and swollen." He tucked her up against his chest.

She laid her head against the size and breadth of him. "But to think the bad guy was winning means he's stronger than she is."

"Whoa, whoa, whoa," Hunter said. "Fill me in here a little, please."

Sebastian shared with Hunter the details Lacey had expressed earlier. "So you see? We're not exactly sure who or what's happening here, but Linnea says her sister is in that space over there. As far as Linnea was concerned, there was a bad guy holding her sister in that room. Lacey assumes the negative force was his."

"Except ..." Lacey said, "I'm not sure that was the same

bad guy."

Sebastian hugged her close. "So close your eyes right now, and tell me which force felt better?" He watched as she obediently closed her eyes and then opened them again.

In a slightly resentful tone she said, "Okay, so the bad guy was behind me. *That* energy was forcing me toward that corner. Linnea was pushing me away from that corner."

"So she doesn't want you where her sister is, but the bad guy does. Is that correct?" Hunter asked.

She gave him a look. "You realize how ridiculous all this sounds?"

He just shrugged. "The thing is, you can't be sure Linnea was the good energy because she was pushing you away from her sister. For all you know, she wanted to keep her sister inside that room."

Lacey shook her head. "No, no, no, no. That's not what she was doing."

"You mean, that's not what *you want her to be doing*," Sebastian said gently. "We can't give these spirits motivations and thoughts to fit our beliefs. We don't know if she was protecting you or keeping her sister safe or if it has nothing to do with anything."

"It has to have something to do with it," she said. "There's got to be a reason why that diagram is missing that corner."

"Is that what brought you here?" Hunter asked.

She nodded. "I came to fill in the rest of the picture. And then I realized this is the room where the woman was kept."

"The sister, you said her name is Sabine?"

Lacey nodded. "But I don't have any contact with her."

"Have you tried?" Hunter asked.

She shook her head. "No, and I'm also not supposed to contact the bad guy either, until you teach me to defend myself against evil spirits," she announced to Hunter. "At least that's the law according to Sebastian."

At that, Hunter laughed. "Not an issue. You're actually already doing a lot right already, but nice to know Sebastian is so worried about you." And he chuckled again.

CHAPTER 15

"**I**T'S NOT FUNNY," Lacey retorted to Hunter's boisterous humor. Hearing noises behind them, she turned to see her cousin walking toward them. "Hey, Chana," she called out.

Chana motioned at the two men. "I get that whatever she's doing is important, but we could use your help at the site."

Hunter sobered and fell into step as they walked away from Lacey. Sebastian turned to look at her and repeated, "Remember what I said."

"How can I forget?" she said resentfully. She watched until they disappeared from sight, then she picked up her camera and turned to look back at the corner.

It was impossible to ignore the fact that she faced the prison room. She felt compelled to go closer but knew, as soon as she did, there would be all kinds of repercussions. What she really wanted to know was why she felt compelled to go over there. Was she supposed to help the sister, knowing it was way too late to help anybody? Or was it more of a trap, and she'd become imprisoned like the sister?

She felt a weird sensation in the air as the two men walked farther and farther away from her. As if a coldness came from the shadows behind her, reaching for her. She studied the corner she had planned to take a closer look at and realized she really needed to follow the men.

She grabbed her camera gear and raced behind them. "Wait up for me," she called out.

Sebastian turned toward her, caught the look on her face and asked, "What happened?"

"Nothing happened," she said. "It's just that whole corner became really, really cold. The farther away you guys moved, the colder it seemed to become."

Sebastian and Hunter exchanged glances.

"Why?" Hunter asked. "What does that mean? Has it happened to you before?"

Sebastian gave a curt nod. "It happened back then too."

She took a deep breath. "I don't think I want to go back there alone anymore."

He hooked her arm through his and said, "Good idea. I'm not sure you should be alone at all."

"Given what I'm doing for you, it's hardly possible to not be alone some of the time," she said.

As they walked up, Chana's smile fell away as she saw their arms linked. Lacey tried to pull her arm free.

Sebastian let her arm go but grabbed her hand. "You got a problem?" he asked Lacey curiously.

She took several deep breaths and said, "We're attracting attention."

Hunter looked at her, down at their hands, and a smirk crossed his face as he picked up the pace, moving ahead of them.

"Does that bother you?" Sebastian asked. "Here I thought you liked me."

"I do," she protested. When he chuckled, she smacked him lightly.

"Don't let them get to you. We're friends. Maybe

more."

"Maybe," she said. "I wanted to be part of the team. And it feels very much like I'm an oddity."

"You are," Sebastian said. "Accept it, and don't let them bother you. You're doing what you need to do. You're here, and something special is happening. They don't know. They don't understand. They're not part of it."

"That doesn't make me feel any better," she muttered.

He squeezed her fingers, then released her hand. "Maybe not," he said cheerfully. "But I can keep my eyes on only so many people. You're the one in danger."

"And who's to say they're safe? You didn't say anything about me being in danger to them," she snapped. And then she sighed. "Something about you makes me crazy."

"That's all right," he said, "because you're making me crazy too." At that, he jumped down onto one of the ledges on the side and made his way to the bottom of the open pit.

She stared at him in astonishment, not sure what she was supposed to do now. Hunter was off with Chana, and Sebastian was making his way toward them but from a lower level. Lacey stood, looking like a fool at the top of the ledge, watching him walk away. Looking like a schoolgirl—a lovesick schoolgirl. She could pin some of her daze on the circumstances but not all. Sebastian seemed to think they had something between them. More than this craziness.

How did she feel about that? Delighted to not be alone, but, more than that, she trusted him. She looked for him when he wasn't here, was at his side when he was. She smiled; he was right—something was between them. Feeling something lighten inside her, she pulled out her camera and took pictures. It was almost a reflexive action when she was looking for something to do or a way to hide. She could hide behind the lens, losing herself in her job. She took multitudes of photos until finally she realized she was being foolish. With a groan she sat down on the ledge, her legs hanging over the edge, just watching them all.

Hunter joined her a few minutes later. "You okay?"

"I really wanted to come and have a wonderful touristy insider look at Pompeii and the site," she complained good-naturedly. "And then all this weird stuff happened."

"The weird stuff sounds like it's been happening for a long time with you," he said. "I get that you wanted to come and have a nice visit, but, for people like us, there isn't anything *nice* about this."

"*Like us?*" She turned to look at him. "In what way am I like you?"

"You're seeing dead people. You're communicating with them. You're drawing 3-D visions nobody else can see." His grin flashed white. "How much odder can you be?"

"Do you see stuff like that too?"

"I see different things," he said in a noncommittal tone. "Sometimes I see energy. Sometimes I see faces. It's hard to describe. And I don't always have a rhyme or reason to explain when one shows up versus another."

"Sebastian said you were instrumental in getting him out of the Mayan ruins. You were pretty young back then, weren't you?"

"I was," he said. "And I'm lucky to be alive, and so is Sebastian." His voice fell silent, and then he looked at the archaeology dig all around them. "What do you see when you look here?"

She studied it for a long moment. "Right now, just rocks and dirt."

"Do you want to see deeper?"

"I could try with my camera again," she said, "but I'm not sure how much value it is. I would see potentially the building that had been here. But then I'll want to draw it, and I didn't bring a sketch pad with me, so that'll just drive me crazy," she confessed.

At that, he chuckled out loud.

Several people talking with Sebastian stole glances their way.

"*That* also bothers you, doesn't it?" Hunter asked.

"What? The sideways looks? The not fitting in? The gossip? Sure. Doesn't it bother everyone?"

"No," he said. "Eventually you get to the point where you don't care anymore."

"I'm not there yet," she said. "I've spent a lot of time without friends. I lost so many people when I stayed home to look after my mom." Her voice was soft. "My friends seemed to fall away. When you find yourself standing at a grave site all alone, you look up and around, realizing how very alone you are, how much you've lost over the last few years. You don't really know how to start again. I hadn't expected to make friends here, but I knew Chana was here. We've always been close, and I figured I would at least fit in. And I did initially. But since Sebastian's arrival, that's changed."

"It's not Sebastian's arrival," he said. "It's that you're opening up to everything around here. Psychics tend to give off an odd air. It doesn't make other people terribly comfortable to be around us."

"And yet, we're no different," she said.

"Our energy is sharper, keener. It makes others uncomfortable."

"I wouldn't have said that about you or Sebastian," she said. "And Jeremiah. I didn't notice anything different about him either."

At Jeremiah's name Hunter turned to look at her sharply. Then he nodded as if she'd said something he understood.

She frowned at him. "You are different. You know that, right?"

He stared at her for a long moment, then gave her a wicked grin. "But you like me anyway, don't you?"

She nodded. "Absolutely." She beamed at him. "I like Sebastian and Jeremiah too."

He nodded. "Right, and that makes total sense."

Just then Chana called over to her. "Lacey, we're breaking for lunch. Are you joining us?"

She nodded. "Coming." She turned to look at Hunter, only to find he wasn't here. She spun around, looking for him. She could see him retreating into the trees behind her. "You've got to stop doing that," she called out.

"Why is that?" he called back in a laughing tone.

"Because you're one scary dude when you can disappear into nothing."

Then he was gone, leaving only his laughter behind. She hopped to her feet, grabbed her camera bag, putting her camera away. Then she walked to where the group was gathered. "I didn't even think about making lunch this morning," she said to Chana. "Did you?"

Chana shook her head. "No, but Sebastian had the guys bring in a bunch of sandwiches."

Lacey glanced at her watch and saw it was almost twelve o'clock. "Where did the morning go?" she exclaimed. "I could have sworn it wasn't even ten-thirty yet."

Chana reached into a large box, pulled out a couple sandwiches and handed one to her. "When you get caught up in your images, apparently everything else disappears around you." She plopped beside the group against a nearby tree.

Lacey nodded. "Apparently." She unwrapped the sandwich, settled back, close to Chana, but not so close she didn't have some space and studied the ruins as she ate. Mark walked up and handed both women a cup of coffee. "Thanks, Mark," Lacey said, accepting it. "Love all this service."

He walked around delivering coffee to the rest of the team.

She let her gaze roam the site. Somebody came around the side of the partially excavated site. Hunter? She looked up with a bright smile. But, instead of Hunter, she saw a dark face inside more of a black cloud. Her smile fell away. She could feel that horrible tensing coldness she'd experienced earlier. Her heart slammed against her chest, and her jaw froze. She stared, unable to pull away her gaze.

A slap on the back of her shoulder had her coffee spilling over the rim of her cup. She cried out at the hot coffee on her legs, but it wasn't bad. She turned to look up at Sebastian, and she pointed.

He nodded gently and whispered, "I saw it too."

SEBASTIAN HAD SEEN the cold energy force approaching Lacey but only as a vague outline—until he'd stepped closer to her, nudging his leg up behind her back. As soon as he came into contact with her, the strange apparition became so much more. Not enough to clearly see any features though but a more defined male form. It was definitely some sort of spirit entity, standing and staring at the group. But no doubt his focus was on Lacey herself.

Every day here with Lacey was something new. Every day it seemed like the spirits got closer and closer to her, touching her, pushing her, trying to get her to do something or not do something. It was definitely concerning. Lacey appeared to be wide open, receptive and completely vulnerable, but not only that—she was unaware of just how much danger she was in.

Sebastian hated to think of her getting injured on this site, like his friends had on the Mayan site, but every day something had happened back then. He couldn't forget the ugly end from ten years ago. It was hard to keep those memories at bay. Everything around him was a constant reminder that people who hadn't paid enough attention to the forces around them had died.

He glanced down at Lacey. Her arm was wrapped around his lower leg, a tremor barely visible in her hand as she squeezed his calf muscle. She stared, her gaze locked on where the apparition was.

"What's the matter, Lacey? You look like you've seen a ghost," Chana joked.

He watched the words hit her almost like a blow. She hunched closer to his leg. He knew she didn't want anyone to think something was between them, but right now she needed comfort.

He jumped down until he sat beside her, wrapped his arm around her shoulders and squeezed her gently. "It's all right, you know."

She twisted slightly so she could look at him. He studied her large pupils, the shock already setting in. In a low voice he asked, "Why this? Why after everything else does this bother you?" He could hear the others walking closer.

"Hey, is she okay?" Tom asked.

"She doesn't look very good," Mark said. "Is this all from that same head injury?"

Sebastian wasn't sure what to say. He hugged her gently. "Do you need to go back to the apartment?"

She shook her head violently.

He sagged back and looked at the others. "She's not feeling well all of a sudden. The head injury is likely causing migraines, and the heat is not helping."

One of the other men from the crew stood behind them. "Maybe she should lie down."

"I'm fine," Lacey said in a faint voice. "I'll be fine."

"At least go lie down in the shade somewhere," Mark said in concern. "Honestly, this heat wave is rough on everybody."

She gave a faint nod and smiled at him. "I think that's a good idea."

"You'd be more comfortable though," Chana said, "if you were back in bed. You hardly got any sleep last night."

Sebastian studied the two women, his gaze going from one to the other, wondering what was behind their restless night. But Chana appeared no longer concerned, and Lacey certainly wasn't volunteering any information. He glanced around the site and found a spot in the shade, which he pointed out to her. "Why don't you stretch out over there for a bit?" Considering it was in the opposite direction of where they had seen the darker energy, he figured it might not be a bad idea.

She studied it for a long moment and then gave him a clipped nod. "Maybe I'll try that."

He hopped to his feet and helped her stand.

She grabbed her camera bag, handed him her half-eaten

sandwich, but did take his bottle of water out of his hand and marched over to where he'd suggested.

As everyone watched, she plunked down her bag and water, then stretched out on the spot. She crossed an arm over her eyes as if to block out the light. The others kind of looked back at him.

Chana whispered, "I'm sorry. She's not normally this easily upset."

"It's not your fault," he said. "She's had a trying few days."

The others waited to see what he would do.

He motioned at the lunch mess. "Is it time to clean up and get back to work?"

They all groaned good-naturedly but cleaned up the mess and then spread out to their assigned jobs.

He wanted to join Lacey but didn't want to disturb her if she was truly resting. Neither did he have any intention of walking away. She shouldn't be alone anywhere. He needed to talk to Stefan, Hunter, or even Bruno about these spirits, to figure out what they wanted and why they wanted her and how to dissuade them from bothering her. If she was stronger, it wouldn't be so bad, but he wasn't sure she had the inner strength to deal with this type of spiritual on-slaught. It was not only dark forces but heavy anger and rage, often hatred, driving these people. It was hard to understand how so much bottled-up emotion could survive through the centuries, but there were cases reported of exactly that happening over and over again.

He surveyed the dig site, wondering what his next move should be, when his phone buzzed.

"Do you have any more pictures for me?" Stefan asked.

"No, she hasn't been drawing any."

"That's too bad," he said. "I'd really like to know more of what she sees."

"I think we all do," Sebastian said. "But she's struggling in many ways. She was eating voraciously, now much less, the same for her thirst. I don't know if it's the head injury, but she's certainly more and more susceptible to the different forces around here. She's also seeing more spirits."

"Sensitives are like that," Stefan said. "Once they're wide open, it's hard for them to filter out the spirits they don't want to talk to. And, once contact is made, you know yourself just how many clamoring voices can overwhelm you."

"I'm not even sure it's so much clamoring voices at this point," Sebastian said, "as much as she's seeing things and feeling things."

"Like what?"

"Cold chills, dark apparitions. She was buttressed between two different forces this morning in a way that was completely bizarre. Hunter saw it as well."

"Interesting," Stefan murmured softly. "I need to connect with him then too."

"I don't know what Hunter has said to you up until now," Sebastian said, "but a lot of stuff is going on here. Like a vortex is building."

"Are you sure?" Stefan's voice sharpened and deepened at the same time, definitely signs that this news had shocked him.

"Yes, I'm sure. Since Lacey arrived, we had some minor incidents before, unexplained. Then a few days of calm. Now we've had incidents every day, sometimes multiples in a day, like today. Her energy is getting spun around. She's doing a great job subconsciously to rebuff it, but, as she's opening herself up to figuring out what's going on, others are taking advantage."

"Have Hunter teach her some techniques to protect herself," Stefan murmured.

"I have discussed a couple basics with her but we need to do more, Hunter could be a huge help, but you know Hunter ..."

"I do indeed," Stefan said, a note of humor entering his voice. "He's a good man."

"Yeah, but a little hard to pin down."

At that, Stefan laughed out loud. "Keep in touch." He clicked off.

Sebastian pocketed his phone, glancing around to see Mark with an odd look on his face. Sebastian studied Mark's expression, searching for signs he'd overheard Sebastian's conversation. When Mark didn't change expressions, Sebastian said, "Earth to Mark. You in there?"

Mark gave a slow nod, his gaze narrowing on Sebastian's features. "Oh, I'm in here," he said. "But something's going on that I'm not sure I like at all."

Sebastian raised one eyebrow and stared him down. Normally Mark was a very nonaggressive, happy-go-lucky kind of guy, but no doubt things going on lately had set them all on edge. Sebastian didn't know how much Mark knew or indeed what Mark might have seen on his own. His behavior was more aggressive but not enough to be a problem, just a cutting tone to his voice, sharp facial expressions. Then everyone was feeling the tension here. Not to mention everybody had the ability to see psychic phenomena. So how many here were? Still most people weren't open or accepting of what their eyes were telling them. And, over time, the images and visions faded. But Sebastian didn't know how anybody here in his site crew stood in regard to psychic phenomenon. "What do you mean, something's going on?"

Mark gave an odd sound. Almost a sneer.

Sebastian jumped off the ledge and walked closer to him. "What are you saying?" he demanded.

Of all the things he understood about a dig like this was there had to be one boss and everybody had to get along. Arguments and strife had to be sorted out at the beginning stages; otherwise it grew into monumental arguments that served no purpose. It caused tension and disruption on a dig site.

Mark stared at him for a long moment and then shrugged. "Maybe it's nothing."

"What is it? Maybe it's something," he said encouragingly. "Tell me what's going on."

Mark shook his head. "It seems like a lot of incidents here I've never seen on other digs before. I am not a superstitious guy, but sometimes you have to wonder just how much somebody is deliberately trying to vandalize our dig and how much of it is supernatural."

"Interesting," Sebastian said, keeping his voice neutral. "Are you thinking you're seeing ghosts or we're being visited by ghosts?"

"It sounds stupid when you ask it like that," he muttered, backing down.

"I'm not sure it's stupid at all," Sebastian said. "It's not like you can do these kinds of digs and not wonder if there's an odd presence when you open up a grave and you see mummies, bodies that have lain there for centuries. You have to wonder if there are spirits, pieces of their souls still around."

"Have you ever seen any?"

"Mummies, graves, souls, spirits? What are you asking?"

"Have you seen ghosts?"

Sebastian contemplated him for a long moment, then gave a clipped nod. "I thought I did once. I don't have any proof of it though."

An expression of relief crossed Mark's face.

Spiking Sebastian's curiosity in a big way. "Have you?"

"I'm not sure," Mark said. "But, in the last few days, I've seen things I don't understand—shapes, lights." The corner of his mouth quirked up. "I figured you'd call me crazy."

"No, I wouldn't call you crazy. I'd say you had a healthy respect for what's going on in the world that we don't understand. I don't think those types of entities can break tools though or can steal them either."

Mark thought about it for a moment and then said, "I guess they can't really pick up anything either, can they? And, if they can't pick up anything, they can't break anything. So, therefore, they aren't the ones causing this trouble." On that note his face lightened and brightened at the same time, and he smiled. "That's good to know. I'll get back to work then." He turned and walked back over to the group.

Leaving Sebastian to wonder how extensive the energy shifts were here, and who all was involved.

CHAPTER 16

LACEY RESTED ON the ground for a good thirty minutes, getting her thoughts together. She hated that she appeared neurotic and weak to the rest of the team. She'd never had a problem holding up her end before, but nobody could have prepared her for what she had found here. Well, even more than that, the coldness, the fear that came with that one particular energy was terrifying.

She sat up and reached for her camera, taking security in that normalcy. She caught pictures of Mark and Sebastian talking, the changes on Mark's face during their conversation before he turned and walked away. Again she caught Sebastian's expression as he turned to look at her. Hastily she dropped the camera, but he knew. He always seemed to know. But, instead of walking toward her, he headed to the Stabian Gate.

That surprised her. After everybody had urged her to go to the apartment or to lie down in the shade, she thought for sure he would want her to return with him. She kept taking pictures of his back, that strong, forward-moving determined stride, that loose-limbed walk of his that implied power, and yet, wasn't threatening. He disappeared into the dark gate's entranceway as she kept clicking.

Finally she put down her camera, lay back down, took a deep breath, stretched for several long moments in her prone position, mentally pushing out all the angst that had been following her this morning and then sat back up again.

Seeing Hunter standing in front of her, she let out a light shriek. "Why do you keep sneaking up on people?" she demanded.

He grinned at her. "Because it's fun."

She groaned. "That's not fair."

"What are you doing?"

"I'm supposed to be resting after another *incident*," she emphasized. "I hate that they are hitting my system with a whack."

"What else do you expect them to do? There's no point in these entities appearing to you if you're not seeing them. It takes them a lot of time and energy to accomplish what they're doing."

"Did you see the one at lunchtime?"

His lips pursed as he studied her face. "I saw the dueling forces earlier. But I haven't seen anything since the time the three of us were together."

She motioned to the corner where she had seen the black apparition. "Then I have to tell you about the one I saw after that." She explained. "It was only about half an hour or forty-five minutes ago. I never even got to finish my lunch."

He squatted down in front of her and checked her forehead temperature.

She made a startled movement. "You can't seriously think I'm sick."

"It's not that you're sick but that entities can play hell with our systems. They can send our body temperatures down or up. Shock is also another major factor. I'm glad you're over here, separated from the rest of them. You need time to yourself right now."

"It's not like I'm getting it. It seems like every day I'm seeing more and more. It's both scary and incredible. But scary is winning out," she admitted.

"Of course it is," he said. "It's all new. It's different. And before, if you haven't seen entities who passed a long time ago, it's pretty amazing to realize that, in some cases, our spirits live on."

"*In some cases* is the real issue. I look around here, and I see these … whatever they are," she said with a wave of her hand, "and then I have to think about my mother, who crossed over. I held her hand while she reached out to grab my father's hand. Is she around still? Or was that doorway her crossing over and leaving this earthly plane forever?"

"That's exactly what it was. You saw the door close behind her …" He leaned forward to study her face as he said that. "Didn't you?"

She frowned, casting her mind back. "I'm not sure," she said. "I was so amazed at everything that I didn't really see a door close, but there was this big solid bright white light, and then I couldn't see the door anymore."

"That's exactly what that is," he said with a note of satisfaction. "The door closes so it no longer appears. It's not like you see a door shut, which I guess some people might, but, in your case, it was just the ball of white light. So your mother has crossed over. She's happy. She's no longer Earthbound. She won't be lingering here to come back and talk to you."

She took a shaky breath and let it out. "And that's both sad and good."

"It's good," he said gently. "What you want is your mother's soul to be at rest. And, although you might be lonely because you don't have her with you, you wouldn't want her with you if it was at a cost to her."

"No, I wouldn't," she whispered. She gave him a small smile. "I really do believe she's happy where she is, with my father."

"Good." Hunter straightened up, reached a hand down and said, "Let's take a walk."

Surprised, she placed her hand in his and bounced to her feet. "What kind of a walk? Where?"

He motioned to the rest of Pompeii that sprawled all around them. "I doubt you've had a chance to explore much, so I thought we'd spend an hour or two."

"Except I'm supposed to be working," she said drily. "I don't know what exactly you do for a living, but, when I have a job to do, I'm not known for shirking my duties."

"I don't think that'll be a problem," Hunter said. "Sebastian's the one who suggested it." He pulled out his phone and wiggled it at her. "I just got off the phone from talking with him."

She smiled. "Then why didn't you say so?" She bent, grabbed her camera bag, tucked her camera back into it, secured it and then put it on her shoulder. "Lead the way."

He led her out through the Stabian Gate once again. They walked around to another entrance where they could see the more touristy area of Pompeii. As they walked, she pulled out her camera, taking pictures.

"These Roman roads ..." she exclaimed.

"They're fascinating, aren't they? To think people laid these by hand all those many years ago ..."

She nodded, fascinated, as she stopped to take pictures of the marks between the lines, the way they fitted together at the sides of the roads. "It's really amazing technology they must have had back then."

"I think it was less about technology and more about hard labor," he said, chuckling.

She nodded. "I can't imagine what life was like."

"And yet, I think you can imagine more than most people," he said with a cryptic note.

He took a left turn and led her into another section, where a lot more people traveled. They could still walk without bumping into anyone, but it was obviously a popular spot. For the next couple hours, they wandered the tourist attractions, taking photos, murmuring, talking, and she smiled.

"Thank you. This is definitely what I needed today."

"It was also helpful for me."

"Why is that?" she asked.

"Because you didn't appear to be affected by any of the other entities we met and saw."

She looked at him. "What are you talking about? I didn't see any of them." She stopped for a moment, thought about it, then shrugged. "I really didn't."

A small smile played at the corner of his mouth. "Good," he said. "That makes it that much more of a touristy visit for you." He motioned back the way they'd come. "I suggest we head back to the dig, but we'll take another route."

Willingly she stepped in beside him, her camera capturing the rocks and the ruins. "I'm not even seeing the 3-D drawings here," she muttered.

"But you're not going to that level either, are you?" he asked. "You're really taking pictures of what's here instead of finding the deeper meaning, as you were on Sebastian's dig site."

"That's quite true," she admitted. "I hadn't realized just how much of a difference there was in my attitude."

"Motivation and attitude are everything," he said.

He led the way forward, but it was darker back here with mounds of dirt and grass. "This is all unexcavated, isn't it?"

"Absolutely. Apparently ninety percent of the site itself is untouched. Incredible wonders are waiting for the world to find them."

"And many more bodies, people who suffered and died await to be found."

"Yes. I think they believe about twenty, possibly twenty-five thousand people perished in that disaster," he said. "But we also have to remember many tens of thousands survived."

That made her feel somewhat better, but it was still hard to consider how so many people had perished so fast.

As they walked, she looked around, seeing how deserted this area was. "I wonder why the tourists aren't all over this section?"

"I think because the tourists come for different reasons. They aren't here to see the geographical area as much as they're here to see the ruins. And, although the ruins are here, they're hidden, so it's not as much of an interest here."

"For me it's much more interesting," she said quietly. "Because I can see the hills and imagine what's underneath. Whereas back there, all the work has been done, and all the surprises have been found. It's like a Christmas present that's already been opened but still having boxes under the tree to unwrap."

That startled a laugh out of him. "That's a good analogy," he said approvingly. His phone rang. He glanced down and smiled.

"Feel free to take that," she said, when he pocketed the phone.

He shrugged. "It's an old friend. I'll give him a call later."

But in a few minutes his phone rang again. He pulled it out and frowned.

"Is it the same person?"

He nodded. "If you don't mind, I'll take this real quick."

She pointed to a knoll on the right. "I'll sit there and enjoy the scenery." She walked over to the small hill, sat down, brought out her camera and took pictures of what was in front of her. She knew she was taking many pictures that she'd end up deleting, but it was almost impossible to know what she would capture until she could look closer at her photographs.

As she sat here, she listened to Hunter's part of the phone conversation, understanding he was talking to somebody named Stefan and that Sebastian was connected. The conversation then turned cryptic as Hunter appeared to turn evasive. She blocked out the conversation, realizing he had a right to his privacy.

As she sat here, the sun seemed to go behind clouds. She hadn't seen many clouds until now. She sighed. "Of course it would rain. All we've had is dead heat so far." But as she watched, she could almost see the clouds march across the sky. She had to lift her camera as the clouds crowded out the bright blue sky, shutting off the sun from the Earth.

When she was done, and the light had turned gloomy and dark, she twisted around to see Hunter standing ten feet away from her, his hands on his hips, staring at her. She frowned back. "Is your call done?"

He nodded. "What did you just do with the weather?"

She gave a surprised laugh. "I didn't do anything," she said. "I was taking photos as the clouds came across. They were moving so fast that I could see them race across the sky."

He didn't say anything but motioned for her to get up. "If we hurry," he said, "we can get back to the dig site before the rain hits."

She nodded and joined him on the path. When he went to take another path to the left, she stopped. "That's not the right way, is it?"

He frowned and looked at her. "Yes, it is."

She shook her head. "No, we have to go this way." She pointed to a small path going to the right.

He studied her face, studied the direction she wanted to go and said, "The dig is over here." He pointed to the left again.

She stared down that path, then shrugged. "Maybe it is. But I have to go this way." She stepped forward ahead of him and walked down the path to the right.

"Not alone you're not," he warned as he fell into step behind her.

She kept walking, hating that the darkness now seemed to have a more menacing air to it. "Why is it I feel I have to go this direction?" she muttered just loud enough for him to hear.

"I don't know," he said. "Maybe you're the one who needs to answer that question."

"Except I don't have an answer," she continued.

She kept walking for another fifteen minutes. And it seemed like they were getting deeper and deeper into the middle of a labyrinth. Hills and hummocks surrounded the area, but they hadn't seen anyone in a long time.

"This place should be bouncing with tourists," she complained, "except this section feels eerie and dark right now."

"This is not a normal path," he said quietly. "I don't

know if you're looking at the ground, but it's hard to discern any kind of a pathway."

"No, I'm following one," she said, her voice certain. "I know I am."

"Well then, lead on," Hunter said. "Apparently you know where you're going." He hesitated, then added, "Or is it Linnea who knows where you're going?"

Lacey froze. "I should be checking that, shouldn't I? I should be finding out why I'm being led this way and why I'm following without questioning where the impulse is coming from."

"You should certainly be double-checking your inclination to follow along blindly," he said softly. His phone rang. He pulled it out and said, "Sebastian? Yeah, we're on our way back to the dig, but she's taking a road going in a different direction."

He held the phone out so she could hear Sebastian say, "Get her back here. Don't let her go off on her own."

She piped up, "Sebastian, I have to go in this direction. I don't know why, but I do."

Silence came from the phone. A worried silence took over Hunter's face.

She gave him an apologetic look. "I'm sorry, but I have to." She turned and kept walking. Behind her she could hear Hunter talking to Sebastian, giving him coordinates so he could join them.

"It can't be dangerous, can it?" she asked.

"You tell me. The skies turned dark, and you're being led into a completely desolate area of Pompeii. How is it that you think this is a good idea?"

She shivered, fear snaking through her body. "I don't know," she whispered. "But I just know I have to go here."

"Which is why we're going," Hunter said gently. "So let's keep walking. Sebastian is coming to meet us too."

With that news bolstering her spirit, she picked up the pace. Another five minutes later, she stopped. "I don't know which direction to go."

"Tell me what you see." Hunter's voice was melodious and calm behind her.

She raised both arms into a *V* and said, "The two paths literally go in that direction. We're standing at the center where we have to split left or right."

"And, if I say *left*, do you say *right*, and, if I say *right*, do you say *left*?"

She shook her head. "No, I can't really tell which way I'm supposed to go."

"Close your eyes," Hunter said. "Reach out to Linnea and ask her."

Lacey closed her eyes, letting her head bow forward, and in her mind she said, *Linnea, if that's you, direct me which way to go*. Her right arm jerked. "She said to the right."

"Good. Now reach out to that other entity and ask it."

She gasped. "I'm not sure I want to bring that one back into being. He scared the hell out of me. Not to mention Sebastian would be pissed."

"Fear is a huge teacher. And you are not alone."

She bowed her head, reached out to the other energy and asked, *Which direction do you want me to go?* Immediately her arm rose to the left. "Of course they each want me to go in different directions." She turned to look at Hunter, a craftiness in her tone as she said, "How about you go left and I go right?"

Hunter laughed at her. "No, that's not happening. We're definitely heading in the same direction together. But, if Linnea wants you to go right, then let's go that direction."

She thought about it and then nodded. "It feels right."

Together they walked in the direction Linnea had said to go.

"Did you ever consider why Linnea wants you to go in this direction?"

"I have no clue," Lacey said. "No more than I know why the other energy wants me to go the other way."

They kept walking for several more moments until she tried to take another step and couldn't. She leaned forward but still couldn't move her feet. "I can't move forward at all," she cried out.

Hunter reached out a hand, and it stopped on an invisible barrier right in front of her. He searched the barrier with both hands, looking for a way through.

She stared at the invisible barrier. "I've never seen anything like this."

"Neither have I," Hunter said. He stepped back, tugging her with him, and tested the strength of the barrier with his foot. But he couldn't seem to nudge it or break it. He stared at it with his hands on his hips. "What do you see when you look forward?"

"Just a blank space as if nothing is there," she said in amazement.

"Can you see where it ends?"

"Oh, I never thought about that." She placed a hand on the barrier and then went to the left as far as she could go. "It's all the way over here," she said, a good ten feet from him. As she glanced back, she realized he'd been doing the same thing on his side. "A barrier is really here," she marveled. "If people could see something like this, it would completely change their view of supernatural events."

"Which is probably a good thing that they can't see this," Hunter said drily. "Mass chaos and panic would ensue."

"Maybe not," she said as she walked back toward him. "What I don't understand is why would Linnea want me to be here? No point in coming if I would get stopped partway."

"So maybe you should ask her," Hunter said gently.

She glanced up at him. "But I can't feel her anymore."

He nodded slowly, his gaze never leaving her face. "If you can't feel her," he said, his voice even deeper and lower, "then what can you feel? Is it the same energy that put up this barrier?"

SEBASTIAN APPROACHED HUNTER and Lacey, wondering what was the subject of their intense conversation. He gave a light whistle. Hunter raised a hand in acknowledgment. Lacey stared at him, then her face lit up, making him smile. She really did sense the attraction between the two of them. But so much else was going on, and he knew she didn't see it for what it was. He did though. He kept walking toward them, wondering about the odd look on their faces.

"Can you walk straight toward me, please?" Lacey asked.

He raised an eyebrow but obediently closed the distance between them. When he stepped right up against her, he leaned over, kissed her gently on the forehead and said, "Is that what you wanted?" He studied her face, seeing the shock as her gaze darted to the side and then back to him again.

She reached around and placed a hand out, feeling something. He placed his hand near hers and could feel the barrier, but he stood right in the middle of it. It conformed to the shape of him here. He stared at Hunter. "Do you have an explanation?"

Hunter very slowly turned his head from side to side. "No, I don't," he said. "But what's fascinating is that you can cross the barrier. You're standing in it."

Lacey crouched and placed her hand between his feet where the barrier should be and sure enough it was there. She gasped and bounced back to stare at him in awe. "You literally are one with the barrier," she said. "I don't even know what it is, but it's fascinating that you are joined with it."

"Did you try to cross it?" he asked.

"Yes," she said. "I can't. Whereas you didn't even know there was one, but you could cross it. Was it because of that mind-set maybe?" she asked in confusion.

He shrugged. The barrier rippled around him.

"If you step toward me, and you're out of the barrier, do you think you can cross back again?"

"I don't know," he said. "I could try to find out."

"No, wait," Hunter said. "Step back on the other side of the barrier first and see if you can find a barrier."

Sebastian did that. He reached up a hand and held it against Lacey's hand flat on the barrier. But there was no barrier for him. His hand went right through it to clasp hers. And gently, ever-so-gently, he pulled her forward, and she walked right through it.

"That makes no sense," she cried out.

"It does actually," Hunter said, but his voice had an odd echo because the barrier had sealed up.

She stared at him and then at Sebastian. "Bring Hunter through too."

"Or we can both go to the other side, to join Hunter."

Sebastian grabbed her hand and stepped through where the barrier should have been. But, for him, there didn't appear to be one. With her hand extended through the barrier, he gently tugged, and she came through the barrier with him again. Once they were both on the same side of the barrier as Hunter, Sebastian reached out a hand, and he could feel the barrier, but, when he pushed, his hand went right through it. The others tried to push their hands through it as well. But, for them, it was solid resistance.

"Interesting," Sebastian murmured. "Why can I enter, and you can't?"

"A barrier that has an affinity for you alone." Hunter shook his head. "Every day I still find out something new and wondrous about this crazy world."

"I don't know about *wonderful*," Lacey said, "because honestly this was intended to keep me out. And yet, Linnea was leading me here."

"Why would she do that?" Sebastian asked. He hated that Lacey followed Linnea's guidance so much, without knowing if she could trust her.

"She led me to the barrier, but I don't know why. I don't know what the barrier would mean for me."

"Who's putting up the barrier? That's a better question," Hunter said.

"But how do we know anyone is?"

"Signatures," both Sebastian and Hunter answered at the same time. They turned to study the energy of the barrier.

"Signatures?" Lacey asked in confusion. "Are you telling me energy has a distinct identification, like a fingerprint?"

"That's exactly what we mean. How you got that from the word *signature* though, I don't know."

"I remember reading something about it," she muttered.

Sebastian studied the barrier, not seeing what he needed to find. "What about you, Hunter? Can you see anything? For me the barrier is invisible, since I can permeate it. But maybe you can see better what's here, because it's a barrier for you."

"I'm definitely getting a sense of the energy," Hunter agreed. "But it's very faint." He placed one hand onto the barrier and closed his eyes. Immediately the barrier vibrated.

"Oh, that's a terrible whine," Lacey cried out, placing her hands over her ears.

Hunter looked at her in surprise. He added more energy to his vibrational call, and she cried out again. He released his hand and asked, "You can hear that?"

She nodded. "At least I heard something. It was a high-pitched whining noise, like a motor running at too high a pitch for comfort."

Hunter looked over at Sebastian. "What about you?"

Sebastian shook his head. "I didn't hear anything," he said. "Interesting that she could hear and feel the barrier but couldn't see or cross the barrier. You could touch it and raise the vibration, but you can't cross it. I can't hear or see it, but I can cross it."

"That's all nice, fine and dandy," Lacey said in frustration, "but what does it mean?"

"It means, we don't know what it is," Hunter said in a laughing voice. "So much of this stuff we don't have answers for. We're exploring and understanding more every day, and yet, every day something new like this pops up."

"Can we carry on this path then? Linnea says I'm still supposed to go in this direction."

"I'd be happy to take you through that barrier, as long as Linnea tells us why she wants you to go there."

Lacey gave a clipped nod. "I'll ask her."

She bowed her head, and he could see her lips move as if she were speaking to Linnea. He exchanged a glance with Hunter, who just shrugged. They'd seen a lot of people communicate with spirits in many ways, from painting scenes, writing down what a spirit needed to say, to standing here and speaking with them one-on-one.

Lacey raised her head and said, "Linnea just says it's important."

"How important?"

"Very important," Lacey said drily. "She's not exactly forthcoming."

"Which is also why I'm a little worried," Hunter said.

"But, if we don't go, we won't find out," Sebastian said. He grabbed both Hunter's and Lacey's hands and walked them carefully through the barrier.

On the other side he led the way forward, in case there were more barriers. He could feel a buzz as he went through, alerting him that an energy field was here. He studied the area around them. "I haven't been in this corner of the site before."

"Linnea is directing this trip," Hunter said in a hard tone. "I'm not sure I trust her."

"I don't trust anyone," Sebastian said. "In a human body or out."

"How can you say that?" Lacey asked from behind them. "My mother was incredibly trustworthy."

"Though we won't see her here," Sebastian said. "She's a happy soul living out a happy soul life until her reincarnation back onto this place again."

"Do we know for sure all souls come back?" she asked dubiously. "I'm not certain I like that idea."

"It depends on where in your soul's evolution you are while on this Earthly incarnation," Hunter said in a cryptic tone.

For Sebastian, who'd heard all this many times before, he understood the confusion on Lacey's face. He explained the little the psychic world surmised about reincarnation and the Akashic records. Sometimes people refused to learn their lessons, saying they would learn it in their next lifetime instead of putting in the work to learn it now.

"Sometimes people are born over and over again because they refuse to learn their lessons the first time," he said. "And then you get people who move very well through their lifetimes, learning the lessons they need at every step of their growth, and this could be the last time you see them because, when they die and go through to the altered plane on the other side, there's no need for them to come back."

"That's also kind of depressing," she muttered. "Who'd want to be the one who sits up there all alone, waiting for the rest of humanity to join them? And who wants to be the humanity sitting down here for fifty lifetimes and still not getting anywhere?"

"But a soul's journey is a soul's journey and is individual to that soul," Hunter said. "That's why it's so important to take the high road at all times on this Earthly plane, so you don't add more negative karma that you have to fix later. Karma can be a bitch, and she always gets you in the end, even if it means adding another lifetime to clear these karmic debts."

"I don't like the sound of that at all," Lacey muttered.

Sebastian approached a copse of trees up ahead. He could feel the coldness emanating from them. His footsteps slowed, and he held out his arms to hold the other two back.

"What is it?" Hunter asked.

"Temperature drop," he said succinctly.

Hunter stiffened and stepped out to the side.

"Is it him?" Lacey whispered behind him.

"Who is *him*?"

"That same energy I felt at noon today. The jailor?"

"You tell me," Hunter said. "Is it him?"

Sebastian stepped slightly away from Hunter so there was room for Lacey to join the two in the middle.

She stared at the trees and then nodded. "I think so. It's dark—evil—energy, and I can feel that coldness. Nervousness. I'm not getting anything nice from it."

"Neither am I," Sebastian said. "But we can't judge it for that alone. Sometimes very old energy that's been lying here for a long, long time gives the same impression."

Hunter whistled softly. "Not sure *I* like this at all." He stepped forward and then took a couple more steps.

"Don't go over there," Lacey cried out.

"Why not?" Hunter asked.

"You're the one who just said you don't like this," she said in exasperation.

"I don't," he said, "and, therefore, I want to find out what it is. Because, when you're afraid of something, it becomes much bigger in your mind until you figure it out." He motioned to the other side of a small hill. "There's some kind of a cave-in here."

The others joined him and looked. "It's a fairly good-size cave-in." Sebastian took several steps to the side to get a better view of what was going on. As he approached, the ground fell away under his boots. He took several steps back as sand, dirt and vegetation crumbled inward.

Lacey gasped. "Come away from there, please," she cried

out.

Hunter looked at her.

Sebastian looked at him, but, instead of listening to Lacey, he walked in a wider circle around to where he could see more of what was going on. "It has definitely caved in," he said. "There appears to be some kind of an anteroom underneath. I don't know how big it is, and we'd have to look on the map to see where in the archaeology site this is."

"I can already tell you," Lacey said, her voice resentful. "It's some kind of burial chamber."

The two men looked at her.

Sebastian said, "How could you know that?"

She shrugged. "Linnea is telling me."

"Is that what she wanted you to find?"

Lacey nodded. "Yes. That's what she wanted me to find here but she's also not happy about it."

"Now that you have, can you leave?" Hunter asked.

That was a good question because often entities, once they had a chance to show something to someone, felt their Earthly mission was done, and they could leave. She shook her head. "No, not yet," she said. "She won't let me leave yet."

"Why?" Hunter asked gently. "Ask her why."

Sebastian watched as Lacey bowed her head as if talking to Linnea. Then she took several steps toward the edge of the cave-in and pointed off to the right. "Underneath, on that side."

"And what will we find if we dig there?" Sebastian asked. He kept his tone even because something was odd about Lacey's movements.

She walked around to join him so they could both look in the direction she indicated. "She is in there," Lacey said softly. "Linnea is in there."

"*Aah*," Hunter said with understanding. "She wanted her body to be found."

Lacey shook her head. "No. That's not it at all."

"Then what difference does it make if she's in there or not?" Hunter asked curiously.

"She's not alone," Lacey whispered. "Other women are in there with her. Lots of them."

"How did they die?" Sebastian asked, his stomach sinking. "Did they all die in the Pompeii disaster?"

Lacey slowly shook her head, tears filling her eyes as she stared up at him. "No, they were murdered. All of them were murdered, except for Linnea."

"Why not Linnea?"

She whispered, "Because she was trying to save them. She went to save them, but they had already been killed. And then the disaster struck, and Linnea died."

CHAPTER 17

LACEY HATED THE words that came from her mouth. She tried to backtrack and said, "But I can't know that for sure."

"But that's what she's telling you?" Sebastian asked in a noncommittal voice, turning away.

"I think so," Lacey said, rushing to catch up. "You're walking toward that spot. Why?"

"I want to see this cave-in from a different angle." He stopped, turned and crouched to look at the hill.

"Are you planning to excavate it?"

Sebastian shook his head. "No, you have to understand the paperwork involved in opening up a new dig site."

"But this one's already been opened," she argued.

"It's caved in," he said. "That doesn't mean everything is close to the surface. Or that we have the right to anything we might find."

She glanced around and said, "Now where did Hunter go?"

Sebastian chuckled. "Hunter is always where you least expect him."

She searched again, her gaze finally coming around to the cave-in. And, sure enough, Hunter's head popped out from the inside. She wanted to rush to him, but Sebastian held her back. "Why?" she asked. "It's not dangerous surely."

"Hunter is looking with his other vision," Sebastian said softly. "Let's not disturb him."

Slowly she let Sebastian pull her back to where he'd been standing. She studied Hunter, who seemed to be turning in a slow circle, looking at everything on the surface. "When you say *his other vision* ..."

"He sees things too. His abilities are different than ours."

"Ours?" she asked in a dry tone. "I don't even know that I have any abilities."

"You just talked to a dead person—isn't that an ability?"

"Did I though?" she asked. "Or was it just my imagination?"

"That's possible too," he said as they watched Hunter disappear for a second time.

She tried to go forward, but Sebastian still held her back. "Is he destroying valuable items?" she asked, looking for any angle that would allow her to better see Hunter. "Ones you're not entitled to excavate?"

"Whatever has been buried here has been buried for a long time," he said. "It would be unusual to have a cave-in like this in the first place, since lava is not picky. Normally it destroys everything in its path. In this case the lava has fallen in below."

"But now that it's caved-in, don't you want to see what's inside?"

"Absolutely I do," Sebastian said with a smile. "But Hunter gets to have his moment first."

She tapped her foot impatiently as she waited and waited and waited. But Sebastian appeared to be completely unconcerned. "What if I'm wrong?"

"There's no way to know for sure," Sebastian said. "We can only listen to the voices from the past and surmise what might have happened. They could be telling the truth, but they might not be."

"But why would a spirit have a reason to lie about something like that?"

"It's hard to say," he said. "Most of the time they believe what they're saying, or they're so hung up on a goal they'll say anything to achieve it."

She smiled. "That makes sense. I know there's a lot of desperation in Linnea's actions and words."

"Anger?" he asked. "Or something else?"

"I'm not sure. Panic and a sense of urgency. I don't really know." And Lacey didn't. The more she thought about it, the harder it was to figure it out. It was almost as if, now that Linnea's spirit wasn't here, her words were drifting away, fading from Lacey's memory. "Is it possible the spirits can erase their words from your mind afterward?"

He made a startled sound. "You mean, like reach into your memory and pull away that memory?" he asked in amazement.

She winced. "Okay, I know that sounded stupid. But I'm having trouble remembering what she said to me."

"That's very interesting. How much of that is because you're tired and worn out and so much is happening?"

"I don't know," she said, pacing aimlessly while she struggled to remember exactly what Linnea had said. "I can't remember her exact words anymore," she said, "and I really want to. I feel like I need to record everything going on around me."

"You have the recorder with you, right?"

She checked her pockets and found the recorder and held it up. "But I should have recorded her words when she first said them to me, not now that my memory is failing."

Sebastian pointed to the red light. "Has it been going for hours?"

She shook her head. "I don't remember turning it on."

He took it from her and hit the Stop button, then hit the Replay button. They listened as conversations from that morning played, somewhere around the time she felt the two entities and was involved in their push-pull actions. The conversation that followed was at lunchtime with the dark entity they'd both seen, then her talking about Linnea.

She stared at him. "I don't normally record conversations with other people," she murmured, afraid he may think she did something devious. "My voice has a weird static element."

He studied the recorder in his hand, a frown deepening the lines on his face. "I don't think you would do something like that. But I'm glad at least your side of the conversations were recorded because now we have something to remember those multiple conversations by."

She backed up when he tried to hand it back to her. "No, you keep it. I don't want anything to do with that."

He pocketed the recorder and reached out a hand, gripping her shoulder. "It's okay, you know. Remember these people have been gone a long time. As much as they're terrifying, the effect they can have on us today is minimal."

She stared at him. "Are you saying the people from that Mayan ruin didn't end up dead because of whatever was happening down at that site?" She watched him take in her words as if they were a body blow.

He bowed his head for a long moment. "Ouch," he said. "I was trying to make you feel better and to allow myself to forget."

"Were the people possessed? Did they kill each other

because of someone else's influence?"

"Something like that," he said, lifting his head, staring off in the distance. "But it sounds pretty horrible to hear you say it that way."

"It *is* horrible," she said. "I'm sorry," she added, "It wasn't fair of me to bring up those bad memories."

He gave a hard laugh. "We need to remember because a repeat here could be devastating." He shook his head. "I wouldn't be alive today if it weren't for Hunter." He motioned at his friend, who's head popped up aboveground again.

She called out, "Did you find anything?"

Hunted nodded. "Lots. Come and look."

With a glance at Sebastian and his nod, she raced over. She fell to her knees just back from the opening so she could peer in. "This is a really large space."

"Be careful. The edge is unstable. I'm not exactly sure what this was. Lava has filled in a lot of what's here, but I can sense the spirits trapped here."

"Were they murdered?"

He raised an eyebrow. "Isn't that what you said?"

"Sure, but that doesn't mean I'm right," she said in defense. "I'm very new to this. I have no clue whether I should even be listening to Linnea."

"It's wise to double-check everything," he said. "Especially what comes from the spirit world."

"Which is really depressing." She focused on Hunter. "You'd think that, after a lifetime and having lost their lives, they would be honest when they finally get a chance to talk again."

"Most of the time they are," Hunter said. "But you have to remember their world has shifted, and they're usually focused on one thing."

"Like, in the case of somebody whose child was murdered, they want that person found."

"Something like that, yes."

She peered into the darkness, but it was almost impossible to see into the corners. "I can't see anything," she complained.

"Maybe you need to look with your vision too," Sebastian said in a dry tone from behind her.

She twisted to look up at him. "But I can't see like Hunter does."

"Then use your camera," Hunter said helpfully. "Think about what it is you want to see and then view it by giving yourself permission to see."

She studied both men's faces as she processed what each had said. "You're right. I only ever really saw when I had the camera at first, when I was looking deeper."

"Chances are the camera was a prop," Sebastian said. "You should try without it."

She turned once more to peer into the darkness, giving herself permission to see what she had always seen before, but nothing happened. Finally in frustration, she reached for her bag, pulled out her camera and took some pictures. She twisted, rolled, crouched, leaned over—completely immersed in whatever had gone on here. It would take time looking at the pictures on the computer to understand what she saw. But, as she delved deeper and deeper, she could see the forms showing up. And then, in the next several clicks, she saw the blue lines.

"It was a prison," she announced.

"What kind of prison?" Hunter asked.

She kept clicking as she viewed. "It was a single room.

Similar to what was in the other area but bigger and a very different purpose."

"And how many people are in here?"

She kept digging into her new vision. "I don't understand," she said. "Linnea said there were several prisoners, but I only saw one."

"Maybe Linnea meant over time there had been several prisoners. Is this where her sister was?"

"I want to nod and say yes, but I don't know that. I thought she meant the other room like this."

"But maybe she was pointing in this direction."

Too confused and turned around to understand which direction Linnea had been pointing, Lacey said, "At least I know she directed us here."

"Except for that barrier," Sebastian said, his tone mild. "Let's not forget that barrier you couldn't cross."

She sat back on her heels, dropped her camera into her lap and stared up at him. "I wonder if I should photograph the barrier now."

He looked at her in surprise. "What are you expecting to see?"

She frowned. "I'm not sure." She picked up the camera and photographed the area around them. She could see other buildings, other homes, walkways, roads. "It was a slum area here," she said, "not even the normal servant level. Or the everyday common man. It seems even lower income than that." She stopped, hearing what she said. "Did they have slums back then?"

"They had the same problems we do today," Sebastian said. "Every civilization does. There are always those who have more than others. And whether they have a caste system within the society or not, there will always be some people who have much less."

She nodded slowly. "That also explains why we're so far away from the touristy areas. This is one of the areas where the people who lived in this house had much less. But I believe, at one time, it was in better shape. I think, over time, these people lost what they had, and the place slowly fell into ruin around them."

"There could be all kinds of reasons why one home is worse for wear," Hunter said as he pulled himself out of the opening. "We also have to consider who was imprisoning these people—were his actions sanctioned by the law at the time or was he just an early sadistic serial killer?"

She nodded. "But there's an odd sense about this one. As if people were afraid of it."

"Again, think about today's society and somebody who's different and strange. Think about somebody who's got a disease that's physically disfiguring," he said. "And think how that would be way back when. People would have avoided that person, would have moved quickly past him, whatever to avoid coming close. They could even have murdered him because of the disfiguration. People were very superstitious, and fear drove many of their actions."

She nodded. "How sad is that though?"

"It's no different than today," Hunter said. "You might want to think society in the Western world is nice and pretty, but it's not. Anybody with a handicap or a very visible disfiguration will tell you people are cruel. That life for them is not the easy life we would like to think they have."

She slowly lowered her camera again. "I see that even in classrooms," she said slowly. "As much as you hate to witness it, there's always a child who doesn't fit in, always a child who has something wrong—whether it's, you know, a disorder, like Tourette's, or coming back to school after cancer treatments with no hair, or even birthmarks that are scarring or very visible." She lifted her camera, seeing in her lens the images from days gone by. "I can envision people racing past this corner. They're almost holding their noses, as if the smell is too strong."

"Which could mean all kinds of things," Sebastian said. "They were very clean people. Imagine if you didn't have any way to remove human waste because you were too poor to have proper tunnels built or any other way to remove it."

What if somebody was murdered here?" Hunter asked. "How would they dispose of the body? Maybe they just buried it in the garden, and the rot is what people would smell."

Her face twisted up at the thought. "You're not making me feel better."

Hunter laughed. "Remember that, whatever happened, happened a long time ago. And there's nothing you can do to help them right now."

She nodded. "I know. It is a good puzzle though." She slowly made her way to her feet and turned to look the way they had come. "Would you both mind walking back to that barrier with me? I'd love to take pictures and maybe see what it is."

"If you can take a picture of it and see what it is," Hunter said, "does that mean the barrier was there way back when?"

She thought about it and looked at him. "I don't know," she said honestly. "I couldn't tell you. I'd still like to see it again." She twisted to look up at Sebastian, realizing he held out a hand. Slowly they made their way to where the barrier had been. She kept a hand in front of her, just in case, so she didn't walk into it. When she stepped up to where she thought it was and kept going another ten feet, she turned and looked at him. "Is it gone?"

Sebastian turned to study the area and then shrugged. "Maybe?"

"That makes no sense. Why would it be here before and not now?"

Hunter came up behind them. "Because you found this area. Somebody was probably stopping you from finding it, and, now that you have, there's no point in expending the energy to keep it up."

"How the hell does one even do that?" she asked in amazement. "As humans we can't, so why the hell would we be able to do it as spirits?"

"When it's your turn to try, you let us know," Sebastian said drily. "You have to remember there is no precedence for this. There is no text we can refer to. No ancient words of wisdom that give us the answers."

At that, she nodded. "I'm sorry. I keep expecting you guys to have all the answers, don't I?" She walked forward a few more feet, then said, "I'm sure this is where we were stopped on the other side. So I think it must be gone." She turned and walked back toward them. Almost instantly she hit the barrier. She froze and reached out a hand. It wouldn't let her pass.

"Can you see me?" she called out.

Sebastian frowned and stepped forward. "I can see you. Can you not come toward me?"

She shook her head. Knowing that he would reach across to help her again, she pulled out her camera, stepped back, taking photographs to see what that barrier was. But the more she took, the less she could see, like everything blurred in front of her. She rubbed her eyes. "Everything's becoming paler and blurry, less distinct."

"It could be that you're picking up the energy buzz," Sebastian said. He grabbed a hold of Hunter's arm and walked them both through the barrier. "I suggest we call it quits for the day or find something else to look at."

She reached up, feeling her head boom. "I think I already did too much." She winced. "My head is really aching now."

He gently lifted the camera away from her hands and pulled the bag off her shoulder while she rubbed her forehead, trying to control the pain now slamming hard against her temples. He put the camera away, put the shoulder bag on his own shoulder, then hooked her arm through his and said, "That's enough for today. It's late. Let's walk back to the apartment."

She glanced at Hunter to see him nodding in agreement. With a final glance at the barrier and then at the hill behind them, she said, "Will you guys remember where this is?"

Hunter held up his phone and said, "I recorded the coordinates."

"Both places?"

He chuckled. "Both for the barrier and for the jail room. Now let's get you back where you can lie down. You're not used to doing all this energy work. And it's taking its toll on you."

She nodded. "I can't say I feel all that great." She took several steps forward and found herself using Sebastian's arm for support. She stopped, took several deep breaths and said, "Why am I so weak? I need to sit down for a minute to rest."

Sebastian helped to lower her to the ground. She sat for

several moments, taking many deep breaths, looking around, trying to understand why she felt queasy. "My stomach is nauseated."

He popped a bottle of water into her hand. "You don't have water with you again. Remember how you're supposed to always have water with you?"

She nodded. "Sorry. I must have forgotten. I didn't remember to bring lunch either."

"Have you not eaten?" Hunter asked sharply.

"Only half a sandwich. But it didn't sit well. That's when I saw the other apparition this morning."

"That was hours ago. As in *many*." Hunter slipped the backpack off his shoulder and crouched in front of her. He pulled out a granola bar and handed it to her. "You can't be without food for so long either," he admonished.

She groaned. "Normally I'm good at taking care of myself. You know that, right?"

"We'll stay here for a few minutes while you eat and get some water down. Then we'll continue so we can get you out of the heat," Sebastian said.

She sat for several minutes and ate the granola bar. When it was gone, she handed the wrapper back to Hunter. "Thank you." Slowly she sipped the water until it was all gone. Using Sebastian's hand again, she stood, giving him a bright smile. "I feel much better."

The three turned and walked back toward the Stabian Gate.

She took another ten steps, then she gripped his arm and whispered, "Sebastian, ... help ..."

He turned as she pitched forward and blacked out.

"WHOA," SEBASTIAN SAID as he caught her in his arms and slowly lowered her to the ground.

Hunter was at his side, already running his hands over her frame.

"I don't know what just happened," Sebastian said. "But something did."

"Look at her stomach," Hunter said.

Sebastian studied her exposed abdomen, going so far as to lift up her T-shirt to her ribs. "Outside of the fact a ton of energy is right here, what am I looking at?"

"The energy is dark, cloudy," Hunter said, using his hand to brush it away from her aura.

"A faint line of black runs all the way through her system." Sebastian did the same as Hunter to remove the cloudy energy. "She had captured some dark energy in one of her earlier photos. Of course she didn't know what to call them yet, just saying they were smudges caught on film. It was the only part of her visions that I could see in any of the photographs. I can only guess it is related to my ability to read auras."

"Are we thinking this particular black energy is from the spirit roaming the Pompeii site? Or from that opening in the ground? Or from the barrier?"

"My guess," Sebastian said, "would be the barrier. She walked right through it from that side to this. I think with me there, when we went the other way, it helped to protect her somehow. Maybe my psychic protections already in place protect her when we touch each other. But, when she went back through, she had no protection. She didn't even feel it, did she?"

"No, she didn't appear to. She walked right through it and turned around. When she tried to come back, she came up against it."

"So it's a one-way gate. Interesting."

"And you held on to me when we came back. But I might have been able to have come through without your assistance, like Lacey did, as long as we are headed in this direction, leaving the jail room cave-in," Hunter said. "But we definitely needed you to open the gate enough to let us through."

"I'm not even sure that I opened the gate as much as the gate let us through on a vibrational level."

Hunter made a strangled exclamation.

Sebastian looked up at him. "What?"

"Look at her face."

The black energy had formed around her chin, like a mask. "Oh, my God! Look at that," Sebastian whispered. He leaned forward, his hand trying to remove the black energy, but it had locked down, the energy firmer, denser, more substantial.

Hunter reached up as well. Together they tried to clear away the darkness. But the mask became almost solid right before their eyes. "We have to get that off of her," Sebastian yelled. He placed his hands along her throat, coming up underneath the mask.

Hunter did the same from the topmost edge of the mask, coming down. "At least if we can block it from forming around her chin, that would be something," Hunter said. "But I've never seen anything like this."

"Neither have I," Sebastian whispered. His hands were busy inching beneath the darkness forming. "You can see the detail. The markings, the detailed metal work."

"Are we really thinking this will become a permanent mask?"

"I don't know," Sebastian said. "But it's giving it a damn good try."

"We have to get it off," Hunter said. He closed his eyes. "I'm calling on a healer to help."

"You can do that?" Sebastian asked looking around for someone he was trying to contact only to realize he was contacting someone on an energetic level. "Stefan?"

"No, Dr. Maddy," he whispered. "Leave me to do it."

Sebastian watched as energy poured through Hunter's hands—clean, pure, loving energy, into Lacey's system. "I don't know what you're doing," Sebastian said, "but do more."

Hunter gave a broken laugh and whispered, "I'm trying. I'm trying."

Sebastian used his own energy to go into Lacey's aura, sliding in as deep and as low as he could to come inside from her skin to the mask. What he didn't want was for the mask to seal atop her. He recognized the markings on it now. It looked exactly like the one she had drawn on him in her sketchbook. The fact that it was in visible form in front of him terrified him. It looked like it wanted to cover both her mouth and her nose. He didn't know if it would stop her from breathing or not, but it was way too dangerous to even consider.

Finally it seemed like Hunter's energy overpowered the darkness, so it was incapable of latching tight enough to seal around her.

Sebastian's own energy was smoothed across her skin, coming up underneath the mask. Then he gave it a hard blast, splintering the darkness up and away from her. He wanted to pick her up and race her back to the apartment, but he knew the energy, being energy, could easily follow them and reform at any time. He placed his hand on her heart chakra and surged more energy into her system, as much as he could, filling it with warm loving energy.

"Can you add your energy to mine?" he whispered to Hunter. "We need to somehow send a message to that darkness that it can't come back to her."

"I'm working on it," Hunter said.

Before long she was completely enveloped in a glowing, healing, healthy ball of energy. The men sat back on their heels and studied her for a long moment.

"She looks much better," Hunter said.

"Yeah, well, what the hell was that mask? And why did it go after her?"

"Either she's more vulnerable or she's connected to something we don't understand here. Whatever it was, we have to make sure it doesn't come back after her."

"And how do we do that?" Sebastian asked in a harsh voice. "Nothing going on here is normal, whether it's psychic or not. I don't know what that mask is all about. No one who's seen the sketches she drew knew of any historical reference to them. I've never heard of anybody in Pompeii or that society using masks like this."

"No. You have to wonder if it doesn't have something to do with the prisoners she keeps talking about."

"And Linnea. Maybe somebody else can contact Linnea and get clarification of what's going on?"

Hunter nodded. "It's possible. I just don't know if it's reasonable. Lots of other people speak with the dead. The fact is, for whatever reason, Linnea has a connection to Lacey. And it's her that she wants to talk to."

"But what if it's Linnea who led us here?"

"Oh, there's no doubt Linnea led us here," Hunter said.

"The problem is, do we trust her? Was she trying to save her sister? Trying to save herself? Or was she in cahoots with whoever is the jailer here?"

"She better not be," Sebastian said. "We have to find a way to separate her intentions now from what happened back then."

"And for that, we'll have Lacey contact her. But Lacey needs to go through some training to help protect herself. She left herself wide open, and obviously something took advantage."

CHAPTER 18

LACEY WOKE UP to find both men leaning over her. She gave a yelp and tried to move away. Both men reared back, and yet, at the same time, Sebastian outstretched a hand and said, "Take it easy. You passed out on us."

She shook her head. "Why would that happen?" The grim look on his face had her heart pounding. She put a shaky hand to her forehead. "I'm not hurt, am I?"

Both men shook their heads.

"But something happened." She hazarded a guess from the looks on their face. "Did you see something happen?"

"You weren't feeling good. You complained about a headache. We made you eat and drink water, and you said you felt fine. We took ten steps, and you collapsed, just pitched forward onto the ground—actually on me." Sebastian crouched beside her. His gaze wandered over her face as if checking her color, seeing how she looked.

"I feel fine." She held out her hand, and he helped her to a sitting position.

"Take it easy," he said. "Don't move too quickly. We don't want you passing out again."

She wrinkled her face. "This is really not like me."

"Maybe not like your life in the US, but it does appear to be who and what you are here."

She hated to hear that. "I'm not neurotic. I don't understand what's going on." As she watched the two men exchange a glance, she narrowed her gaze. "Tell me. What did you see when I was out?" When Sebastian hesitated, she shook her head at him. "Don't hide anything from me. It just makes what I'm imagining much worse."

He gave a one-shoulder shrug. "A black energy formed around your face. For several long moments, we tried to brush it away. Then it appeared to be the mask you drew in the pictures."

She stared at him in confusion. "A black energy mask?"

Hunter picked up the story. "You definitely had black energy in your belly region after you passed through the barrier the second time, alone. And then we could see a streak of it running down to your toes and up to your head. But, at your head, it seemed to collect and form into a mask. It was hard to move. We only freed it off your face by sliding our energy under and through it, then filling your heart chakra so full of light that there wasn't room for any of this darkness."

She dropped her gaze to stare at her fingers, wondering how her world had gone so completely off-the-wall crazy. "I don't even know what to say," she murmured. The thought of that mask she had drawn on Sebastian's face was just recently on hers had her terrified. "I didn't feel anything, or at least I don't feel anything now."

"And that's a good thing," Sebastian said cheerfully. "Remember it was energy. It wasn't like there was this big metal mask on your face."

She smiled at that. "Thank heavens, but still it's very disconcerting. Let me try walking about." She stood slowly, then took several tentative steps, turned and smiled. "The world isn't spinning. I feel fine. Not faint at all."

Hunter handed her a bottle of water and said, "Have some more water. Then we'll get you back to the apartment."

She took several sips of water, relieved when it went down her throat just fine. She returned the water bottle to him. "Thanks. That was good." She turned around, looking to see where they were headed and frowned. "I'm not sure which direction we're going in."

Sebastian gently slid an arm across her shoulders. "You're coming with me," he said. "I'll get you home."

She nodded and walked beside him, Hunter on the other side of her. "What do you think it all means?"

"I'm not sure," Sebastian said, "but, if I have to hazard a guess, I'd say somebody was using these masks, potentially on prisoners for whatever reason, and is now hunting the Earth, looking for more victims."

Her footsteps faltered. She could hardly catch a breath. Her chest clamped down so tight that she could hardly breathe.

Hunter slapped her hard on the back and ordered, "Don't panic now. Breathe."

She stopped, took several deep breaths and said, "I know I asked for the truth, but, holy crap, that's scary shit." Her gaze went from one man's face to the other, and both of them looked at her solemnly. "Do you really believe something so bizarre could be happening?"

Hunter shrugged. "Yes. I've seen it before."

"No," she corrected, "you've seen something *like this* before. But you haven't seen *this* before."

He tilted his head in acknowledgment. "But, once you see something weird and bizarre, you don't dismiss other incidents quite so fast or so easily. Life isn't that simple. We don't know all the answers."

"It would be nice if we did." She took several more slow steps forward, relieved when her body stood strong and firm. Feeling slightly better, she took several more steps, continuing in the direction they had been headed. "But to even think an entity's out here—and, I mean, a *nasty* entity—trying to find more potential prisoners is dumbfounding."

"Remember that serial killers, pedophiles—God-only-knows-what kind of dredges of society they were back then—even as spirits, they're still who they were when they were alive. Just because they died didn't make them miraculously wonderful people."

She wrinkled her nose. "And here I was, believing everybody who died had a golden gate, like my mother, and would step across it and be so much better off."

"A lot of people don't find that golden gate or cross over."

"Even if they did cross over, you're saying they still don't necessarily become perfect beings?"

"Exactly. As far as we can tell, everybody is here to learn along their journey. What part of that journey you have made it to determines who and what you get to come back as."

"Scary thought," she said. "I've never really believed in reincarnation myself."

"No, but you probably will now," he said. "Think about it. What's the chance you are Linnea?"

That was another hard physical blow. She was left gasping in its wake.

He took several steps forward, but she couldn't even begin to move. "That can't be possible," she cried out. "That would mean I was talking to her spirit, which would also be me."

He quirked an eyebrow at her and grinned. "Mind-bending, isn't it? Maybe you are connected in another way—like her reincarnated sister Sabine? Or one of her other sisters?"

"Maybe. That's a better explanation than being the reincarnation of Linnea. Because, if I were her, it would still be her spirit inside me. And I wouldn't see her outside myself." Even that confused the hell out of her. She twisted her mouth into a grimace, figuring out what she was saying.

Hunter said, "It is possible but not likely. But it would be a snapshot of her who you were speaking to. Almost like a holographic image. And she'd be connecting to something in your own mind, pulling out this past-life information."

She stared at him, shook her head and walked away. It was just too much. All of it was too much. *A holographic image snapshot?* Wasn't it enough that they were already talking about past lives, invisible barriers and black energy masks without going further? She didn't know what to say and figured silence was the best bet while all that information rolled around in the back of her head. It was so far-fetched that she struggled to believe any of it. And yet, no doubt she had passed out. What had happened while she'd been unconscious? Well, she didn't know.

Also a weird buzz continued in the back of her head, but she didn't dare mention it to the men. They already looked at her strangely, as if afraid some sort of black cloud would take her over again. The thought terrified her. Especially since she had been insensate at the time. It was one thing to consider facing evil while you were awake and aware and yet another thing entirely to be vulnerable while you were not yourself or unconscious, where the evil-doer could do whatever they wanted to you. She kept touching around her mouth, as if afraid the energy of the mask would return. She could visualize it all too easily because she had drawn the sketch of it.

Why not a mask on her face? Why a mask on Sebastian in her drawing, for that matter? What did the mask mean? "There were two masks."

"Yes, you drew two masks," Sebastian said. "I did get some information from Bruno." He filled in about the jailer, Tialox, possibly being the grave his team had opened at the Mayan ruins.

"That's terrifying. How can the two even be related?" She shook her head. "No, I don't know why. Did you see one or two on me?"

"Only one," Sebastian said. "The same one you drew on my face."

She stared off in the distance but kept her feet moving forward. "There must be different meanings behind the masks."

"That would make sense," Hunter said. "But what the meanings are is a little beyond me at the moment."

"I want to see those images again," she snapped.

"We can do that."

She shoved her hands in her pockets and then froze. She spun around, caught sight of her camera on Sebastian's shoulder and sighed with relief. "I forgot. I thought for a moment there I'd lost my camera."

He patted the strap on his shoulder where it hung securely. "No. I wouldn't do that to you. We've got it safe and sound."

She gave him as bright a smile as she could and spun around to keep walking. Now if only that damn buzzing in the back of her head would go away. She slowly rotated her neck to ease the tension building with every step she took. "Do we need to stop at the site to talk to the others?"

"By this time, they're packing up for the day," Sebastian said calmly. "We'll see them at the apartment. If we don't meet up with them on the road."

"That would be good," she said. "I feel bad if I'm not pulling my weight."

"You need to worry about yourself in a whole different way," Hunter said. "Forget about the camera at the moment."

"I can't do that," she said simply. "I have a job to do. I'm not about to let it be forgotten because there's so much other chaos."

"I appreciate that," Sebastian said mildly. "But we can't have you making yourself sick with all this other stuff. You can't do your work if you're sick."

She winced. "Good point. I have to admit I'm hungry now too."

"Again?"

She shot Hunter a puzzled look. "It's been hours since we ate." When the two men exchanged looks, she frowned. "Now what?" she asked in exasperation. "It's really irritating when the two of you have this private conversation, and then you don't share it with me."

"You just ate a granola bar," Hunter said gently.

She waved her hand at him. "That was completely nothing. I could easily eat ten of them." Up ahead she recognized one of the main tourist areas they had come through. "Now that I know where we are, we weren't all that far away from the dig itself, were we?"

"No," Sebastian said. "Maybe that was the same room

Linnea had been pointing out earlier, the doorless one."

"I don't know," Lacey said. "I'll have to think on it. Maybe, when I come in tomorrow, I can see if that's what she was talking about. The thing is, we did locate another unique find, and maybe that's important archaeologically?" She twisted slightly so she could look at Sebastian's face. But the thunderous expression on his features made her doubt it.

"No," Sebastian said. "That's not something I'm willing to open up to the public. And we can't excavate because permits are required first."

"But we just explored it on some level," Lacey argued.

"It's typical government bureaucracy," he said with a shake of his head. "You have to have permits for everything. And a whole new dig site area requires permission."

"But it *is* open," Hunter said. "I'm not advocating making it an excavation site. But it wouldn't hurt to have a little more in-depth look."

"I'm in," Lacey said.

"No," both men snapped.

Sebastian added, "*You're* not going down there."

She glared at them. "Why not?"

"You're too susceptible. The energy wants you. Therefore you are the last person allowed to get close to it." Sebastian said. "I don't know what's going on with you yet, but I don't want you anywhere close to that place."

"I would like to go back, once the black-energy masks are completely taken care of," she said. "I also want to see what my photos captured. That should be interesting." She turned to look at him. "You never thought to take pictures of my face with that bloody mask, did you?"

He shook his head. "No. We were too busy saving you."

She smiled up at him. "Nice to know you care," she

teased.

He just slanted a look at her.

That had heat rolling up her cheeks. "I didn't mean it *that* way."

He chuckled, wrapped an arm around her shoulders and tugged her close. "You can't know how I feel about you."

She pushed away from him. "No way I would know how you feel about me." She shook her head. "Outside of the fact that I'm an oddity and some kind of a magnet for this bullshit energy, I can also see images that might show how buildings looked back then. But other than that, no. Hell no. I don't know anything about how you feel about me."

Hunter chuckled and took several steps away from the pair so he was farther ahead.

"You don't have to run away," she said.

"Oh, yeah, I do," Hunter said. "These kinds of conversations are painful when it involves two people. It's even more painful if three are here. I'm no third wheel for anybody."

"Chicken," she called to his receding back.

Sebastian squeezed her shoulders gently.

She turned her glare at him. "You shouldn't be chasing him away."

"I didn't chase him away," Sebastian protested. "He left on his own."

She rolled her eyes. "But you turned this into a personal conversation."

"Good," he said. "It's time."

She deepened her glare. "There isn't a relationship. You hardly know me."

He smiled the sweetest of smiles and said, "True, but I do know what I like, and I know what counts."

She shook her head. "You can't be serious?" She paused

275

long enough for him to argue with her, but he didn't. "So far, I've been nothing but a weak, fainting, crazy woman. Who wants to spend time with someone like that?"

He laughed out loud. "Me, for one."

"Or is it that you think I can tell you something about the civilization from a long time ago," she said, suddenly very tired. "Because I like you. I have to admit you're a very sexy beast, but I'm not sure I'm ready for a relationship."

"We'll deal with that one step at a time," he said calmly. "But you need to understand it has nothing to do with what you can see or can't see. I like who you are, just as you are." He slipped his fingers through hers, as he had many times before, and held her hand as they walked forward.

She stared at their linked fingers, wondering, because he had done this right from the first moment. "Do you think past lives matter in relationships today?"

"They do indeed," he said softly, squeezing her fingers. "And I like the *sexy beast* comment."

"Did you have a past life here?"

He nodded. "Absolutely. But I haven't ever been able to get any details."

"Would we have known each other back then?"

"Experts say, if you're drawn to certain people, that you still have things to work out. In that case it's likely karma rearing its head. The other possibility is that we're drawn to people we had strong relationships with back then, and that bond is still with us."

"Karma is a scary thought," she said with a laugh. "Because you can do your best and still feel like you're doing a shitty job. I've always tried to be a nice person. But you don't know what you've done in past lifetimes. To think there's this big cesspool of behavior you didn't know about—some crap that you might have done when you were a less-than-nice person—yet it's coming around to bite you in the ass. That is not something I want to contemplate."

He chuckled. "Trust you to think along that line. Everybody else wants to know whether they were royalty or pirates or politicians or movie stars."

At that, she laughed out loud. "I doubt I was. I was probably what I've always been—a simple woman with simple tastes."

"Oh, I doubt it." His voice was serious. "We can take on both female and male physical forms in past lives, in order to experience in greater depth the human life as we live it."

"That would be fun," she said, laughing. "I guess you can do a past-life regression too. Or maybe not. I'm not sure I would want to. What if my past was explosive and difficult?"

"Why would you say that?" he asked, frowning down at her.

She shrugged. "Because nothing about this Linnea stuff is easy. I want to believe she is everything I feel she is. But I don't know how she could be, and yet, still have all this darkness around her. Or this mask stuff and that wall, that barrier. What the hell was that all about? So much here is hard to understand. And how does any of it relate to the dig and things like the broken tools and stolen tools?"

"I don't know," Sebastian admitted. "That's what brought me here this last time. To keep an eye on the site and to figure out what exactly was happening. Instead I got sidelined with you."

"I'm sorry," she said. "I didn't mean to take you away from your work."

"It's not taking me away from my work," he said gently,

"because I'm pretty damn sure it's all connected. I just have to figure out how. And, like everything, when tearing stuff apart, it looks messier until you put things back together again. It's only then that we'll find out exactly what's going on here and who's behind all of it."

"You think somebody's behind it all?" she said, her footsteps slowing as she turned to look up at him. "Is it one of us?"

He shrugged, his lips twisting into a lopsided grin. "Maybe," he said. "It definitely involves you. That we know for sure." He leaned over and kissed her.

IT WAS ALL Sebastian could do to get her back to her apartment building, especially when she demanded to walk on her own two feet. Sebastian frowned at Hunter but otherwise kept his gaze locked on her. She was groggy and shaky still. By the time he had her inside, he'd taken her to his place.

She sagged onto the couch and shot him a look. "I can't say I'm feeling very good again," she confessed.

"Just rest," Hunter said, sitting down beside her.

Sebastian walked into the kitchen and poured her a large glass of cold water and brought it to her. "Do you need to see Juan?"

She looked at him blankly.

"The doctor?"

She shook her head. "No. Unless he's a spiritual doctor."

"No," Sebastian said, "he's not. He's a regular flesh-and-blood doctor."

"I don't think whatever's wrong with me is a flesh-and-blood issue."

"You don't know though," he said. "It could be your electrolytes are off balance, making you dizzy."

Her grin slipped out, charming him, even as it disappeared quickly again. "He's more likely to label me a lunatic when I tell him about the things I see and that barrier I went through, even before I get to the black-energy mask."

Sebastian frowned, tapping his foot gently on the floor as he contemplated the issue. "We really do need somebody who is more of a psychic healer."

Even as Hunter nodded, she chuckled at the thought. And then she realized they appeared to be serious. "Are you for real right now?" she asked.

Sebastian nodded. "Absolutely. I mean, if there are psychic investigators and mediums and all the rest of the psychic specialties out there, there must also be psychic healers."

"I do know somebody," Hunter said, "but she's extremely busy."

"And we won't bother her," Lacey said firmly. "Nothing's wrong with me."

"Something is definitely wrong with you," Hunter said. "But I'm not sure it's serious. I think it's more about your energy needing to rise to the vibrational level being required of it."

She stared at him, her mouth dropping open, and then she slowly closed it, reached for the water and drank half of it in one gulp. "I'm going to forget you just said that." She looked at Sebastian. "I need food. Remember how I had almost no lunch. I'm probably just feeling the effects of the heat and the lack of food and water too." She held up the half-empty glass, then finished the rest of the water and handed it to him. "Refill please."

He obediently refilled it for her and came back watching

as her energy faded quickly.

"I'm not sure I'm up to going anywhere right now." She glanced around and yawned. "Maybe I should have a nap instead of food."

"No, you need food," Hunter said. "At least another granola bar."

"Do you carry anything else in that backpack of yours?"

He shrugged. "Only food that's packable and easy to travel with."

She nodded. "The others are all going out for dinner soon, right?"

Sebastian checked his watch. "They should be showering right now."

She thought about it. "If I have a quick nap and a shower, then we can all go together."

"I'm not sure that's a good idea," Sebastian said.

"It is a good idea," she insisted. "You need to make things as normal as possible."

"Why is that?" Hunter asked.

"Because there's already unrest with me supposedly too attached to Sebastian. It's never a good idea for the newest employee to come and have an affair with the boss man," she said drily. "And, although that might be fun, it isn't exactly what's happening, and I don't like the insinuations or the suspicions that something like that is going on."

"Work romances happen all over the place," Hunter said. "It's hardly an issue here. And what does anybody else care? You're both consenting adults."

Sebastian was interested in her answer. He was also interested in what she'd said earlier because he thought an affair would be just fine too. But he wasn't sure she was ready for that.

"We are consenting adults, but I do get a sense of unrest because of us being together so much," she said. "The jokes are more pointed, as if people are not happy about it. I didn't come over here to cause trouble. I had hoped to have a wonderful vacation, fulfilling a dream for me, not living this nightmare I'm currently embroiled in."

"Understood," Sebastian agreed. "But, like Hunter said, even if we were dating, there's no reason anybody else should be upset about it."

"But they are though, aren't they?" She put him on the spot.

He nodded slowly. "From the sideways glances, the nudging and some of the tones when people speak with me, potentially yes. But I'm not sure why."

"Neither am I," she said, stifling a yawn.

"Let's get you back to your place so you can nap, take a quick shower, then we can all go out for dinner," Sebastian said. He turned to Hunter. "Do you want to join us?"

Hunter was already up and walking toward the front door. "No, I'm fine. I'll see you later tonight." And he walked out.

Sebastian helped Lacey to her feet and walked her to the door. Outside he led her down the hall to the other apartment.

"You know if we walk in together that they'll say something."

"It doesn't matter what they say," he said briskly. He opened the door, and the conversation that had been light and jovial came to a screeching halt. He led Lacey inside and motioned to her bedroom. "Remember what the doctor said. Take a nap, then a shower before we go out for dinner."

Chana jumped to her feet and came running over. "Did

she have another accident?"

"No, but she passed out on the trail," Sebastian said. "The head injury appears to still be an issue."

Chana led Lacey into the bedroom and out of sight.

Sebastian turned and looked around at the rest of them, gathered together before dinnertime. "It seems like the entire gang is here," he said lightly. "That's a good thing. I'm asking you to keep an eye on Lacey, in case she passes out again."

"Should she even be out there if she's in danger?" Mark asked. "That's hardly safe for her or for us."

"I don't think it'll be an issue after this, but she didn't eat her lunch and neither did she have water." Somebody snorted in the background. He wasn't sure who. "She wasn't prepared, and we all know what that means. In this case hopefully she's learned her lesson, but, combined with the head injury, I don't want any more incidents." He checked his watch. "I've got time to grab a shower myself. I presume dinner is at the usual time?"

"We're thinking about pushing it back a bit, if that's all right with you," Tom said.

"Better for Lacey definitely," Sebastian said, "and easier for me too, considering I haven't showered yet. I'll be back in about an hour and a half then."

He walked out, staying close to the door in the hall, but he couldn't hear the conversations going on inside. In his own apartment he stopped at the door, surprised to see Jeremiah in the living room. "Hey," Sebastian said, striding forward. "I wondered where you got to."

"Bloody business stuff," Jeremiah said. "How's the girl?"

Sebastian shrugged, not sure if Jeremiah meant after today's incident or just in general. "She's improving," he prevaricated. "But we certainly had a bizarre day."

"I hear you there." He motioned at the books on the table in front of him. "That mask drawing is downright freaky."

Sebastian flipped a chair around and sat on it backward, facing Jeremiah. "Let me tell you what happened." And he told him about Lacey's experience with the black energy and the mask forming on her face.

Jeremiah was stunned. "Holy shit. This is happening all over again, isn't it?"

"I'm hoping not. But I can't tell yet. Although there were no masks back then – at least none I saw."

"We don't want to wait until it's so bad that we *can* tell," Jeremiah said.

"But what can we do?" Sebastian's tone was heavy. "We saw it happen in front of us ten years ago, and we couldn't stop it then. What are you expecting we can do this time?"

"She's going to die, you know," Jeremiah stated.

Sebastian's heart clenched. He gave a hard shake of his head. "Not if I can stop it."

Jeremiah searched Sebastian's gaze. "You're sweet on her, aren't you?"

"I'm not exactly sure what I am," he said in a short-tempered tone. "But I would like to know where our relationship stands and what we have and where we may be going, and I need time for that to develop."

"That energy didn't give us any damn time at all at the Mayan site. From the very first, we knew something super-natural was going on. We had people dying shortly thereafter, like in a handful of days."

"I know," Sebastian said. "And, from that time frame perspective, it looks like we're heading into more serious events than minor accidents and broken or missing tools. However we have no proof that these two events are going to follow the same timeframe."

"How can you say that?" Jeremiah asked. "Since she first saw these buildings, it's already been six days. For all you know, people will start dying tonight."

"Things are similar but different. Nothing from then can be used as anything as a guide. No one has died yet, for one."

Sebastian hoped not. He hoped nobody would die. But he knew he definitely didn't have any plan in place to stop an attack so fast. After all, at the Mayan site, all they saw was the negative energy. One very strong and powerful male energy and very, very, *very* angry. "I have to send a message." He pulled out his phone and sent Stefan an update on the situation. As he pocketed his phone, Sebastian said, "I'll grab a shower, and then we'll join the crew for dinner."

Jeremiah nodded. "I'm not going though," he said. "I don't like being around so many people. And I don't want to get to know anybody any better. They're all going to die."

CHAPTER 19

SOMEHOW LACEY MANAGED to grab a fifteen-minute power nap. When she woke up, she had to admit that she felt a hell of a lot better. She made her way to the shower and adjusted it to a cool-water spray, quickly rinsing off, not wanting to hold everybody up for dinner. By the time she was dressed again and went out to the living room, it was to find the others impatiently waiting.

Chana jumped to her feet. "There you are."

Lacey smiled at her. "Done and ready to go."

The others grumbled a little, but they all raced to the door.

"I gather everybody's hungry," Lacey said lightly.

Mark nodded. "Absolutely."

They filed out one at a time. Chana waited for Lacey to go ahead of her and then locked up the apartment behind them. Lacey couldn't help looking down the hall to see where Sebastian was.

Chana grabbed her arm and pulled her forward. "Forget about the boss."

"I get that nobody's happy we're friends," she said, "but I don't understand why anybody would really be against it. It's not like we're sleeping together, even though we are consenting adults. We're both single and available."

"I think it's that *currying favor* kind of thing that pisses

285

them all off," Chana said.

"I'm only here for a couple weeks or so. It's hard to curry lasting favor when I'll be gone before the month's end. I'm not on the payroll. I'm not trying to climb within the foundation," Lacey said in a dry tone. "And, to repeat, we *aren't* sleeping together."

Outside the heat wave slammed into her again. It took her several moments of deep breathing to catch her breath; then she followed along behind Chana.

"Good point but, for some reason, ever since you've gotten here, there's been nothing but problems."

"That's not fair either. The problems started before I arrived," Lacey said quietly. "And I would do anything to have changed the impression of me as being some weak, scatterbrained, accident-prone female because that's not who I am. But, since I've been here, I know I've given nothing but a bad impression to everyone."

"Well, the longer you stay without any more problems on the site," Chana said, deliberately keeping her tone light and bubbly, "that perception will change."

"Like I can stop the things happening on the site," Lacey grumbled.

They walked into a new restaurant for Lacey. "What do you guys have, a group of favorite restaurants you rotate through?"

"Absolutely," Chana said. "We're going upstairs on the balcony. It's beautiful up there."

Lacey was happy to know they were headed upstairs where there was room for all of them, and she found Sebastian already seated. He patted the chair beside him. She glanced at Chana to find her studiously looking away. Lacey thought about sitting elsewhere, for all of a split second, then realized she really did want to sit with him. And, if everybody else had a problem with it, well, that was *their* problem. Too bad. She walked over to Sebastian and sat down.

"You look better," he said.

She smiled. "Thanks. I feel better."

And, for the rest of the meal, things seemed normal. She could eat, and her stomach wasn't touchy. The heat didn't bother her; the conversation appeared to be light and friendly. All in all, it was a great social gathering.

When they were done, she went to stand up with the rest of the group, heading off to a pub. But Sebastian held her down in her chair. "I need to speak with you."

She glanced over at Chana, who shrugged and walked away.

"Go with them if you want." He stared deep into her eyes. "Is that what you want?" He withdrew his hand.

She sighed, and, being honest with herself and him also, she said, "No, that's not what I want. It always seems so awkward, and I don't like that."

"I don't either," he said. "And I don't know why it would be."

"Maybe if they just accepted that we're friends, it would be easier."

He gave her a warm grin.

"What did you want to speak to me about?"

"I suggest you don't go to the site tomorrow."

She frowned up at him. "That would not make me happy," she said in confusion. "That's the whole reason I came here."

"I get that, but you keep getting injured. And your body needs a chance to heal. A day of rest would do that for you."

Inside she could feel something urging her to ignore

him. She frowned, her finger tracing the pattern on the tablecloth in front of her. "See my mind says that's okay, but my heart is disappointed. And something inside me says I have to go."

"Where's that feeling coming from?"

She placed her hand over her solar plexus.

He nodded. "If you're going tomorrow, I want to go with you," he said shortly. "I don't want you alone at any time."

She wrinkled her face up at him. "When I get caught up in my pictures, in my photographing daze, it can last for hours, which would be boring for anyone tagging along."

"I've seen you," he confessed. "I often wondered what you see behind that lens."

"Very different things than you apparently," she said with a light laugh.

Just then their waiter came back around, offering more drinks. Sebastian ordered more wine for the two of them.

She smiled and said, "This is almost a date."

"We can classify it as a date, if you'd like."

"I don't think dates are supposed to be optional. Either it is or it isn't," she said with a laugh. "As it started with a gathering of coworkers, I hardly think this classifies."

"But sitting here and having a glass of wine under the moonlight definitely does." He lifted his glass, clinking it gently with hers. "To us and many more interesting conversations."

She smiled, clinked her glass back, and they both took sips of the wine. Her face scrunched up. It still tasted off. Placing her glass down, she settled back. "What do you think it means that I have to go in tomorrow?" She played with the long stem of the wineglass.

"I don't know, but I suspect whatever is happening is building to something big," he said.

"Is that what happened at your old site ten years ago?"

He nodded. "It seemed like there was nothing, nothing, nothing, and then things happened that we couldn't really get a handle on. So we didn't think they were major at first. But, all of a sudden, things became major, and then they became deadly."

"And how does that correlate to what's going on right now?"

"I'd say we're in the major stage."

She could feel all the heat blanching from her skin. "That doesn't leave much time before things get deadly."

"In the first case, it was very fast," he said. "I can't guarantee that this dig site will suffer the same scenario, the same time frame, or if, indeed, this will exactly follow the same pattern, but we had less than a handful of days from the time we really clued in to the strangeness of what was going on before things got deadly."

"And how many people died?"

He took a deep breath and said, "Four."

She could feel the breath leaving her chest. "That's a lot of people."

He nodded softly. "It is indeed."

"And did you also have multiple spirits back then?"

He dropped his gaze to the table, and then he shook his head. "I'm not sure because we weren't really aware of what supernatural events were going on. We didn't recognize the signs early enough. And, by the time we did, all we saw was the negative energy. One very strong and powerful male energy as far as we could tell. A very, *very* angry energy."

"Because you opened his dig site?"

"Who knows? It's not like the entity discussed any of this with us."

"Understood." She took another sip of her wine and thought about how strong that feeling was that she had to go back there tomorrow. Then the vile taste hit her—and her stomach curled. *Ugh.* She slowly replaced the wineglass on the table, then looked up at him. "Not only do I have to return to the site tomorrow but I have to go back to that same hole in the ground Hunter was in today."

Sebastian shook his head. "Hell no."

She slid her fingers over his hand, entwining their fingers together. "I have to. I have no choice."

His glare worried her until she understood the fear in it – the fear for her.

He gripped her fingers tightly and then nodded. "Then I'm going with you."

She stared up at the sky. "Maybe Hunter too."

"What are you supposed to do there?"

"Find something," she said.

"Find what?"

"Find a mask," she whispered, unable to help herself.

SEBASTIAN'S HEART DROPPED. "Find a mask? You're expecting to find a mask there? One of the ones that you drew?"

She puzzled at his words for a moment. "I don't know. I feel like a mask was there, but I highly doubt it's there after all this time. I don't know if its Linnea telling me to go get it though."

"It certainly could be, from her–or the other entity. If you can't tell, I certainly can't." he said, "considering how much Pompeii was completely enveloped by lava and dust. Just buried. But it's a major excavation to get a mask like that, and we're not allowed to do it."

"Right. I forgot about that." She looked at him. "I don't understand what these masks are all about. Did you have a mask in the Mayan expedition?"

He shook his head. "No. I only heard about the mask from Bruno. Then just because I didn't doesn't mean it wasn't there. I didn't see the men die so I can't know."

"Do you think it's the same energy, but now it's connected to something here, although how it could, I don't know? I mean, what does this dig site have to do with whatever happened ten years ago at a completely different location?"

"I'm not sure," he said gently. "I was told, once the negative energy from the Mayan site had seen me and knew my signature, that it could find me and recognize me later." He watched as her pupils widened. He gave her a lopsided grin. "Right. I know it all sounds very strange and, in fact, a little on the unnerving side …"

"Skip the unnerving side," she said, "that's downright terrifying."

"I just don't know why the energy would care."

"How many people escaped back then?"

He took a deep breath. "Just me with Hunter's help."

"Oh, my God."

She said it in such a way that it was almost like a prayer. She squeezed his fingers and pulled his hand closer to her, so she could hold it with both of her hands. "It's coming back after you. You escaped. It's trying to take you out this time."

"Not likely." He chuckled. "First that was a long time ago—why wait ten years?"

"But you're at a new dig site, and now we have the same things happening."

"Yes. It was also suggested that it's potentially another pocket of evil energy that has been released. And, because one was released ten years ago, it might have found this one, or this one may have somehow contacted the old one, or they were attracted to each other, so it's stronger."

She started to shake.

He tucked her up close and said, "I didn't want to bring this up."

"But you have to," she cried out. "Otherwise I could be walking into a trap."

"That's what I want you to realize. We don't understand what's going on here, and you are in danger."

"Hell no," she said. "You're the one in danger."

"No. I've learned a lot about myself and my talents. I think I'm the one who may have brought them into being last time. I'm the one who opened a Mayan tomb, at the guidance of the people with me. We didn't find any valuables at the grave, just the sarcophagus inside. We didn't get very far down. We didn't excavate the site. Everything blew up in our face soon afterward and we left."

"But that sounds exactly what we just did hours ago, in the caved-in area behind that weird energy barrier."

"For the longest time I wondered if there was like a spidery network of dark energy underneath the Earth's surface, and, if you happened to be unlucky, you're the one who opens up a pocket where it's closest to the surface and lets out some of the dark energy," he said. "I spent a decade studying this topic to find out what the hell was going on at that Mayan site. And honestly I found no answers to support my theory—but that's not proof either."

"Unless it can travel," she said softly.

"I thought of that," he said. "But how?"

She winced. "It would travel with objects or with … people."

He stared at her. "What do you mean, by people?"

She glanced around at the almost empty balcony and whispered, "Possession."

He shook his head in denial. "No, no. That's not the way it was."

"Who else escaped with you?" she asked.

"Just Hunter, but he was brought in to rescue me or rather to rescue all of us but I was the only one left," he said calmly. "And, as you can tell, he's as normal as anyone."

At that, she laughed aloud. "There is *nothing* normal about Hunter," she said.

He chuckled. "Hunter's a very capable person."

"He's a very *dangerous,* capable person," she corrected. She waited a long moment and then added, "Any chance he's possessed?"

Sebastian shook his head. "No. I think I'd have seen it."

"Because of the auras?"

He nodded.

"Could you be mistaken?" Not giving him a chance to answer, she asked, "What if you were possessed? Would you see it?"

Again he nodded. "Just like I can see our combined auras when we hold hands, I can see my singular aura by holding up my hand too."

"Amazing," Lacey said.

"I used to play around with all things supernatural before I went to the Mayan expedition. But afterward, it became a major focus of my world," he said absentmindedly.

"Of course you did. It explains why, maybe, this entity came toward you. It understood you had some abilities and might see him, might be able to communicate with him. Did you ever wonder what he wanted back then?"

"No," Sebastian said. "It seemed so angry. Whether it was irritated because we had opened up his grave or just because we were there or because he was no longer alive … I mean, how does anyone know?"

"I guess one doesn't," she said. "I don't get the same feeling of anger here. Maybe with the negative energy but not with Linnea."

"The fact that two people, with very different energies, are involved in this is also very odd," he said. "It makes no sense."

"It does if you consider that one might be protecting something or trying to save something, and the other one is trying to stop her."

"It's possible," he said doubtfully. "But that's a lot of energy to be utilized to try to save someone."

"I think Linnea loved her sister a lot."

"Maybe," he said. "That's still an awful lot of energy to stay around the Earth for centuries and then to try to save her once we're here digging up the site."

"I think the energy came once I was here. And then with my arrival you came."

"And we both arrived later on the same day the tools were vandalized and some were missing, and that event brought me in. Although we didn't meet until the next morning at the site."

She nodded. "So who's to say who is responsible for what's going on? We'll find out tomorrow."

"But, for now," Sebastian said, "we'll just enjoy our

evening together."

And indeed they did, at least a little bit more.

IN THE MORNING Lacey got up, dressed and walked toward the dig site with the rest of the gang. She could feel them studying her a little more with every step she took. She gave them all a bright smile. "I was stupid yesterday. I didn't eat, and I didn't have enough water. The heat got to me. I'll do better today, so I'll be fine."

They looked at each other and over at Chana.

Chana said, "We decided that, because you're my cousin, I'm the one who should look after you. We can't have you passing out on the site."

Not sure where this had come from or why Chana would choose now to tell her in front of everyone, Lacey nodded slowly. "So what is it that you're asking me to do?"

"Stay close."

Yet Lacey knew inside she had to return to the other place. "I can as much as I am able to," she said, "but the boss wanted to take me to another section and get photographs."

A snicker came from one of the guys.

Lacey glanced over at Brian. "I understand you all think something is going on between the two of us. But there's not—at least not yet. However, if this should develop into something more, it would be interesting to see where it goes," she said calmly. "I don't understand why this rumor has been treated like some teenage high-school romance. We're all adults here. What difference does it make if I end up having a relationship with Sebastian?"

There was only silence around her.

She nodded. "Exactly." And she picked up the pace until

she was ahead of them. She walked through the Stabian Gate on her own. As soon as she got to the other side, she felt a sense of peace. She tilted her face up to the sun and smiled.

The walking was rough because of the Roman road. Rocks were easy to trip on. She had to watch her step. She did have boots on, and that made the going a little easier, but it was easy to catch her foot on an uneven flagstone.

She carried on to the dig site and stopped for a moment at the top. She pulled out her camera and took a picture of the empty site before the start of the day; she then waited until they all caught up and discussed the tasks for today. She turned to Katie. "Do you have more items for me to photograph for the catalogue?"

Katie shook her head. "Not right now. By the end of the day I should get on that again."

Lacey nodded. "Let me know when you're ready then, please." She walked around parts of the dig, taking pictures of new sections, looking for something different. She'd already taken hundreds and hundreds of photos of every individual rock. But she knew she hadn't included any that were the view from the inside out. She walked down to the deepest section and snapped pictures, looking skyward as the walls rose up and around her. It was an interesting perspective with the trees in the sky.

As she turned around to face the group of workers, she saw Sebastian, standing with his hands on his hips, glaring at her. She raised both hands in frustration. "Now why am I in trouble?"

"You were supposed to wait for me this morning."

"I was?"

The others chuckled.

She opened her arms and said, "Well, I'm here. You

found me easily anyway."

He motioned at her to get out of the pit. "Hunter is here too."

The others looked at each other and then around the dig site.

She ignored them, climbed back up to the top and said, "What does he want me to take pictures of?"

Sebastian glanced at the rest of his crew, saying, "I'll be back in about an hour." And he led her away to the section where they had been yesterday.

When she realized exactly where they were going, she smiled and picked up the pace.

CHAPTER 20

"**T**HINK ABOUT HOW you feel as you approach this area," Sebastian said. "Think about who may be affecting how you feel. Think about voices in your head, voices around you, people urging you to move on, people urging you to stop." He paused. "Imagine yourself surrounded by white light—pure love."

She nodded. "I know what you're saying in theory," she said slowly. "But I'm not sure I know how to tell the difference between the voices."

"Which is why I want you to think about it. Stop here and"—he pulled her to a halt—"close your eyes. What is it you're doing here, and where is it you need to go?"

She stood for a long moment and turned slightly, then pivoted a little more. She held out her right arm and said, "I'm going there. I'm going there because Linnea wants me to."

"Is it Linnea who wants the mask?"

Lacey thought about it and then nodded. "Yes. Linnea wants the mask."

"Good. Why does Linnea want the mask?"

"And that's when the answers stop," Lacey said with a frown. "I'm not exactly sure why."

"It's up to you to find out," he said. "If these spirits want our help, they have to give us answers."

"Okay," she said slowly. "Linnea says I'll know when I get the mask."

"Interesting. Ask her what happens if we can't find it."

"She says we will." She winced, looking at Sebastian. "Honestly that's all I can tell you. She seems to think we'll trip over it."

"And you probably will, considering what I can see from here," Hunter said as he stood at the opening to the cave-in.

She wanted to rush toward him, but Sebastian held her back. "Oh, no you don't," he said. "You stay here and continually register how you feel and who you're getting these feelings from. Stay in the ball of white light."

"Okay." She slowly stopped again, turning to look at him. "You think the only feelings I have are ones other people are putting in me?"

"It's certainly possible," he said. "If you think about it, they affect everything we do. I want you to be sure you can separate Linnea's feelings from your feelings and from this other entity's feelings."

"Is there any chance only Linnea is here?"

"There's a chance for all kinds of things," he said. "So I want you to be very careful. You have to take in the information, but you must also take a moment to digest who it came from and why."

She nodded, as he led her toward Hunter.

As they approached, Hunter squatted down and pointed into a section of the cave-in. "I see something down there."

She peered in beside him and could see the glint of something in the darkness. "I have no clue what that is though," she said.

"I'll check it out," Hunter said. "I was already down there once yesterday. I know how unstable it is."

She nodded. "Can you retrieve it?"

He shrugged, walked back around to where the cave-in was more of a slope and carefully made his way down. Once he was in the center of the hole, he turned and said, "I can't see it from here."

She studied the interior and then pointed out where a glint of metal was.

He followed her directions and then crouched. "Something is definitely here. I don't know that I can lift it out though."

"You've got to try," she urged. "For all we know, when we come back again, it'll be missing." She watched but could only see his back as he tried to pull something from the dirt.

Sebastian frowned, standing at her side. "This should be excavated properly."

Hunter turned and grinned up at him. "Then get your shovels and come on down here and join me."

"You know how much trouble we'll get in, right?" Sebastian growled. He made his way around to the opening Hunter had used to get in. As he descended, he turned and looked up at Lacey. "Don't you move."

She stuck out her tongue at him but stayed where she was.

Apparently satisfied that she would listen to him, Sebastian descended to Hunter's side.

She shifted a little so she could watch the men. Sebastian leaned over, grabbed whatever item it was Hunter was fighting with, and the two pulled. A weird popping, sucking sound followed, and then dust rose all around them followed by a low rumbling. She could hear the men cry out.

"Hunter, Sebastian, get up here right now. Hurry, hurry."

She could hear the men scrambling up out of the hole, but they were hidden in the cloud of dust. She couldn't stop thinking about Sebastian's theory about unleashing a spider network of evil from inside the ground, ugly rumbling shifted beneath her feet.

"It feels like an earthquake," she yelled. "Get out! Get out while you can!"

She raced to the other side and tried to peer into the caved-in area. A hand landed beside her. She reached down, grabbed the arm and pulled.

Hunter came up first. "Move back so we can get up."

"What happened?" she asked, backing up.

"I don't know," Hunter said. "But it's like the ground fell away from us."

She looked down to see Sebastian clinging to the edge of a rock. He moved very carefully, using his feet and hands, but the ground beneath him was gone. The additional further cave-in had taken away the rocks and surrounding vegetation farther down.

Now that he was almost on safe ground, Hunter grabbed a hold of Sebastian's arm, pulling him to safety.

As soon as Sebastian stood on solid dirt again, she threw herself into his arms, hugging him tight.

He held her close, his heart slamming against his chest and her ear, and said, "That was not fun."

She leaned back to look up at him. "What happened?"

"As soon as we freed the stupid thing from the ground, it's like everything underneath it collapsed," he said. "The ground has fallen another good twenty feet deep, as if another big cavern were underneath the first cave-in."

"Which doesn't make sense," Hunter said. "But I can't say I feel like going back into that hole again."

"It's not just a hole now. Anybody who falls in that will have a hard time getting back out again without a rope and a friend to help," Sebastian said. "We have to put up warning signs to stop the tourists and even fence it off so animals can't fall in."

Lacey crouched at the edge of the hole. Instantly her shoulders were grabbed, and she was pulled back.

"You stay away from there," Sebastian ordered, holding her hand as the trio moved several yards away.

She turned to look at him and gasped when she saw blood streaming down from his temple. She reached up to touch him. "You're bleeding. You need to get that looked at," she said.

"Maybe," he said, "but I'm not doing it right now." He dug in his pocket and pulled out a handkerchief, which he held at his wound to slow the bleeding. He glanced at Hunter. "Do you have it?"

Hunter reached into his shirt and pulled out a dusty metal object.

She grabbed the mask. "Oh, my God," she whispered in awe and involuntarily shook. "It's exactly the same as what I drew on your face."

"Exactly," Sebastian said. "The question is how did you know what it looked like and what relevance does the mask have?"

She lifted it up high and studied it. And then, unable to help herself, she placed it over her face.

Both men yelled out, "Stop! Don't!"

But it was too late. The mask wrapped around her face and sucked her in. She cried out and tried to rip it off, but it wouldn't budge. Both men reached for it, but it wouldn't move.

She screamed, "Help me! Help me!"

"Calm down," Sebastian said, gripping her fingers in his. "We're trying to help you. I don't know how you're breathing in there," he said, "but you need to stay calm."

She closed her eyes, hating the claustrophobic feeling as the mask covered her nose and lower jaw. Her eyes were uncovered, but the mask came up to her temples. She tried hard to breathe slowly, but it was hard to breathe at all. "I hate this thing," she whispered, her voice trembling.

The men gripped either side of the mask and pulled, but it only pulled her skin away from her face.

She could hear them discussing what to do about it until a voice spoke in front of all of them. "She has to get it off herself."

She stared at a faint white outline of a male. "Why?" she asked cautiously, not sure what or who she saw.

"Because it's your challenge," the newcomer said, "not that that's an easy answer."

"They use this for their prisoners," she said suddenly, getting an inkling of Linnea's panic.

"Exactly," the ghostly figure said. "And they too had to free themselves. It was a trial to discern who had abilities and who didn't. Or who was a witch and who wasn't. Who was guilty of the crime and who was innocent?"

She stared at him. "Who are you?"

Hunter supplied the answer. "His name is Stefan Kronos. He's one of the most capable psychics in the world and my boss."

"Well, okay. I guess," she said cautiously, not knowing what to say in this situation. "Have you seen masks like this before?"

The golden figure shifted. She'd take that as a nod.

"Some civilizations have a similar test. In the witches' trials, they used to throw the witches into the lake, and, if they drowned, they were deemed innocent. But, of course, nobody knew how to swim back then, and they were flung in fully dressed and sometimes weighted down. So the chances of them being a witch were pretty slim. History has many other examples used to determine guilt or innocence."

"That's possible I suppose," Hunter said. But he looked at the mask now. "It's on very tight. And it's *metal*." He tapped the side with his nails; a sharp *ping* could be heard.

"I want this off," Lacey cried out.

"Then take it off," Stefan said gently. "The mask is your connection to another world. It's like a directional map. If you can utilize it to see those who came before you, plus whatever it is you're meant to see with it, then you'll be acknowledging your own skills and your own abilities, and you'll be able to pull it off."

"And if I can't?"

"Then you would not be psychic, and you would suffocate. Or in other words, you'd be guilty of whatever transgression you were accused of."

"But ..." Then she fell silent. She could almost see something.

"The trick is to stay calm," Stefan said, "and to not let your panic overwhelm you."

A broken laugh escaped. "Too late," she murmured. She could feel everything splintering inside her, a sense of captivity, being the victim, taking over. She hated the weakness already infiltrating her system. "I feel funny," she whispered.

Sebastian helped her to a sitting position.

She could see the worry and panic in his eyes. She

reached out and clung to his fingers. "How long do I have?"

"Longer if you don't panic. Possibly a long time. We don't know," Stefan said. "But honestly, if you sink into it, sink into the energy that comes from it, you should be able to get the mask off faster."

"And how do I do that?" she whispered.

"Close your eyes and breathe in your white loving energy and exhale into the mask. Don't suck your breath away from it. Understand that many people before you have worn this as well."

She took a deep breath and nodded. "Okay. Let me try it." She bowed her head, hating the sensation of having everything around her head confined and constricted. She tried to inhale then exhale as instructed, feeling the warm air bathe her face as she told the mask, *I'm here. What is it you need me to see?*

Instantly she could see things all around her. She could see back to the time right before the eruption, the people, the villages, faces upon more faces. And there, on one side, was Linnea's face. Linnea stared at Lacey in worry, her hands wringing, as if waiting for Lacey to do something. She mentally called out to Linnea. *What is it you want from me?*

To survive, Linnea answered.

To survive?

Not knowing what the hell that meant, Lacey kept seeing other visions and other faces. She could feel her body swaying. She didn't know if she was about to faint from all the sensory overload or if she was ready to pass out from lack of air. Yet it seemed like she had air. She was breathing normally, but she had dizzying moments, seeing and feeling so much going on around her.

Finally she closed her eyes and reached up to touch the

mask. "I acknowledge that I have these abilities. I am one who gets to wear the mask." And she grabbed the mask on either side of her cheekbones and pulled.

The men's cries of surprise rose up around her as she pulled the mask free of her face to stare up at them. She very carefully placed the mask on the ground beside her. "The next time I go to put that sucker on my face, stop me."

Sebastian grabbed her hands, helped her to her feet and tucked her tight against his chest. He stood there with her, rocking, swaying slightly side to side, holding her close. "Oh, my God," he whispered. "That was way too scary."

She gave a muffled exclamation and squeezed him tighter to her. When she could, she slowly turned around and looked at the mask on the ground. "I don't know what that looked like from the outside, but, from the inside, it was terrifying."

That faint outline of somebody remained, the ghostly spirit. "Thank you, Stefan. I don't think I would have gotten it off on my own."

"Which is also why many people died in that mask," he said calmly. "But you do have abilities, and you did see many things while you were in that mask, did you not?"

She nodded. "I also saw Linnea, and I asked her what I was supposed to do. Her answer was even more surprising." Her gaze went from one to the other and then the other. "She wanted me to survive. She said the whole focus of this was for me to survive."

"To survive?"

She nodded. "The message was very clear. She was looking at me with the mask on, wringing her hands in worry."

"So maybe that room we were talking about," Sebastian said, "was where those were kept who were chosen to wear the mask. That's why there was no door."

"Possibly," she said. "But how they got people in and out, I don't know." Then she stopped and smiled. "No. I *do* know. They were lowered down with a rope. The mask had to come off, and the only way to get the mask off was to acknowledge your abilities," she said softly. "So they would leave them in there to die. If the mask came off, then they could call out for the rope, and the rope would be lowered."

"And Linnea's sister?"

"I think she might have been the one in the closed in room," she said softly. "And Linnea was trying to help her survive."

"But she didn't?"

Lacey shook her head. "No, she didn't, because *I was* the sister of Linnea. I was Sabine." The truth was painful as she realized how Sabine's life had ended. Her heart filled with pain and dread at what Sabine had done to the others.

At that Stefan spoke. "Good. Recognizing a past life is huge. To interpret the symbols and your surroundings, as you do so, is even more helpful. Linnea is caught in a time warp. She still thinks you're a prisoner. That's why she cannot leave this Earthly plane," he said gently. "You can teach her to let go, so she can leave."

"And the mask?" Lacey asked. "What about the mask?"

"I suggest it go into a collection," Stefan said. "Where somebody can look after it properly. It's dangerous. Write up some history on it because it will be important."

"But that doesn't say anything about the darkness," Hunter said. "A lot of dark energy is here. In that pit, it surrounded the mask at the time it was buried."

"Think about it," Stefan said. "Think about the type of people who'll allow somebody to die a slow death caught within the mask. Imagine how many hundreds died wearing that mask and how few would have survived."

"And that energy?" Sebastian asked. "Are you saying that's the energy of the souls who survived or the energy of the souls who died?"

"In a way it's none of the above," Stefan said softly. "It will be the energy of the anger and the fear of what was done to them, the energy of the person who did this to them. It's full of emotions. It's hatred. It's anger. It's panic, and it's terror because death has no survivors."

SEBASTIAN DIDN'T KNOW what the hell had just happened, but he knew it would show up in his nightmares for the rest of his life. Seeing that mask form, then lock around her face was … absolutely terrifying. He'd seen her drawings of himself in the mask, and that had felt extremely uneasy to view, but to see something like this happening to her, well …

He exchanged a hooded look with Hunter. The two of them had no experience at this level. Sure they'd had a horrific time in the Mayan ruins, but they hadn't seen any masks. That didn't mean they weren't there but he hadn't seen them.

A disturbing thought.

He stared at the mask with loathing. "That sucker is dangerous," he whispered.

Stefan agreed. "But it's energetic. So it needs a special case to hold it. While it's in metal form, it's all well and good, and we must ensure it doesn't come in contact with somebody with psychic abilities. Apparently it's attracted to that, for starters."

"And yet, it didn't come after me or Hunter," Sebastian said, his arms clenching tighter around Lacey.

"No, I think you'll find it's after the innocence, after the unaware, after the pure of form," Stefan said softly. "It might need that."

Lacey's head reared back, and she stared at the man. "Me? Is that what you're saying I am?"

"It tends to be those who have not utilized their powers much. Yours are just awakening," Stefan said. "And it's attracted to that pure energy. Maybe sensing the power there. Maybe it has more control over those who are una-wakened. Maybe because it senses you were Sabine and it knows—recognizes you."

Her gaze flew to Sebastian's gaze, remembering what he'd said about the energy signature recognizing him again in the future. So did the mask want her more than him? Obviously, but that should mean it wasn't the same energy here as at the Mayan ruin, which should have him feel better but it didn't.

She asked in confusion, "But what can it do with that energy?"

Sebastian stiffened. That was, of course, the crux of the matter. If it wanted all this energy, what would it do with it? And he was afraid the answer would terrify him. He could see from the look on Hunter's face that it was bad.

Silence took over for a long moment, but she wouldn't let it go. "I don't understand," she said. "How is this related to Linnea or me?"

"It's possible this person was after Linnea before," Hunter suggested.

Lacey shook her head. "Wouldn't think so. Her sister wore this mask, and either she didn't have abilities or she didn't figure out how to unlock it."

"Well, Linnea is connected," Stefan said. "And, therefore, you're connected. But the energy has found you now. And it wants what you have."

Sebastian watched the puzzled expression grow on her face.

Stefan hummed in place for a moment, and then he said, "The energy wants to feed on it. And, whether you accept it or not, there are ways for entities to come back to life. They can move in and take over others. As long as Lacey has an energy it wants."

Lacey stepped out of Sebastian's arms and cried out, "Are you saying it can possess me? Because …" She shook her head. "Because that's not what it felt like. It felt more like it was draining me."

Hunter nodded. "Yes, absolutely. *Draining* you is a good word for it. Because they can't step into your system because you're full of light. It repels them, but, if they can drain away that goodness, they can step in the void left behind."

She took several deep breaths, her hand patting her chest as if hyperventilating.

Sebastian clenched her shoulders. He needed her to know she wasn't alone. "We're here to help protect you," he tried to reassure her.

She just stared at him. "I presume, if somebody drains my energy, I'm going to die. Is that correct?"

Sebastian stiffened, but there was no denying Stefan's immediate "Yes."

She asked Sebastian, "Is that how the people died in the Mayan site?"

"We don't know for sure how they died," he admitted.

"Meaning, you woke up to find them dead?"

"In one case, yes," Hunter said, "but not in all cases. Remember those, Sebastian? You're the one who told me about them. There were accidents, lots of accidents. And if severely injured, possession is much easier. But some people are weaker anyway, in heart, mind, or soul making them more susceptible to otherworld entities."

"Did you stop that entity back then?" she demanded. "Because that has to be stopped. We can't have spirits running around injuring people and then stealing their energy."

Hunter shook his head. "We left. We were hoping the entity would dissipate with no other victims to prey upon."

She stared at him, and her hands trembled. She brushed her hair off her face. "But it could feed on animals, isn't that correct?"

"Potentially, if it had enough of its own energy to do so, yes," Stefan said calmly. "But it's unlikely. They were tuned into human energy. Once they fed at that much-higher vibration, animal energy wouldn't be the same."

CHAPTER 21

LACEY DIDN'T EVEN know what to think anymore. It was early in the day, although it seemed like she'd lived a lifetime in just a few days. Her time here in Pompeii was passing so fast, and yet, when weird and scary things like this happened, it seemed to slow time to a stop.

With Sebastian's help, she sat on a large rock near the barrier and the caved-in find. He passed over a bottle of water.

"I'm not sick, you know," she muttered as she drank nearly all the water at once. She caught sight of Sebastian's hard look at Hunter. She then asked the glowing ball in front of her, "What does my thirst and hunger have to do with any of this?" As long as she acted like everything was normal, she figured her reality would catch up with what was happening soon enough.

"It's often a sign of your energetic systems being under attack," Stefan said gently.

She turned to stare, hearing almost a weird echo. "Talking to you like this is so bizarre."

Laughter rolled freely around her as Stefan chuckled.

"It is," Stefan said. "But only for the first couple times. Once you get used to it, you'll find it becomes the norm."

"Is there some kind of secret underground society of people who know how to do this?" she asked. "Because I've never even heard of this, and yet, here we are, discussing topics so far beyond *normal* that any rational person would consider me ready for the nuthouse." She took a deep breath. "I've heard and read of people like, you know, repeating mantras and stuff, will that help protect me?"

"The best way is to surrender your energy to one of love," Stefan said. "In this case, however, you also need to lock down your energy because that love energy is attracting this darkness. It needs your light, your energy, because it can do so much more with it than it can with its own dark energy. And, in order to protect yourself, you must create a sensor to alert you when somebody is after your energy, or one that will rebuff them completely."

She stared at the empty water bottle in her hand, passing it back to Sebastian. "Both of which sound like crazy stories." She didn't want to call Stefan a liar because it was already beyond ridiculous that she was talking to this glowing space between the two men. She glanced from Hunter to Sebastian. "Do you guys do that?" Her stomach sank when both nodded. She scrubbed her face with her hands. "You know how ridiculous this sounds?"

"We do," Hunter said. "That moment of awakening, that moment of realizing you have abilities you didn't know about and that people were utilizing and feeding on your system because you didn't know to stop them, ... it's the end of innocence."

"*Awakening?*" she mimicked in disbelief. "It's terrifying. It's scary as shit. And what you said doesn't tell me anything useful. I need to know how to create that sensor."

"The initial lesson is awareness," Stefan said. "Now that you're aware of what is going on around you and that somebody is helping himself to your energy, whether a little bit or a lot, you need to do something about it. First, become aware. You know how you feel great and energized when you're with certain people, and then how you can be with another group and walk away feeling drained? That's because people subconsciously reach out and help themselves to the energy they need. Some people use that as a way of communication. The reason they're with people is because they're attracted to that energy, and so they help themselves to our energy to make themselves feel better. But, as an end result, *you* feel worse."

"Oh, wow," she muttered. "I really don't like the sound of that. And I still need to have an early alarm system."

Sebastian chuckled. "Whether you like it or not, you have to realize this is exactly what you're dealing with now. *Awareness.*"

"It's a lot to take in," she admitted.

"It is," Hunter said. "This is a crash course in getting up to speed."

"Or else this entity will suck me dry? You've been watching too many vampire films."

"We do understand," Sebastian said, crouching in front of her. "But consider how much food you're inhaling. Consider how much water you're drinking. Consider the fact you can't sleep anymore, and your system is under extreme distress."

She covered his hand with hers. "Since I arrived, I've had nothing in my life *except* stress. This mess being one of the final straws of so much that started with that accident."

"And what accident was that again?" Stefan's voice was sharp.

Almost in an absentminded voice, Sebastian explained about her getting hit by a vehicle on her second evening here.

"Interesting."

Hunter turned to look at Stefan. "Why?"

"Remember in the Mayan ruins, injuries were this entity's way of getting into the energy system."

Silence fell.

Her gaze went from one to the other. "Are you saying, after that accident, I became even more susceptible?"

Sebastian nodded slowly, adding, "We did wonder if that accident had awakened Lacey's abilities."

Hunter nodded. "That would make more sense."

"But it doesn't make sense to me," Lacey said. "Is the entity slipping into my body through my injuries, my wounds?"

Stefan shook his head, smiling sweetly. "It's more invasive than that. The spirit waits for your body to divert its normal processes of protecting your body from foreign invaders, whether germs or this black energy spirit, into an all-out healing mode. So your body is more interested in healing itself than in protecting itself from further invaders. Think of the last time you had a bad case of the flu. It knocked you out, kept you in bed for days, right?"

She nodded.

"You were too out of it to eat or drink. Just sleeping. Until the body healed itself." Again Stefan smiled sweetly at Lacey. "The black energy is aware of this human process and takes advantage of it. Even to the point of creating these injuries to begin with, to divert your body's protection process to a more focused healing process."

Lacey rubbed her temples. "What about the headaches? Are they all connected?"

"Explain the headaches," Stefan ordered.

She shrugged. "What's to explain? They're headaches. They're always at the back of my neck, right where my head joins my spine. It's like this ... *tension* bubble."

"No," Stefan said softly. "It's likely a hook."

She stared at him, dumbfounded. "There's no hook in the back of my head." She turned to face Sebastian. "Is there?" She watched as this weird glowing entity moved around her, barely noticing that Sebastian held both of her hands.

Stefan murmured, "Definitely a hook is in here. I'm not sure I can release it. You'll have to do it yourself."

"What are you talking about?" Lacey released Sebastian's hands, then threw her braid over one shoulder. She searched the back of her neck. "There is no hook. I don't know what you're talking about."

"A spiritual hook," Sebastian said. "It's like a direct line into your energy system. At the spine, it hopes to tap into the Kundalini energy at the base of the spine, as well as the other energy in your chakras."

She stared at him. "What's really scary is that this concept doesn't seem all that foreign to me."

Hunter gave a bark of laughter. "That's good because we want you to disconnect that hook."

She shot him a look. Her stomach churned. "How do I do that?" she asked cautiously. "I can't feel anything."

"Close your eyes," Stefan ordered.

She obeyed but winced at the fact that she did so. "Since when do I listen to a ghost," she muttered.

"I'm not a ghost," Stefan said. "I'm as alive as you and Sebastian are."

She doubted that, but this wasn't the time to argue.

"Close your eyes. Think and feel about what's going on

from the top of your head down to your shoulder blades," he instructed. "Feel whether it's heat or whether it's cold or if it's tension."

She tried to sort out the sensations running up and down her back. Right now she was so confused and terrified at the thought of this hook in her neck and what it might be taking from her that it was hard to find a neutral position in which to assess her system. Eventually though she could tell there was no pain but kind of a tug on the right side of her neck. She reached around and touched it with her fingers. "My neck feels like it is being pulled here at this spot."

"Good," Stefan said. "That's the hook."

She explored the area. "I really can't feel anything though."

"But you can. It's just you don't know what it is you're sensing," he said. "Now I want you to think about that hook. Imagine a vacuum hose is attached to that part of your neck, taking with it whatever it needs from your system. So, while you're drinking and eating, you're feeding that thing too."

"And how do I get it out of my system?" she cried out.

Sebastian leaned toward her, placed a hand on her knee and squeezed. "Just remain calm," he said. "You have to realize everybody has hooks, and most of them we allow."

"We always allow it," Stefan said. "But sometimes they come in with other hooks. Because you've agreed to the first, the second one is like a leech. Several other kinds of hooks are in your system, and that's normal. There will be friends, family members."

"Okay," she said, slightly calmer. "How do I get rid of the one I don't want? I presume the ones I allowed or I do want, help me to have a better relationship with people?"

"Exactly," Stefan said. "But it's still not healthy to have them if these people are controlling you, manipulating you. We must set boundaries even with our friends and family. Getting rid of those isn't today's issue. Getting rid of the one sucking the life out of you is."

Hearing it described like that made the bile rise in the back of her throat.

"Now I want you to reach out mentally and disconnect that line," he said. "Not because it's hurting you, not because you're afraid of it, but because you have the power to decide who and what can have your energy. From a position of a calm sense of knowing that you have the right to do what you're doing, detach it."

She tried to get into that mind-set, but doubt and fear warred inside. "I can't quite get that sense of being allowed to do this," she said with a wince.

"That's because you're coming from a victim mentality. You feel like he's done this to you," Stefan said, "and that he's taken advantage of you, so you're being terrorized, and you've put yourself in victim mode. You need to realize somebody was taking advantage, and you have to slap them back into their place. Think about when you're in a store, and somebody cuts in front of you in line. You speak up and say, *Excuse me. The line is behind me.* Have you ever done something like that?"

She shrugged. "Not for myself but for my mom I have, when others have stepped in front of her when she needed to get to the front of the line as soon as possible because she was so tired."

"That's fine. Use that analogy now. Not coming from a victim mentality but coming from a sense of knowing they're in the wrong."

"*Aah*," she said and tried again. She could feel herself straightening her back, stiffening, almost as if getting bigger.

"That's it," Stefan murmured. "Keep doing that. Find out who you are inside. Stand up straight and tall and be proud of it."

She followed his instructions to feel through her toes with this great energy from the earth, pulling it up, filling her system, her arms, her fingertips, through her neck and her head. And then she hit the top of her head. This Earth's energy bounced back around to where this hook was, and, as if with a flick of her finger, she kicked it out.

Instantly the sensation of being freed from a heavy weight on her shoulders fell off her. She stretched her arms high above her head, rolled her neck and her shoulders, and said, "That feels much better."

"That's because you released it," Stefan said. "Now go to where it was and fill the space with a warm loving energy but also put a cap on it. Visualize snapping it in place so this person cannot, under any circumstances, reopen it."

She could see a great big manhole cover coming down over the space where the hook had been. She looked around in surprise, took several steps, shaking out her legs and her neck. "I really feel different right now."

"Good," Stefan said. "Now you need to be aware if other attempts are made on your system."

She turned to face him. "And what about the other hooks in my system?"

She could feel Stefan's warm smile reaching out for her, the pat of approval on her back.

"When you did what you just did, you released all the hooks," he said. "So you might find some relationships a little off right now. But a lot of these relationships and hooks have been in there since you were a child. It was definitely time to release those threads, those connections, to let other people grow and be who they are, to let yourself grow and be who you are without that neediness."

She stared at him in astonishment, but he slowly faded before her. "Wait. How do I contact you again?"

A warm chuckle filled her mind. "Now that we've connected, the connection will always be there."

She asked suspiciously, "Does that mean you have a hook in my system now?"

His voice, ever-so-gentle, whispered back, "No, my dear. You have a hook into my system." And he disappeared.

She turned to stare at the other two men. "He said I have a hook in his system," she cried out. "I didn't mean to do that."

Sebastian just grinned. "If he wanted to get rid of it, believe me, he'd get rid of it. And it wouldn't matter in the least what you tried to do about it."

She nodded slowly. "Well, that makes me feel a little better because I didn't know I did that."

Hunter nodded. "Relationships are like that. They are two-way streets. A hook is a connection between the two of you and is something you can build and agree on. And, if you're very lucky, you can open that connection so you communicate through it. Hooks don't have to be bad, and they can be turned into these tunnels, these doorways between people that will allow you to communicate much easier."

"I really like that idea," she admitted. "With my mother's passing, I lost a really intense part of my life. For the six months before she died, it seemed like I could read her thoughts. I could understand what she wanted without her even asking for it."

"That's probably because you had already forged that tunnel between the two of you," Hunter said. "And that's a good thing. That was a loving daughter connected to a loving mother. When everything is right, it's the most beautiful thing. What you have to watch out for is when things feel off or wrong, or if you get into an abusive situation. It's subconscious behavior, but, when somebody becomes a bully and pushes people around, you have to realize they're utilizing that kind of energy to make you do their bidding. Whether it's threats or intimidation, it doesn't matter. Often it's just pure emotional blackmail. You have to detach from those hooks so you can see clearly what's going on. As long as those hooks are in place, it's hard for you to get clear of all that manipulation. But it's important that you do, for your own safety."

She took several more steps around the area. She studied the mask with distrust. "And how do we fence that off so nobody from the team touches it?"

"I'll take it back," Sebastian said. He bent down and opened up his backpack, carefully put the mask in it, closing it over the object.

"How do we know it won't just disappear into black energy?" she asked. "It came, and it changed, and now it's returned to its former form."

Hunter added, "Yeah, Sebastian, we want to make sure nothing unlocks it again."

Sebastian nodded. "We need a secure glass case."

"Silver welds would be good too," Hunter said. "Making sure it's hermetically sealed, so it can't change form again."

"In any case, we better go now," Sebastian said. He stopped, turning to look at her. "Are you okay to leave?"

"Leave? Go where? I've done no work at all today."

"Good thing there wasn't a whole lot for you to do, isn't it?" He held out a hand. "Come on. Let's go. We need to take the mask somewhere safe."

When they were talking about, *locking it up securely*, they had meant it. She thought they were returning to the apartment. She'd been through enough that morning already that she'd be quite happy to return there. Even though she'd said she needed to get to work, she'd secretly wanted to just be alone in her room. But that wasn't happening either.

Instead they ended up going to the rear of the apartment building where Sebastian had his vehicle parked. With her and Hunter both inside, the mask carefully stowed in the footwell, he drove to another building.

She studied the area, fascinated. "I wish I had time to take in the tourist sights. I really hate to leave without having seen some of the most famous attractions."

"You're working in the most famous attraction of all," Hunter said.

She smiled, thinking about it. They passed a small market. She twisted in her seat to see everything offered in the crowded booths.

Sebastian commented, "Don't worry about it. We'll get you out here at least once before you go home."

At the thought of going home again, she settled in her seat and muttered, "When will that be, two days?"

He shot her a look through the rearview mirror.

She just shrugged. "I'm hardly doing the job I came to do."

"Remember that it's a volunteer position," he reminded her. "It's not like you're on the payroll."

She brightened. "So you can't fire me then."

"Hardly," he said. "You're the best photographer we've had."

She grinned. "I'm glad to hear that. I teach photography at the high school too, but, at that level, most of my students only have point-and-shoot cameras. We do mostly photo editing, so they can understand composition."

"And you are a history teacher?" Hunter asked.

She nodded. "History, photography, sometimes math." She wrinkled up her face at that. "The more subjects you have, the more hours you get to work. For the longest time, I just taught history and worked only part-time to be able to help my mother."

"At least you had that," Hunter said. "It gave you a chance to get out of the house."

"It did, but, every time I left, I felt guilty and worried about her. I used to phone her on my breaks all the time, send her texts, and then I'd rush back home again to see if she needed me."

Hunter smiled. "You don't need to feel guilty for being a loving daughter. It's that kind of love that makes the world go around."

She stared out the window, wishing she didn't feel, in a sense, that she'd pulled the short straw in that deal.

"Were you caring for a loving mother?" he asked, as if studying the unrest on her face.

She glanced at her hands and nodded. "I was—and I hate to speak ill of the dead—but no doubt my mother was only waiting to return to my father, who had passed away ten years earlier. So, although she loved me, I was second in her life."

Hunter's gaze was intense as he studied her face and the depths of emotions in her eyes. "That's not an easy situation for either of you."

She grinned. "I don't hold any illusions about it. I was loved, being an only child, but, once my father passed on, it's like my mother was doing her duty by sticking around. She wasn't terribly unhappy about dying. She was looking forward to seeing him again. When I became an adult, I think she felt like she had fulfilled her role as a mother."

"Still, it had to make you feel like you were less than your father."

She settled into her seat and thought about that. "I think it was more an understanding that something stronger than her love for me existed. That, although she did love me, her love for him was bigger. In a way her love for him was even bigger than her love for her own life. I understand losing somebody to the extent that you're overcome with grief, because that was me with my mother. Yet I'm not sure how it feels to be so overcome with grief that all you can do is put in time until you can rejoin that person." She spoke as honestly as she could. "I went through a fair bit of trauma, sorting out my own feelings about it all. But no doubt I needed to make her as comfortable as possible to the end, if only to fulfill my role as her daughter and to show her my gratitude for raising me."

"And you shouldn't feel ashamed for any of that," Sebastian said from the front seat. "Or any sense of guilt for the few moments you may have been away where you were happy, or for a sense of wondering what was wrong with you that she didn't want to stick around to spend time with you."

At that she gasped. "How did you know I felt like that?"

"I think one of the hardest things about death is it leaves us with a confusion of feelings we have to sort out. From a relief that it's over and then the sense of guilt for being relieved. I don't think anything is quite so confusing as watching a person you love die."

"How long did it take her to pass?" Hunter asked.

"Interesting you ask it that way," she said with a smile. "Most people ask how long she was ill."

Hunter turned to stare at her. "I view death a little differently. Once you become horribly ill, and you know death is coming, some people walk toward it with open arms, embracing it, and other people drag their feet, kicking and screaming. So my question was more about how long it took from when she got very ill to actually dying."

"Getting to the point of being very ill took her a couple years," Lacey said, thinking back. "But, about three months before she died, she was like, … *Leave me alone. Just let me go.* At the time I told her no, no, no, and I went away and cried, but then I finally came back and told her that, anytime she was ready to go, I was okay with it and that she didn't need to stay with me."

"Did that make her happier?"

Lacey nodded. "I think it did. I think she lingered because of me, caught between her duty as a mother and her love for me versus her need to go and her wish to exit a very painful existence."

Hunter nodded. "It sounds like you have had quite an intimate experience with death. Although it might have been extremely difficult, I think you were also blessed to have lived through such a thing because it changes your perspective on life."

"It did," she said. "But I'm not sure it changed my perspective as much as these last couple weeks here has."

At that, he laughed. "So very true."

They'd pulled into a large parking lot and headed into an underground parking garage. Sebastian brought the car up to a security gate, where he punched in a key code. The gate opened, and he drove down below the building.

She's frowned. "Where are we?"

"A secure building," Sebastian said. "We keep a lot of archives here. They have to be kept in special oxygen-sealed rooms."

Interested, she perked up when he took a parking spot close to the elevator. "You think the mask will be safe here?"

"I'm hoping so," Sebastian said. "I'd like to keep this locked down for the rest of humanity, so it doesn't kill anyone else."

"But it didn't kill me," she reminded him.

"No, it didn't," Hunter said. "But that doesn't mean it won't kill somebody who doesn't have abilities or who doesn't know enough to free himself or herself. Imagine if you hadn't had Stefan, who knew and could tell you how to free yourself, even though you have psychic abilities."

"It was terrifying even with his help," she said. "I still can't believe it went from being this metal mask to something of a dark energy and then a metal mask again around my face. Are you sure that's what happened?"

Both men turned to look at her.

She shrugged. "Okay. Just checking."

Soon they were out of the vehicle and walking toward a large elevator. Inside, instead of going up, they went down.

She looked around. "Do you own the whole building?"

Sebastian didn't answer.

She mentally buttoned her lips to stop the rest of her questions from bursting forth.

When the elevator doors opened, Sebastian led the way

to a large room with a metal door. When the metal door opened, he walked inside, and they found one man sitting at a desk.

The man looked up, stood and said, "I didn't expect to see you here this morning, sir."

"At ease, Henry, please. We have something to secure in the vault."

Henry nodded, brought out a ring of keys and what looked like an iPad and headed down the hall. They followed as he punched codes in a door on the left, and it opened.

Lacey followed Sebastian inside a small room. It appeared to be lined with stainless steel and had a pedestal in the center. He very carefully removed the mask, placed it on the pedestal. From the ceiling came down a long tube of glass, and he sealed the mask inside the tube.

She was stunned as the glass filled with smoke. "What are you doing to it?"

"It's going through a process where we test to make sure it's not carrying any diseases and that nothing strange is on it. It'll go for more intense testing later, but, as we already know how very dangerous it is, we need to make sure nobody opens this without the proper preparation—not to mention proper authority."

"Should have to wear a full hazmat suit," she said, "so it can't grab onto their face."

"That's an interesting idea," he said. He motioned her back out of the room.

The door closed, but a window was in the door. They watched what was going on inside. Within, the glass tube flashed.

She gasped. "What's that?"

He shook his head. "I don't know," he said, "but it can't

be anything good. It will give us a computer scan of the results when complete." He turned to Henry. "Make sure this door stays locked. Nobody gets in but me. Do you understand?"

Henry nodded. He tapped the iPad in his hand and held it out for Sebastian.

Sebastian signed his name, apparently on some kind of order, and then Henry took the iPad, swiping the order wherever it needed to be.

She watched all this as close as she could, but it wasn't close enough to read the writing.

Then Henry led the way to another room, giving Lacey a quick tour as they passed several glass doors. "This room has computer-coded security," Henry said, pointing, "like a bank vault full of safe-deposit boxes run by a computer." He used one of the big ornate keys he had to unlock the next door that they came to, opened it and said, "I have them all locked in."

Henry remained in the hallway. Sebastian entered first, Lacey next, with Hunter bringing up the rear. Inside was a large lab.

"So why is this under lock and key, and the others are all computer coded?" Lacey asked.

"This is part of the original building," Sebastian said walking through another door. "The computer-coded areas were all upgrades. In this section though, a key is just fine."

She turned, looking around, realizing it was a big office and sitting room. "It's homey here at least." She spotted her sketchbook on the desk. "Why is that here?"

"We were trying to scan in the images, remember?"

"Right. Your friend Bruno wanted a copy."

He looked at her but didn't say a word.

She walked over and flipped through the pictures until she came to the one with the masks. "This blows me away," she muttered, "that I could have drawn this."

As she finished speaking, a huge explosion vibrated the area. She stared at Sebastian for a second. They bolted for the hallway. Henry lay on the floor, breathing, but bleeding from a head wound.

She dropped to his side and motioned to the others. "Go, go, go! Find out what happened." But, as she returned her gaze to Henry, she saw that the previous room they had left the mask in was open. She stared in shock. "Tell me the mask is still in there, please?"

Sebastian checked out that first room, his face grim when he shook his head. "No, it's gone."

She took several shaky breaths. Her heart slammed against her chest as she thought about all the damage that mask could do. She tried to stop the bleeding on Henry's temple. "He's either been hit, or the blast sent him flying back, and he hit his head on something." He was breathing fine, so she hoped he was just knocked out.

"I've got somebody coming to help him," Sebastian said, "and security will be here shortly."

In fact, uniformed guards rushed down the hall toward them now.

She stepped away from Henry as two men dropped down beside him, wearing the same uniforms as Henry did. She searched around, but Sebastian was gone. Frowning, she walked over to the open room where the mask had been but was stopped by one of the guards and taken back to the nice office room she'd been in before the blast happened and was told to wait.

Collapsing onto a chair, she frowned, wondering what

the hell was going on. Did the energy in that mask take offense to being held captive inside that glass container, or was it something else? Like was the explosion caused by the sparks?

She sat in front of her sketchbook, studying the drawing of the masks, hating that one was on Sebastian's face and the other on Hunter's. As she stared at the sketch it came to her that they'd found one mask—but only one. Was the second mask still intact? Was it here? Or still at the Mayan ruins? Considering Sebastian had never even seen a mask she wondered if there even was one. Maybe she'd drawn two masks because both men had abilities? They'd only found one mask, and that worried her even more.

She continued to study the drawing. She wanted to go back to the cave-in and see if it was there. She knew Sebastian and Hunter would both fight her on that. But, given what was going on with this first mask, it was more than important that they find the second one.

If it was even here …

She paced the room, wondering what she was supposed to do. Should she wait for Hunter and Sebastian to come for her? But, after twenty minutes, she couldn't stand it anymore. She marched back to the door of this room, only to find she had been locked in. She took several deep breaths to still the panic already crowding her mind. She pounded on the door. "Open up! Open up!" she cried out. "Let me out."

But she heard nothing. She walked back to the desk, and, of course, there were no windows because they were underground. She threw herself into the chair and again studied the masks she had drawn.

A horrible thought formed as she considered what else was housed here. "What if that energy wanted to be in here?

In this secluded building full of other artifacts? What if that energy wanted those other artifacts? Could it sense them?"

Then she raised her gaze and studied the walls, seeing framed pictures from the old Mayan ruins and realized quite possibly that Sebastian had relics from the Mayan ruins stored here as well. Maybe that mask energy wanted to connect with those. Could it know? Maybe something needed to pull itself together amid the Pompeii finds and the Mayan finds kept in this facility.

Just thinking these crazy things made her cringe. How far had she come in a few days?

She got up and studied the images on the wall. It took her about ten minutes before she finally saw what she was looking for, on one of the temples still three-quarters buried. It was a tiny carving in the wall, and damn if it didn't look like a mask, like the one she had drawn around Hunter's face—the second mask. She leaned closer, wishing she had had that photograph enlarged, so she could see the details better.

She wandered the room looking for more pictures of it. And froze. There appeared to be one of the same location– only minus that rough carving. She pulled out her cell phone but there was no signal. Of course not, being down as far underground as she was. So no way to contact Sebastian and ask him.

She walked back over to study the mask in the framed picture and then murmured, "Is that mask here? Maybe it doesn't need to be the whole mask... Is there a piece of that mask here? Are you trying to connect with it? But then how would you even know if it were?"

Just then the door opened, and Sebastian walked in.

She raced to him and threw herself into his arms.

His arms closed around her securely, and he just held her tight.

"Are you okay?" she demanded, grabbing his face so she could look into his eyes.

"I'm fine," he reassured her, gently hugging her close. "And Hunter is too."

She looked around him, but the door was shut again. "Where is he?"

He gave her a crooked smile. "Hunting."

She tried to step out of his arms, but he tucked her closer and just held her. "Just stay here for a moment," he muttered thickly. "I need this."

She gave a broken laugh. "I need to show you something."

He looked down at her inquiringly, and she led him to the framed photos, tapped the carving she'd seen in the picture then pointed to the similar image only minus the carving. He studied it for a long moment and then shrugged. "I don't know what you're trying to show me."

She walked over to her sketchbook, picked up the drawings of the masks and brought it so he could compare the two. His sharp indrawn breath said he got the message.

"I don't know what it means," she said softly. "But what's the chance the mask wanted to come here? That it was attracted to whatever else was here? That it *needed* to come here and used you to get here?"

He stared at her. "And why would it do that?" he asked cautiously.

"What's the chance"—she raised her drawing alongside the photograph on the wall—"that there's another mask here?"

"No." He shrugged. "I know all the pieces here. I would

have recognized it."

"What if one of the little pieces which came back with you from the Mayan dig was part of another mask?"

"We didn't bring anything like that back. Remember we barely got out with our lives, let alone any artifacts."

"Maybe, but it wouldn't have been a very big or a very identifiable piece." He motioned at the two pictures on the wall. "And that doesn't explain why the image is there in one picture and not in the other."

"But if you did, it would have an *energy* signature, right?" she asked slowly.

He stared at her with respect. His gaze changed suddenly. "Right, it would at that." He turned to study the drawing in her hand and then the photograph. "Come with me." He held out his hand.

She grasped it tightly. "Shall I bring the sketchbook?"

He shook his head. "No, leave it behind." He led the way out in the hall, down in the direction where they'd passed the security guard, then deeper into the hallway. He brought up his cell phone and punched in a code. A clicking in the lock on the door in front of them was heard. He opened it enough to peer inside and then opened it wider for her to step in with him. The air was cool, chilly even. He left the door open on purpose, putting a doorstop wedge on the floor, so it wouldn't close by accident.

She frowned as she watched him. She was going to say something but held back the words. He led the way to a vault.

He used a combination to unlock the vault, pulled it open and looked at her. "Stay here."

She shrugged and said, "Sure, no problem."

He walked inside and returned with a small bag. At a

nearby table he gently dumped out the contents.

She peered at them. They appeared to be broken pieces of metal and rock. "What are they?"

"Everything I brought back from the Mayan site ten years ago—which as you can see is very little," he said in a hushed whisper. "Four men died there. I didn't have any reason or desire to catalogue the inventory from that trip. We had a hard enough time trying to explain the deaths of our team members. We put it down to accidents, and there was no way to retrieve the bodies. It was as if the site itself swallowed them whole."

"Considering the cave-in where we found the mask, I hope you don't mean that literally."

He shook his head. "In a way, I do ..."

She stared up at him to confirm he was serious, then took in a deep breath. "Well ..." She gently moved the pieces around on the table. "So they're nothing important?"

"Only one." He picked out a couple and placed them to the side. Then handed her a four-inch piece of black metal.

"I carried it as a good luck piece for having survived that massacre up until a few days ago, when I put it back in here. At the time I didn't understand why it was there. I figured that maybe one of the other men had dropped it. I picked it up and I tucked it away in my pocket without thinking about it."

She looked up at him. "Did you pick it up before the men died or afterward?"

He frowned at her, then shook his head. "Oh, I don't like where you're going with this at all ..."

"It doesn't matter if you like it or not," she said gently, "but you need to answer the question. Because what if picking this up caused those men's deaths?"

"Then I'll feel guilty for those men's deaths. I'll carry that grief for the rest of my life. So it's a good thing I picked it up afterwards."

She covered his hand with hers and whispered, "What we need to do is solve that nightmare, so we can solve this one." And that was a tall order. "It's why you could cross the invisible barrier," she said suddenly. "That's suddenly making sense. We need to know how this piece got to the Mayan site."

"I don't know how," he said, staring at the piece of black metal. "At the time, I wondered if one of the men hadn't taken it into the Mayan ruins on his own. In which case, I needed to bring it back out."

Rocked by that suggestion, she settled back on her heels and nodded. "In a way, that would also make sense. Maybe he knew about something at the site. Maybe taking it there triggered something. Maybe it was a piece of energy from here that started something there."

"We're grasping at straws with these theories."

"It doesn't matter," she said gently. "Maybe this was all accidental, and nothing could have avoided it. Maybe one of your friends took this piece of metal from Pompeii, as a keepsake. Maybe he didn't intend it to cause any kind of destruction. What if he had been in Pompeii years ago— before the Mayan dig—working here, and found the piece and kept it as a memento? Then took the piece to work on the Mayan dig with you ten years ago."

He stared at her in growing alarm.

She studied him, and then she knew. "That's exactly what happened, isn't it? One of the four men who died ten years ago at the Mayan dig had been in Pompeii earlier. And he removed the metal pieces, taking it to the Mayan ruin and, for whatever reason, started a cycle of cataclysmic events. Maybe adding the carving to the spot himself either on his own or under the influence of the mask? Someone had to as it's not there in both photos. There wasn't a Mayan mask at all. It was part of the Pompeii masks. That's why you never saw the mask there."

His mouth opened and then closed.

She whispered, "Who was there with you at the Mayan site who had been in Pompeii before that?"

He closed his eyes, shook his head and whispered, "Jeremiah. My other partner, Jeremiah."

"That doesn't make any sense," she frowned. "you said Hunter rescued you. That only the two of you survived."

"That's correct," Sebastian whispered. "Jeremiah died at the ruins."

She frowned up at him. "No. How could that be? Isn't that the man I met?"

He opened his eyes and stared at her steadily. "Yes, absolutely it's the man you met."

She took a step back and shook her head. "Then you have to be wrong," she said, "because the man I met wasn't dead."

"Jeremiah is definitely dead. You were speaking with his ghost."

CHAPTER 22

LACEY STARED AT Sebastian, swallowing hard as her mind wrapped around what he said. "I know you believe he's a ghost," she said slowly, wondering if maybe he was the one off *his* rocker.

He gave her a lopsided grin. "I'm not crazy," he said. "Sweetheart, I was there with him when he died."

"But he looked like flesh and blood, sitting right beside me," she whispered.

"He does, doesn't he?" Sebastian said with a gentle smile. "It doesn't change the fact he is no longer on the Earthly plane." He held out his hand containing the small black metal fragment.

"So how old is the site buried in the Mayan ruins?"

"Dates back to about 900 AD."

She studied the piece. "How could an energy from 900 AD live long enough to care about a piece of metal from its Mayan ruins that's now here in a Pompeii ruin, in the twenty-first century? Answer? Because it doesn't. It's all part of the same Pompeii ruin."

"For that, I have no explanation," Sebastian said slowly. "This is all very confusing as it is, but, right now, we have to protect this piece and I think your sketches and the mask itself."

"But the mask is gone. So is the piece of the second

mask safe here?" she asked cautiously. She glanced around at the secure underground space he had built. "You have one guard injured. How many others are as well?"

Pocketing the piece of metal, he walked to a wall panel, pulled it back to show a monitoring system of other rooms. Grimly they studied each monitor as he counted four other men down.

She shook her head. "This is terrible."

He tapped one of the screens as black energy filled the room in view. "It's in there."

"*It?*"

He slid her a sideways look. "Either the mask or whoever is part of the mask."

Her breath sucked back against her throat. "That is a scary thought. Where is that room located?"

"Down the hall," Sebastian said, while the two of them looked both ways.

The hallway had several men collapsed on the floor.

In her heart of hearts, she knew some were dead. Whatever was going on here, it was too deadly to leave alone. There was no immunity here. "What if you gave it that piece you've been carrying around?" she asked.

"I have no idea what would happen. It could be good. It could be very bad." Sebastian grabbed her hand. "I want you to stay here. I'm going after it."

She looked at him and shook her head. "I think you're missing a very important factor here. I can control that mask. At least when it's on, I can take it off. I don't know about any of these other people. And I think *it* is after that piece in your pocket," she said, motioning to his leg. "It might decide to attack you to get it."

The secured door slammed open as the words fell from

her lips. She jumped closer to Sebastian as one of the guards staggered in, blood pouring from a head wound. She raced to him as he cried out, "The mask ... Don't know what happened but the mask got loose."

Grim-faced, Sebastian nodded, helped the man to sit on the couch, while Lacey checked his head wound.

"What about the others?" she asked urgently. "Are they alive or dead?"

He stared up at her, his eyes haunted. "I don't know how they can still be alive," he whispered. "It looks like they've been butchered."

She shot Sebastian a look.

He nodded. "Yes, that's the same as what happened at the Mayan site."

She nodded, checked the head wound while the guard pulled out a handkerchief from his pocket. She used that to put pressure on the bleeding area and said to Sebastian, "We have to go after it."

The guard grabbed her arm. "You can't," he said urgently. "It will kill you too."

She smiled down at him. "It's after me, remember?" She didn't know that for sure because, in her mind, that piece Sebastian had was maybe what it ultimately wanted. But how this all fit together, she didn't know.

Sebastian looked at her, clearly hating the idea.

She stared up at him and said, "You know there's no other way."

He gave a clipped nod and reached out a hand.

She reached back as she told the guard, "Keep applying pressure. We'll be back." And she dashed out into the hall with Sebastian.

Once their door had been breached, chances were the

mask was on its way toward her. She bent down and checked the guard at the desk. He was alive but unconscious. She couldn't see any visible wounds. That, at least, meant he wasn't going to bleed to death.

At the far end of the hall was yet another fallen guard. Sebastian checked him, raised his gaze to her and shook his head. Her heart sank. Somehow she'd still hoped maybe they could get out of this with just a few casualties. But now that there was one confirmed death, it was a completely different story.

He motioned at the door in front of them. "It should be in there. That's where we put it when we first arrived."

"But these men on the floor in the hallway may mean it's not there anymore." She shrugged, reached for the doorknob and pulled on the door. It was unlatched, so it opened easily. As she stood in the open doorway, she could see the glass case was shattered and empty.

Behind her a voice roared. "It's not gone."

She spun to look at yet another of the uniformed guards. He held a knife in one hand and a gun in the other. The knife dripped with blood. He tucked the gun into his waistband, shifted the knife to his right hand and stared at her.

Her gaze was locked on his face and the mask that covered it. She could feel the claustrophobia reaching up to choke her. The feeling of having that mask on, not able to get it off, remained with her. That sense of suffocation, of wrongness. "How do you like the mask?" she said in a conversational tone. "It's quite something, isn't it?"

The man just stared at her, his eyes hot, feverish. She hadn't had the mask on very long, and Stefan had helped her get it off. What would have happened if it had stayed on longer? Would she have ended up looking like this man? Acting like this man?

She took a step toward him.

He held the knife in a ready-to-attack position.

"Have you tried to take it off?" she asked.

He stared at her and shook his head. "I don't want to," he growled. "It's fantastic. It's all-powerful."

She sighed. "So you have psychic abilities then?"

He waved the knife around. "I don't have any psychic abilities. But I'm happy to gut you regardless."

"Not in the market for a death today," she said, studying the mask. "Mask, are you sure you want to be with him and not with me?"

An odd silence hung in the air. The man grabbed the mask, as if to hold it on his head. "You can't take it from me," he roared. "I'll kill you first."

"And why would you kill me?" She backed up ever-so-slightly. "Why do you want to hurt me?"

The man looked confused, but he was in some kind of a rage, running on primitive emotions, desires, not thinking clearly.

She studied the mask. It glowed or was it her seeing the energy of it? "What's the chance that, if you don't have psychic abilities, you have to keep the mask on until you're vanquished? Maybe the mask fills you with bloodthirst. The mask, instead of making you stronger with your psychic abilities, maybe it makes you enraged instead?"

She heard Sebastian sucking in his breath. "That's quite possible," he said. "It might also explain why they had to imprison those with the mask. But you managed to get the mask off your face."

She nodded. "Because I am psychic," she admitted for

the first time. "And it's a mask geared for people like us. So this guard possibly has some unknown powers, or maybe the mask had few options and thought this man would give it the best chance of survival."

"I think you're giving it more human consciousness than it has," Sebastian said. "I don't think it has the ability to make cognitive decisions."

"No," she said softly. "It's running on instinct. It's in a negative position. It needs power. It'll take negative power if that's its only option. And, from the looks of the guard in front of us, I'd say that's what he's producing."

"Hence the attacks?"

She stepped a little closer, Sebastian grabbing her arm.

"Mask," she whispered out loud but spoke stronger in her mind. "Come to me. I have the energy you want. I have energy that feeds your soul, not this nasty negative energy that hurts everyone."

Sebastian, realizing what she was doing, squeezed her arm. "You have to be careful. Just because you got it off once, doesn't mean you can again."

"My choices are limited." Her full attention was on the mask again. "Mask, come to me," she said with an air of authority.

In front of them, the mask slowly dissolved, like a series of metal plates receding before it disappeared into a black energy. The guard stared at them for a moment before falling to his knees, then flat on his face to the floor.

She motioned to the guard. "Sebastian, check him out."

"No," Sebastian said, his voice hard. "Look."

The darkness slunk around her feet, going higher and higher up her body until it totally encompassed her, except for Sebastian's hand connecting the two of them. The dark energy kept gyrating around where his hand was, as if trying to find a way to separate her from him.

"Don't let me go," she cried out.

The mask formed around her face and then locked in tight. She opened her eyes to stare mutely at Sebastian. She took several long, slow, deep breaths, hating the claustrophobic feeling, but it wasn't new this time. She'd been here before. She could do this. She took several steps forward, still hanging tight to Sebastian's hand.

"How do we secure it?" she whispered to Sebastian. She could feel urges running through her. The vestiges of energy from the guard. She could almost see the visions as he had attacked his friends, killing two, mortally wounding another. She tried to cleanse away that energy, remembering what Stefan had told her: that love was the answer to all. She may have opened this door, but this mask had been waiting.

She didn't know who had broken the glass case or whether the mask itself had done the damage, but it would take something very special to keep this black energy contained. Sebastian led her ever-so-slowly toward the room where they had originally placed the mask for security.

She could feel the mask warring with her. It was still on a blood hunt, the thirst of that violent energy rippling through its being. She kept pouring out love, purity, joy, happiness, anything to help combat the viciousness surging through her—remnants of its pairing with the guard.

Sebastian still hung on to her. The mask was telling her that he was her next victim, to reach out and take what she wanted.

That was the last thing she wanted—to hurt Sebastian. If this mask truly was one used for psychic abilities, it should know her. It should know she had the abilities and that she was of sweetness and light … And it should be easing back on the viciousness and the bloodthirstiness, though it was even now calling for more.

In the same room, Sebastian reached into his side pocket awkwardly—because it was on the side where his hand was holding on to hers—and pulled out the missing piece of metal, placing it on the table with the shattered glass tube. She stared at it, sensing the mask, wanting, gloating the piece it was after.

"It's not part of this mask," she whispered. "It's part of the second mask."

"What can it do with it?"

"I don't know," she cried out. "But it wants it."

The mask tightened down around her throat and neck. She gasped.

Sebastian stepped in front of her. "Remember how you can control it. It had control of the guard, but you're the one with abilities. *You* control *it*." Still holding on to her, he brushed the busted glass off the pedestal and walked to a safe, unlocked it. "Maybe they were forged of the same metal," Sebastian theorized.

She watched Sebastian, her breath heavy as anticipation coursed through her.

He pulled out a metal box. It looked like a minisafe. He opened it.

She saw it was empty.

He looked at her, looked at the mask, but didn't say a word.

She whispered, "Put the piece of metal in the box."

Surprised, he did as she requested. Almost instantly the mask began to detach from her face. As, soon as she could, she pulled it off and slammed it into the metal case, shutting the lid securely.

She looked up at Sebastian and said, "I heard the metal hit the inside of the metal box, so I presume it's still in mask form."

He nodded, his fingers busy closing the latches on the side of the box. "What do you think it wanted that metal piece for?"

"I think it belongs to the sister mask," she said. "As if they're a pair. Possibly separated a long time ago."

He looked up at her in surprise.

She shrugged. "I don't know what I know. All I can tell you is the words that keep coming out of my mouth."

"Good enough," he said. "It'd be nice to have all this recorded though."

"It would," she said, "because I'm not sure I'll believe any of this afterward."

With the box now secured, he replaced it inside the safe and locked it.

"Did anybody see what we just did?"

He shook his head. "No. I shut down the monitor to this room before we left."

She took several long and deep breaths, staring at the safe. "Even now it's calling to me. Asking me to free it."

He gently led her from the room. As he stepped out, he locked the door securely.

"We should clean up that glass," she murmured.

"First off," he said, "we have injured men to attend to."

She walked back to find the one guard sitting up, holding his head.

His face lit up when he saw her. "Are you okay?"

She nodded. "I am. But several men aren't."

The guard's face collapsed. "I saw him. I've never seen

him look like that before. He had something weird over his face."

No point in explaining. She checked his head wound, found the bleeding had slowed and said, "You need stitches."

He brushed it off. "My brother is a doctor. I'll go to him." He got up and staggered to the door, looking around at the bloody devastation. When he saw Sebastian bent over one of the guards, he said, "I don't think I care to do this job anymore."

"Understood." Sebastian straightened, then stepped away, pulling out his phone to make several calls.

Lacey sat on the couch the guard had vacated, her mind wrapping around all the details she'd just seen and felt. The mask had taken on such a bloodthirst within the guard that he had killed almost everyone around him. So many people had lost their lives because of that mask.

And yet, when she'd had it on, it was all about psychic abilities. It was almost as if there was no way to know how the mask would react until it was on someone. Though she didn't think the guard was a bad person, the combination had been brutal, and, while wearing the mask, the guard had killed his friends.

Explanations would be a bitch.

Ten minutes later Sebastian walked into the room, relief on his face when he saw her. He crouched in front of her, reaching up to brush her cheek. "How are you?"

She gave him a sad smile. "Dazed, in awe and shock. But I will be fine."

"Come on. Let's get you home safe and sound."

She gave a startled laugh. "After what I've seen tonight? I'm not sure there is any such thing as *safe and sound*."

Standing, he tugged her into his arms and held her close.

"I know the feeling," he whispered. "It took me a long time after I came back from the Mayan ruins to understand what my new reality was. I'd always seen auras, but I had never seen the dead before. But, after that energy back then, and I think maybe because of Hunter too, it seems like I've seen nothing but, since."

She shook her head. "And yet, you didn't see the man at the restaurant?"

"I did see him," he corrected, "but he was a ghost. No living man was on that restaurant rooftop. I could see him—or his aura rather. Same as the table of well-dressed couples."

She groaned. "They seemed so real."

With a chuckle he led her out to the hallway. She could see first responders arriving. "Can you leave?"

"No," he said. "Bruno is coming to take you home."

Surprised, she looked at Sebastian. "Bruno?"

"Yes, he'll take you back to the apartment."

She frowned. "Is there a bedroom down here?"

He shook his head. "No."

"I don't want to leave you behind."

He frowned. "The thing is, I will be here for several hours."

She motioned to the couch behind her. "I'll be happy to stay there."

He studied her for a long moment, then tilted her chin up and kissed her, a long sweet kiss so unlike the little pecks he'd given her up until now. She reached up, her fingers stroking along his neck, sliding into the curls at the base of his nape.

When he lifted his head, he murmured, "Then lie down on the couch. I'll wake you when I'm done."

She smiled, walked over to the couch, curled up and was

asleep almost instantly.

SEBASTIAN WASN'T SURE what to do with her. In his heart of hearts he wanted to send her back to the States so she stayed safe. But he didn't know what *safe* meant anymore.

She was so damn special, and she'd come so close to getting hurt tonight, possibly even killed.

His gaze surveyed the EMTs coming with stretchers to collect the dead men. The police were here as well. He had already called two of the people he knew on the force. He wasn't sure how to explain what had just happened.

A guard went unexpectedly berserk and killed his buddies. That was all he could really say, but was it fair to the poor man who'd been caught up with the mask's evil energy? As it happened, he had been a disgruntled employee. Another man had been promoted above him. Maybe that energy had attracted the mask to him, had expanded on it, had helped the guard act out his darkest thoughts.

If it couldn't have the good energy, it would take the negative. Sebastian had seen that time and again in civilization. If they couldn't get kind appreciation, then they would often take a kickass fight.

The police walked toward him, and the questions started. He gave the statement as best he could. When they wanted to wake up Lacey, he refused, saying he'd bring her to the station the next day, that she was exhausted and in shock still. They'd been content with that.

The injured men had been taken to the hospital. Sebastian walked up to the guard who'd done all the killing. The paramedic was crouched at his side but looked up as Sebastian approached. "He's dead."

"I'm sorry," Sebastian said. He couldn't say it aloud, but it was almost a relief. The man would get blamed, but he likely wouldn't have a clue how or what he'd done. In this way, it was easier, though not for his family. They wouldn't understand.

The paramedic looked at him. "And you saying he just collapsed?"

Sebastian nodded. "He fell on his knees, then fell face forward." He pointed to the man's nose, broken from hitting the floor.

"He must have had a heart attack," the paramedic said with a frown. "There are no obvious wounds anywhere."

Sebastian nodded. "It did happen fast."

"It happens like that sometimes," the paramedic said. "They just drop dead."

Sebastian had never seen it before, and he never wanted to see it again. He stayed until the bodies were collected and the forensic team came in. One of his friends, a police officer, walked toward him. Sebastian asked him, "May I leave? I want to take Lacey home."

The officer turned to look at the sleeping woman and nodded. "It sounds like you two have had a horrific afternoon."

"We did indeed," Sebastian said. "Not much fun for any of us."

"Take her home but bring her to give a statement tomorrow."

"I will," Sebastian said. He looked around at the building, wondering where the hell Hunter had gone. Sebastian hadn't thought of Hunter in hours, but, last Sebastian knew, Hunter had been outside on guard duty. He must be wondering what the hell was going on by now. As Sebastian walked over to Lacey, he called Hunter on his cell phone. "Where did you disappear to?"

"I was hunting," Hunter said in a succinct voice. "Black energy left the building. Even left some psychic footprints."

Sebastian froze, his heart slamming against his chest. "Seriously?"

"Yeah. I'm serious." Hunter sighed heavily. "But I lost its trail. It's like it evaporated in front of me. And so did the footprints."

"Where are you now?"

"Back at the apartment," Hunter said. "Are you coming?"

"Yes, and I'm bringing Lacey, but I hate to wake her. She's sleeping on the couch."

"Protect her," Hunter said. "I'll watch out for you."

Sebastian crouched beside Lacey and tried to lift her up. She awoke instantly, flung her arms around his neck and hugged him tight. He stood with her in his arms, but she fought to stand on her own two feet.

She smiled up at him. "Nice thought," she said, "but we've both been through too much to need any extra physical exertion."

With her at his side, they returned to the apartment. As they walked into the third floor, he tried to lead her to her apartment.

She shook her head. "No, I'm sleeping with you tonight."

He smiled, tucking her close. When they walked in his place, they saw Hunter lounging on the couch.

She looked at him and frowned. "Where did you disappear to?"

He gave her a warm, sleepy smile. "Apparently you were

having a hell of a time inside."

"Yes," she said. "We could have used your help."

"And I would have," he said, "but I've been hunting energy that escaped the building."

Her shoulders sagging, she whispered, "Are you saying it's not over?"

He shrugged. "I'm not sure if it's over or not. I couldn't track it any farther, but I have a decent idea where it's going." He motioned toward her. "Go to bed. You're asleep on your feet. We'll talk tomorrow."

She looked around the apartment and asked, "What bed am I taking?"

Without a word Sebastian led her down the hall to his room. She looked at the large bedroom, nodded and headed to the bathroom first. She came out, stripped down to her underwear and crawled in bed.

He followed suit, stripping down to his boxers, then he joined her in bed, tucking her closely against him, and they both crashed.

CHAPTER 23

L ACEY ROLLED OVER. Her body was sore and achy. She couldn't quite figure out why. She opened her eyes and frowned. She bolted upright, not recognizing the room she was in. The sheet fell away, and she saw she was in only a bra and panties. Shaking her head, she looked around to see Sebastian curled up beside her. And then the evening's events came flooding back.

She crashed back down onto the bed, tears welling as she thought about the poor men who had lost their lives last night. How many other lives was that mask responsible for? Or would be responsible for in the future? She could feel the compassion and empathy in her heart for the poor guard who'd been wearing the mask. It wasn't for the faint of heart, and neither was it for anyone not of pure heart.

She didn't hold herself in any higher regard than anyone else. But she'd spent her life fairly blameless. She'd always tried to do good versus bad, to help others versus hurt them. And the mask was getting more from that energy than from the destructiveness of the man it had been on earlier. She vaguely remembered coming home. But not the details. She was so exhausted. She remembered snoozing on the couch at the office building, then Sebastian waking her up.

In the back of her mind she remembered a conversation about not wanting to leave him. And it had been the truth.

In her state of mind, that was the only thing she could have given, the truth. She didn't want to play games. She didn't want to make a competition out of her relationship. She wanted honesty, and the honest truth was, she wanted to be with him. Now and, God help her, forever.

She curled back under the covers and slid her fingers into his. Immediately his fingers closed around hers. She smiled and let her eyes drift closed.

He whispered against her face, his warm breath bathing her cheeks, "You should still be sleeping."

"I woke up in a strange bed in a strange room," she said with a chuckle. "That brought me wide awake."

He smiled, snaked an arm around her and tucked her closer.

She twisted so she was curled, spoon side against him, and laid her head against his arm. She worried about Hunter's words last night. "Is it really not over?"

Sebastian squeezed her gently. "I'm not sure stuff like this is ever over," he muttered. "But it should be the end of our involvement."

"I hope so," she said. "Are we supposed to go to work today?"

"We'll be doing something. I have to take you to the police station later to give a statement. But you don't have to feel like you need to go to the dig."

"The team is due some days off, aren't they?"

Sebastian thought about it and nodded. "The next two days are free time anyway. A festival is in town, and everyone has the time off."

"I need to tell my cousin. Though I don't want to explain too much to Chana. Not sure I even could."

"Send her a text," he said. "Your purse is beside your

clothing."

She thought about it and then nodded. She got up and made her way to the bathroom. When she came back out, she grabbed her cell phone and sent her cousin a text, then slipped back under the covers.

"What did you tell her?"

"Unexpectedly spent the night somewhere else," she said with a laugh. Her phone buzzed. She read the message out loud. "Hope you and Sebastian have a good day together. If you need me, text me." Lacey smiled. "That's what cousins are for."

He smiled and kissed her on her cheek. "It's nice to see you're close."

"I never asked," she said. "Do you have any family?"

He chuckled. "Parents both live in Illinois."

"No siblings?"

He shook his head. "No siblings but the men in the foundation were like brothers. We did a lot of traveling together, a lot of working together, a lot of living together at these sites."

"You mean, Jeremiah and Callum?"

"Yes. Now Colin, Callum's brother, is my partner."

"I haven't met Colin."

"No. He's far away, looking at something in the Amazon."

"All under the same foundation umbrella?"

"Exactly. It still works out well for the two of us though," he clarified.

"Who inherited after Jeremiah passed on?"

"Technically his part of the foundation was split between the two of us."

She nodded. "I guess that makes sense."

"Yes." He snugged her closer against him. "Can you sleep some more?"

She shook her head. "I'll be tired later, but I'm wide awake now."

"Good," he said, rolling her over so she was on her back, pinned beneath him.

She raised her eyebrows, and a smile formed on her lips. "Why?" she asked in a gentle voice. "What do you have in mind?"

He lowered his head gently, his tongue tracing the outline of her lips. "I don't know," he said, his warm breath bathing her face as he dropped kisses beneath her chin and down her neck. "It seems like we have an opportunity to spend a little time together without the rest of the world intruding."

"I'm always open to that." She laughed. She stroked his hair and whispered, "I should have realized we'd end up here."

He nodded, surging up a little bit higher so he could kiss her nose, her cheeks, her eyelids. "You should have," he said. "From the minute our energies blended together, you should have known."

"Well, give me a break," she said on a laugh. "It's not like I have much experience seeing energy."

"Not a problem," he said. "I'll teach you." He lowered his head and kissed her.

They shared such a connection, such a meeting of two energies, it was almost like she could feel the sparks. Heat flowed from his mouth to hers. She lay here, stunned, as she felt not passion but his energy soothing the inside of her system, her muscles, her tissue, before reaching the end of her fingertips and the end of her toes. "Is it supposed to be like that?" she asked in wonder.

"Absolutely," he whispered, his voice thick, guttural. "When it's right, it's right." And he kissed her again, this time his tongue sliding inside her mouth to tangle gently with hers.

She wrapped her arms around his neck, wanting to experience everything he had to offer. This was such a new world for her. Not just the energy stuff or this weird feeling when his kisses slid all the way to the base of her toes but just knowing she was with a man who she could respect and care for like she did Sebastian.

It had been a long time since her last relationship, and it had ended with her not hating him but hating what her ex-boyfriend had become. Somebody too selfish to help another. And she knew Sebastian would never be like that.

Soon her bra was off and tossed to the floor. She chuckled. "You're not just great with history. You're also great with the present day, aren't you?"

He loomed over her and gave her a snarky smile. "Sweetheart, with you, I will be the best I can be anytime," he promised.

And he proceeded to show her—his hands hot but gentle as they caressed every inch of her, smoothly divesting her of the last of her clothing. She moaned and twisted in his arms, loving the feeling of being connected in such an intimate way. Sparks flared at just the touch of his hands on her skin, sending her senses into overdrive.

Finally she wrapped her arms around him, demanding he come to her. He chuckled and took off his boxers, and she reached down to grasp his erection—sliding up and down to explore the full measure of it.

He pulled her hands away and promised, "Next time."

His voice was thick. "I can't wait this time."

And without any more warning, he slid inside and kept going right to the hilt.

She lay stunned as the energetic weird sensation that had flowed through her body with his kisses now floated upward through her soul with his possession. She arched her back, crying out, "I've never felt anything like this."

"I haven't either," he said. "Send that same energy back to me."

And she did. She closed her eyes and let all the energy in her heart, her body and her passion flow down her body into his, back up to his head and down to his toes. He cried out as the energy circulated from one to the other. They were both locked in a loop of an energy force field so much bigger than they were. And yet, it was here because of them, because of who they were and who they became together.

When he could, he started to move. With his arms shaking, he slowly pulled out and then slid all the way in. She wrapped her thighs high up around his hips to stop him from pulling out too far. Then, as if something inside him snapped, he plunged deep, his back arching as he drove faster and faster.

When he reached down between them to touch the tiny nub, she cried out as her climax rippled through her. But it wasn't a normal climax. It was as if their combined energy had amplified every sensation. Every bit of her skin buzzed; the inside of her throbbed and pounded as her life took on a whole new meaning. She heard him cry out above her as he slowly collapsed atop her, still holding his weight on his arms to protect her. She wrapped her arms around his neck, her body thrumming in joy.

He whispered, "Are you okay?" His hands slid up,

touching the tears in the corner of her eyes.

She could barely speak. "I'm much more than okay."

He wrapped her up tight, fell to her side and pulled her close. "Good," he whispered. "Because I'm absolutely fantastic." He pulled the sheets over them and whispered, "Now sleep, if you can."

And she didn't need any more urging. She closed her eyes and let sleep take her back under.

SEBASTIAN WOKE UP an hour later. Somehow Lacey had shifted to the far side of the bed, the covers tossed off her, and she lay spread-eagle across the mattress, completely comfortable in her skin. And a beautiful skin it was. He leaned over and kissed her gently at the nape of her neck. Then he got off the bed, went into the bathroom and had a shower.

It was later than he had expected, but he wouldn't get upset about it. This time spent with Lacey was too special. When he stepped out of the shower, she was still sleeping. He dressed and walked into the kitchen, finding Hunter sitting there. "Did you make coffee?"

Hunter shook his head. "No, I haven't been up very long." His voice was groggy, tired.

"Did you go back out hunting again?"

Hunter nodded grimly. "Honest to God, I tracked that energy back here to the apartment building."

In the act of making coffee, Sebastian froze, then turned to look at him. "Here?"

"I don't know how," Hunter said, "but it came upstairs."

Sebastian slowly finished putting the coffee on to brew and collapsed into the chair beside his friend. "Did you see black energy and psychic footprints in the hall?"

Hunter nodded. "I did."

"This far down?"

Grimly Hunter nodded. "Yes. But also at the other apartment door."

"What the hell?" Sebastian tried to think, tried to clear the glorious fog he'd been in all morning. "Did you recognize it?"

"Normally, I'd be able to, yes," Hunter said cautiously. "But, as you know, you cannot always count on what you thought you could."

"Explain," Sebastian demanded.

"Sometimes energy can mask itself, which is appropriate in this nightmare. Sometimes spirits or people have the ability to take on somebody else's energy, so it looks like theirs. If this dark energy is possessing somebody, then I wouldn't recognize it because it would have merged its signature with the person it was possessing."

"Oh, Jesus," Sebastian said, staring at Hunter. "So is there any way to know where and what that black energy is doing and who it is originally or who it is possessing?"

Hunter slowly shook his head. "Not for sure. Not unless we have a confrontation with it."

"I need to talk to the rest of the team."

"Most of them left to go to the festival downtown," Hunter said.

Sebastian stared at him blankly. "Oh, right. I forgot about that."

"You haven't been thinking clearly lately," Hunter said with a wry smile. He nodded toward the bedroom. "How is she this morning?"

"She's fine," Sebastian said absentmindedly.

"There's a chance she's the one carrying the dark energy. You know that, right?" Hunter said.

Sebastian froze. He thought about it and then shook his head. "No, that's not possible. I would see her aura changing. I would feel her energy changing too. I'm so close to her, my energy knows her. More than that my heart knows her."

"I'll trust you for that," Hunter said. "But then you need to consider it could be one of the team."

"Maybe, but who? I've worked with these people for months, some for years. Why would they or the energy do this now?"

But he and Hunter said the same answer at the same time. "The masks."

Sebastian focused on Hunter. "One of the things that came out last afternoon was that the mask was attracted to that piece of metal I brought back from the Mayan ruin ten years ago," Sebastian said. "It was just a small piece that I kept in my pocket. I took it out a few days ago and put it safely away."

"I don't remember you mentioning this piece before." Hunter leaned forward, studying Sebastian's face.

"No, I probably didn't. Certainly not back then. There was no time or thought for something as unimportant as that when we were in constant danger," Sebastian said. "It made no sense to me at the time. I thought someone dropped it, whether on purpose to salt the site or to discredit the site or some lazy visitor did it without malice. Lacey suggested someone who'd been at the Mayan ruin might have previously been to Pompeii, had taken it from here and had lost it at the Mayan site." He winced. "And then she noticed something on the photos I have on my wall from that trip." He quickly explained about the carving in the one and not on the other."

For a long moment Hunter just stared.

"Wow. That means someone scratched that on the wall and that someone was down there at the same time as you were. Which limits the options tremendously." Hunter nodded. "Lots of theories, now we need to prove something. Also we've seen things we can't explain numerous times, and, when it comes to this type of energy, time has no meaning."

He nodded. "But I don't understand something. Why that mask? Why did Linnea want the mask awakened?"

"That would explain maybe why we found the mask. Did you have that piece in your pocket while we were in that other part of the Pompeii dig?" Hunter asked.

Sebastian nodded. "I kept it with me every day as a memory of what happened to those men in the Mayan ruins. To remember to be grateful that I survived and to make something out of my life. But, when I saw what was happening to Lacey, I put it away for safekeeping."

"Jesus." Hunter rubbed his face. "Why?"

"Everything was so strange. I wasn't sure whether Lacey was the catalyst or whether this was all intended to happen the way it happened, I don't know," Sebastian said. "It certainly seems that the two wanted to be together."

"Was one energy attracting the other?" Hunter asked.

"Lacey says the little piece of metal that the mask wanted to be with was part of the other mask she drew. With your face."

Hunter stared at him. "Do you have the sketch of that?"

Sebastian walked over to where her sketchbooks had been dropped last night when they returned home. He brought one back with him. He opened to where the masks drawings were. Hunter looked at it, a frown forming on his face. "So the question is, where's the rest of that mask?"

"Honestly I think it was destroyed," Sebastian said. "I had just a small piece. I don't know for sure it's from that mask. I only have Lacey telling me it is, from whatever source is telling her."

"That's good enough for me," Hunter said.

"Me too. But she also said Linnea wanted that mask to be found."

"So what we have here is a mask that, if it's with a psychic, then it's all good things. They can control it. They can take it off. But, if a person who is not a psychic gets this mask, they can turn into a vicious killer, correct?" Hunter asked.

Sebastian nodded. "Yes, that's true as far as we can tell."

"So that doorless room we found likely had somebody's energy there who had on the mask but didn't have the ability to take it off, and they turned violent?"

Sebastian thought about it and then nodded slowly. "That makes sense. The person would have been walled-in there, jailed, and either a friend, family member or somebody who cared for them kept them alive, but they couldn't figure out how to get the mask off. Not forgetting that it would have been a witch hunt most likely, victims chosen for a reason and forced to prove themselves."

"True. And the person who wanted you to find the mask was Linnea."

"I think," Lacey said from the doorway, "that Linnea wanted us to find it and to keep it safe. She must have known the energy had reawakened and was dangerous." Lacey smiled at Hunter as she walked forward. She leaned over, gave Sebastian a kiss on the forehead and sniffed the air. "Just in time for coffee."

"So, if Linnea's sister was in the doorless room, was Linnea trying to protect her?"

"She was," Lacey said. "Linnea was the psychic. But her sister had told everyone that *she* was the one with the abilities—in her own misguided way to protect Linnea—so the tribunal set up a test, and Sabine failed in a big way. She was then put into this room. If she could take it off it would prove she was the one with the abilities. At the same time Linnea's pleading kept Sabine alive while Linnea tried to figure out how to help her sister get out of the mask. But, the longer Sabine wore it, the more out of control she became. In the meantime somehow she got free from the room and murdered a group of women as Pompeii exploded."

Lacey brought the cup of coffee over to the table and sat down. "So Linnea was hoping, when we found the mask, it would release her sister's spirit, and she could be freed once and for all. And if possible, keep it locked up and safe from everyone."

"Commendable on Linnea's part," Sebastian said. "But why the other mask?"

"I don't know anything about it. Neither does Linnea presumably." She frowned. "Unless it's because of the same usage, same energy, same something," she said, "they were attracted to each other. Maybe they needed two and she only saw one."

"True," Hunter said. "Maybe forged of the same metal?"

"Is it over with now?" Lacey asked with a smile. "Because I really want to hear both of you say, *Absolutely*."

Sebastian looked at Hunter. Hunter looked at him. They both turned to look at her, and her smile fell away.

"It's not, is it?"

Hunter shook his head. "Last night I left, and I tracked

dark energy complete with glowing psychic footprints from that nightmare yesterday afternoon at the security facility to this apartment building. It came up the stairs to the hallway. It also came down here to the apartments."

"What are you saying?" she asked hoarsely. "Because it's not me."

Sebastian gripped her fingers. "It's not you, and it's not me."

Relieved, she settled back. "It can't be my cousin, and I can't see it being any of the other workers." She turned to look at Sebastian. "You would have recognized that energy. And so would Hunter."

"Possibly, yes," Hunter said. "There are ways to disguise the energy by wrapping it around another person. It's also possible this energy was *masked* for a long time, and we're just now seeing the reality of who it really is."

She turned her gaze on Hunter. "Who is it then?"

He stared at her, opened his mouth to say something, when another voice came in the kitchen behind them.

A man spoke. "Funny, you are all specialists, and you still can't figure this out. It's me," Mark said. "It's always been me—at least the me inside."

And there, right beside them, Mark stood, with a silly grin on his face, but laid over his physical form was another entity—Jeremiah.

Sebastian's partner who died at the Mayan expedition.

CHAPTER 24

L ACEY STARED AT the man in front of her, her mind confused with what she saw and with what she heard. "I'm sorry?" she asked. "What are you saying?"

Mark sat down at the table with the rest of them—his gaze going from one to the other.

She studied his face to figure out what was wrong with it. It looked like somebody needed to tug it into place properly. She leaned forward and stared at him.

"Can you see me?" he asked.

She nodded slowly. "Well, I can certainly see something. What is it? I'm not exactly sure."

He laughed. "That's because I'm using Mark," Jeremiah said. "Poor Mark, he doesn't even know he's being used. He looked so confused that morning after he had damaged some of the tools and had taken others. At the time he had absolutely no problem busting them up. You'll find the stolen ones hidden in his room too. And he'd be horrified to realize he had nudged you into the street and into the path of that vehicle. But, of course, he knows nothing about it."

She shook her head in confusion. "Why? None of this makes any sense."

"Well, it does, if you understand what this is all about."

She sat back, her hand sliding over toward Sebastian. He gripped her fingers hard in reassurance. But she wasn't sure there was anything to be reassured about. "Then please explain," she said. "I'm new to all of this. I don't understand what I have to do with any of it."

"I'm not so sure it's you as much as it's Sebastian. You see? I went on that Mayan trip with him. There were three of us. Callum didn't make it. He died. Callum's brother, Colin, inherited his brother's share of the foundation."

"So you were one of the four men who died on that trip?"

"Yes, both of Sebastian's partners died. Very convenient, huh?" His laughter rang through the room, but there was a horrified twisted cackle to it.

She winced at the sound. "I highly doubt back then the foundation was very big or worth enough for *anyone* to be interested in killing off his partners so soon. It would have been much better to wait until millions of dollars were involved. Then kill you both," she said smoothly.

The men froze.

Mark/Jeremiah looked at her and chuckled again. "I like you," he said. "That's very smart."

"So why are you using Mark right now?" she asked. "You know you don't need to. I've seen you before."

Instantly Mark's face smacked into the table as Jeremiah stood separate from Mark. She looked at him clearly for the first time. This time she recognized that, for all the incredible job he'd done appearing real, she could now see he was indeed only a shadow of his former self. She stared at Mark, who appeared to be breathing but completely unconscious.

"Did you hurt Mark?"

Jeremiah shook his head. "Nope. I'm decent at getting in and out of bodies at will. Of course they have to be the right ones—the weak ones."

"I have no idea why I didn't recognize that before," she said. "Of course you're a ghost."

"But I fooled you at the beginning, didn't I? It took lots of energy. And, by using *your* energy, I could keep you confused and distracted."

Slowly she nodded, her hand instinctively going to the back of her neck and the hook she'd removed. "But what have you got to do with these masks?"

"You see? I wasn't very happy to be dead," he said bitterly. "Even worse, to see Sebastian go back home again safe and sound, on top of the world, having survived the most horrific events we'd ever seen."

"And you blame him for that?" she asked incredulously. "Why the hell wouldn't you want to see your best friend and partner survive? It's not like he wasn't completely torn up over everything that happened. Terrified too, I'd imagine."

"Sure. But he got to live, didn't he? He got to carry on as if nothing had happened. Whereas Callum and I were dead."

"It was the masks, wasn't it?" she asked suddenly. "Did you find a mask?"

He glared at her. "No. I had found several small pieces of metal here in Pompeii. I took them on the Mayan trip, hoping the others could help me figure them out. I tried to put it together. I accidentally put it on my face one night, just laughing while I was in my tent, all alone. But it caught hold of me. Before I understood what the hell was going on, Callum was dead, and the last of our guides was dead. I can't remember his name now."

"You killed them?" Sebastian gasped, staring at his best friend in horror. "All this time you've been coming here, visiting the site, visiting me, and you're the one who killed them?"

"But I didn't mean to," Jeremiah protested. "You know that."

Sebastian sank into his chair, staring at his best friend's spirit.

"Then why are you haunting Sebastian?" Hunter asked. "And why are you here now?"

"Because he took the piece I had of that mask. The one I had taken to the Mayan site. After I died the mask kind of disappeared but that was one of the original pieces. I recognized the design on it. I'd actually carved it on a rock down there as a joke. So I guess it's a good thing that whole area collapsed so my meddling didn't show up for the history books." He gave a deprecating laugh. "I never was a good archeologist, was I?"

He glared at Sebastian as if daring him to agree. When Sebastian stayed silent he continued. "I didn't realize why I was following him around until I saw that piece of metal again, and I recognized what it was. If he had one, there was a good chance he had others as well. There was a lot of power in that mask. Maybe with his help I could have controlled it. I could have taken it off. Maybe it wouldn't have been a slaughterhouse that night. Maybe I would have survived."

"How were you killed?" she asked slowly.

He turned to look at her. "The mask suffocated me I think. I remember the killing spree—the rage. I think it must have shattered around the same time. It seemed like an ugly explosion all around me. The cave-in happened at the same time but that's all I remember. I woke up the next morning as a ghost.

She stared at him. "So you found several pieces of this second mask at Pompeii, took it to the Mayan site and, as a joke put it over your face. Even though it looked innocent enough, it locked down on your face, and you couldn't get it off. You went into a mad frenzy. You ended up killing several people, and, when you couldn't get the mask off, it continued on its bloodthirsty quest and killed you. It's only in ghost form, some ten years later, that you saw Sebastian had a piece of the same mask in his pocket the whole time, and realized that's why you've been unable to leave him. Because you connected to that powerful mask energy back then and it's still dragging you around as it tries to return home. Only you're blaming him because you think he should have helped you years ago. That if he'd come to your rescue you'd have been freed from the mask and you'd still be alive today?"

He sat back in his chair and stared at her. "You laid that out pretty well. Surely the mask wasn't functioning properly, and the more pieces available, the better it would work. He'd found one piece that I dropped. So if he'd contributed that piece then I'd be alive."

"It worked for *psychics*." Lacey snorted, shook her head. "But why here? Why now? What do you have to do with Linnea?"

He looked at her in astonishment. "Nothing. Linnea's trying to save her sister. Her sister wore the mask and was suffocating, but she was dangerous, so she was forced to stay there until she could free herself of the mask or die. By chance that happened to be when Pompeii came crashing down. Linnea went to save her sister, hoping that, in the chaos of the volcano erupting, she'd get her out of that room, and they could find a way to get the mask off." His lips twisted. "She did release her sister. You don't really understand how Linnea died, do you?"

Lacey stared at him. "She said she got caught as she ran back to her own home."

"Oh, she got caught, all right. But guess by whom?"

She stared at him, feeling sick to her stomach, her hand going up to her throat. "Did her sister catch her?"

He slowly nodded. "She did indeed. Sabine killed Linnea, plus several other women. But Linnea also wounded her sister. They both fell into a pit and were burned by the lava flow. Where you found the first mask was where the sister died and so did Linnea. I have no clue where I found the pieces of the second mask or how it was destroyed. Likely the volcano."

"She doesn't seem to know she died in that pit though."

"That's because she's terrified of the mask living on and hurting someone else, and worried about her sister's fate."

"I haven't seen Linnea since we found the first mask," Lacey said suddenly. She glanced around the room. "Why is that?"

"Because, when you found the mask, Linnea realized her sister *was* free, not still caught in the mask as she feared," Jeremiah said quietly.

"And you?" Sebastian said. "Why is it you're still here?"

"I figured that, if I had the mask, maybe I could find a way to get back to life again," he said. "It caused my death and was obviously supernatural so if it did all that, it could also give me a chance to live again."

Lacey shook her head. "But how does that make any sense? It hasn't brought anybody back to life."

"But now you have the whole second mask *and* this piece of the other mask," he said persuasively. "Let me have them. Maybe the process needs both to reverse the damage done, they probably have to work together. And, if not, nothing's lost. But, if it does work, then I get a chance to live again."

She stared at him. "But you had a chance," she said slowly, carefully. "And when the mask had you, you killed everyone around you."

"That's not my fault," he cried out. "Besides that was back then." He slowly rose above her, his frame getting larger and larger. "You don't know that it would happen the same way again," he roared. "I know more now. It's a different mask too. It's so powerful. It just needs to be controlled and I can do that. I did it once."

"I still don't understand the connection between getting that mask and living again. Whatever you were trying to do didn't work the first time. Why would you think it would work now?" Sebastian said. "I'm so sorry you're not here beside me in your physical body. You have no idea what I went through."

As if Jeremiah lost what little control he had, he yelled, "You have no idea what I've been through all this time, watching you succeed, just a shadow at your side, coming at your beck and call. We were young, just starting out a new partnership, with so much possibility ahead of us … Only you got to live."

"That's not fair," Sebastian said. "I wanted you to go find the light and to leave this Earthly plane so you weren't trapped here. But you're the one who refused to move on."

"Wait," Lacey said slowly. "You said if you controlled the mask once before and if you had it you could do so again—that means you *wanted* to kill those men. They did die at your hand, not because of the mask." Her voice dropped to a hush. "The mask loved you because instead of the goodness and light energy of psychics, it found a willing recipient of the dark energy."

His smile was terrible to behold. "I want another chance to live..." He switched his gaze to Lacey. "Get me the mask."

"Because then you'll be powerful enough to kill Sebastian, right? You wanted to kill him that night when you killed everybody else, didn't you? You tried to kill him that night in the Mayan dig. But you couldn't find him. Instead you found Callum." She shook her head. "This is all about revenge, isn't it?"

Finally she was getting it. "The mask was only part of the perfect storm. Maybe the carving you did, like some magical rune, called to the energy of the ugly soul from the grave you'd just opened up... bringing the mask you carried to life. The energy could feel your ugliness. The hate inside you. It helped you hone it, target the ones you wanted to kill. Your partners. Both of them. You reveled in your true nature. Instead of fighting it, it was helping you do what you wanted. Oh, it must have loved that. The mask wasn't to blame. Sebastian wasn't to blame. Instead that ugliness inside you was your own undoing."

"Callum was my best friend next to you," Jeremiah said, his head bowed, seemingly talking to himself. "I'd have done anything to not hurt him. It was supposed to be Sebastian. The three of us were supposedly equal partners, but everybody, including Callum, looked to Sebastian as the lead boss. It was always about him. I hated him even then. I'd hoped to find a way to get rid of him on that Mayan trip so it would be just Callum and me. Sebastian had the money though. But, if he died, the foundation would be ours without him."

Wow, his own hate had contributed to his downfall. Once he'd opened up that pus of negativity ... Lacey looked at Sebastian and the glazed look in his eyes, the shock of these words draining the blood away from his skin. She pinched his hand hard.

He jolted, gave her a hard look and said to Jeremiah, "Well, you failed to kill me. Now I'm alive, and you're dead."

Jeremiah's gaze bored into Sebastian's. "Only until I can figure out how to change that. I've spent all these years making sure I was right here at your side, so, when the opportunity arose, you could change places with me. I wanted you to be caught in-between like I am in this perverted existence that's neither living nor dead."

"Just because he dies doesn't mean he's caught in-between," Lacey said. "You're so full of poisonous thoughts of revenge and anger, you can't even see common sense."

He drew himself up to his full size and turned to glare at her. "I don't like you."

"That's too bad," she said with a smile. "I'm sure I would have liked you. But then I like most people. I understand they are who they are, good and bad, and that they need to have outlets for both. But murderous intent is not acceptable whether you're alive or dead."

Sebastian laughed.

"And just what do you think you'll do about it?" Jeremiah asked. "I'll spend the rest of my unnatural life haunting you."

She nodded. "Well, you might, except for one thing."

"And what's that?" he snapped.

She smiled at Linnea, standing off on the side. "Linnea is here to say goodbye."

Linnea reached out a hand. Lacey reached back. The two women connected, and an ethereal door opened behind

Linnea. She stepped through the door, and, in that moment, the two women, their hands still gripped together, wrapped around Jeremiah and dragged him toward the door.

Sebastian stepped up behind her placing his hands on her shoulders, adding his strength to hers.

"No," Jeremiah shrieked, fighting the women's loving hold. "No, no, no. You can't do this."

"The door between life and death is right there," Lacey said, her voice calm, controlled but authoritative. "Face your music, step toward that light and cross over. Or at least try. I have no idea what happens to evil souls like you."

He gave a cackle of laughter, but Lacey placed one hand on his heart and gave him a hard-mental shove, with Linnea on the other side, her arms wrapped around him. Together Jeremiah and Linnea went through the door. As she stepped through, Linnea gave Lacey a wave. A flash of gold wrapped around her—but only her. And instantly the door closed.

Almost numb but strangely at peace. Lacey sank back down, picked up her coffee cup and took a sip.

Hunter looked at Sebastian. Sebastian looked at Hunter. They both turned to look at her.

"Did we just see what we thought we saw?"

She lifted her gaze. "I'm not sure what you saw, but I helped Jeremiah cross over, whether he wanted to or not, and no, I'm not sure where he went. I only saw Linnea in the light," she said. Seeing their shock, she shrugged and added, "Honestly I've worked very hard to get to this point in my life. I wasn't about to let some idiot like him ruin it for me." She reached out and squeezed Sebastian's hand.

He picked up her hand, bringing it to his lips, and kissed it gently. "Did I ever tell you what an incredibly beautiful person you are? Inside and out?"

She opened her eyes wide and shook her head. "No. I'm not. You see? If I was, I wouldn't have sent him off to the other side. I would've understood it was his lesson still to learn and have left him alone."

Sebastian shook his head. "No, you wouldn't. Because you didn't do it to save us or to stop yourself from being haunted by him. You did it to stop any threat against me."

She stared at him for a long moment, a soft smile on her lips, and said, "You figured that out, did you?"

Sebastian nodded his head.

She shrugged. "I look after what's mine very, very well. And nobody, absolutely nobody, gets to hurt those I care about—on this side or the other. He had to leave. No way would I constantly look over my shoulder to see if he was coming after you again."

Sebastian tugged on her arm, pulled her into his lap and just held her close. Over her head he whispered, "You are the best."

She chuckled. "I don't think so, but you can spend the rest of our lives convincing me of that."

He tilted her chin up and whispered, "Challenge accepted." And he kissed her.

That kiss was for more than just today, for more than just tomorrow. It was for all time, both on this side and on the other, so that they could spend forever together.

Hunter slowly clapped and cheered across the table from them. "I guess my job here is done." He stood. "I'll carry Mark here back to his bed and let him sleep this off."

"Will he be okay?" she asked anxiously having completely forgotten about the poor man. "Will he remember any of this?"

"Not likely. And yes, he should be fine. Likely wake confused and with a hell of a headache." He walked over to where Mark was slumped. "Even better, he won't have a clue what happened."

"Well, that's a relief." Lacey stood staring down at the unconscious Mark as Sebastian opened the doors for Hunter. "You'll come back after and have breakfast?"

He grinned. "Well, maybe." He walked out to the hallway, calling back as Sebastian walked ahead to open the other doors. "But I don't want to disturb the two of you."

"You won't." She chuckled. "We have more than just this lifetime to spend together now. You're more than welcome to be a large part of that."

His laughter floated toward her. "In that case, can you put on more coffee please. It's been a hell of a morning already"

"Done." She watched as the three disappeared into the other hallway. Then realizing they'd be back in just a moment, she raced to put on more coffee. It might have been a hell of a morning already for him, but she'd never had a better one. And given where they'd started, the future had never looked brighter.

This concludes Book 14 of Psychic Visions: Unmasked.
Read the first Chapter of Deep Beneath:
Psychic Visions, Book 15

PSYCHIC VISIONS: DEEP BENEATH (BOOK #15)
CHAPTER 1

W HIMSY CONNOR PADDLED her kayak forward across the ocean. She loved the way the waves lapped over the front of the bow and came up along the side. She couldn't resist stopping her strokes and dragging her fingers through the cold water. She stared into the blackness underneath. That was one thing about the ocean. You never knew what floated just beneath the kayak. It could be a whale; it could be a shark, or it could be a million different schools of small fish, depending on where you were. It was fascinating. A lot of marine life populated this area, but she hadn't been lucky enough to see any yet today. She glanced over at Mark, feeling a heavy gust of cold wind biting at her face. *The squall Mark had mentioned earlier.* She studied the skies, then the path they had to travel back, and frowned.

"You still up for this, Whimsy?" Mark asked. "We have a way to go, if you want to reach the spots you were looking forward to. But, with the weather turning ugly, we won't have much time."

She was beginning to have some misgivings about this trip. She could see Sarah and Wallace, now small figures in the distance, and realized that maybe she and Mark should have turned back with them. Looking at the nearing squall, she said, "That is coming our way and building."

"Yes, it is," Mark said calmly. "Let's get closer to the shore. Then we can reconsider."

She nodded.

He turned and struck out strongly.

The trouble was, by the time she turned and followed him, the squall was almost upon them. "Wow, that came up fast," she said, pulling hard on her paddle and examining her every strike.

They paddled hard toward the shore, where the waves should be a little bit calmer. Instead they broke on the beach with an exuberance that normally she would have loved. But fighting those waves in this kayak wouldn't be much fun. She stared back out at the deep water. "Maybe we should go back out there, out of the reach of the storm," she shouted. "I'm not making much progress."

"The tide will be too strong," he yelled back at her over the waves.

She put her back into her strokes. "We need to go in closer ..."

But the waves and winds stole her words. If she could just make it to shore ... They could always camp out and wait for the squall to pass, then get back in their kayaks and paddle home again.

She put her head down and just focused on moving one arm and then the other. The rain started then, pounding on her head and her shoulders, adding a gray sleet to the horizon around her. The bad weather had come up so damn fast and had overtaken her world. She could barely make out the shore ahead, yet the force of the current pulled her farther and farther out into the ocean.

Mark was closer to the shore and still fighting the elements. But he was stronger and in better shape.

She angled her kayak's nose toward the shore, but almost immediately the waves turned her kayak away. She couldn't keep it on a steady course.

Panic roiled inside her. She glanced around for any possible way to get to shore quicker, to get out of this until the world calmed down. There were no boats on the water as far as she could see—which wasn't very far in this squall. They had been smart to stay away from this harsh element of Mother Nature.

It would only get harder from here on out until the storm died down or turned off in another direction. Meanwhile, she was in for the fight of her life. She kept paddling, but the storm pulled her right back out, deeper and deeper into the churning ocean.

She was at a point of no return. Each kayaker was paired up, and each pair carried a megaphone with them, in case they got caught up in fog or whatever, but their megaphone and flare gun was in Mark's kayak, not hers. She had her cell phone—doubted she could get reception out here—but that was it. She preferred to travel light. She didn't even have the thermos of coffee. He had that too.

As she peered through the sleeting rain, the dark clouds whirled around her. If she weren't so intent on her imminent survival, she could make some curious shapes out of the blackness crowding in on her. With a shake of her head to get that fanciful notion out of her mind, she focused on finding her kayaking partner. She could barely see Mark now. He was farther ahead and still paddling, his head down, fighting his own battle against the waves. He couldn't reach her now. If nothing else he should be able to blast over those waves and beach himself safely.

And that's what she was determined to do as well. Keeping her focus in check and her panic at bay, she once again turned so that she directly faced the shore and gave it her all.

When the lightning lit the clouds and the thunder cracked overhead, she barely heard anything. Not so odd as she was drowning in the pounding rain and the heavy waves slashing at her and at her kayak. The latest swell swamped over her vessel. If she didn't have a proper rubber skirt, she'd have already abandoned her sunken kayak and been floating alone in the channel. As it was, the waves kept breaking over her again and again. Paddling at this point was almost impossible. Yet, if she didn't paddle, she would be taken farther and farther out into the sound.

She looked up and around to find a couple small sailing crafts coming into her view, heading toward the marina themselves. They couldn't hear her screams nor did anyone appear to notice her panicky waving arms.

She thought she heard yelling and screaming, but it came from behind her a distance. She glanced back at one of the small yachts there. People were on the bow, fighting. Whimsy had bigger problems than they did.

Exhausted, she turned her face toward the shore. Paddled right, left, right and left.

Another wave slammed into her, twisting her sideways and sending her even farther from shore. When the next crack sounded overhead, she cried out, terrified, wondering if she could win this fight ... Her arms were too weak now. Her body no longer answered her orders to paddle. She was soaked and freezing and terrified that she'd flip over and out of her kayak and end up floating out into the ocean with no one the wiser in those early crucial moments.

She was a decent roller in the kayak, when needed, and, as long as she kept her paddle, she'd have a chance to right herself and to possibly steer at some point. She couldn't see the shore any longer and had no way to orient herself. But she wouldn't think on that. All she could do was concentrate on staying afloat. To that end she tucked the paddle tight against her chest and just waited out the fury of the squall. Even though cold and wet and miserable, she was still capable of surviving a storm out here.

The trouble was, her vision was fading, and her muscles were cramping to the extent that she was afraid she couldn't hold on to the paddle much longer.

Another huge wave caught her kayak broadside.

Under she went.

She still had her paddle, and, holding her breath, she braced it up and used her hip motions to flip herself and her kayak back upright again. As soon as she did, another wave washed her and her ride back under again, and the paddle was wrenched out of her hands. Upside down, strapped securely into her kayak, her vessel was tossed about in the waves above as she was tossed about underneath. She was fine with a quick once-over dunk into the waters as she flipped her kayak back upright. But submerged in this weather? No she'd have to detach from the kayak and that would leave her floating out in the ocean trying to survive until she could be rescued. And drowning was not the way she intended to die. And especially not now. Her love of water refused to contemplate that end, despite her current circumstances.

She quickly slipped out of the rubber skirt edging in the kayak. Hanging on to the frame, hoping it would stay afloat, she popped up to the surface and gasped for air. Another wave broke over her head. She tried to flip the kayak upright, but it was taking on a lot of water. And in no way could she empty it in these squall conditions. A big wave tossed her up and separated her from the kayak; she cried out as she went underwater again, her breath sucked out from the repetitive blows of the churning ocean. She struggled to return to the surface, and a buckle on her life jacket snapped.

Finally she made it above water, gasping for air, only to have more unrelenting waves crash down on her before she could fully fill her lungs. The life jacket then twisted, tugging. So many swells crashed upon her, forcing her under the current, catching her, then pulling at her, that she could feel the air being forcefully expelled from her. A black haze filled her mind. Her lungs burned. Her arms and legs weren't working.

Blackness overtook her as something bright slid by, then beneath her, lifting her from underneath. It should have terrified her when she crested the water, coughing and gulping, gasping for air. And finally, when she could breathe well enough, she looked around to see what had brought her up to the surface. But it was gone. Whatever it was, it wasn't here now. *How interesting.*

Another wave crashed over her.

Something brushed against her back, nudging her in a different direction. She could only see a massive form in her peripheral vision but couldn't tell what it was.

Or was it just her imagination? Or more likely her nightmares ...

Water once again cascaded over her, filling her mouth and lungs, and she choked on it, coughing to clear her passageways.

She was tossed high over the water, gasping for oxygen, before she fell again, to be engulfed by the ocean. At one point in time she blacked out, only to find herself waking up once again, floating on the surface of the ocean. The next time it happened, she opened her eyes to realize the storm was off to the side, and she was even farther away from the shore. Coughing and gasping still, she tried to preserve her heat by pulling her knees to her chest and holding her body tightly together, hoping for a quick rescue.

The beacon on my life jacket. Remembering that, now realizing that maybe somebody could pick up her signal, she punched the button to set it off. On her shoulder a light flashed. She curled up in a ball, the life jacket high on her neck, and just tried to hang on, hoping that help was coming soon. Then the second buckle on her life jacket snapped.

She panicked.

If she lost the life jacket, she was lost in a bad way. She could float on her own for a little while but not for very long.

She grabbed it against her chest, holding on as best she could. But no longer secured around her chest, it could be taken from her with one more wave, still powerful even amid this retreating squall. She had made it this far. She refused to lose this battle in the last round. She hung on tight. Her world narrowed to one focus: staying on the surface. Too numb to fight, she felt the waves still tossing and turning her.

Her arm was through the opening of the life jacket, trying desperately to keep it against her chest, but the next wave ripped it free, and she sunk deeper and deeper and deeper into the frigid disturbed waters. And again she felt that same presence—the huge strong back—sliding underneath her legs, lifting her, pushing her higher and higher. She reached down with a hand, feeling the silky smooth form beneath her fingers, as it pushed her to the surface yet once more.

This time when she came up, gasping for air, another

killer wave sent her spiraling, tumbling toward something that she couldn't see. But she felt it when she contacted it. Oh, she felt it.

All of a sudden her knees felt the harsh impact, then her face landed among barnacles and rocks. She inhaled a scream. Her knees pulled up into her as she crawled forward onto the sandy shore. Two feet later, she collapsed, unconscious.

SAMSON CARTWRIGHT FIDDLED with the dials of his ham radio, trying to get reception but with only a noisy buzz filling the air. "Damn weather." The dogs, King and Queen, barked in agreement. The storm had knocked out the power, and, of course, Samson's satellite internet was hit-or-miss at the best of times. But, given that he was here for as much peace and quiet as possible to do his research, the slow spotty internet was sufficient for his needs. Except for now when, absent the internet, he needed his radio to work for sure.

He rubbed the back of his neck, a pricking there quickly turning to an ache which then slammed into a throb without breaking.

A groan ripped free. He got up, gasping, as the cry ripped into his mind. He clasped his head, desperately trying to handle the influx of noise and pain.

Through the din, he heard the urgency. The screams ordering him to obey.

Unable to move, he yelled, "Stop!"

But the voice didn't. It got worse—louder, more demanding—until Samson was crippled, slowly crumpling to his knees. "Stop," he roared. "I can't help if you do this."

Silence came.

Samson stood, shuddering as his body slowly recovered. Then, understanding the urgency, he raced outside, thankful he was mostly dressed. The sky was dark, the rain a light soaking. The storm crackled above; the sky would open soon, and walking would be treacherous. Running, lethal.

But he had no choice. The noise in his head started up again. He needed it to stay calm before it killed him as he navigated the rocks. He couldn't function when the voice took over. The rain pelted his head, blurring his vision, making the rocks slick under his bare feet.

The cliff edge loomed in front of him. The dogs, silent this whole journey, stopped on either side of him. Then turned and headed along the cliff edge. He trusted their senses over his. He could barely see for the gray sheets of rain blinding both his long and short vision, and the lightning cracking overhead gave him a partial but eerie look to the world in intermittent flashes. It was late afternoon, yet it looked like minutes from midnight.

King barked once.

The more dominant dog and the more psychically connected of the two, King led the way to the beach. Queen, her nose in the air, was the better physical hunter. And much more compassionate. The beach was too far away for Samson to see if anything was there yet.

Samson made his way to the outcropping that jutted into the ocean; the waves rose and crashed over the rocks, soaking him. The noise was deafening as Mother Nature unleashed her fury at the world, and, boy, was she pissed. He squinted at the angry waves that churned close to him. He noticed … movement. A darker mass in the water. But was it just a normal storm or something else?

And, if something else, … what? He'd been searching for

months now, not finding what he sought.

"Focus," roared the voice in his head.

"I am," Samson shouted against the storm, but the wind picked up his words and tossed them behind him. In the distance he heard Queen howl.

She was never wrong.

Samson turned, slipped and slammed into the rocks. He straightened, used the rocks to stabilize himself and moved as quickly as possible toward the beach. There, close to the rocks, a rag-doll form was pushed forward with the tide, then pulled back as the ocean refused to give up her prize.

The dogs reached it first. Both dove into the water, grabbed hold and backed up, dragging the form with them.

Samson hit the beach, running now on sure footing to their sides. He reached down and scooped the tiny woman into his arms. Enough water twisted around his ankles that he had to fight its pull to drag him and his burden back into the ocean. Further inland on the beach he laid her down. He collapsed at her side, reaching for a pulse.

The dogs whined beside them.

"And?" the voice roared through Samson's mind.

"She's alive," he whispered. "Barely, but she's alive."

"And you need to keep her that way," the voice roared, splitting the words into white noise as they crashed through Samson's mind. "She's important. Don't lose her."

And, for the first time since this latest intrusion started, the noise in his head disappeared, replaced with a sense of peace.

Book 15 is available now!

To find out more visit Dale Mayer's website.

smarturl.it/DMDeepUniversal

Author's Note

Thank you for reading Unmasked: Psychic Visions, Book 14! If you enjoyed the book, please take a moment and leave a short review.

Dear reader,

I love to hear from readers, and you can contact me at my website: www.dalemayer.com or at my Facebook author page. To be informed of new releases and special offers, sign up for my newsletter or follow me on BookBub. And if you are interested in joining Dale Mayer's Fan Club, here is the Facebook sign up page.
facebook.com/groups/402384989872660

Cheers,
Dale Mayer

Your Free Book Awaits!

KILL OR BE KILLED

Part of an elite SEAL team, Mason takes on the dangerous jobs no one else wants to do – or can do. When he's on a mission, he's focused and dedicated. When he's not, he plays as hard as he fights.

Until he meets a woman he can't have but can't forget. Software developer, Tesla lost her brother in combat and has no intention of getting close to someone else in the military. Determined to save other US soldiers from a similar fate, she's created a program that could save lives. But other countries know about the program, and they won't stop until they get it – and get her.

Time is running out ... For her ... For him ... For them ...

DOWNLOAD a *__complimentary__* copy of MASON? Just tell me where to send it!

http://dalemayer.com/sealsmason/

About the Author

Dale Mayer is a USA Today bestselling author best known for her Psychic Visions and Family Blood Ties series. Her contemporary romances are raw and full of passion and emotion (Second Chances, SKIN), her thrillers will keep you guessing (By Death series), and her romantic comedies will keep you giggling (It's a Dog's Life and Charmin Marvin Romantic Comedy series).

She honors the stories that come to her – and some of them are crazy and break all the rules and cross multiple genres!

To go with her fiction, she also writes nonfiction in many different fields with books available on resume writing, companion gardening and the US mortgage system. She has recently published her Career Essentials Series. All her books are available in print and ebook format.

Connect with Dale Mayer Online

Dale's Website – www.dalemayer.com
Twitter – @DaleMayer
Facebook – dalemayer.com/fb
BookBub – bookbub.com/authors/dale-mayer

Also by Dale Mayer

Published Adult Books:

Lovely Lethal Gardens
Arsenic in the Azaleas, Book 1
Bones in the Begonias, Book 2
Corpse in the Carnations, Book 3

Psychic Vision Series
Tuesday's Child
Hide 'n Go Seek
Maddy's Floor
Garden of Sorrow
Knock Knock...
Rare Find
Eyes to the Soul
Now You See Her
Shattered
Into the Abyss
Seeds of Malice
Eye of the Falcon
Itsy-Bitsy Spider
Unmasked
Deep Beneath

Psychic Visions Books 1–3

Psychic Visions Books 4–6

Psychic Visions Books 7–9

By Death Series

Touched by Death

Haunted by Death

Chilled by Death

By Death Books 1–3

Broken Protocols – Romantic Comedy Series

Cat's Meow

Cat's Pajamas

Cat's Cradle

Cat's Claus

Broken Protocols 1-4

Broken and… Mending

Skin

Scars

Scales (of Justice)

Broken but… Mending 1-3

Glory

Genesis

Tori

Celeste

Glory Trilogy

Biker Blues

Morgan: Biker Blues, Volume 1

Cash: Biker Blues, Volume 2

SEALs of Honor

Mason: SEALs of Honor, Book 1

Hawk: SEALs of Honor, Book 2

Dane: SEALs of Honor, Book 3

Swede: SEALs of Honor, Book 4

Shadow: SEALs of Honor, Book 5

Cooper: SEALs of Honor, Book 6

Markus: SEALs of Honor, Book 7

Evan: SEALs of Honor, Book 8

Mason's Wish: SEALs of Honor, Book 9

Chase: SEALs of Honor, Book 10

Brett: SEALs of Honor, Book 11

Devlin: SEALs of Honor, Book 12

Easton: SEALs of Honor, Book 13

Ryder: SEALs of Honor, Book 14

Macklin: SEALs of Honor, Book 15

Corey: SEALs of Honor, Book 16

Warrick: SEALs of Honor, Book 17

Tanner: SEALs of Honor, Book 18

Jackson: SEALs of Honor, Book 19

SEALs of Honor, Books 1–3

SEALs of Honor, Books 4–6

SEALs of Honor, Books 7–10

SEALs of Honor, Books 11–13

Heroes for Hire

Levi's Legend: Heroes for Hire, Book 1

Stone's Surrender: Heroes for Hire, Book 2

Merk's Mistake: Heroes for Hire, Book 3

Rhodes's Reward: Heroes for Hire, Book 4

Flynn's Firecracker: Heroes for Hire, Book 5

Logan's Light: Heroes for Hire, Book 6

Harrison's Heart: Heroes for Hire, Book 7

Saul's Sweetheart: Heroes for Hire, Book 8

Dakota's Delight: Heroes for Hire, Book 9

Michael's Mercy (Part of Sleeper SEAL Series)

Tyson's Treasure: Heroes for Hire, Book 10

Jace's Jewel: Heroes for Hire, Book 11

Rory's Rose: Heroes for Hire, Book 12

Brandon's Bliss: Heroes for Hire, Book 13

Liam's Lily: Heroes for Hire, Book 14

North's Nikki: Heroes for Hire, Book 15

Anders's Angel: Heroes for Hire, Book 16

Reyes's Raina: Heroes for Hire, Book 17

Dezi's Diamond: Heroes for Hire, Book 18

Vince's Vixen: Heroes for Hire, Book 19

Heroes for Hire, Books 1–3

Heroes for Hire, Books 4–6

Heroes for Hire, Books 7–9

SEALs of Steel

Badger: SEALs of Steel, Book 1

Erick: SEALs of Steel, Book 2

Cade: SEALs of Steel, Book 3

Talon: SEALs of Steel, Book 4

Laszlo: SEALs of Steel, Book 5

Geir: SEALs of Steel, Book 6

Jager: SEALs of Steel, Book 7

The Last Wish: SEALs of Steel, Book 8

Collections

Dare to Be You…

Dare to Love…

Dare to be Strong…

RomanceX3

Standalone Novellas

It's a Dog's Life

Riana's Revenge

Second Chances

Published Young Adult Books:

Family Blood Ties Series

Vampire in Denial

Vampire in Distress

Vampire in Design

Vampire in Deceit

Vampire in Defiance

Vampire in Conflict

Vampire in Chaos

Vampire in Crisis

Vampire in Control

Vampire in Charge

Family Blood Ties Set 1–3

Family Blood Ties Set 1–5

Family Blood Ties Set 4–6

Family Blood Ties Set 7–9

Sian's Solution, A Family Blood Ties Series Prequel
Novelette

Design series

Dangerous Designs

Deadly Designs

Darkest Designs

Design Series Trilogy

Standalone

In Cassie's Corner

Gem Stone (a Gemma Stone Mystery)

Time Thieves

Published Non-Fiction Books:

Career Essentials

Career Essentials: The Résumé

Career Essentials: The Cover Letter

Career Essentials: The Interview

Career Essentials: 3 in 1

Made in United States
North Haven, CT
26 January 2022

15315799R00243